25 Minnesota Writers

25 Minnesota Writers

EDITORIAL DIRECTOR
SEYMOUR YESNER

EDITORIAL BOARD
STANLEY KIESEL
PHEBE HANSON
ANNETTE DAHL
EDIS RISSER

PHOTOGRAPHY
LARRY RISSER

ACKNOWLEDGEMENTS
Jon Hassler by Ray Erickson
Patricia Hampl by Kay Bonczek
Peggy Harding Love by Dr. John Love

ACKNOWLEDGEMENTS

Event: "Gainfully Employed" by Alyce Ingram.

Mademoiselle: "The Jersey Heifer" by Peggy Harding Love.

Many Corners, Preview, and *Worthington Daily Globe:* "Marriaging," "Love and Crime," "How Are You Going to Keep Them in Paris After They've Seen the Farm?" by Mike Finley.

PREFACE

The book derives from its precursors, 25 Minnesota Poets 1 and 2, in which we attempted to assemble a compendium representative of the poetic work of people living and writing in Minnesota and somehow, because of that fact, bestowing on their poetry a special flavor. The books were also an effort to highlight the work of several well-established poets and to uncover the work of others. Our goals were modest; and in a modest way we succeeded. Also, because of the circumscription *25* and because of the varied and individual tastes of the selection committee, guided to a large extent by an overriding utilitarian schoolroom purpose, many excellent poets were excluded — with considerable anguish on our part.

No such schoolroom mandate binds this book although the idiosyncrasies of taste still persist. Within those idiosyncrasies, a remarkable concurrence bonded the selection around work exhibiting the sensitivities of young and old, male and female, rural and urban. We sought a richness of diversity in style, in background, in humor and sobriety. In large, we were after anything that seemed true to the Minnesota writing scene of relatively recent times, and, in a surprising way, though the locale of the stories were "Minnesotan", and some facets seemed culture bound, we found the themes were easily assimilated as universal.

We are delighted by the range and variety of topics and of narrative forms. But mostly, we are overwhelmed by the remarkable literary talents at work in this state.

I want to thank the members of the selection committee for their willingness to give of their time and to test continually and openly their individual judgments against the judgment of others. Finally, I need to acknowledge my gratitude to Norton Stillman who continues without fanfare to support these, and other, endeavors that quicken the artistic life of the Minnesota community.

Seymour Yesner

CONTENTS

ALYCE INGRAM: was born in St. Paul, Minnesota. Her stories have appeared (or are forthcoming) in *Vagabond, North American Review, Mediterranean Review, Mundus Artium, Eureka, New Renaissance, Short Story International* and others. She also has had published by Vagabond Press a chapbook of short stories titled *Blue Horses* while two of her stories have been included in the *Moving to Antarctica* and *Vagabond* anthologies.

In 1964 she received the McKnight Foundation Award in the field of short fiction.

Alyce Ingram

GAINFULLY EMPLOYED

It was a rainy twelve o'clock noon on Saturday in a converted rooming-house called *The Manor*. "Some manor," Ellie's sister Rose had said on that first visit to the place six weeks ago when Kate, the owner, had answered their knock, let them into her apartment and told Ellie in a little room back of her kitchen (that years earlier had probably been occupied by the family's hired girl) to take off her pants and climb up on the chrome-and-yellow table that matched the one off which Ellie now ate her lunch except that hers was red-topped.

She tried hard never to think about that rainy day in Kate's back room but now, because of the letter in her pocket, she permitted the whole frightening experience to wash over her afresh. It had not taken Kate long to do the job, she remembered. Then afterwards Rose had said to Kate: ". . . and to think her own father kicked her out of the house calling her a *hoor* when it was her first fella and the bastard was his very own hired man" so then Kate said, "Well, if Ellie didn't have some place to stay why not come here to The Manor and work for room and a couple of bucks a week because the best way to put something like that behind you was to keep busy and gainfully employed where there wasn't someone around to throw it up in your face." She had helped out a lot of girls like this, Kate said, until they got on their feet and the last one left just the night before to try Hollywood so pretty soon it was all arranged for Ellie to start the next morning.

After they left The Manor, Rose said all men were bastards. "Piss-off inside you and then they're off to the ballgame," she said and then she had treated Ellie to a Strawberry Super-Duper across the street at the Drive-In where Kate's son Earl worked behind the soda fountain and finally fixed their order himself saying when they finished and Rose paid up he'd see Ellie around and she'd be just fine now — almost as good as new — if she'd just learn to keep her legs crossed. (Earl used to be a bus boy at The

Red Rooster where Rose worked as a waitress and it was through him that Rose found Kate.)

Ellie wished often she hadn't been born such a muddlehead. It would have been nice to work at The Rooster with Rose but Rose said she'd never be able to keep the orders straight and she was too fat to fit behind the dishwasher. She was glad, now, Kate had hired her to work at The Manor that accommodated (besides Kate, Earl and Ellie) five elderly gentlemen who spent most of their time down the street at Pete's Place drinking beer and playing pinochle so with Kate off calling Bingo when she wasn't tied up in the back room there was no one breathing down Ellie's neck making her nervous. No one to tease her the way they did at home because her hands shook when she had to remember two things at once and could never time it to come out right when mashing potatoes and making gravy at the same time.

"My rules are simple," Kate had said at the outset when breaking Ellie in. "One, no sticky fingers. Two, no dilly-dally. Three, no fooling around with anything private and that includes a gentleman's jiggle stick." The last had taken Ellie a few minutes to understand. Whenever anyone said something to her that she could not soon comprehend she would blink her eyes rapidly several times and then, light dawning, would break into a slow, moist smile as though proud of her accomplishment. (But if, on the other hand, she did not after a few moments grasp the meaning of the words then the slow, moist smile would not appear and, instead, she would frown heavily while gnawing on her left little fingernail that was by now chewed to the quick and hurt when she bumped it.)

Ellie had another sort of smile, however, besides her moist, happy smile. This second — infrequent — smile was a brief, peculiar twist of the upper lip that revealed, for only an instant, her right eye tooth before it disappeared leaving an expression on her somewhat large face of almost sly gratification and it was this smile she wore as she now reread with moving lips a letter received from her mother in the morning's mail. The letter with newspaper clipping enclosed stated in pencilled writing that Oscar Peterson had been killed down-state as the tractor he was driving overturned.

Ellie was never quite sure in her mind these days whether she hated Peterson more or her father for calling her that word and kicking her out. Peterson's teeth were large, jagged and yellow and she had not liked him from the beginning when he came to work on the farm as hired man. But still when everyone else in the family was gone off somewhere on Saturday and Sunday afternoon (not wanting to drag her along), it was nice having someone for company even though he never did anything after that first box of chocolate covered cherries but sneak up to her room, unbuckle his overall straps, let them drop to the floor and climb on top of her huffing and puffing like a steam engine except for once when they did it out in the barn on the hay instead as the cows looked on and that was the time that for some reason or other she felt afterwards like stabbing him with the pitchfork.

Now, suddenly, Ellie felt like having a good, long cry but instead she cut herself another piece of chocolate layer cake and ate it standing by the sink. She bought most of her food at *The Deli* down the street gorging alone in her green-painted-over wainscot quarters that consisted of a large room and butler's pantry that held a two-burner gas plate and shelves for her plastic dishes and staples which were mostly boxes of cookies and sugar-coated cereals. Perishables she kept in an old-style refrigerator turned the color of cream that stood next to a chipped kitchen sink fixture. She hung her clothes in a metal wardrobe in the corner and she slept on a Hollywood-type bed that doubled by day as a davenport bolstered with fat red and yellow cushions.

Evenings, when not upstreet enjoying a double-feature, she would sit in a wine-colored frieze overstuffed chair watching black-and-white TV that she wished Kate would replace with color. While viewing the picture she would alternately crochet and flip through movie magazines when she wasn't mending one of her red uniforms that came from Rose. These uniforms (she now wore one) fit her somewhat tight and revealed far too much of her thick white thighs when she stooped but she loved them more than any of her dresses and would patiently mend the thin spots under the arms which is why Rose had discarded them in the first place and bought herself new.

Sometimes, while occupied in this fashion evenings, she would remind herself that she was happy. At least, she would think, she was happier than when living at home where the bad thing had happened. Happier than when in school where the kids called her Big Butt and Tootsie Roll until she had dropped out. And certainly happier than when she had tried out baby-sitting in town but would always fall asleep before the people got home and that made them mad. "What if the house had caught on fire?" they would say with shrill voices as though they, themselves, stayed awake all night and kept watch when they didn't have some place to go.

Yes, it was much better living here at Kate's except that she got so lonesome. Some day, though, she believed she would meet a nice boy friend . . . some day . . . and he would telephone her and make an honest-to-goodness date (something she had never once in her life had though Rose had had so many she couldn't keep track of them and sometimes stood them up). Yes, this fellow would come driving up to Kate's door in his polished automobile — it could be second-hand — and he would take her out to dinner and dancing afterwards and some day they might even get married. Yes, some day she would find just such a man while sitting in the park which she did almost every afternoon — unless it rained — after she finished her work.

Sitting in the park afternoons waiting for this special person to turn up was both a source of pleasure and disappointment to Ellie. Dressed up in one of her freshly ironed uniforms she would tell whoever happened to share her bench that she was a beauty operator and had her own shop called *Ellen's*. "I got me ten girls now," she would say to a total stranger while holding up ten reddened fingers. ". . . it's why my hands look so bad . . . the strong stuff we got to use giving perms." Sometimes, while visiting like this, she wished people would stay longer and not be in such a hurry always having to rush off and do this, that or the other when she tried her best to hold onto them relating bits of gossip gleaned from her movie magazines and make-believe beauty parlor customers even offering them jelly beans from her pocket while urging them to come and visit her at Kate's evenings. ". . . but not to my shop, y'unnerstan . . . it's best not to mix business and pleasure, I always say." Yes, sometimes it was like the whole world was in one great big hurry and she was the only one who had time to sit and get acquainted as she waited for him to come along and even that little twerp Earl these days was always in a hurry where at first he used to stop nights for just a minute when her door was open and he was on his way to the alley to air his cat. Would then call out if he caught her crocheting: "Well . . . and how's the happy little hooker making out."

He was some clown, all right.

And she didn't need Kate to tell her he didn't like women at least not *that* way. Kate said he didn't like anyone except Taffy, his cat and sometimes he was even mean to her. Thinking about Earl always made her feel all muddleheaded. Now here was Taffy who crept up on helpless little birds and killed them and even worse was the way she sneaked up on poor little mice who didn't have wings to fly away and never did anyone any harm. Made so little noise. Did not yowl at night and snag draperies. Yet she herself was already crocheting Taffy a red and green sweater for Christmas (months ahead) just to keep on the good side of Earl and Kate when whoever heard of anyone crocheting a mouse a cute little outfit . . . and when you stopped to think that all a mouse ever got out of life was maybe some stale cheese in a trap and then he was flushed down the john or tossed into the incinerator . . . well, it made you stop and think. And, as she told someone in the park just the day before, there were plenty of cat and dog hospitals in the world but where, she'd like to know, was there ever a mouse doctor and did they ever see on the news where someone left a lot of money to a mouse the way they did to cats? Nosirree, she had said to the antsy woman who kept scratching her head and then got up and hurried away without even saying goodbye.

And people were so changeable.

You just never knew from one day to the next what to expect so that you felt like a dummy some of the time and Earl was getting funnier than the rest of them she thought while gathering together the necessary things to clean his room-and-alcove on top floor. Why, just today before lunch while dusting the front stairs she had said to him in friendly fashion *howdy-doody* as he passed her by on his way down but he had not so much as answered leaving her stomach feeling all sick and funny but then, five minutes later, he was back carrying an ice cream table and had called out like his other self *hi-ya, Ellie . . . gettin' much?* and everything was fine again as she triggered back (proud of her spunk): "T'aint's none of your gol-darned business, you daffy doodler" for he was taking a correspondence course in drawing and had pictures of naked women tacked all over his place but had spoiled all of them by drawing smoking cigarettes coming out of all of their openings.

Sometimes he would say crazy things just to make her laugh but Ellie's laugh was not the usual fat person's sort of laugh. It was neither a chuckle nor a chortle and it did not come from way down deep and then explode like her sister Rose's. No, her laugh was more like a drowning person's *glub-glub* that seemed to hurt her throat where it got stuck for it would invariably bring a rush of quick tears to her eyes and then her nose would begin to drip and she always found herself without a hanky.

Now it was almost 2:00 o'clock.

She usually saved the cleaning of Earl's room until the very last and now she climbed the two flights of stairs to his quarters carrying dust cloths over right shoulder, fresh linen on left, a shaggy oil mop and carpet sweeper in one hand and yellow plastic bucket of scouring aids in the other. Almost always by the time she reached the top landing, puffing heavily, she would remember something she had forgotten and for just an instant her pale plump eyes would look bleak and sometimes spill over before she would drop her burden, sigh and lumber back down the steps to the supply closet on first floor. Today, however, upon finishing the climb she smiled her moist, happy smile upon discovering that she had re-membered everything and would not have to retrace her steps.

She found Earl sketching at his new ice cream table seated upon one of two matching wrought-iron chairs. He said he had bought the set at a fire sale down the street. Now he stopped drawing and picked up his cat Taffy nuzzling her nose-to-nose prompting Ellie to say (almost enviously): "You sure are crazy about that there little snot, ain't cha?" to which Earl quickly replied, "You can bet your sweet bippie, Dippy . . . and if this place ever caught fire in the middle of the night you guess which one around here I'd grab and run with."

Ellie told him shucks, nobody could be that mean and not warn their mother but she knew he spoke the truth for she had heard the way he spoke to Kate. After changing his linen she folded his Murphy bed to the wall and began dusting his furniture. She then filled her bucket with hot, sudsy water and knelt down heavily to scrub the linoleum in the corner reaching behind herself occa-sionally to pull down her skirt for she was backed to him and sometimes he teased her about her fat exposed thighs saying they looked ike nice white hams.

". . . say . . . how'za'bout you modeling for me, Ellie," he said now suddenly. ". . . maybe holding Taffy . . . or better yet eating an ice cream cone sitting on one of my new chairs."

Ellie felt herself flush with pleasure at his suggestion that she pose for him but then gradually like a slow motion camera unreeling before her eyes there appeared a picture of herself seated on the tiny round white disc her fat thighs spilling over and she said maybe she would some other time after she started on her new diet which was not true for she did not ever diet, only planned to sometime in the future.

"Why don't you get yourself a by-pass?" Earl said after a time.

Ellie looked over her shoulder, saw that he was again sketching and said she didn't know what he was talking about. Earl replied that his aunt had got one and gone from two-hundred-and-seventeen to one-sixty-nine in just a couple of months believe it or not.

"In a pig's eye," Ellie said. Then, almost cautiously, she asked while continuing to scrub: "How'zit work anyways, Dr. Smarts?"

"Ever seen a picture of your gut, Ellie?" Earl said.

"Not lately," Ellie answered.

"Well," Earl said shaking Taffy from his lap. "Let's see now how to explain . . . well, you saw that tuba someone left here once instead'a rent . . . well, they look a little like that. So they go in and they take and they cut an' then they sew the first two feet of your upper . . . to the last coupl'a . . . so your chow travels only a few feet. The rest stays back and doesn't go through the plumbing . . . or something . . . get it?"

"Got-cha," Ellie said even though she hadn't and thought maybe he was just having fun. But still . . . his own aunt . . . and he sounded serious . . . well, she would wait and ask Kate tonight when she came back from calling Bingo. Kate could be depended upon to tell the truth and to tell her how to go about finding a good sawbones who would let you string the payments out so much each month without sending around bill collectors to give you a bad name because if there was one thing Ellie was proud of (and boasted of when sitting in the park) it was that she didn't owe anyone a cent.

"Now will you please move them big feet of yourn," she said to Earl as she came closer to where he sat. ". . . or do you want me to scrub them, too."

Earl said it was O.K. He was going to work now and he slammed the door on his way out.

The noise seemed to jar Ellie's brain loose and she thought suddenly for the very first time as though the Lord had sent her a message that maybe Earl was hinting at something. Maybe he was hinting that if she'd just take a little better care of herself . . . not that she wasn't as clean as a new sponge . . . but maybe if she'd lose some weight . . . he might take a shine to her. Not a very hard shine because he wasn't what you would call woman crazy as Kate had said. But maybe the gut operation story was really on the level and coming to The Manor was the Lord's way of bringing someone into her life. Not that Earl was anything to write home about . . . skinny and pimply . . . and he was awfully tied to Kate's apron strings . . . but still it would be better than nothing . . . better than nobody . . . better than sitting alone in her room nights when she ran out of movie money . . . and she could fix this room-and-alcove up real cute if given a chance besides which it would be better sleeping with someone on a Murphy bed than on a Hollywood by yourself . . . and nobody ever got everything they planned on in life Rose said just lately. You learned to cut your dreams first in half and then smaller and smaller until you were satisfied with just slivers, Rose said and Rose was one smart cookie everyone said.

Now, with an almost beatific yet thoughtful look on her face Ellie got up to move the table to scrub underneath when glancing down at Earl's sketch she saw that he had doodled a tuba, a large tuba with a woman's head (looking very much like her own) coming out of the beginning and a fat, fat rump with a crack down the middle coming out of the end. Through this fat rump Earl had drawn an arrow.

After a longer than usual pause during which Ellie's eyes became bleak but did not spill over she began chewing her left little fingernail until it suddenly spurted blood and then she continued with her cleaning as though nothing at all had happened.

JON HASSLER: At the age of 37 I began to write, and after a few years of self-imposed apprenticeship (85 rejection slips) I began to produce readable fiction, most of it set in fictional Minnesota towns resembling the several I have lived in. I was born in Minneapolis. My father was a grocer, my mother a schoolteacher. When I was not yet a year old we moved to Staples, where we spent ten years, and then to Plainview, where we spent eight. From Plainview High School I went to St. John's University, and from there into the teaching of English — ten years in high school (Melrose, Fosston, Park Rapids) and the past fifteen years in college (Bemidji State University and Brainerd Community College). Along the way I picked up a master's degree at the University of North Dakota.

With the publication of *Staggerford* (1977) and *Simon's Night* (1979) in addition to two novels for young adults (*Four Miles to Pinecone* and *Jemmy*), I have been asked when I plan to quit the classroom. Probably never, for two reasons. One, unless your novel is a best-seller (one of say two dozen titles among the 15,000 published each year) you will not support yourself with your fiction. And, two, the society of the classroom serves as an agreeable counterpoint to the solitude of writing. Further, teaching and writing have a lot in common. We teach and write by imitation and by instinct. Teachers and writers, given a modicum of talent, are stimulated and rewarded pretty much in proportion to how hard they work. Teachers and writers are students of the human spirit.

Jon Hassler

ROSS'S DREAM

Ross was ten years old when Alan Romberg died.

Alan Romberg was fifteen.

The accident happened on a hot Sunday afternoon in early September, 1943 — cicadas buzzing, the air heavy with corn pollen — and Ross, lying on the grass in his shady back yard, was struggling through a dull story in *Boy's Life* when he noticed the first sign of alarm at the Romberg house across the alley — Mr. and Mrs. Romberg rushing, stumbling, out their kitchen door and climbing into the Canning Company pickup. Ross had never before seen Mrs. Romberg in the pickup. Indeed, he had scarcely ever known the Rombergs to speak to one another; it was hard to think of them as husband and wife. Mr. Romberg was the Canning Company field man, which meant that six days a week all summer he went out and did something in the fields, coming home only for meals and bed, and six days a week all winter he played cards in the pool hall. He was a fat man with a blustery temper; Ross frequently heard him shouting at his three sons (Alan, Sam, and Larry the Twitch); twice he had seen him chase Alan across the yard in anger, once flailing his belt in the air like a lasso, the other time wielding a willow switch. Mrs. Romberg was a bony, silent woman whose perpetual smile looked to Ross more like a facial cramp than a sign of pleasure. She had spent the summer on her knees in the several garden plots that surrounded her house, and she had very little to do with Ross's mother or with any of the other women of the neighborhood. The only words Ross had ever heard her speak were the names of her sons when she called them to supper.

A dusty haze hung over the alley for several minutes after the Rombergs sped away, and Ross, watching the dust shift and settle, had a hair-raising premonition. He sensed that whereas years ago only something very wonderful, like love, could have brought this unlikely couple together in marriage, now only something very horrible, like death, could have reunited them in the pickup. But because hair-raising sensations (most of them unfounded) are common in boyhood and quickly pass, Ross turned back to his story — turned to the continued part at the back of the magazine where the print was small — and spent a long time scouting with Kit Carson in the arid foothills of the Sangre de Cristo Mountains.

Half an hour later a red car came down the alley and parked where the pickup had been. At the wheel was a young man Ross didn't know, apparently Ruthellen Romberg's boyfriend, for both the young man and Ruthellen got out on the driver's side and hurried toward the house. Ruthellen, the older sister of the Romberg boys, was enrolled in nurses' training in Rochester, twenty miles away, and she wore her student uniform. The young man wore a bell-bottomed sailor suit. Sam Romberg, Ross's age and classmate, emerged from the kitchen and held the screen door open for his sister and her boyfriend. The three of them stood there for a minute, half in and half out of the house, speaking and nodding and glancing nervously up and down the alley. They noticed Ross; Sam waved; then they went inside and the screen door, its spring weak, slowly pulled itself shut. Ross sat up, leaned back against the trunk of the elm that shaded him, and rejoined Kit Carson.

In a few minutes Mr. and Mrs. Romberg returned in the Canning Company pickup. They were followed by a maroon car containing Mr. and Mrs. Browning and their son Earl. The Brownings, who owned Browning Appliance and Bottlegas, lived on the other side of town, seven blocks away. The pickup and the car stopped in a swirl of dust. Five doors were opened and slammed. The two women walked woodenly toward the house, Mrs. Browning massaging or caressing Mrs. Romberg's left arm.

The men, as though to separate themselves (as far as Sunday decorum would allow) from their wives and children, went directly into the tomato patch that occupied the vacant lot next to the Romberg house. This lot was directly across the alley from Ross's house; it was the first thing he saw each morning when he raised the shade in his bedroom. In the spring Mrs. Romberg had set out a hundred tomato plants in orderly rows; through the summer she had nurtured them and pruned them and staked them up; and now, like a dwarfed orchard, they stood hip-high and heavy with the ripening fruit of her labor. The tomato patch was open to the sweltering sun, but Mr. Romberg and Mr. Browning seemed oblivious to the heat as they moved steadily up and down the rows, smoking cigarettes. Something about their gestures — restrained, jerky movements of hand and head — suggested to Ross that they were suppressing great emotion.

Earl Browning, having got out of the maroon car, remained beside it, turning in a circle — disoriented or dizzy, thought Ross. Earl was sixteen and a friend of Alan Romberg's. On his cheek was a strip of white tape. He was short and muscular and his hair was freshly watered and combed. The white T-shirt he wore, like the tape, was piercingly bright in the sun. In a few moments Sam Romberg came outside to join Earl, and Ross noticed that although they stood face to face, they averted their eyes as they spoke. Then they moved over to the hammock which was slung between two apple trees and where Mr. Romberg would have been lying were this an ordinary Sunday, and the boughs above them, studded with reddening winesaps, dipped slightly as they sat down side by side.

Larry the Twitch, the youngest Romberg, came running home from the Sunday matinee (his mother had phoned the theater) and came to a stop beside the hammock. He scratched his chest and ankles and head as he listened to what Sam and Earl were saying. Larry the Twitch was nine and nervous. He picked an apple off the ground, brushed off a speck of dirt or an ant, took two small bites, and threw it away.

Ross wondered where Alan was. And he wondered what the Brownings were doing over there — the Rombergs never had company. He closed his magazine and was about to stand up and cross the alley and ask what was going on when Sam left the hammock (Larry the Twitch bounced into his place) and came over to Ross's yard and sat down under the elm. Sam had inherited his mother's even disposition but not her smile; his face — fine-featured and swarthy — was serious.

"I've got to get away from there for a while," he said. "I can't stand to be around a bunch of people bawling."

"What's going on?"

"My ma and Earl's ma and Ruthellen are all in the kitchen bawling. I think Ruthellen's boyfriend is even bawling. Listen, you can hear them."

Ross cocked his ear and heard what might have been soft wailing — or a strain of music from a distant radio. "What happened?"

"Alan got killed. After dinner he took his bike out for a spin on Highway 42, and Earl Browning came along in his dad's pickup and asked Alan to ride with him. Earl just got his driver's license last week, and he was on his way out to some farm to deliver a tank of bottlegas. So Alan put his bike in the back of the pickup and got in and rode along, and Earl swerved for some reason and got his wheels over on the shoulder where the sand was loose, and they tipped over in a ditch. Alan broke his neck."

Ross felt a general rising of his innards, as though his lungs and heart were crowding into his throat. It took him a moment to find his voice. "What about Earl?" he asked, hardly aware of what he was saying, his eyes neither on Earl nor on Sam, but on the two men sauntering through the tomatoes.

"Earl cut his face. He says his head feels funny, but the doc says he's okay. The doc was at the accident when Ma and Dad got there. A cop was there too — and the undertaker. The undertaker's got Alan at the mortuary now, fixing him up." Sam's voice neither wavered nor cracked. If Larry was the Romberg's twitch, Sam was their stoic.

Ross was shaken. He didn't know how to absorb news of death when it struck this close. Death, until now, had remained safely afar, working its way among grandparents, soldiers, and distant great-uncles. But Alan Romberg was somebody you saw every day — a lanky, blue-eyed boy whose high spirits amused and irritated his friends. Ross had shot enough baskets with the older boys of the neighborhood to understand that Alan was the Romberg clown. He cavorted and joked and seemed incapable of earnest competition. He thought up nicknames for people who seemed to need them. It was Alan who had attached "the Twitch" to his brother's name. Next week Alan would have turned sixteen. Now he was dead.

Ross, his eyes on the tomato patch, closed his arms around his knees and pulled them toward his chin. Instead of feeling a sense of diminishment at the news of Alan's death, he had the curious impression that the neighborhood was suddenly overcrowded. Death had moved in. Ross didn't imagine Death in the black cloak of the Grim Reaper or in any other mortal guise, yet he had a strikingly clear sense of Death's airy, expanding presence, and if he had been asked to pinpoint the source — Death's home base — he would have pointed to the tomato patch. Why, he wondered, had Death chosen to reside among the tomatoes? Did Death have a nose for the dusty, fecund aroma that hung over gardens on hellishly hot afternoons? Or was it simply because the tomato patch was central to the neighborhood? Or because that was where Ross's eyes had been fastened when Sam told him about the accident?

How much time generally passed between victims? Who was next? The odds were against Death's visiting the Romberg house again in the near future. With the Rombergs ruled out, the chances were slightly greater that Ross or his father or mother might be next. Ross's parents were napping this afternoon, and he had a sudden urge to run indoors and see if they still breathed, but he overcame the impulse, unwilling to let Sam, so tight-lipped and tough, learn of his fear. No, Ross reassured himself, Death for the time being was probably satisfied with Alan. Death would be feeling a lot of self-esteem right now, content to be hiding over there among the soft leaves and the whiskery stalks of the tomato patch, where Mr. Romberg and Mr. Browning, smoking and moving about with their heads bent, seemed to be searching him out.

Larry the Twitch left Earl in the hammock and came loping across the alley singing, "Alan got killed."

"I know," said Ross.

"I already told him," said Sam.

"Can I go in and tell your folks?" Larry the Twitch had not yet broken the news to anyone, had not yet drawn upon himself the glamour of his brother's death.

"They're asleep," said Ross.

"Scram," said Sam.

Larry the Twitch threw himself to the ground and paged, very fast, through Ross's magazine.

Again the Romberg's screen door opened and Ruthellen stepped outside with her boyfriend. Holding hands, they walked over to the hammock and said something to Earl, who got up and walked off with them around to the front of the house and down the dirt street toward the center of town. Perhaps they felt the need to mingle with a few of their contemporaries — the bowling alley would be open, and the drugstore soda fountain.

"How would you like to be Earl about now?" said Larry the

Twitch, probing his nose with a twig.

"That's a dumb question," said Sam.

Larry the Twitch showed his tongue to his brother, then said to Ross, "How would you like to be *us* about now? How would you feel if *your* brother got killed?"

"That's dumber yet," said Sam. "Ross hasn't got a brother."

"But if he did."

"Then he'd feel like we do." Sam put his head back against the rough bark of the elm and looked up at the dusty leaves. "He'd feel like hell."

Ross nodded. He wanted the Romberg brothers, especially Sam, to know how bad he felt even if he was brotherless, indeed how sick to his stomach he felt. He wanted to tell Sam that he hoped all this was a nightmare and not really happening, because if it was really happening he didn't see how he could go on living in a world where Death struck you down while you were out riding your bike on a Sunday afternoon. He wanted to explain that Death was not in the tomato patch, savoring his last victim, pondering his next. But not having the words to convey all this, yet feeling obliged to fill up the silence, he said, absurdly, "What about the bike?"

"The bike's got some bent spokes, is all. It flew over a fence and landed in a cornfield."

"It's in the back of Dad's pickup," said Larry the Twitch. "You want to see it?"

"No, I have to go in." Ross picked up his magazine and went into the house, leaving the Rombergs under the tree. He felt somewhat safer with the door closed behind him and the sound of his mother moving about in the bedroom. He settled into a deep chair in the living room, where his father was sleeping a deep, open-mouthed sleep on the couch, his arms thrown up over his head, his wrists crossed. Finding his place in the magazine, Ross pressed onward through the tedious story of exploration, benumbed by the long, neat columns of print, comforted by the soft whisper of his father's shallow snoring.

But Death, though formless by day, took shape in Ross's sleep. That night he dreamed he was down the basement fetching something for his mother — a jar of preserves — when he heard a scratching at the window where the coal chute was. He went to the window and saw a hand or a paw moving across the glass, the fingers human, the nails talons. Ross had come into the basement by daylight, but now it was suddenly dark. Luckily a flashlight materialized in his hand. He shone the beam up at the window and saw a snarling, hairy-faced creature peering down at him. The window, hinged to open inward, came unlatched, and the creature put in its head. Ross was unable to scream. He kept the light shining in the creature's eyes, which were red and watery. They were strange eyes. Everything else about the creature — the snarling, the matted hair, the claws — indicated voraciousness, but the eyes were oddly neutral, even vulnerable, and when Ross gathered up his courage along with his voice and said, "You're at the wrong house! You don't want anybody here! You want Mrs. Feeney next door!" the creature's motions were stilled. Ross woke up sweating and tangled in his blankets. The creature's face was etched in his mind and hs saw, though awake, something he had missed in the dream: plastered on the matted hair of Death's snarling face were the seeds and skins and dried juice of tomatoes.

On Monday morning Alan's body was put on display in the Romberg's sitting room, Mr. Romberg having decided that mortuary rent was more than he could afford, and there it remained until the funeral on Tuesday. Larry the Twitch stayed home from school on Monday and received, along with his mother and Ruthellen, the condolences of the townswomen who showed up, one after another all day, bearing cakes and pies and rolls and macaroni hotdishes, as though carbohydrates were bereavement's only known antidote.

On Monday Ross was surprised when Sam joined him on the way to school. "It's okay if Ma and Ruthellen and my runt of a brother want to stand around the coffin all day and bawl," he said, "but that's not for me. The way I see it, Alan's dead and I'm alive, and what good would it do Alan if I stayed home? And what good would it do me? The undertaker brought the coffin while we were eating breakfast. Dad had to go out and help carry it in. He says it isn't very heavy, even with Alan in it. Made out of wood, I guess, with this fancy cloth covering it. A deep red color." They were walking along the alley beside the tomatoes. "You going in and see Alan?"

"I suppose I should," said Ross, certain that no force on earth could make him do so. "Probably after school."

"I don't know why you should. He doesn't look like Alan."

"He doesn't?"

"He looks like somebody a lot older."

Earl Browning was in school on Monday as well. Ross saw him in the hallway, moving among his fellow sophomores but seeming separate from them, seeming to hold himself rigid as he walked, seeming deep in thought. On his face, where the tape had been, was a red scab.

Ross did not pay his respects after school, nor did his parents urge him to accompany them after supper when several of the Rombergs' close neighbors (close only by location; the Rombergs were without close friends) paid a group call. Ross's mother came home from the visit with her eyes wet. She said it was a dreadful, dreadful business — Alan looked so skinny and old, the rest of the Rombergs looked so forlorn. Ross's father said nothing, but picked up the Minneapolis *Star-Journal* and read it very intently until Ross's bedtime.

That night the hairy-faced creature came to Ross's bedroom window, opened it, and had one paw and forearm already inside when Ross became aware of him and shouted in terror, "Not here, not here, you want Mrs. Feeney next door!" Death backed away into the darkness. This time when Ross awoke he suffered a pang of guilt concerning Mrs. Feeney, a hump-backed, white-haired widow who took in washings. What if tomorrow morning Mrs. Feeney were discovered dead? Surely Ross would be to blame. Well, he could learn to live with Mrs. Feeney on his conscience. At least, living with that, he would not be lying in a coffin, skinny and old.

The Lutheran Church was crowded for the funeral on Tuesday (the sophomores went as a group), but though teachers declared absence excusable for this event, no one from the fifth grade attended but Sam, no one from the fourth grade but Larry the Twitch. On Tuesday night Ross did not dream of Death.

On Wednesday Mr. Romberg went to work, Ruthellen returned to Rochester, and both boys went to school. All quiet on the Romberg front. Neighbors remarked how quickly, after tragedy, life returned to normal, how easily (said Ross's mother, who sometimes wrote poems) death was absorbed in the fabric of Time.

But by the end of the week it became apparent that something was wrong with Mrs. Romberg. Though her cucumbers, corn, beans, tomatoes, squash and potatoes were ripening fast, she was making no attempt to bring in the harvest. Normally she would have been at work from sunrise till dark, boiling, pickling, canning, freezing; but now she let it be known (through Sam) that the neighbors were welcome to whatever they wanted from her gardens; it didn't make sense (she told Sam to tell the neighbors) for her to slave away at putting up vegetables when her husband was entitled to buy canned goods wholesale, and damaged cans for a lot less than that. The neighbors, however, had gardens of their own and all they could do to reap what they themselves had planted, and so as day followed autumn day the only visitors to the Romberg gardens were birds and rabbits, and Mrs. Romberg closed herself up in the house, coming outside only to hang clothes on the line or to call her two sons to supper. Soon neighbors were remarking how slowly, after tragedy, life returned to normal, how irregular (said Ross's mother) was the weave in the fabric of Time.

Walking past the tomato patch by day, Ross was infused with a powerful sense of the world's plentitude (those thousand or more fat orange globes breaking their stalks with their juicy weight), but seeing the tomato patch in his mind's eye as he lay in bed each night, he was vividly aware of the world's waste (the globes bursting their skins and rotting, the juice seeping into the earth), and very often his first moments of sleep were terrorized by the hairy-faced creature on the prowl.

After the first hard frost of October, the tomatoes rotted quickly, turning the color of prunes, and Ross's dream, though no less frightening, became less frequent. Through the winter — the black and leafless plants sticking up through the snow — Ross had the dream about twice a month, and each time he narrowly saved his life by reminding Death of Mrs. Feeney.

One night in the spring Ross had the dream twice, the second time (a particularly horrible vision of the creature reaching up from under the bed) just before he was awakened by the roar of a gasoline engine. This was a sunny morning in late April. Ross raised his shade and saw Mr. Romberg guiding a roto-tiller through the vacant lot across the alley, Mrs. Romberg moving ahead of him and pulling up last year's stalks and throwing them into a bonfire. When Ross came home from school at lunchtime, the vacant lot had been thoroughly plowed and raked; the moist, pulverized soil lay flat as rippled water — a sign to Ross, whose breast expanded with relief, that the hairy-faced creature would never again trouble his sleep. Home once more in the late afternoon, he noticed Mrs. Romberg on her knees, setting out her sprouts.

Old Mrs. Feeney died the following autumn. Ross and a few of his friends, including Sam, were playing football in the back yard when the undertaker arrived. The boys stopped their game to watch the body being borne from the house on a stretcher. By this time Ross's recurring dream was a memory so dim that Mrs. Feeney's part in his nightmares, as well as the part he might have played in her final nightmare, never crossed his mind. The undertaker and his helper slipped Mrs. Feeney into the back of the hearse and slammed the door and as the hearse moved off down the street the boys resumed their game.

BARBARA JUSTER ESBENSEN: I was born in Madison, Wisconsin in 1925, and attended elementary school, high school, and the University of Wisconsin there. At the university, I majored in Art Education, but from earliest childhood, I have considered myself "a writer." For most of my life, my writing concentration has been in poetry.

After graduation from the UW, I taught art, and had the pleasure of seeing my watercolors in juried shows in Wisconsin. In the fifties, we moved to the Trust Territory of the Pacific Islands. While there, I had a chance to teach creative writing to Micronesian students who spoke English as a foreign language, and it was from this experience that I developed the strategies for encouraging young people to take chances with language — to write "daring" poetry. All of this resulted in a book, *A Celebration of Bees: Helping Children Write Poetry,* brought out by Winston Press in 1975.

Another book, SWING AROUND THE SUN, a collection of my poetry for children, was published earlier by Lerner Publications, and recent poetry has appeared in such literary journals as *Moons and Lion Tailes, Sing, Heavenly Muse, Alembic, Great River Review, Poetry NOW, Identity,* and the forthcoming *Milkweed Chronicles.*

I am married to Thorwald Esbensen, and we have had six children, presently ranging in age from eight to 29. We have two grandchildren as well. THE GONIFF is my very first attempt at writing fiction for adult readers.

Barbara J. Esbensen

THE GONIFF

"He's got a tootsie somewhere," my grandmother is saying. She fills her sister-in-law's glass with tea and puts the teapot back on the copper samovar. They are sitting at the round table in the front-room window, watching the house across the street.

"How do you know this?" Yenta leans expectantly toward my grandmother who is still peering out into the early spring morning. My grandmother lets the lace curtain drop back across the glass and faces Yenta. She flings her arm out in an extravagant gesture.

"He's too *fine* with her. He's too *good* with her. He is too full of presents. For nothing he gives her little gifts. What kind of a man does these things, I ask you? He's got a tootsie hidden away someplace and he's full with guilt." She wraps a napkin around the steaming glass and pops a cube of sugar into her mouth. She sips the tea. Her grey eyes narrow against the steam.

Yenta is disappointed. She is ready to hear juicy facts, not opinion. She wants evidence. Names. The body. Or, in this case, bodies. The implied weapon, she already knows.

"Well!" she explodes, banging her glass down on the white crocheted tablecloth. Tea splashes out and stains the petals of a lacy flower. Yenta moves her arm casually, and covers the stained place. "What do you mean, 'What kind of a man does these things?' My God, Golda, what's the matter with you? Your Albert is exactly this kind of a man! Your Albert is good to you, he gives you plenty of presents. More than I ever see, I can tell you. Everything you say about Minna's Sam we could say about your Albert." She is becoming agitated, and her head shakes from side to side, as if it is saying, no-no-no. "So tell me, *dear* sister-in-law-with-opinions, what are you talking about? Can't you make sense already this early in the morning?" Long strands from her thick pile of black hair have come loose. Impatiently, she jerks her head to one side and raises both arms to twist the stragglers into place, jabbing a big hairpin into the high coil on top of her head.

"My Albert? My Albert we don't mention in the same breath with the name of Sam Kaler, Yenta. *Yenta*! What have you done to my cloth? Oy! It's staining the whole thing!"

Yenta's face looks surprised. It is the face of a person seeing this stained flower for the first time. She is deciding whether or not she should look insulted and stalk out of the room. But there is this business about Sam Kaler. So, instead she says, calmly, "A little cold water and lemon juice will take it out. Here, I'll do it. Go on already, Golda. What were you saying about Sam?"

My grandmother is standing now, and the light glints off her reddish hair and the little gold-framed cameo pinned against the dark cloth at her throat. She is forty. Her fair skin is unwrinkled and firm and her wide cheekbones are tinged with color. She is big-boned and strong. When she is older, people will say she is 'heavy-set.'

"I am saying," she measures out each word, "I am simply saying Albert is good to me because he is a good man. He gives me presents because it is his nature to give me presents. He loves me. Not anybody else. Me. He wouldn't *look* at another woman. Not Albert." She stops for breath. The placid face is pink, her grey eyes look dark under their pale lashes. "That Sam Kaler over there," she gestures with her raised chin," he don't love anybody but himself. He is *so* good, oh *so* sweet to Minna *for a reason*. Any man with eyes like that — they slide over a woman like a snake. Pftui!" She spits out the word. "When he tips his hat to me, I cross the street." She nods her head for emphasis. "I don't even like to go into the store alone when he's at the butcher block. That's how much I trust that *goniff*!"

Yenta has finished with the stain. "You don't *know* he has a tootsie, Golda. I sit here listening to you. I expect to hear the woman's name, her initials, at least. And you don't tell me nothing. You're just making it all up. Is it because he is such a good-looking fella?" She glances sideways at my grandmother. "One of these days poor Minna is going to hear what you say, and then what will you do?"

"One of these days, Minna is going to figure it out for herself. Then what will *she* do? That's the sad part. There are plenty men with women stuck away for fooling around with. And where are the wives? At home, suffering. What woman wants the shame of a divorce? Take Rose Mandlebaum for example, Yenta. You remember her?'' My grandmother leans across the tablecloth.

Yenta certainly remembers Rose Mandelbaum. Everybody knew about the women her Abe fooled around with. One of them, he had tucked away for years and years and Rose knew, Rose *knew*! But hard as it was for her, humiliating as it was for her (they tell each other over and over), she stayed in that man's house as his wife. They remember what Rose kept saying.

"That's the last thing I would do," Rose told everybody. "Why should I give him exactly the thing he wants from me? I ask you! He stays married to me. *Me*! I make every minute of every day HELL for him!" It's true. A divorce . . . that shame is worse than death . . .

My grandmother is standing, and has moved to the window again. She eases back the curtain, "My God! Look at that! He's at it again, the liar!'' Yenta and my grandmother stare across the street at the tableau, framed like a valentine, in ecru lace.

When summer comes, the Kaler front porch will be nearly hidden by the spreading leaves of the wide-branching maple tree that stands alongside the frame house. But this is only the beginning of the Wisconsin April and the little green fists on the branches are barely open. The women can see the entire porch.

Sam has one arm around his wife. In his other hand, he holds a derby hat against his checked coat. Below the edge of the coat, his butcher-apron hangs down to his knees. He is saying goodbye. He has bent his whole body into hers, so that her back is curved like a dancer's, and her skein of shining hair nearly sweeps the porch floor. He is kissing her eyes. Her mouth. Her neck.

"My God! He don't care *what* he does, and she is like a lamb to slaughter. What did I tell you!''

Sam releases Minna now, and she leans weakly against a pillar as he clears the last two steps with one leap. He turns to wave at her, and then he swivels around on one heel to face my grandmother's house. He looks directly at the front-room window whose lace panels fall shut at the same moment. He tips his hat.

"Now *that's love*,'' Yenta sighs. "Oy! What a love they have. She loves him. He loves her. And you, Golda, *you* are crazy if you don't admit this — a real mishugeneh.''

"That's guilt,'' says my grandmother, snapping the curtain into place. Her face is burning. She has seen Sam Kaler tip his hat.

Now the day settles into its routine. Yenta has gone and my grandmother moves to the kitchen. Albert is already at the scrap-iron yard, and all the other men in the neighborhood are off working someplace. Thank God in this country there is always some honest work a man can do, and no soldiers on horses to tell a man what he cannot do.

The hired girl trails into the yard, dreamily twirling a dandelion between her fingers. My grandmother sets her to work at the washtubs standing on the back porch, and goes inside to stir up the bread dough. A nice plump hen, newly killed, is already simmering in a big pot on the woodstove, and it makes a comfortable plopping sound as it turns itself into soup.

Yenta is next door in her yard. My grandmother can hear her singing offkey as she whacks the dusty rugs hanging over her clotheslines. It's much too early for spring cleaning, but Yenta has energy she doesn't know what to do with — doesn't know how to use in any other way.

Spring mornings are predictable. The vegetable man's little pony cart comes clop-clopping past, filled with early lettuces and greens. His name is Harry Tomato. That's what they have always called him, these Russian Jews of Mound Street. Harry Tomato. Nobody remembers his real name anymore. To them all it sounds like a real American name. His wife they call Tomaychika. It means a lady tomato. Depending on the day of the week, Yankel the Milchiker will stop by, with his cans of cool fresh milk. The ragpicker appears on their street every once in a while calling out, in his torn voice, his plea for old clothes.

My grandmother saves for him the clothes she can no longer mend for her growing family. Once a month the scissors-grinder walks past, pushing his tinkling wagon before him. The grinding wheel turns as the wagon moves, getting itself ready to whirl up showers of sparks against the sharp-tongued blades of the neighborhood knives and scissors.

On Mound Street, at the beginning of the twentieth century, spring mornings are comfortably predictable.

Yenta in her back yard, and my grandmother in her kitchen, hear the sound at the same time: the heavy blowing and stamping of two big horses, stopping right in front of the Kaler house. This is not part of the ordinary predictable morning. My grandmother hurries to the front-room and shoves one lace panel aside with her elbow. Her hands are powdered with flour and she holds them stiffly in front of her as she peers out.

Two overstuffed chairs, two large men, Minna Kaler, and little Dollie all appear simultaneously on the proch. The two chairs and the men continue down the steps and disappear inside the big covered cart. Minna Kaler is running down the stairs and up again, crying and waving her arms. Dollie sits on the top step and sucks her thumb, her head turning from the men to her mother and back again.

The men enter the house once more. A moment later they emerge, balancing Minna's worn horsehair sofa between them. By this time, Minna has collapsed on the stairs, Dollie is crying, and my grandmother is whipping off her apron. She is across the street like something shot out of a cannon, and pulls poor Minna up by one shoulder, shaking her and yelling her name.

"Minna! Stop this bawling! What is happening? Who are these men? Tell them to put your things back in the house this minute! YOU!" She hooks her floury fingers in the suspenders of one of the men. "What do you think you are doing?"

The man, a gigantic Swede, with a good-natured bland face, ignores my grandmother's question, but she has wound her other arm around the porch pillar, and he finds that he cannot move. Yenta and a cloud of dust are flying toward them from the other side of the street. The man twists out of my grandmother's grasp. She lurches toward him again, trying to get a new hold on his shirttail.

"LIS-sen LA-dy," he shouts, holding her off with one huge paw, "MIS-ter KA-ler hees PAY-in' oss tew take owt hiss FUR-nichure. Ve are FUR-nichure MEW-vers. Ve are MEW-vin Fur-nichure. Now git OWT off are vay!" The sofa bumps against my grandmother, and she stumbles down the steps, colliding with the advancing Yenta, who has the big wire rug-beater clenched in both hands, brandishing it above her head.

"Minna! Stop crying and run to Sam down at the store. And YOU! Don't you touch another stick until she gets back!" She has changed the position of her arms as she launches herself up the porch steps toward the men. The rugbeater is now cocked over her right shoulder like a baseball bat, and its wire scrolls and arabesques vibrate with her fury.

"Don't worry!" she shouts to my grandmother as Minna staggers to her feet and runs, sobbing, to the little grocery store where Sam works as butcher for his cousin, Ben Kaler. "There is some kind of good answer. Sam Kaler has the answer to this thing with these men taking out from his house these chairs. Don't worry. It will be explained. I know Sam already seven, eight years!"

Sam has the answer. "It's all right!" gasps the returning Minna. She is trotting toward them, her long skirts held up off the street with one hand. She is waving with the other. Sam is at her heels, gesturing wildly at the waiting men.

Darling Sam wanted it to be a surprise, but now the secret is out, she tells them. These men are removing all the furniture because — OH! such a man is Sam — because Sam has gone and bought everything new! Imagine this! Little Dollie will not be sleeping in that shaky old crib tonight. NO! Her Papa has bought for her a lovely bed. Probably the very bed — the white iron one with the twisted hearts at the head and the foot — that she and her darling Sam have looked at so many times at Mr. Schwid's store.

Everything will be delivered later this afternoon. Minna is ecstatic. Yenta has lowered her arms and is holding the rugbeater directly in front of her face. She nods triumphantly at my grandmother through the tears that well up in her black-olive eyes, and turns to gaze at Sam Kaler, handsomest man in town.

He has brought the miracle of affluence to Mound Street. Who could suspect that the young kosher butcher should be able to save so much money already from the salary his cousin Ben pays him? And to do such a lavish and such a loving thing . . . no wonder Yenta is overcome. It's beautiful, *beautiful*!

Through all this, Sam has been directing the men, in a lowered voice, to continue their work. He saunters over to Minna, throws an arm over her shoulder. His little girl holds onto her mother's skirt. He looks at the women, who have moved out of the way, and are standing at the foot of the steps.

"Ladies," he salutes them with his free hand, "now you see what is happening here, you can go home. The secret is out. My Minna knows now what kind of a man she has." Minna blushes. The women turn to leave. What more is there to do here? Even my grandmother has to admit that a man who does such a thing for his wife is a real mensch. A human being. A gentleman, probably.

"Mrs. Dubrov," he calls after her. My grandmother turns around, and shades her eyes against the spring sunshine. The light twinkles along the row of tiny buttons that chase themselves down her dress from throat to waist. "You are looking very nice this morning." Sam's eyes slide up, down, across her body. She can feel the little buttons trying to unfasten themselves.

"Rasputin!" she breathes, fleeing down the path and across the street to her safe house. She can hear his mocking laughter, but when she and Yenta are inside looking out, there is only Minna on the porch with Dollie. They are watching the horses strain at the heavy load that moves slowly away under budding branches. A violet network of sun and shadow slips over the big dray-wagon as it drives out of sight around the corner. Minna takes Dollie inside. The porch and the street are empty.

In my grandmother's kitchen, the chicken soup gives off its perfume, and the bread dough breathes under a clean cloth near the stove. Yenta can't sit down, and strides around and around the table where my grandmother is laying out some strudel and glasses for their tea.

"You see, Golda, you see. All that talk about Sam. And for what? Now you see where your mind is wrong about him. You got to admit he don't have any tootsie at all."

My grandmother sits down, and pours out the tea. She motions to Yenta. "Sit, sit, sit. I suppose so. But this kind of man . . . I thought he had a woman somewhere. I felt he had a woman. But . . ." Her voice trails off.

"But! Yes, *but* is right! There is no *but* . . . how could a man spend a fortune on brand new furniture for his wife — enough for a whole house — and have anything left over for a tootsie? We close now the case!"

It is three o'clock, and the smell of baking bread finds its way through the open front door, and the screenless front-room window. My grandmother is on the porch standing on a wicker armchair. She has washed the pane with ammonia water and seems to be focusing all her attention upon polishing it with a dry cloth. Actually, she is a little surprised to find herself beginning her spring cleaning so early. The weather is still apt to turn chilly — it could even snow, as everyone glumly tells one another at this time of the year. There is a gentleness in the air this afternoon, though, and Golda has already scrubbed the wicker porch furniture that the hired girl lugged around to the front of the house from the shed out back. Might as well have it nice and clean and ready for summer's most popular pastime: front porch sitting.

My grandmother shifts her body a little, before the glass. A wavery reflection of the house across the street appears. She can see the steps of the Kaler porch and the two pillars supporting the roof. Standing on the top step, framed by the pillars, is Minna Kaler. My grandmother watches the blurred figure arrange itself against the lefthand pillar. Minna's face, reflected in the glass, looks greenish and out of focus.

It is "later in the afternoon" — the time of day Minna has been waiting for ever since Sam confessed his wonderful secret about the delivery of the new furniture. My grandmother nonchalantly lowers herself from the chair. Now, still with her back to the street, she lifts the screen from the floor and hooks it into place in front of the sparkling glass window. She turns the chair around, so that it is facing the street. She shifts the other two wicker chairs and the matching white table, and dumps the pailful of dirty water over the railing. She looks up, and as if just discovering Minna that very instant, waves.

Minna waves. She bends her head forward and pulls out a watch that hangs on a chain around her neck. My grandmother can see her shoulders raise and lower in a great blowing-out of breath. They both turn their heads to look down the street. The delivery wagon from Schwid's Fine Furniture will be coming from that direction. Despite her attitude toward Sam Kaler and anything connected with him, my grandmother is filled with nervous excitement at the prospect of seeing all this beautiful furniture arrive.

Minna looks across at my grandmother and spreads her empty hands apart in front of her. Her hands are saying, "Nu? So how long will we have to wait, already?"

"It takes time to get here from Schwid's over on the East side, Minna," my grandmother calls to her. "Here comes Yenta. Wait. I'll bring out a little lemonade and something to nosh — a piece of sponge cake, a little this, a little that. You'll come over here and have something to eat. The time will pass better."

It is pleasant on the porch. There is a little breeze and a loamy smell comes from the freshly-turned earth in my grandmother's flower beds. Minna chatters nervously at Yenta and my grandmother. She wonders, her voice shaking a little, what kind of dining room table Sam has bought for them. She hopes he remembers how much she has wanted to have a really comfortable rocking chair, so that she can rock Dollie when she wakes up at night. At the mention of the rocking chair, Minna begins to laugh uncontrollably. It seems to sum up for her just what riches she is about to enjoy, and she laughs and laughs, throwing her head back against the edge of the chair, tears streaming down her cheeks. She is laughing and crying and choking on the lemonade.

"My God, she's going to make herself sick," cries Yenta. "Golda, she's historical!"

"Come, Minna, come." My grandmother takes the glass of lemonade out of Minna's limp hand, and makes her stand up. "Be a little calm now, and take a deep breath. There! Are you all right?" Minna sits. She makes little gestures of apology and dabs at her eyes. The three women gaze toward the east end of the street again. Nothing moves.

"Oy! Such a suspense," Yenta sighs. Minna looks again at her watch. My grandmother stands up. "I hear the children out in the back yard," she says suddenly. "Belle and the boys are home now from school. They'll have some of my bread and a glass of milk in the kitchen. Relax. I'll be right back. In two shakes, I'll be back. By then, who knows . . ."

Now the street rings with the calls of children returning from school. They saunter past, arm in arm, or whiz by on rollerskates, books flying out behind, caught in midflight by leather bookstraps held tightly in their hands. The spring sun has moved behind the tall synagogue at the west end of the street, and the air has turned chilly. Minna stands and pulls her arms tight against her chest. She shivers. She walks over to the front door and sticks her head inside.

"Thank you, Mrs. Dubrov, for the lemonade. I think I'll just go and sit on my porch for awhile and wait. It is still sunny on my top step. Maybe Belle would like to come and play with Dollie? She should be waking up any time now from her nap.

"I had to put her down to sleep on the parlor floor, on top of my heavy coat. You know how babies are — well, of course my Dollie is not still a baby, but she can sleep any place. And just think, tonight . . . !" She laughs and trots briskly down the steps and across the street, reveling in the anticipation of the glories to come — all the new things, and the little white iron bed for Dollie, most especially.

* * * * * * * *

It is twilight. Belle sits on the porch with Minna and Dollie and no one speaks. One by one, lights in the houses are beginning to go on. First in the kitchens, then in the living rooms, and soon all the dining room windows will light up. It is getting cold. My grandmother comes out into the front yard and calls across the street.

"Minna! Come over here, now with Belle and the baby, and Sam can find you here when he comes home. Come! It's too cold to be outside with the sun gone out of the sky. It's not summer yet! Belle, bring Minna and the little one, and come. Before you get good and sick already. Come! Sam will look for you over here, Minna. Something happened they didn't bring the furniture today. So you'll come now. Please."

Slowly, Minna stands up. Belle takes Dollie's hand and the three of them walk into my grandmother's house.

Darkness settles down. From the busy kitchen come the good smells of vegetables and chicken broth and fresh bread. The plates and bowls are brought out and set around the table in the dining room. My grandfather and the older boys and Belle and the younger children are all at home now, and there is a great deal of noise — laughter, crying, and general commotion — from every part of the house. Minna helps set the table and carry in the platters of chicken and the big tureen of hot soup. Her face is tired and white and her hands shake slightly. Sam has not put in an appearance yet. Sometimes his job as butcher keeps him at the store a little longer than usual, but he is never this late. And there is this matter of where they will all sleep tonight, since there is nothing to sit on or sleep in at their house . . .

My grandmother seems to read Minna's thoughts. "You'll stay here, in that big front bedroom tonight, Minna," she says quietly. "There is plenty room up there, and we have a nice cot for Dollie and plenty blankets, don't worry." Mina protests weakly, but she is glad to have this much of her strange situation settled so easily.

Dinner is ready and although Minna at first wants to wait and have her supper when Sam arrives, the family loudly convinces her to eat with all of them. "Dollie will eat her food better if you are eating too," they tell her.

While Minna and Belle and one of the boys wash the dishes, my grandmother and grandfather are speaking in low tones in the back bedroom. My grandfather tugs on his bushy moustache while my grandmother speaks to him in fierce whispers. Then he puts on his coat and goes out the front door. He walks down Mound Street, lit by a pale rind of moon, and turns the corner.

There is no light in the front part of the little grocery store, so my grandfather walks around to the far side where he can look in a window. It is pitch dark inside.

At midnight, they are still sitting around the table in the warm kitchen. Yenta, for once, is silent. Her husband has gone next door again to get some sleep, but he was here for hours trying to help the others figure out what has happened. This is a situation which has no answers, only questions. What has happened to the old furniture? And, most baffling of all, where is Sam Kaler?

Minna sits staring at the tablecloth. Her tea is untouched. She seems unable to move. Even her eyes are unblinking. Her fine skin is bleached, ashen. Under the light cast upon her face by the lamp hanging over the table, are the wavering shadows of her bedraggled hair. No one has spoken for some minutes.

From upstairs comes the wail of a child. "S-h-h-h-h! The little one. . . !" my grandmother whispers. She starts to get up but checks herself. "Minnaleh, go to her. She wants you. Go. Comfort her. She has a bad dream. She wants her mother. Go!" Like a puppet, Minna walks stiffly through the house. They can hear her trudge heavily up the stairs.

When my grandparents look in on them, sometime later, both Minna and Dollie are nestled down in the big bed, sound asleep. My grandfather turns down the lamp and my grandmother throws another blanket over the two of them, and opens the window. The cold spring breeze stirs the curtain.

The next morning, my grandfather doesn't go to the scrap yard. Instead, he storms down to the grocery store to confront Sam Kaler. But Sam is not there, and his cousin, Ben, doesn't seem to know anything — not about Sam's whereabouts or the furniture — nothing. He says he came to work as usual this morning, unlocked the store, and has been waiting for Sam ever since. My grandfather storms out again.

Days go by. My grandfather has spoken to the police captain, and they are keeping a half-hearted eye out for Sam, now listed as a *missing person*. The neighbors all have their own favorite theories about the disappearance of Sam Kaler. Maybe someone came in the night and killed him. Or *stole him*! There are bands of gypsy caravans travelling through town every now and then. The neighbors are still talking about the time, a couple of summers ago, when Mrs. Stein came out into her side yard in time to see her husband, Herman, streaking down the alley after a swarthy man wearing a bright bandana wrapped around his head. Herman made a grab for the small bundle the man had under his arm and wrenched it free of the man's shirt. At the same time, he stuck out his foot and the man went flying into the rose bushes that hang over all the back fences. The bundle turned out to be the Stein's 10-month-old baby girl, who had slept through the whole thing!

Of course it would be quite another thing to try to steal Sam Kaler, everybody agrees. But he is gone — without a trace, and one crazy explanation is as valuable as any other. The police stop by each evening to tell my grandfather there is no news. Minna's family in Milwaukee writes to tell her she should be brave — that Sam will come back. And even if it turns out that he is dead, she must be brave . . .

Then, one hot, muggy June morning, Harry Tomato comes past in his little pony cart full of early garden produce. My grandmother comes out on the porch to see what he brings, and to chat with Tomaychika who has ridden along. Minna is giving Dollie a bath in the room off the kitchen. Their voices drift through the house, with the sounds of water splashing. There is an occasional protesting cry from Dollie.

"Beautiful tomatoes I have for you, Mrs. Dubrov," Harry calls to her. "And lettuce, and nice green onions." He holds them up. They glisten like jade in the sunlight. He apologises for his rather long absence from Mound Street. For the past month he has been peddling his vegetables to the new neighborhoods out on the East Side. "Expending mine clientele," he explains. "Selling to them Lutheran and Catholic gentile ladies." And he has found a few farm women with nice vegetable gardens out there, east of the city limits. He can get all the fresh vegetables he needs, and will have enough for his customers on *both* sides of town!

Tomaychika climbs out of the wagon to stretch her legs. "Oy! Mrs. Dubrov, we are awful sorry to hear about what happened to that nice little Minna Kaler and her Dollie," she says, under her breath. She looks over her shoulder at the house across the street. Her husband gives a sorrowful sigh.

"My, my, my! Such a terrible way for them to die — slipping through the ice like that . . ." His voice trails off and Tomaychika brushes at her eyes with the corner of her skirt.

My grandmother, listening to the sounds of bathing and the clear voices of Minna and Dollie, is not sure she has heard what Harry Tomato is saying.

"*What*?" Now she is sure that she has heard him quite correctly indeed.

She advances toward the woman, her eyes narrowing, trying to keep from shouting. Every syllable is spoken deliberately.

"What are you talking about, Tomaychika? Who told you such a story?"

"Why, Sam Kaler, himself," Tomaychika replies. "Poor man. He told us with tears in his eyes. We met him in front of his gate, 'way out there east of town. He has that cattle place, of course you know that. Used to be it was the old man Svendson's? Maybe two, three weeks ago we saw him and the widow Svendson. A good-looking *shiksa*, and plenty smart, running that cattle business now all by herself. But I guess she will be the new Mrs. Kaler pretty soon. Such a ring she has on her hand. My Harry's tomatoes should only be big like that ring, I'm telling you!"

* * * * * * * *

Through all the days that follow, my grandmother tries, for Minna's sake, not to look triumphant. But when Minna and her child finally go back to the relatives in Milwaukee, there is no longer a need to be diplomatic.

"I told you! I knew she was hiding in the pickle barrel, this tootsie of his! You wanted a name, Yenta. That I didn't have. Now we all have her name. And Sam has her dead husband's cattle business. And She has Sam. And the money from the furniture," she adds bitterly. "And Minna? Minna has nothing!"

Yenta feels betrayed. Such a fine-looking hard-working man as Sam Kaler has no business being a — a — snake. That's what Golda calls him — daily. And this *shiksa* of his — how can a woman stoop to such a thing? To ruin a nice little family. And Minna? What will become of her now?

Yenta can only look sadly at Golda and shake her head. She feels like crying. Actually, no one doubts what Minna will do now. She will live in Milwaukee. Her crowded family will have to support her. She will have no husband, but she'll always be married to Sam. She'll be chained to Sam, and Sam will not even feel the shackles. He will live with the widow Svendson and people will forget, and neither one of them will ever give poor Minna another thought. On Mound Street, divorce is never an option. Nobody even considers it. People stay married. For better or worse, no matter what happens. A woman puts up with things. She is expected to suffer, if circumstances call for it. Not necessarily in silence, God knows, but . . . to suffer.

The news of the divorce action brought by *Kaler, Minna G.* against *Kaler, Samuel*, reaches Mound Street with the force of an earthquake. There is even a moment or two when the neighborhood seems to forget whose side they're on.

A divorce! Oy, such a mess it makes! What kind of woman would go through with such a thing? In a *court* she had to go! And little Dollie, too, thumb in her mouth, telling the judge, "My Papa took my crib . . . down . . . the . . . steps . . ."

Who ever heard of such a thing, I ask you — a baby in front of a judge! But Minna, soft and pretty Minna, looking so helpless up there in the courtroom, everything she owns . . . gone . . . gone . . . There is not a dry eye when she steps down. They remember whose side they're on.

Soft pretty Minna takes Sam for everything he's got. Guided by a relative who is a lawyer, she sues and sues and takes and takes.

* * * * * * * *

Milwaukee is such a cultural place. Minna moves away from her relatives and rents a pretty apartment near the Normal School. She takes English lessons, and elocution lessons, and has big plans for Dollie in music and dancing. Maybe a fine career on the stage — who knows? In this country, everything is possible. She loves to think about the money, growing bigger and bigger there in the red sandstone bank building downtown. She loves to think about the money and all the things she can do with such a glittering heap of it.

She buys her clothes at Chapman's, where the doctors' wives shop for their dresses and their coats, and their lacy underwear. She goes to the hairdresser and has her tawny hair fixed like the beautiful Lillie Langtry's. People tell her that she is even prettier than the English actress whose pictures are in all the store windows these days. She doesn't believe them, of course. Still, she is aware of her magnificent hair and fine figure. She knows that heads do turn to look at her when she walks down Wisconsin Avenue in the brisk autumn air, her arms loaded with packages.

Sam must borrow the money from his *shiksa* and people say that things are never quite the same there again.

It took a long time for Mound Street to settle down after the events that rocked it that spring and summer. After Minna and Dollie had left, my grandmother and Yenta, from force of habit, would sit by the front-room window, drinking their morning tea and gazing at the porch across the street.

The house was eventually rented to a Litvak family, who filled it with noisy red-headed children. But it took a long, long time before my grandmother stopped looking over there, expecting some morning to see once more the famous Sam Kaler kissing scene . . .

This story is affectionately
dedicated
to my grandmother, and to
her children
and to all the people who
lived on Mound Street when
this century was newly turned

DEXTER WESTRUM: I grew up in Albert Lea, Minnesota, where my father taught me to trap muskrats. I also lived for long periods in Vermont and South Dakota. In all three places I knew old timers who insisted on living their lives according to their own rather elemental rules of self reliance.

Dexter Westrum

TRAPPING

He was a man not as old as he appeared to be. Coming through the rushes onto the lake, his foot had tangled with the rope of the sled, his balance had given away in the loose shore-line snow and for a finite second, he had been adrift, disjointed in the universe, above the ice. Shoulder tucked, he rolled out of his suspension, the sky becoming earth, and landed, upright, bent at the hams, the sound of his feet slapping the earth carrying in the distance. His eyes focusing, he turned to double check the count of his traps.

Forty of them, wired to poles, lay piled within a roughly fachioned box affixed to an old sled, once belonging to his elder child. As he knelt above the box, his shorn hair shone blue in the early morning sun. His count completed, he fastened his collar and pulled his parka hood over his head. As a second thought he made sure his hatchet was under the poles. Then he took the wooden handle of his iron hook in one hand, lifted the sled rope over his head with the other and moved out.

Once he was beyond the rushes, the wind picked up. His cheeks, worn down to the blood vessels and protected by lonely gatherings of black and gray hairs, wrinkled up to keep the water in his eyes.

He had never been forced to trap this county before and was not sure how things would go. It is a public lake, he thought to himself. So far nobody else has come. I have to set these traps before anyone does.

Coming to a feeder house, a brown pimple of mud and reeds frosted with snow and ice, he stopped. Stuck in its base was a pole with a strand of red cloth, twitching now and then in the wind, tied around it. He loosened the pole and played with the wire going from it into the house. He heard a splash, some scratching, and metal against ice. This one was alive. With the hatchet he whacked through the frosting, cutting a triangle in the house top. Over night this piece, removed yesterday when the trap was set, had refrozen in place. Returning the hatchet to the sled, the man picked up his hook.

A slick, soaked muskrat, trapped at the tail, sat center feeding table, glistening eyes looking over tobacco colored teeth out the hole. The man began to play the hook at the rat's nose. The angry rat clamped it behind his teeth. The man lifted pole and hook. Animal and trap followed, for a brief moment afloat in the universe. Jerking the hook and letting loose of the pole, he whipped the animal, belly flop first, to the ice. Scratching for traction, it tucked its feet under itself and lifted its nose toward the man. The side of the hook landed on its crown; the animal twisted to its back, hind legs pumping. Rich blood, brightly shining in the sun, streamed from its nose and mouth into blotches on the snow.

"Rat," he said, "I need you worse than you need life."

After he had reset the trap and secured the house, the man shook snow and blood from the rat. Then he dropped it, its pliable body curling, into the box among the poles.

Although pelts were now up to a dollar thirty-five, the first three weeks of trapping had been slow. Usually in a two month season, he could count on picking up a thousand to fifteen-hundred dollars. And, as always, he must again earn that amount if his family were to eat this winter and spring. The pheasants and ducks from last fall were almost gone. But until now the prices had stayed below seventy-five cents and his income to date was scarcely above three hundred dollars. He must stay at the lake late today, set the new traps and run the line two, perhaps three, times.

Within two hours there were twelve new rats and he was nearing the place where he hoped to make the new settings. And, he calculated, he had only fifteen sets yet unattended to.

Laying his hook down, he sat on the poles and traps and rats. Half unzipping his parka, he took a cigarette from the pack in his shirt pocket. He lighted it and inhaled. Closing his eyes, he saw himself in the evenings, sitting at his table, peeling the fur from the purple carcasses and snapping their tails. Hides were in piles at all reaches of the cellar and he would be proud as he walked through them to go upstairs and sleep. His toes wiggled and small patches of snow squeaked under his vibrating boots. After another, longer, drag, he opened his eyes to see three bodies emerging from the rushes near the end of the line of his marked houses.

From their rhythm and bounce, he judged them to be high school boys. Then perhaps the tallest, the one with the hand ax, could have been somewhat older. He didn't know. The two shorter boys were of thick build. One carried a gunny sack, the other ribbons of blue cloth.

He did not believe them at first. He was less than a hundred yards from them and still they walked up to the final feeder, the tall one cutting a wedge in its top, took out his trap, relieved it of its catch and remade the setting. One of the thicker boys replaced the man's red marking with a blue one. The third boy lifted the drowned animal by its tail and dropped it into the sack.

In less than half an hour they were up to where the man sat. At first they laughed or commented on the size of a caught rat. One rat was alive and had to be killed with the blunt end of the ax. But as they neared the trapper, they were quiet. Never did they turn their heads to look at him.

He studied them as they worked. In cowboy boots, blue jeans and athletic award jackets, they were not dressed for the lake, yet they did not behave as if they were cold. They wore no neck scarves and their wool stocking caps sat at the backs of their heads. They work in too much of a hurry, he thought.

After putting out his cigarette against the sled, the man picked his hook off the ice and stood up. The tall one gingerly rapped his ax into the feeder house right next to where the man was standing. The man laid his hook over the handle of the ax.

"We had better talk," he said.

The boy let go of the ax and looked down at the man. The shorter boys, standing behind to either side of him, completed a triangle.

"I want to thank you for the seven rats you've got in that sack," the man began, taking his hook off the ax. "But, so I don't have to call the sheriff, I think you'd better find those red markings and put them back on the poles."

"Go hump yourself, old man, we're taking over," answered the boy. A light sparkled obnoxiously in his eyes and his smooth face stretched widely into a smile.

"That's right, Mister," the boy with the ribbons added. "You're wrong to have been here."

The boy with the sack looked down at his boots.

"Our family farms this shore," the tall one went on, "and we always trap this side of the lake."

Seeing the boys were eager and their bodies agile, the man became aware of how tired he was. His calves had tightened during his rest and there was a pain at the bottom of his back.

"The lake is public property," he began. "My traps were the first set. I started at the other side and have worked over to here."

"Look, old man, if you've got any sense, you'll take your stuff and get out of here before the three of us get rough," the tall one cut in. Letting out a snort, the boy with the ribbons grinned.

The man stood expressionless. He was too tired to make a stand. Impatient, the leader came face to face with the man and with both hands pushed him toward the sled. The one with the ribbons started to close in.

After giving a step, the man pushed off his right foot, cocked and unleashed his right arm from underneath, catching the boy in the mouth with the backside of the iron hook. The boy dropped as if he were unpeeling from a banana, hit on his back, rolled to his stomach, spun and came up on his knees, his face in his hands. Blood strained through his fingers and clotted in the snow.

The man silently regarded the others. The one with the ribbons began backing up; the remaining boy dropped the sack and stared.

His eyes emitting hatred, the bloodied one looked up at the man. With a moaning growl he started to rise, his hand stretched out toward the ax still stuck in the feeder. The man hooked the ax where the head meets the handle and backhanded it out over the ice. It landed and slid, scraping up small swirls of snow. Frustrated, his energy spent, the boy sagged and collapsed on the ice. Cautiously the man stepped back and set himself for the remaining two.

The ribbons shaking in his closed fist, his eyes filling with tears, the second boy screamed:

"You didn't fight fair, ya son of a bitch, you didn't fight fair."

MIKE FINLEY: has published five books of poetry and prose. His work has been featured in *Rolling Stone, New: American and Canadian Poetry, The Midwest Quarterly, Pebble Prairie Schooner, Poetry Now, The Lamp in the Spine, Invisible City, Steelhead, Midatlantic Review, Grub Street, Rockbottom, Falcon, Abraxas, Northeast, Ironwood, Moons & Lion Tailes, Calliope, Chowder Review, Manroot, Truck, Beyond Baroque, Shore Review* and many others.

In addition, Finley has worked as television producer, aerial photographer, zookeeper, talk-show host, farmhand, soda pop bottler, graphic designer, book/theater/music reviewer, and storefront minister.

He is currently employed as publisher and editor of The Kraken Press, a small company specializing in unusual literary and graphic work, and as editor of the Worthington, Minnesota, *Daily Globe.*

Mike Finley

HOW ARE YOU GOING TO KEEP THEM IN PARIS?

I worked for a while as a proofreader for a typesetting firm. It was my job to notice mistakes and correct them. The office was on the ground level of a twelve-story building in downtown Minneapolis, but what we published was farm magazines. There I sat, the city around me, the panoply of agriculture, the language of the farm spread out on my desk.

It was slow reading for me: only a farmer, that impossible ordinary man, would understand the difficult words. What the farmer had to know covered everything: chemistry, mechanics, medicine, agronomy, economics, law.

I scarcely understood a word! But it was a job, day in and day out, the eyes on the lookout for error.

When I thought of the city, I thought of a couple of months earlier, when at a meeting of the editors of a radical magazine, there was a big bitter kid, upset about the city.

Make other plans, he said, forget about those people. Something is wrong with their minds. The way they're all connected, they always think something will save them, some ambulance, some last-minute pardon or something. Our revolution is rural, tribal.

When the others looked at one another, he rose to leave. Look at this rawhide coat, he said. I made it myself. I live in a teepee. Don't you understand what I'm telling you?

I think of the downtown of Minneapolis, of the tallest building there, the IDS Tower. From a long distance off, it looks like the key to every other small midwestern town, like the plain gray grain elevator standing like the phallus of every simple town.

And so it is. There is our wealth. You can imagine its translation from dirt and water and sun into wheat and soybeans and corn into hard cold cash, the clatter of combines on a hot day in August, suddenly the mental hum of cybernetic circuitry.

It's the old story.

There is a feeling city dwellers sometimes have that somehow, in some mysterious way, something important is being kept from them. A major cover-up of a glaring truth. Have you never had this feeling?

It turns out that among the conspirators are the cement truck, the glass-man, the shrubberies dotting every green suburban lawn. What happened to dirt — the common, the ordinary, that which was below? Who is protecting us from our earth?

Bored with my galleys, drumming my blue-pencil, I am thinking these things.

I think it has something to do with excrement, how the living blend into the unliving, how consciousness that is us becomes earth. Down there. Forever. Fear!

I take the elevator to the top of the IDS building. From the 52nd floor, Minneapolis is what it always was, a forest once again, trees obscuring the boulevards and homes. Only the forest from on high is a mat of wet moss. It is hard to see properly.

It is as if — it is as if we are all skycrapers now, as if we all wear 52-story stilts at will. How mighty of us: it is as if we are all of us now giants, magicians, minor gods.

A century ago a man wielded his own weight, plus what his horse could pull, his axe bring down. But now, with these long legs of ours, these lungs like great flapping canyons, our voices heard across oceans, outer space . . .

Some are so powerful here in this provincial capital that rising from their chairs nudges the planet in its orbit.

Down in the street, away from the noise of the composition machinery, I follow a retarded man in a checkered suit. He is singing a song, "The Impossible Dream."

He enters the bus station. There on a poster is Fred MacMurray. See America for all it's worth, he says.

The bus station is honeycombed with safes. (Some safes! At midnight they all get emptied out.)

Going for a trip is the opposite of having 52-story stilts; it's like taking a pill that shrinks you down, that makes you so small you can thread the narrow eye of the city limits. Another pill and the city's conveniences shrink to the dimensions of several pieces of luggage.

Buses go out to Chicago, San Francisco, Seattle, Kansas City,

Winnipeg. Buses come in from Elbow Lake, Owatonna, Worthington, St. Cloud.

There is a man with a funny cloth veil around his neck. It hides his laryngectomy hole. When he breathes, the veil puffs out. When he inhales, it goes flush against his throat. He is tearing the cellophane ribbon off the top of a pack of cigarettes.

A man wearing two pairs of pants wears a button saying Smile, God loves you. His zippers are both open.

Middle-aged people put their parents on buses and send them away.

A pale young woman who is passing for white kisses her blacker mother good-bye.

Good-bye.

Outside on a corner is a building with Chinese characters emblazoned on the facade. A camper with a million important messages on it zips by. Believe in Jesus Christ Who Is Our God. Through Our Lord and Saviour Jesus Christ Who Is God.

On the other corner is a sign that says SIGNS.

A bus unloads a group of blind men and women. They gather to cross with the light. Their legs mesh in a motion, they are a centipede of women and men.

Saturday night in the city in the country. Two overweight teen-aged girls pause by the river, looking down. In the one world, the world of air, they see the sign that says GRAIN BELT BEER in fifteen foot letters. In the other world, the world of the river, the sign is a poem in green and red phosphorescence. The girls are creatures from the urban pastorale: two bridge-nymphs waiting for the next long train.

The birds of morning sing, they throw off their dew. A swallow soars, then crashes into an invisible windowpane. It crumples, it falls dead onto the sidewalk

But no! It picks itself up again! Yes, embarrassed to the marrow, it jumps back living into the air!

Sunday morning, overtime, I labor in the downtown gray. The buildings are gray, the sky is gray, all the streets are gray concrete, gray earth.

Down the gray sidewalk, just past the office where I'm reading my galleys, a man is walking, and under his arm he is carrying a potted plant.

In a recurring fantasy I return to my apartment, find everything gone, all but a message smeared in soap on the bathroom mirror:

Thank you for your things, we were all of us struck with the care shown in your selection. Not everyone shows such care these days. Try not to feel like a victim.

All my things, my books, my pictures, my music, gone. What a feeling! Like awakening with a start in the dark of night, I check my body to see if all the parts are still there, or if just my head is resting on the pillow, making all this up, the rest of me gone off to try its luck elsewhere.

It was only a fantasy. Every time I put lock to key, I have it all over again.

So I sit on the stoop and watch who passes. More fantasy; my brother visits.

"I forgot to mention," the dream-brother says, "I lost my key, so I left your place unlocked."

"It's all right," I tell him, the vacuum of my living room cool upon my shoulders, "it's all right."

Other times I imagine the sound of footsteps overhead. Or the sound of a drawer sliding open in the dark. Or the curl of smoke loosening in the air.

I worry. It's fun. "It's all right."

Yesterday the neighbors packed off for San Francisco and a new life. There they go: mother, father, three kids, a midget, a dog, two cats, a TV, trailer, furniture, motorcycle, dolls.

Waving, they depart, driveshaft sparking against the cement.

An old love telephones. "It's been five years. I wanted to chat. Tell me about your life."

She tells me about hers: happy, and married, a mother now, such darling children, approval raining down upon her from this direction, that.

Yet in the midst of it, this mysterious phone call.

"Tell me I didn't ruin your life. Or did I?"

"Absurd," I tell her, the thought fresh all over of being seventeen, the impossibility of it.

"The idea," I tell her, and I am gripping the receiver now.

I glance about my one-room apartment. Another fantasy: Books, pictures, music still there.

Still the sensation of robbery.

A week in the country with family. I recall how the doors there swung open year-round. Even on vacation the doors never locked. I pull down the driveway late one night. The door, locked. I climb in through a torn screen window.

"More tea, cake," my mother offers. How jealous I used to be of the hours of her day, and how envious she now is of mine. Our lives, I consider: the things we would make of one another's.

I stayed a week there. It could not last. One morning, still dark, I made my farewells.

We kissed on the stairs overlooking the creek. I walked to the car, I licked my lips in the black of the air.

MARRIAGING

My friends and I keep putting off marriage until we find a person to marry. All the people I know, know their parents want grandchildren.

Lately I've been breaking rules I don't have to break. After two years of toothaches and waiting in unemployment lines, I found work.

Now I wake up at 6:30 a.m., do my teeth, bike the dog through the neighborhood. The sun is just rising then, and the air seems particled, like a painting of Seurat's. Or else it's just my eyes.

We want to sneak her into the park wading pool, but there is a sign that says no plus a man raking beer cans out of the water.

Work isn't hard. I thought it would be but it isn't. Sometimes I wonder if I'm doing it right, whether I'm good or whether I'm not good. It's not always easy to tell.

My new clothes don't fit exactly right. I was at a wedding and the minister said for everyone to take oaths with the two getting married. All the strangers looked at each other. Some smiled, some didn't. My new clothes didn't feel exactly right.

I bought a queen-size bed. I carried it home from the store on my head. I told the dog she's not allowed on. At night I stretch out on it like an X.

I telephoned my mother long distance. We talked.

I leave big tips. I pay my way to everything. I read the ads. I want a car. I bought some sunglasses.

I like to bicycle around the university and look at people through my new sunglasses. The relationships I have with the people I see are almost complete. First I see them from behind. Then I see them from the front.

My dog and I share supper. Now that I'm rich I eat more cheaply, more eggs, less meat, lots of vegetables. I don't drink much and won't smoke cigarettes now.

Everyone I know is putting off marriage, but we're all getting married anyway. Things begin to solidify. I feel I'm getting drawn into it more and all that's left to do is meet someone, give some of it away.

I could go on and on. A picture I have, of a house of crystal, my own quartet of violins, black satin everywhere, the clink of champagne — laughter, more music, and after dinner, dessert. It's like that now.

A friend calls up, asks how am I. I have the flu. It's going around, he says, but I know you're taking care of yourself.

Late at night I wake up. A stereo is shouting country songs next door. My dog is on the couch. She can't sleep either. We live in a terrible neighborhood.

I step out onto the porch. There's a Ford covered with crepe paper, now limp with dew. Just married. Between the shade and the window ledge I can just make out two rear ends waltzing.

The whole block is on the phone to the police. I have to be up early for work, but I stand a while longer on the porch. It's noisy, but it's quiet. The breeze feels nice.

Everyone I know is getting married whether they want to or not, and that includes me. I go inside and get in bed beside the dog.

COLLEEN TRACY: Although I lived less than one-third of my life on a farm, the land, as enemy-and-lover, has been a dominant influence on my life and my writing. I grew up in Sioux City, Iowa, but my parents came from endless generations of farmers. They had grown up on farms and were farmers even when they lived in town. The stories they told of their struggles, frustrations, and occasional triumphs with the land became my stories. When I was eighteen, we moved to the farm near Worthington, Minnesota, which my maternal great-grandparents had bought in 1890. The place was saturated in family history. I lived there until I married six years later.

After a ten-year residency in Minneapolis, my husband, our children, and I returned to the farm. Most of my life I have tried to assimilate the material it presented. In my tortoise-like way, I have been trying to turn the stories of the diverse people who live in harmony or disharmony with the land into fiction.

I no longer live on the farm, but the old affinity is still strong. Our present home is very near the Kasota prairie, which acts as an everpresent stimulus to my memory. I am working on a long autobiographical piece; I hesitate to call it a novel. I am not sure what it will turn out to be.

52

Colleen Tracy

AN ACCIDENT

Laura could not see him beside her on the bed in the smothering, hot darkness, but she could feel the angularity of his bones: elbows and knees like jutting rocks; knew how the ropy veins rode the long muscles of his arms and how black bristles sprouted on the backs of his hands. In time her son would have looked like him.

Bert lay sprawled in sodden sleep; only random twitchings and the sound of his deep breathing identified his state as sleep instead of death. She wondered how he could sleep like that. It had been ten nights now and each night he slept. Each evening, even the first evening, he said, "What's for supper?" Like an old plow horse, he moved through the habit of his days, although he was not an old man.

Her hands clenched and her legs stiffened. Stiff as a corpse she lay while fire burned behind her eyes. She knew she must have slept some time during those last ten days, but her mind, whether asleep or awake, was like a bird that has flown into a house and batters itself against the windows trying to get out.

Now, lying there on the sweat-stained sheet, she felt a movement, like fairy wings, in her belly, just as she had when she carried her son inside her. She held her breath, waiting. The flutter came again. Her belly seemed to swell, the skin becoming taunt as a violin string. Her fingers crept down, gently probing. Beneath her skin, she could feel a round head that fit the palm of her hand. She cupped it lovingly but it turned slowly like a sleepwalker feeling his way. Now she could feel the head deep in her pelvis pushing against her cervix. She gasped as the first contraction came like a giant's hand squeezing her distended abdomen. The contraction peaked and she took a shuddering breath.

How could this be? What was happening to her? She panicked when the next contraction turned her belly hard. Biting her knuckles to keep from crying out, she abandoned her body to this process of birthgiving. Unconsciously, she filled her lungs deeply and watched that imaginary second hand move around the white clock face.

How long she lay there, her body remembering each step of birthing, she did not know. Finally she felt the pushing, expelling motion of her muscles. Her knees spread wide and she felt the mouth of her vagina stretch and tear with a burning sensation. The little head was out. She pushed once more and the slick, sticky body wiggled out.

Panting from the exertion, she lowered her quivering legs and they came together upon nothing. So real had been the illusion that she sat up in bed searching between her legs for the baby. Her legs were dry and cold. She patted her slack belly; it was empty as a bird nest in winter.

She had lost her child again, and the sense of bereavement was as sharp as the day her son had died. She turned on her side and began in haste to pray, "Help me, oh God, for I am cold and alone."

When Laura awoke in the morning, a dream was vivid in her mind. Dressed in her wedding gown and satin slippers, she was hurrying across the yard to the barn. A feeling of expectancy made her feet light like a robin half running, half flying across the ground.

She wanted her husband. Her breasts swelled with her desire, and she compared them with the udders on the long row of Holsteins in the barn. They were shifting their weight from side to side, lifting one back leg and then the other, lowing deep in their throats with suppressed impatience.

She searched for Bert in the many rooms of the barn. Then she realized he must be in the hay mow, and she tried to climb the ladder, but her long skirt impeded her. As she struggled with her gown, she spied a cuddly kitten in the straw on the barn floor, and she dropped down and caught it. The kitten's eyes were round with alarm, and it struggled in her arms. Reluctantly, she let it go and it dashed down the row of cows. One of the huge bovines raised her hoof and came down on the kitten, crushing it impersonally, never turning her head.

Laura opened her mouth to scream but it was not her own voice she heard but that of her son, Joey, as he fell from the hay mow window, a cry, thin and high pitched, not very loud.

As she broke the eggs for Bert's breakfast, her voice said, "I wish I were dead." She knew she had not spoken aloud, but the words were very plain. Her hands began to shake until the spatula made a tattoo on the frying pan.

"I wish I were dead." That had been her mother's refrain when in her blue moods. On her mother's good days she sang popular hits like "I'm Gonna Wash that Man Right Outta My Hair." On other days, if the soup boiled over or the wind blew too loudly, she'd mutter, "I wish I were dead."

One day when Laura was four or five, she'd been playing a game, a modified hopscotch over the linoleum pattern, and unconsciously whispering, "I wish I were dead." Her father had stopped her, knelt down in front of her, holding her upper arms in his big hands. Sternly, he had said, "Don't ever say that again."

"I wish I were dead," she whispered now, caressing the words. "Father, I wish I were dead."

She put her husband's eggs on a plate with toast and bacon and set it on the kitchen table. The food odors made her feel queasy, as though she were two months pregnant, and her experience of the night before surfaced. She hadn't forgotten it, but had been holding it at bay like a hungry wolf. She didn't want to think about it now.

Bert padded in on stockinged feet, having left his barn boots in the entryway. He washed at the sink before beginning his breakfast. He'd always been neat, considerate within his limitations, a person content with routine.

"You're not eating?" he asked. She shook her head. She poured a cup of coffee and stood looking out the window. She had no words for him — had not spoken to him since the accident, but she did not think he had noticed.

They'd never talked, not really. When they met he had just taken over the family farm after his father's death. She was a senior in high school and knew little about farming. When Laura tried to talk to him, she sounded, to her ears, like a twittering school girl; and she soon stopped. But Bert had been the fantasy lover she'd longed for all through her adolescence, and his silence allowed her dreams to continue.

After their marriage a form of communication evolved that consisted of stock phrases, code words and gestures. For her part, even those had broken down now.

A puzzled frown was making the diagonal line between his eyebrows deeper; she knew this without looking at him.

"Maybe I should take you to the doctor," he said, his voice hoarse as though he were forcing the words past an obstruction in his throat. "Maybe he could give you something."

Her hand fell to her side — a gesture he interpreted correctly as a negative reply.

He finished his breakfast and left without another word. Through the window she saw him mount the tractor. She leaned her head against the window frame and the day stretched ahead of her like a trail across an endless desert.

She dragged along, forcing herself from one routine task to another, most of her energy going into an effort to suppress thought; but the vacuum cleaner growled, "I wish I were dead"; the clothes in the washer swished out the same message.

A part of her mind realized she had to talk to somebody, that she could not go on in this frozen silence without going mad or worse; but her dominant self panicked at the thought. Her mouth worked like a beached fish and her breath came in ragged gasps just thinking about trying. She knew she could never initiate her salvation.

When the telephone rang she answered it automatically.

"How are you getting along, today, dear?"

"Oh, it's *you*, Mother."

"You sound surprised, Laura. Were you expecting a call? Should I call back later?"

"No. I'm sorry. I . . . I don't know why I was surprised." She could see her mother sitting on the small chair before the telephone table, plump shoulders slumped and wisps of gray hair falling across her face. She knew she'd be pleating her apron nervously with her left hand. From long habit, Laura wanted to protect her mother, or herself, she was never sure which, so she tried to make her voice brighter, less dead. "How are you, Mother?"

"Oh, I'm all right. I was just thinking about you, wondering how you are. Are you keeping busy?"

"Sure, Mother, you know there's always something to do in a house. I'm okay."

Their soft voices, like goldfish in a shady pool, slid past each other, coming close but never touching.

"I saw your friend, who moved to California, Susan? She's home on a visit. She asked about you. She might come out to see you."

"That'd be nice," Laura said, but she thought, no, not Susan. She remembered a friend in high school named Susie, but the smartly dressed woman who flew around the country and had a career instead of children was a stranger she didn't want to talk to.

"We missed you at church on Sunday." Her mother sighed. "Are you coming to prayer meeting, tonight?"

"No, I don't think so."

"Should Dad and I come out?"

"There's no need. You can, if you want to, but," she faltered, "Bert'll be working late . . ." Laura's voice trailed off into silence, then quickly before the silence became too painful, said, "How's Pudgie and Ditto?"

"Fine. Just fine. How's Shep?"

"He's okay. Well, I gotta go now, Mother. Thanks for calling."

"Call me, sometime." Her mother's voice had become a whine, but she caught herself and continued in a conversational tone, "You know I don't like to call you; I might get you away from something, but I'm never very busy. I wish I were. I wish I could help you some way."

"That's okay, Mother. I have to hunt out enough jobs for myself. But thanks. Bye, now."

"Your Dad and I think about you all the time, dear. Remember to call."

"I'll do that. Good-bye, Mother."

"Good-bye, honey."

Laura could tell her mother was crying at the end of the call, and the old ambivalent feelings of anger and guilt flooded her mind. She knew her mother wanted to hold her and share a good cry, but the ingrained patterns of control prevented this. How could she say, "Mother, I'm going crazy and I wish I were dead."? Wouldn't her mother be frightened out of her wits, this woman who'd been cared for all her life? But maybe her mother had hidden strengths, maybe she could teach her how to grieve. Her mother's tears came easily, she knew. She had a memory of her mother, like a scene from some old movie: she could see her sobbing, tears falling on her quivering bosom, collecting in the crevice between her breasts, while in her hands she held the dead canary and she crooned, "Oh, Dickie, poor Dickie."

Now Laura remembered her crying with the same abandonment at her grandson's funeral. But that wasn't fair. Suddenly she realized she'd never been fair to her mother, had always treated her like she was the child and not the mother. She knew her father had taught her that, and she felt sick from that knowledge.

That evening after the work was done, Laura slumped in a chair in front of the television. She stared at the screen but she could not understand the story, wondered what the studio audience was laughing at. Bert came in and sat beside her. He held her hand but it remained as lifeless as a plucked flower.

"I'm going up to bed," he said. "Are you coming soon?" She knew what he was asking and she shook her head.

She sat there long after the screen went blank, afraid to go to bed, afraid to breathe. When she felt the first contraction she ran outside and walked down the lane in the dark. But she could not out-walk her body. When she reached the road, she started back toward the house, whose lighted windows she could see through the trees. As the pains got worse, she stumbled and fell to her knees in the gravel. She could not feel her skinned palms or knees, she was so engrossed in the birth process. She crawled into the grass damp with dew at the side of the lane and waited with the patience of an animal for her body to finish the monstrous joke it was playing on her.

In the nights that followed, she lost her fear and came to look forward to the experience, especially the beginning when she could feel her son's small head, trace the tiny feet when they kicked her. He was hers again for a little while. But this was always followed by catastrophic disappointment when it ended and she was alone again.

Sunday, when Laura did not want to go to church, Bert hitched the mower to the tractor and rode off to cut the alfalfa. By mid-afternoon, Laura had worked her way to the front porch, where she found Joey's toy tractor behind the rocking chair. She picked it up and traced the intricate details of the tractor with her fingers. It was a replica of Bert's tractor that her father had given Joey. She sat down and continued rubbing the toy as though it were a tailsman; it held a painful comfort, and she drifted in time.

When her parents appeared she was startled and hid the toy in the folds of her skirt.

"Oh, honey," said her mother, embracing her, "you look awful. You've lost so much weight. Dad, look, she's wasting away."

Gently, Laura pulled away from the soft flesh and smell of sweet talcum. "I'm all right, Mother."

Her parents sat in the glider and her mother fanned herself with her hankie and talked about how hot it was and about her neighbors and her sisters and their families. Her father studied the trees and the lawn and the fields in the distance. "That elm'll have to come out, Laura," he said, pointing. "I'll borrow a saw from work and cut it down, next Saturday."

Laura looked at him and saw a body still strong from constant labor, but the lines of age were showing like the veins on an autumn leaf. The collar of his white, church shirt looked a size too big for him and wrinkles furrowed his cheeks. He's old, she thought, he's grown old and I never noticed. Now he'll never achieve his dream. All his life her father had wanted a farm of his own and had planned and saved for the day when he could buy a piece of land. His family farm had been lost during the depression, when he was a young man, and he'd lived all his life wanting to return to that farm.

Laura looked from her father to her mother; she wondered if they bickered less now. When Laura had lived at home, her father had been critical of her mother in many little ways; and she had called him a "stick-in-the-mud." He'd said she had a vulgar laugh, and Laura had thought so, too, and had been careful to laugh in a lady-like manner. On the big issues, her mother had acquiesced to her husband's judgments: she had never held a job after she got married, she voted for his candidates, and she cooked the food he liked. In return, he indulged her passion for the movies, the cluttery bric-a-brac she bought, and the "hen parties" she held in the afternoons.

When her mother's chatter lapsed into sighing silence, her father leaned forward and said, "Now, Laura, I'm going to tell you a story, a true story, and I want you to listen well and think about it."

Oh, lord, he's going to tell me the story about his Aunt Kate, thought Laura, I know he is.

"What I'm going to tell you about happened a long time ago, but I remember it like it was yesterday. My father's brother John and his wife, my Aunt Kate, lived just across the road from our place. They had one son. His name was Kenneth, and he was the apple of his mother's eye.

"Well, Kenneth was seven years old when an outbreak of small-pox hit our community. He hadn't got vaccinated. Uncle John didn't believe in it — a lot of the older people didn't then. I hadn't got the shots, either. Aunt Kate kept Kenneth out of school and wouldn't let him play with any of the kids, but still he come down with the pox and he had it real bad and he died.

"Well, Aunt Kate took his death so hard she went out of her mind; that's what people were saying. Every night she'd sneak out of the house and Uncle John would wake up and find her gone. Every night, he'd go looking for her and find her in the cemetery laying across Kenneth's grave."

"Oh, Dad, stop telling Laura that old story. Can't you see how you're hurting her?" her mother said.

"Don't interrupt me, Mother. There's a reason why I'm telling this story and it's not to hurt Laura. Well, to make a long story short, Aunt Kate got over her craziness when she realized she was in the family way, again. Uncle John told my father he'd insisted she have another child because he knew it was the only way she'd recover. And he was right. She went on to have three more children and she was the best wife and mother anybody'd want to meet."

Laura looked searchingly at her father. "Why did you tell me that story, Daddy? Do you think I'm going crazy? Sometimes I think so." There it was — out in the open; she'd actually said it, and she waited for an answer.

"You know better than that, Laura," he said gruffly.

"What a thing to say," laughed her mother.

She looked from one to the other and knew they couldn't take her seriously. "Oh, God, I wish I were dead," she said, leaping from her chair. With a clatter, the toy tractor fell from her lap to the floor. Father and mother rose simultaneously, and all three stood looking at the toy on the floor.

"Joey's tractor," said her father softly. "I never saw him play with it."

"No," said Laura, bitterly, "he had no time to play; he was always working." She bent and picked up the toy. "I'd have him still if Bert hadn't taken him away from me and put him to work."

"You can't blame Bert, Laura. What happened was an accident and nobody's fault," said her father.

"Yes, an accident, because he was too young to be doing a man's work."

"I harnessed the horses when I was seven, even when I had to stand on a box to do it."

The futility of their conversation fell like a heavy yoke across her shoulders and she grasped the back of the chair to support herself. "I can't talk to you any more, Father."

When her parents had left, Laura began to prepare the evening meal. She waited for Bert to come in for supper, but he did not come. This was very unusual as they always ate at a set time. She could hear the cows mooing at the pasture gate, and she waited with increasing anxiety. When she could endure the waiting no longer, she walked out. It was the first time she had been to the barn yard since the accident. Now she stood by the open barn door calling Bert, but the barn was empty. She walked along the path to the pasture. The cows were bunched together like restless demonstrators, their tails switching, their necks outstretched. She didn't know if she dared open the gate as she was still intimidated by the beasts, never having worked with them enough to become accustomed to them.

Laura was still hesitating when she saw Bert lying face down in the long grass beside the path. In each hand was a clump of grass as though he had to hang on to something. Strangling noises were coming from his throat.

She understood the situation in an instant and knelt beside him, gently turning his body to face her.

"I miss him so much," Bert whispered. "We always went to get the cows together."

"Oh, love," she said and her tears flowed for the first time. She covered his face with kisses, their tears mingling. Suddenly, with the energy of a tormented bear, he tore at her clothing, seeking the comfort her body could give him. Mindful of his pain, she started to yield, but the image of Aunt Kate appeared before her, and her hands turned into fists. Furious, she pounded on his chest and face. Wrenching her body from beneath him, she staggered to her feet.

"I'm no Aunt Kate," Laura screamed and took off running across the hay field.

FREDERICK FEIKEMA MANFRED: was born January 6, 1912, on a Siouxland farm north of Doon, Iowa, in Rock township, just a few miles from the Minnesota and South Dakota borders. Mr. Manfred is the oldest of six brothers.

He was educated in northwest Iowa until he attended Calvin College, Grand Rapids, Michigan, from which he graduated in 1934. For the next three years he wandered back and forth across America, from New York to Los Angeles, stopping off now and then to take on odd jobs to pay his way. In May, 1937, he became a reporter for.the MINNEAPOLIS JOURNAL. In 1939 he did social work and opinion polls. In 1942 he married Maryanna Shorba; they have three children, Freya, Marya, and Frederick.

In 1943, after working as an abstract writer for MODERN MEDICINE for several months, Mr. Manfred decided it was now or never and began to devote his full time and energy to writing. He has written twenty-four books, which include *Lord Grizzly, Conquering Horse*, and *Green Earth.* He has received several grants and writing fellowships from such sponsors as the American Academy of Arts and Letters and the Huntington Hartford Foundation. He is currently writer in residence at the University of South Dakota at Vermillion, South Dakota. Until 1951 he wrote under the pen name of Feike Feikema, an old Frisian family name.

Frederick Manfred

HIJINKS WITH THE MINISTER'S SON

When Ma got to the bottom of the story about what the consistory wanted, she wasn't satisfied. She was afraid of the Beast in Man and was always worried that He might show up in one of her sons. The Devil was always looking for natures He could turn to his own ends. She didn't believe with Pa that their boy Free, for having tackled two big mean devils, was now going to grow up to be a real man. She was concerned that the lords of the barnyard might win out and then where would that leave kind women and gentlemen ministers?

Ma fell into a talk with Domeny Donker about the matter after church, and Domeny suggested they visit him the next Tuesday evening at eight o'clock and at that time they would talk about it.

Free wasn't sure he wanted to go. Domeny had one son, Billy, who was his age, but that Billy was a hard one. Billy was a boss on the school grounds. As the minister's son he thought himself something special. He wasn't very good at running games, threw a baseball like he had a dislocated shoulder, and to make up for it, always was the first to raise his hand in class, even when he didn't know the answer. Free was glad he had moved out of Billy's class, from the sixth to the seventh.

Billy Donker had one bad habit that made him hated by just about everybody. He claimed he had the soul of a cock. When the kids'd correct him, "You mean rooster, don't you?" he'd get mad and say, "No, I mean cock, like this," and he'd spread his arms out like they were wings, crack his heels together, and jump up against a fellow's legs like a real rooster, as though he was chasing a fellow off of one of his hens. And he'd crow, "Cok-it-d-do-do!" and peck at a fellow. He'd roar out over the school grounds, "I'm Gamecock Bill and I do what I will! Whoops! Cok-it-d-do-do! I can lick the whole of creation, if not the nation. A ringtailed roarer of a cock I am. Ftt! Ftt!"

The next Tuesday evening Free for the first time found himself in the church parsonage. Ma had often talked about how important the parsonage was. Ladies Aid sometimes met there. It was kind of a palace all right. It smelled like one, too, as of cinnamon perfume. All the floors were golden quarter oak, the doorknobs a shiny bronze, and the colored panes in the big bay window were the biggest he'd ever seen: scarlet, water blue, pasture green, lemon yellow. Surprisingly, Billy, while in the house, behaved like a model boy.

Around nine Billy asked if he and Free could play outside.

Domeny fumbled his watch chain. At last with a company smile he said, "All right. But don't leave the parsonage grounds, you hear?"

"We won't."

Mrs. Donker said nothing. She just looked at her wild son and rocked in her rocker. She had rolls under her chin like double horse collars. Her face was always set in a smile. The runners of her rocker made loud cracking noises.

The minute they were outside Billy took Free by the arm and led him out through the gate onto the street.

Free hung back. "Your pa will get mad."

"Ftt. I'm not afraid of him. He never licks me."

"What about your ma?"

"Ftt. She just sits there like a tea cozy." Billy had on blue knickers and every time he jumped up and went ftt like a cock he looked exactly like a big fluffy Minorca rooster. "Listen. I want to pull something on somebody." From his pocket he dug out an empty thread spool and a ball of string and a long nail. "I've cut notches along both edges of this spool. See? We're going to scare the pee out of those Shutter girls with it."

Those cute little Shutter girls? The Shutters had only just moved into town that fall and lived in a small stone house across the street from the parsonage. In school they were scared to death of everybody. Poor Mrs. Shutter wearing her bright blue apron had to walk her little girls all the way to the school door because they were afraid to walk past the church barn where Clarence Etten and Tommy Holtup hung out.

"C'mon, let's go," Billy urged.

Free shook his head. The father of the little girls, Mr. Shutter, was not someone to fool with. Free had seen him sitting in church with his shirt sleeves rolled up and his arms folded across his chest. His forearms were each as big as a quarter of beef. Once in a while, when Mr. Shutter worked his fingers a little, the muscles in his hairy forearms rippled like there might be mice running around under the skin. Mr. Shutter was probably twice as strong as Pa. If Mr. Shutter got hold of someone with those powerful mitts of his, he'd grind him into toothpicks. Free said, "If Mr. Shutter catches us, he'll kill us."

"Nah. He's too scared of people in town. C'mon."

"I dunno now."

"C'mon. We'll first try it on Mrs. Holtup. She lives across the alley from the Shutters. I want to get even with her for tattling on me once. And you gotta help me because it takes two to run this notched spool. We'll practice on her bay window."

"How?"

"I'll show you. C'mon."

Free had a score to settle with Mrs. Holtup himself. She'd raised that fuss about her darned Tommy with the consistory. Free decided to go along.

They took the alley behind Mrs. Holtup's little town barn where she kept a cow and a few chickens, crossed her yard in back, and on all fours crept up to her bay window. They could see her rocking. A reading lamp was on and she was knitting. She had on her glasses and was wearing them at the end of her nose.

Behind Free and Billy, across the alley, someone was slowly chopping wood in the half-dark.

"Now," Billy whispered. He quickly wound the string around the spool and then slipped the long nail through the hole in the spool. "While I hold the nail this way, with the notches against the window, you take the end of the string and run. And I want you to really run. Fast. And keep on running. Until you get to my house. Just worry about yourself. Make sure you get away without anyone seeing you. I'll take care of my end of it. Because I'll be right on your tail. We don't want to get caught."

Free took a turn of the string around a finger for a good grip.

"Go. Run!"

Free took off lickety-split.

There was a burr, then a louder r-d-d-r-r-r, then a high whine like a rotary saw. Wow. What a racket. If there was anybody sleeping in Mrs. Holtup's house they sure as heck were going to be wide awake now. Then the string ran out. Silence.

Free could hear Billy running behind him, catching up. Once Billy accidentally tripped on the dragging string and almost ripped off Free's finger. Both dove for the grass behind the bushes on the parsonage grounds.

It didn't take but a couple of seconds for Mrs. Holtup to come scalding hot out of her back door. "You darn rascals! Scaring the daylights out of an old lady at night. Yes, and I know who you are too, you Billy Donker you. And I'm going to tell your pa on you too. Him that's a minister of the gospel whose family is supposed to set an example for the rest of us poor sinners." She went on and on, stomping her high heels on her wooden stoop.

Billy smothered laughter in the grass.

Free wondered where Tommy Holtup was. Probably out chasing girls with Clarence Etten.

After a time Mrs. Holtup cooled off and went back into her house.

"Wow, it works real good," Billy said. "Now to try it out on a Shutter window and make those girls pee all over the floor." He sat up and took the string from Free and began to wind it around the notched spool again. "Their ma always makes them pee in the pot first before they go to bed. And it's just when they squat down over the pot that we'll rat-a-tat their bedroom window."

"How'd you know that?"

"I've seen them, you dumbbell. Their curtain don't quite come down to the window sill and you can peek in under it."

Free saw those huge bare arms of Mr. Shutter again. If those great machines ever got hold of him . . . man alive.

Funny too that Billy should want to torment the very man in church who sang a lot like him. Mr. Shutter sang in the Old Country way, especially Psalm 42, whose melody rose and fell like the sun rising and setting. Mr. Shutter would sometimes slip in an extra note, a short one, between the long notes. "As the hart panteth after the water brooks uh, so panteth my soul uh after thee, O God uh." Mr. Shutter had a big pink mouth and when he opened up and let go in bass, his tongue quivered like a thrasher's. It sometimes looked like he had three fat lips, all of them vibrating. He drowned out everybody around him for at least ten benches. Ma always smiled to herself when she heard him. She said that in the old days when Grampa had his health he would sometimes sing like that, even at home, especially if a storm was coming up. Meanwhile, in the front part of the church, from the bench where Domeny's family sat, across the aisle from the deacons and the elders, Billy Donker was drowning everybody out for ten benches around too with his yowling soprano, also with the little extra note thrown in sometimes. With those two singers the church hardly needed a pipe organ. It was probably because Billy could sing psalms so piercingly, with such wonderful Christian fervor, that Domeny and Juffrouw, and everybody else, had trouble being mad at him and could forgive him all his cockalorums. "Ain't he a real Domeny's son, singing the way he does in God's house of worship?" people said.

"Let's go," Billy urged.

"Boy, but if Mr. Shutter ever catches us."

"He won't. I'm gonna first roll a hoop in front of his door. Then when he comes charging out, he'll trip over the hoop and fall down. And by the time he gets to his feet, we're gone."

"All right, if you think it'll work."

The bedroom of the Shutter girls was on the street side. Billy and Free approached the one-story cement-block house from the sidewalk. The yard was enclosed by a high fence and they had to go through the gate. The curtain on the living room window was up and they could look inside. The curtain on the bedroom window was drawn and just as Billy said, it didn't quite come down to the window sill.

Billy picked up one of the girls' hoops lying in the grass and rolled it in front of the door. Then Billy came back and he and Free peeked in the bedroom window.

Mrs. Shutter was bustling the little girls off to bed all right. The little girls were in their nightgowns and Mrs. Shutter made them kneel beside their bed and pray. She helped them with some of the words. She was kind to little children like Ma was. Then she pointed under the bed. The oldest little girl, the one with the white hair and red cheeks, reached under the bed and pulled out a big white thundermug. The little girl lifted her white nightgown and settled her pink butty on it.

"Now!" Billy hissed and he placed the notched spool against the window at the same time handing Free the end of the string. "Go! Run."

"Rrraw-rrh!" went a voice like a bull's. Around the corner of the house a man came running. He was carrying a flashing axe.

Mr. Shutter.

Free stiffened, petrified.

Billy took one look, yeeked, dropped the notched spool, shot to his left, and in one great long bound, so that he looked like a pheasant cock taking off, sailed completely over the top of the high fence. And disappeared into the dark.

Mr. Shutter grabbed Free by the neck. He gripped him so hard Free's tongue came out. Mr. Shutter made a little motion with his round blond head that he regretted Billy had got away but at least he'd caught one of the rascals. With his one hand he shook Free like a Newfoundland dog shaking a pullet. "So you're gonna make my little girls piss on the floor, huh?" With his other hand Mr. Shutter waved his flashing axe around as if he intended to cleave Free in half. "Scare the piss out of them, huh?" Mr. Shutter spotted the notched spool Billy had dropped. He set his axe down and picked up the spool. "With this fiendish instrument of the devil, eh?"

"No, no," Free gasped. "Billy and I made it so Tommy Holtup could use it as a sprocket wheel for a threshing machine he's making."

"Tommy Holtup! Well, what are you two doing in my yard then?"

"We was taking a shortcut across your yard to Tommy's house."

"And you weren't going to make my little girls piss on the floor?"

"Oh, no. We wouldn't do that." Why hadn't Mr. Shutter tripped over the hoop? Then Free recalled that while he and Billy had been serenading Mrs. Holtup with a notched spool on her bay window, there'd been someone chopping wood in the half-dark nearby. In the direction of Mr. Shutter's yard. So Mr. Shutter had heard everything. Mr. Shutter knew then that everything he'd said was a plain flat-out lie. Man, was he in for it.

Mr. Shutter stuck the notched spool with its string in his pocket. He picked up his axe again. He waved his axe around. It glittered something fierce. "I've got half a notion to chop your . . ." He paused. "No, that's too good for you. What I'm gonna do is call the sheriff."

Go to jail? My God. "Oh, please, Mr. Shutter—"

"That was Billy Donker with you, wasn't it?"

"Who where?"

"The kid peeking in at the window with you. Yeh, I'd know that rascal anywhere."

Free wriggled around to get some breathing room inside Mr. Shutter's squeezing fist. "Please don't."

"Putting a hoop in front of my door so I'd trip over it . . . pretty clever all right. Well, there's only one thing to do and that's to turn you over to the marshal."

Free noticed that Mr. Shutter had come down from the sheriff to the marshal. Maybe in a minute he'd come down to just telling Pa and Ma and that wouldn't be nearly as bad as going to jail.

"What's your pa's name?"

Good. There it was. "Mister Alfred Alfredson."

Mr. Shutter shook his head. "How can a boy like you, born to such nice people, how can you think of tormenting my little girls?"

Free thought of asking Mr. Shutter not to tell Pa, but decided Pa wouldn't like it that a son of his had begged for mercy. Pa would like it better if he just took his medicine and shut up.

Mr. Shutter held Free a little less tight by the neck. It was as if Mr. Shutter was hoping Free would try to escape so that then he could really pounce on him, like a tomcat with a mouse. "This really was Billy's idea, wasn't it?"

Free shook his head diagonally, not quite yes and not quite no.

Tears showed in the corners of Mr. Shutter's blue eyes. "What's wrong with my little girls that you kids don't like them?"

"They always act so scared," Free said out of the middle of Mr. Shutter's grip, "and that makes the kids really sic after them."

Mr. Shutter stared down at Free. "You mean, if my girls was a little meaner, the other kids would respect them more?"

Free nodded inside Mr. Shutter's fist.

"But they're just little girls and there ain't a mean drop of blood in 'em."

Free raised his shoulders with a slight shrug.

"You look like a nice boy." Mr. Shutter's fist relaxed even more. "Why don't you protect them?"

Free wondered if he should make a break for it.

"Listen, boy, if you promise to talk those kids at school out of teasing my little girls, I'll let you go."

Free decided he shouldn't promise Mr. Shutter something he couldn't live up to. "I can't do that, Mr. Shutter. It's bad enough I got to protect my horse Tip against those big boys in school."

"You mean like Clarence Etten?"

"Yes."

"Yeh, he's a son of Beelzebub all right." Mr. Shutter let go of Free. "G'wan home. Don't ever let me see you around here again. And tell that Billy Donker that I'll deal with him later." Mr. Shutter suddenly turned, and carrying his glittering axe disappeared around the side of his cottage.

Free rubbed his neck. It sure hurt where Mr. Shutter's thumb had dug in. Free hoped Mr. Shutter's fingerprints wouldn't show.

Free wasn't sure what he should do next. He could hardly show up at the parsonage without Billy. After dawdling alone on the sidewalk a while, he decided to look for Billy.

He found Billy two blocks from main street. Billy had been hiding behind some bushes on Garrett Tillman's place.

"Wow," Billy said, "you got away alive."

"Yeh, and you deserted the ship."

"Why, heck, what else? I wasn't about to let him chop off my head. He's been laying for me for weeks."

"It was a dirty trick though, Billy."

"What'd you tell him?"

"Nothing. Pretty soon he felt sorry for me just like he felt sorry for his poor little girls."

"His poor little pissers, you mean."

"Oh, I think they're pretty nice little kids."

"Hypocrite. You're just saying that because he scared the poop out of you."

Free shut up. He turned and headed for the parsonage.

"Hey, wait up," Billy called after him. "We better show up at the house together."

When they entered the parsonage, Free could see that Domeny had settled Ma's mind about that Beast in her son. Ma had a big smile for him.

"Well, boy," Ma said, "are you ready to go home?"

"Sure am."

"Hey," Billy said, "we didn't get any chocolate cake."

Domeny sat at the head of the table. "Where were you, Billy?"

"Out'n the yard."

"We called you to come in for your cake."

"Welll . . ."

"Too bad. The chocolate cake's been put away. Not, huh, Ma?"

Juffrouw Donker nodded a company smile out of her collars of fat.

On the way home, Ma half-turned in her seat to ask, "What did you two boys do, Free?"

"Played around. I met Mr. Shutter and halfways promised him I'd watch out for his little girls at school. To keep the others from teasing them."

"Good for you." Ma sighed. "It does look as though the Lord of light is overcoming the forces of darkness in you."

Pa drove the purring old Buick with a steady set of hands.

MARY FRANCOIS ROCKCASTLE: Words, language and stories have been enduring preoccupations. At least, they have remained consistent while other things have changed. I have made my connections to writing and literature in different ways — as a teacher, editor, student, reader and writer. I grew up in New Jersey, went to school at Rutgers and worked summers in Manhattan. The only period of time I spent away from the New York area was a seven-month stay in Oxford, England, during my junior year in college. For the first time in my life I fell in love with a city and knew what it meant to feel intimately bound with a place. "30 Chilswell Road" is in a way my hymn to the city and to the people who mattered. Afterwards, I looked again for other cities and came to Minneapolis. I entered the graduate program in English but midway through decided that studying literature was not making me a writer and that the two don't necessarily mix. I began writing seriously and transferred into the M.A. in Writing program. During this time I taught literature and writing in high school, at the Loft, and at the University, where I still teach Freshman Composition. I am now writing a novel, an excerpt of which is being published in *Fallout*, a new magazine.

While teaching, editing and reading bring me into contact with people and literature, writing leads me inward — to my own images, my own pain, my own preoccupations. In looking for stories I have crawled into my past and shaken it with greedy fingers. The writing suspends me in a time capsule where past, present and future coalesce.

Mary Francois Rockcastle

30 CHILSWELL ROAD

He looked at his watch. It was 8:30. The glare of the lamp made it impossible to tell who was there. He straightened the curtain and walked to the front door. They whispered to each other, bikes scraping, clattering metal in the narrow walkway. The white bulb rushed at him and he stepped back, waiting for the dark to mute the glow and bring the faces forward. They watched him, the two silent and holding their bicycles still.

"Yes?"

"We came about the room. We saw your notice in the post office in Summertown."

He noted their dungarees and hiking boots. The first girl was blonde and soft and the other was fuller, eyes dark. He was glad they weren't British.

"Come in . . . please."

He smiled, feeling his lips part. In the sitting room, he motioned them to sit. It was heavy with cooking odors. Worn furniture with gnarled wooden legs crowded the small room, maroon brocade against green walls. They said they were students and wanted a cheaper place to live.

"When are you returning to the States?"

"In the summer."

The blonde one spoke first, her voice musical and high-pitched. He showed them the two adjoining rooms upstairs, the small back one facing the garden. The rent was only 10 pounds per mouth, and they said they would take it. But they would be on a holiday and couldn't move in until the first of May. He was silent, vacant, then nodded.

"I will hold the room until the first of May."

He watched as they wheeled their bicycles into the street. The dark one laughed, and he stepped outside, eyes glued to her receding back. When he heard the wheels touch gravel, he knew they'd turned onto Abingdon. Quiet sat on the black-rowed block like a hood and he listened until the gravel settled. Then he went upstairs to the two rooms and walked through them, fingers streaking dust across the bureau tops. The blonde girl with the voice like his wife's would have the front room, which he would paint yellow to match his best flowered rug.

When the record was ready, he listened for the poised needle to touch the disc. The orchestra played his favorite melodies, and he slept, curled into the big bed.

The gate unlocked, and he heard the blonde voice laughing. Purple sprayed from his hands as he walked from the garden into the walkway. He smiled, glad they had come. Her face moved like water when she spoke to him. He helped them carry their boxes into the house, and in the yellow room, watched her face. She walked to the back room and put her suitcases beside the bed. Quickly he took her arm and motioned to the front room.

"No. This is your room."

He waited, empty, but she turned from him and said she liked the smaller room better. They agreed between the two that Cassie, the dark one, would take the yellow room. He could do nothing and moved to the window, explaining about the latch. The yellow had been for her, and now it was ruined. His good rug would lie there and the other would look at the flowers every day.

He left. The two voices rose and fell and he listened, hearing pieces of sentences that held him as he lay on the big bed. The giggling began faintly and fluttered in the darkening room. His hands formed walls to hold it close, not wanting them to hear. It was good they were there across the hall. All the others had gone after a short while, but most of them were British. They looked into his face, and their eyes defined the brown skin and the hatred which ground him like bits of glass. But he watched them also, silent and polite and not ever speaking unless it was to answer yes or no. He didn't want to rent to them, but he couldn't live without their money. And it was only fair because they'd taken all of him already and he only wanted to get some of it back. His daughter, Marina, waited for him in Devon. Only when he had enough money could he go to her and save her from those others who'd stolen her, right in front of him, worse than any thieves. Stolen her and his mind too when he was younger. It was the hatred and the watching that stole his mind, and so he'd taken what was left and hidden it behind the silence and unwrinkled brown skin that never showed the thirteen years since it happened. He would study and study, and eventually trick them and pass the exams at the polytechnic. They could not always be watching to fail him whenever he handed in the grid sheet with his name neatly written in small letters at the top.

The record dropped, and he walked from side to side passing himself growing darker and darker as the night progressed. He reached out each time in the other's eyes until he met the tiny globes of light that held him knowing everything. The floor creaked as he turned, seeing the face in front of him and then again as he paced to the window. It was always different at night because then all he could see were the light specks but even during the day when the other had a full face and body and smiled when he smiled the eyes knew the same things as the small light circles. Only there could he look without being sent away by the slow glaze that told him he wasn't British. People in the shops saw his ageless face that made no sound and the grey suit, always pressed. The voice quietly asked or answered but inside he was giggling and watching and safe.

The needle rubbed dully until he took the arm off the warm disc and black shutters dropped in front of the red beam. He could no longer see the double, only slivers of light beneath filmy curtains. The bed was warm under the windows and his face on the pillow caught the moon. Her child face moved farther and farther away, veils of water drenching eyes like his. Pulling at his chest, he felt the bits of glass they'd put there to make sure he'd never get her back.

In the morning Cassie left early, piling books in the bicycle basket. At ten he began his toilette. While the water ran in the sink, he tried to shave, but the giggles stopped him. Because the blonde one, Maly, was upstairs, he tried to control them but couldn't until the soft hee hee giggling made him gag and spit up into the sink. Splashing, he washed his face but the giggles rushed again from his mouth until he choked.

The front door slammed and he checked himself, looking out the side window. Maly flung the gate shut and walked rapidly away from the house. Turning back to the sink, he wondered why she'd gone out in such a hurry. Slowly he moved his face to the mirror until it floated, the two almost touching. Water beaded on the brown skin, hovering on the tips of his mustache. The double pairs of eyes gazed without speech or movement and then the thought of how alone they were and how safe from all the others started the mouth to move and giggles flew into the garden once more. Together they would get his daughter back and she would be happy. Perhaps she would be friends with the blonde one upstairs, whose voice was his wife's, and whose eyes were clear and without the wanting to grind him down.

Outside in the garden, he chose two of the little purple and yellow flowers to put in her room. The key fitted noiselessly into the lock and he walked through the first room to hers and placed the vase under the open window. He liked to stand there, looking out on the flapping wash and the row of back yards where dark-skinned women hung white garments. These were to have been Marina's rooms until they came and took her away from him. Her small face stared over the white shoulder as he screamed. The room circled, and he caught the bureau, knocking over the vase of flowers. It lay on the rug, purple and yellow sprays broken in a puddle. After leaving the house, he pulled his chair from the toolshed and sat in the sun.

Maly hesitated in the walkway and he lifted his arm, beckoning her into the garden. Hurriedly he readied another chair and asked her to sit with him. She wavered only a minute before sitting, book held in her lap. The sun lit the long braid that hung like a golden arrow over her shoulder.

"What are you reading?"

"*Henry IV* by Shakespeare."

"Don't you have a boyfriend?"

She smiled. "Yes, at home. I write him several times a week."

"Will he write you here?"

She shifted in her seat. "He writes me at my address at school. Mr. Hassan, just now I found a vase and flowers on the floor of my room."

"I put them there. But they must have fallen from the wind."

"I don't think you should enter our rooms when we're not there."

"But, Maly, I wanted to give you these lovely tiny flowers. Don't you like them?"

"That's not the point. I would prefer if you did not come into my room when I'm gone."

He didn't understand why she didn't like the flowers. Perhaps

Cassie had said something.

"My wife loved these purple ones the best. They have such a sweet smell. I planted them when our daughter, Marina, was born."

"I didn't know you were married."

"We bought this house shortly after we came to Oxford from Pakistan. My wife was pregnant and I had a good job and we were happy. After Marina was born, we sat here like this in the garden and she watched me plant these little purple ones. But they took away my job and no one would hire me and my wife stayed for hours in that room not even looking out the window when I called from the garden. Then they took her to that place."

"What place?"

"The hospital. They said she died but I never believed them. Soon they put me there too because I could not eat or sleep and the headaches. I looked for her there, listening at night for her voice, but they hid her so well I couldn't find her. I started classes at the polytechnic but they failed me. Then they came with their documents and faces wanting to crush me and they stole Marina. A letter said she had been placed with a foster family in Devon."

He felt the hand on his arm and looking up, the blue eyes.

"I'm sorry, Mr. Hassan. Do you ever see your daughter?"

"No. They won't let me. But I am saving to get her back, once I pass the exam."

"How long has it been since you've séen her?"

"Thirteen years."

He did not hear her leave, but later, in the kitchen, he smelled the little flowers she had arranged in a vase by the window.

Most evenings they were gone. Then he unlocked the door and touched the objects on their bureaus, the clothing that hung in mahogony wardrobes in each room. The front room, Cassie's, was untidy. A large photograph of her boyfriend collected dust. Clothes packed the wardrobe and a wooden box with a faded black and white photograph under glass opened to silver jewelry and beaded necklaces. But in the small back room, painted lavender, and which smelled of the garden through the open window, he stayed the longest. Maly's books, in rows on the desk, were organized according to size. Papers with dated notes lay in a pile. She had no jewelry box and the wardrobe was half-empty. Carefully, so as not to disturb the papers and pens on the desk, he opened her journal, which he read by flashlight, less they come home unannounced and see a light in their room. Poems, dated daily, spoke to him of the loud cry of birds at dawn and of her mother, who died suddenly, and whose face in the riot of flowers had not yet aged. She'd written one poem about a brown-skinned woman who planted purple and yellow flowers in the garden behind 30 Chilswell Road.

He waited for them no matter how late they came home. One evening, he walked to the Turf for a beer. He saw them at a table with two men. At twelve they said goodbye and he followed. They were passing the police station walking their bicycles downhill on Abingdon when he hurried forward and dropped his hands on their shoulders.

"Let me walk with you awhile. They think I can't be trusted with young girls. I want them to see that two pretty American girls want to talk with me and aren't afraid to let me touch them."

He giggled, thinking of the police. When they reached the bottom, he removed his hands and walked behind them.

"Maly, if anyone approaches you and asks you what I say, don't tell him. The police have a record of everything I've said since I moved to Oxford."

When Maly turned to him, he smiled at her soft face which looked scared, like Marina's when they took her away.

"I'm sure the police don't keep records of what you say."

"Yes, Maly, they do."

At home in his room, he turned on the music. When he turned round, he saw the other facing him. Falling falling falling until they met and knew each other without speaking. It wouldn't take much longer before he'd saved enough money and could go to Devon and get her back. Then they would sail to the United States and he would be safe. Inside he bled more and more each day from the broken glass and if he did not hurry he would be too weak to make the trip. Without the other he could not do it because someone had to say the right words and answers to the people on the train and in Devon.

The door slammed. Why they had to slam so hard every time . . . it hurt his ears, and he'd told Maly about it several times. They did it because they knew about his ears, at least the dark one knew because she was always saying she couldn't hear well, which was a lie to make fun of him. Voices and loud laughter. He opened the door and saw another girl with Maly and Cassie.

"Mr. Hassan, this is our friend, Liz, who'll be staying with us for a few days. She's going back to the States this weekend."

As tall as he, she was beautiful. Black hair and large almond eyes and olive skin that would feel like moist petals if he touched it. Not white and not black but perfect. He said nothing, only watched them as they carried knapsacks and packages upstairs.

He was meditating in the sitting room when Liz came in the next morning. Returning his smile, she moved past and into the kitchen. Her black hair shone against a green robe. When she passed again, he wanted to touch her flower skin and ink hair. But afterwards the others came with her.

There were so many people in the house and he hated it and told Maly so and she promised not to invite any more friends in. He wanted only the dark-skinned one and Maly to stay. Wanting her disturbed even his chanting so he went to a movie. Later, alone in the sitting room, he choked on the giggles but couldn't stop them, not even when Maly set her groceries on the table.

"I went to see *Last Tango in Paris* today, Maly."

Quickly she replied, "Yes, I've seen it, a good movie, isn't it? And that wonderful music."

"Yes, you're right." He held the giggles in control.

"But Maly, they do strange things today, don't they?"

She rattled pans in the sink. "I'm glad you enjoyed the movie."

He hid his face and giggles flew round the room. When he finally stopped, she was gone. The door slammed and he heard their bicycles in the walkway, all three. They did not come home for hours and he stayed in his room with the music. For years he had not touched a woman, not since his wife, and when they accused him of molesting a white girl he told them politely that he would never touch a white girl. Often, he peeked through the crack in the bathroom door when Cassie sat in the bath. They went together, one sitting on the rim of the tub while the other bathed, always talking. He giggled at Cassie's large breasts and black curls but looked away when Maly bathed.

From the window, he saw them turn onto Chilswell, their bodies wheeling like ghosts past the brooding wall of houses. Voices mingled with splashing water. Later, hearing no noise, he put on his bathrobe. In his slippers he slid like silk down the carpeted stairs and stopped inside the door to the living room.

The green robe hugged her body as she knelt to wrap a vase, long fingers bending and twisting the paper. Suddenly she cried out and backed away from the package, her body brushing his. Feeling him, she turned, eyes black and big.

"A spider, on the floor." She pointed and he walked slowly to the hairy bug and crushed it with his slipper. When he again looked at her, he could barely swallow, feeling himself hard inside his pajamas.

"Thank you . . ." As if in a dream, he rolled his lower body. She stepped back, her hands twisting and untwisting. The soft green shoulders flinched under his grip and he smiled to calm her, pressing his lips to her mouth. She screamed and broke away, running upstairs. He studied the smashed center of the spider, then felt a touch on his arm and heard Maly's voice.

"Come on, let's go upstairs."

With her propelling him, he climbed the stairs and heard the door click shut behind. The music and white glow of the stereo enclosed him like a warm body. He felt the wet on his pajamas and covered himself with the blankets.

Maly told him the next day she didn't like the way he'd scared her friend.

"But Maly, she wanted me to kiss her. And how could I scare her? She's been all over Europe traveling and American girls are like that, anyway."

"What's that supposed to mean?"

"Never mind. I told you not to allow overnight guests in my house."

"I know. We're leaving today. Cassie and I will stay at the school for a few weeks before we return to the States."

"No, Maly, please. I don't want you to go."

"It's better this way, Mr. Hassan."

"But, Maly, won't you stay with me?"

"No, I want to leave."

He watched them carry boxes to the taxi. On his knees he weeded the green shoots climbing up near the purple flowers. He did not want her to go, only the others. The blue eyes and voice like his wife's slowed the glass from killing him.

"Mr. Hassan." She stooped beside him to say goodbye. Fumbling in his pocket, he put a pile of coins in her hand.

"Maly, when you get to the States take these to a coin

specialist and he will give you a thousand dollars."

Looking at the coins, she tried to give them back. "No, Maly, keep them." Then he asked if he could kiss her goodbye. She leaned forward and kissed him on the cheek, her hair like evergreens. At the gate he waited as the taxi door closed and she waved behind the window. Then she was gone.

The house was silent and the bright sun gilded the rooms and hurt his eyes. Now they were empty again and he would have to advertise and see the hate in their eyes and know they were grinding him even when they asked the price. Her child face moved farther away and he screamed until no more sound came. It hurt inside with all the pieces rubbing against his flesh.

Upstairs he turned on the music. In the back room the window was still open and sunlight trickled over the vase of flowers and dropped pools on the rug beside the bare bed.

JOHN CALDERAZZO: Born in Brooklyn, lived in New York and Florida before coming to the Twin Cities four years ago. I started writing during my senior year of college and have become increasingly committed to it. I write poetry as well as fiction and have a special interest in children's literature.

I worked in the Poetry in the Schools program in Florida; for the last several years I've supported myself by a variety of teaching jobs; am currently finishing an MFA degree in the writers' workshop at Bowling Green State University.

I've recently published a chapbook of poems, "Ropes of Blood," from Blue Lights Press, and have had fiction in *Carolina Quarterly* and *Harbinger.*

I believe, as Kafka said, that a good book or piece of literature is "an ax that breaks the frozen sea within us."

John Calderazzo

THE WINE TRICK

The evenly spaced cracks of the Belt Parkway thumped like a great heart beneath the back seat of his father's Buick, and Joseph was getting excited. They had just passed under the two-tiered rusty el, a sure sign they were in Brooklyn. Ahead loomed the massive Pyrofax gas tank, and then, beyond a wilderness of rooftops, the elegant silhouette of Coney Island — the two giant ferris wheels, the Cyclone, and the delicate mushroom of the Parachute Jump. Then one more exit, in Bensonhurst, and they'd be at his grandfather's house, which was better than Coney Island and Jones Beach rolled into one. He wished his father would step on it a little.

He squirmed uncomfortably in a new shirt and tie and made a half-hearted attempt to tease his younger brother, Billy, who was absorbed in a Little Golden Book. When they passed Coney Island he noticed with dismay that the view was partly blocked by the rising steel skeleton of an apartment project; by the end of the summer, when the floors were bricked in, there wouldn't be any view at all. Frowning, Joseph let his mind drift elsewhere. He leaned forward and thrust his elbows over the front seat between his parents, and asked, "Hey Dad, is Grampa the oldest guy you know?"

"Sure, next to Methuselah," said Mr. Santinori.

"Does Methuselah live in Brooklyn, too?" Billy asked.

"Used to. He moved."

"Stop it," said Mrs. Santinori. "Don't listen to him, kids, that's just another of Dad's bad jokes. Grandpa's eighty today, and that's old enough for anyone."

Billy slammed shut his book. "He'll *never* blow out all the candles."

"Sure he will," said Joseph. "Grampa can do anything, can't he, Dad? He's gonna do the wine trick tonight, too, 'cause I'm gonna ask him to."

His mother turned quickly. "You most certainly will not."

"Why not?" wailed Joseph.

"Because he's getting too old for that sort of thing, that's why not," said his father. "Remember last year, when he almost fell down? That's not gonna happen again." He poked a finger at the rear view mirror. "So don't even mention it, understand, Mr. Bigmouth? You know how stubborn Grandpa gets."

Joseph slumped back in the seat.

"Aww-ww, we want the wine trick," he and Billy whined.

"Shut up," said their father, so they did.

The wine trick was not a "trick" at all, but a test of muscle and will power, and it was the most impressive thing Joseph had ever seen. Usually it took place on a festive occasion, such as a birthday or a wedding anniversary, with the entire Santinori herd gathered in the backyard of the ponderous three-story brick house his grandfather had built himself in 1910, less than a decade after he had immigrated to Brooklyn. At such times, children and food could usually be found everywhere. Dark-eyed youngsters darted under tables and bushes. The braver ones ventured into the forbidden vegetable garden adjacent to the trellised patio, while others explored the house or walked to the corner candy store to buy baseball cards, or if they were older, to sneak a smoke or two.

Seated at the long center table would be nine of the ten living Santinori children and their spouses — all but Dominic, the oldest, who lived far upstate and who had spoken to no one in the family since shortly after the war, for reasons that were never explained to Joseph.

Everyone smoked. And here and there were family friends from the old days in Reggio Calabria — grim little women in black dresses and sweaters, their hair wound in tight buns, and shriveled men who smoked gnarled black cigars in absolute silence.

At the head of this table Grandfather Joseph Santinori would gaze fiercely over the kingdom of food his wife had spent days creating. To young Joseph, the man was a giant, though he was not tall. His neck and shoulders, however, were still massive, his fists were clubs; but the real power radiated from his face, framed by white hair combed straight back, and a waxed moustache —

tobacco brown — that flared like tusks around a beaked nose. Joseph thought he sometimes saw his eyes glow as red as the cigar stub he twirled endlessly in his fingers. They were eyes that seemed capable of incredible malevolence. As they roved over the backyard they asserted, quite simply: All this is mine.

After the food-mountains had diminished to hills, one of the grandchildren would invariably get around to mentioning the wine trick. And while some of the grownups rolled their eyes or stifled deep groans, and the children tittered with excitement, the old man would ritualistically grind out his cigar. From this point on it would have been easier to stop the earth from spinning. By the time he rose proudly to attention there'd be total silence.

"Vino," he would then demand hoarsely.

And his wife would move to his side to take the jacket, vest, tie and gold pocket watch he was removing with the insolent care demanded by such occasions. Next, a gallon jug of wine was brought up from the cellar. It was fine wine, legendary in the neighborhood, and had been crushed from grapes whose vines now withered on the trellises around the patio. It had fermented in great wood vats some twenty years earlier. A gallon of it was so heavy that young Joseph, a hefty nine-year-old, still had some trouble lifting it with both hands. When the old man finished rolling up his sleeves to his still-firm biceps he would announce, to nobody's surprise, "A test. To proof how strong."

Then he'd set himself, throw back his shoulders, grab the gallon jug by the neck with his right hand and lift it stiffly in front of him, as though he were aiming a pistol.

And he'd aim and aim and aim — his arm ramrod stiff, his face an ivory mask — for five impossible minutes. Meanwhile, forty or maybe fifty Santinoris held their breath and Charlie, the youngest son, obediently barked out the passing minutes, feeling only a little silly for a 36-year-old, twice-married, father of three.

While Joseph looked on in amazement, all the fantastic tales he had ever heard about the great man, and had passed on to disbelieving schoolmates, seemed undeniably true. Such as the time his grandfather stepped onto the shore of the New World with a pregnant wife and only two pennies, and threw the coins into the East River, vowing he'd just as soon start with nothing but his family. Or the time, soon after, when he was a railroad construction foreman and once snapped a railroad tie over his back with a crack that could be heard a mile down the track. Or the time, on one of his frequent returns to Italy to contract more laborers for the railroad, when he single-handedly lowered from the ship a lifeboat laden with men and supplies during a storm when the engine conked out. The truth of all this seemed undeniable.

There was no doubt in Joseph's mind about any of it: How, back to stay in Brooklyn as landlord, grocer, banker — *Padrone* to the scores of immigrants he had helped bring over — he was once approached by a courier of the dreaded *black hand* and promptly kicked him into the street, and, to the astonishment of everybody, was never bothered again. How, when a high school teacher one day appeared at the front door twisting the ear of Joseph's father (Joseph II), Grandfather Santinori took the poor man, kicking, and lowered him head-first into a garbage can as a lesson never to touch one of his sons, and then grabbed Joseph II by the collar of his overcoat and hung *him* on a meat hook in the freezer — as a lesson to never talk back to his teachers.

And much more. It didn't matter how inflated the truth had become in the telling and re-telling, Joseph believed it all. Nor did it matter — since Joseph never heard about it — that his grandfather had once been able to fight the wine for *ten* minutes, that he volunteered the trick less often than he used to, and that in the last few years, especially, Charlie barked out the minutes with much more speed than the clock did.

It didn't matter at all. When the time was up and the jug slammed to the table (making even the lasagne jump), the children responded to their grandfather's gigantic smile with wild, foot-stomping applause, the relieved adults clapped politely and nodded their heads with great respect, and while the wine was uncorked and hurried around the table, the old men sucked impassively on their gnarled black cigars.

Joseph and his parents were among the first to arrive on the tree-lined street. His grandfather was too absorbed weeding the small front garden to notice the Buick pull up. He worked standing — after the years on the railroad he vowed his knees would never again touch the earth, except in prayer of course, though he had nothing against dirt on anyone *else's* knees. So, he was bent double, his firm jaw practically scraping his kneecaps. Even from the car Joseph could hear the sound of roots tearing, being ripped by those powerful arms.

"The old boy *lives* in that garden," muttered Joseph's father, shaking his head. Then he called out, "Whaddya trying to do, Pop, break your back?"

"Giuseppi!" He snapped up like a sapling, his huge grin all but obscuring the stab of pain he felt from the too-sudden movement.

There was much kissing and hugging, redolent with the scent of garlic, followed by effusive words of praise. The old man beamed approvingly at the boys' posture, which they had spent much of the afternoon perfecting.

"You look a little pale, Dad. Feeling OK?" said Mrs. Santinori, with as much tact as possible. She knew he had been battling a cold all spring.

He dismissed this with a wave of his hand.

"No sun," he grunted, and pointed at the culprit, a gleaming six-story apartment house next door that bathed the entire street in shadow. It stood out in the faded neighborhood like a huge white brick. Joseph remembered playing on the construction site a couple of summers before.

"I never shoulda sold that house to that Jew," the old man philosophized. "In two day that bastard knock down what took me six-months-a-build."

"Now, Pop . . ."

"Now, You," he went on hoarsely. He picked a shrunken tomato from the garden and looked at it with obvious disgust. "This you call a tomato?" His hand flew toward the apartment. "That monster blocks all-a sun. Jewish miracle, turns tomatoes into cherries!"

Inside the dark house, Billy bee-lined for the kitchen, where his grandmother would be putting the final touches on desk-size trays of lasagne, two-inch-thick pizza, veal parmagiana, and a bakery-ful of pastries. At the age of six, he was already a veteran Taster.

Joseph followed his grandfather to the first-floor bedroom, where he would bounce around on the creaking bed while the old man slowly changed his clothes. Grandfather Santinori made no secret of the fact that Joseph was his favorite grandchild, but what passed between him and the boy could hardly be called conversation: "Hey, Grampa . . ."

"Hay is for horse, not me."

"Think the Dodgers can win it this year?"

"What Dodgers?"

"The *Brooklyn* Dodgers, Grampa, the baseball team. Win the Penn . . ."

"Baseball? Bah! Big men run around-a chase little ball. Don't bother me with!"

And Joseph would dissolve with laughter while the old man grumbled. This dialogue was repeated two or three times a year.

On the ancient bed, Joseph sometimes felt as though he'd fallen into a history book. Perhaps it was the pink light diffused by the fine silk curtains on the room's only window, or the shiny gramophone yawning in one corner, or the piercing smell of garlic. Whatever it was, it drew him into the past. When he lay back, it was not difficult to hear horse-drawn carriages clopping by on the cobblestones outside, or model-T's cranking up, things his father talked about over and over. Above the mahogany dresser was a large photograph of his grandfather shaking hands with the great LaGuardia himself — the Little Flower — and as Joseph's eyes darted from the picture to the old man, now stripped to his waist, the past overwhelmed the present: his grandfather's hair darkened, thickened, his skin unwrinkled, flesh was trimmed from his middle. Over the bed was a crucifix. The wracked Christ figure was skinny. Joseph wondered how He could be stronger than his grandfather. How *anyone* could.

By nightfall the house was bustling with people. Santinoris poured in from every borough of the city, from New Jersey, Connecticut, Long Island. Tessie, the youngest daughter, simply walked across the street with her brood — the old man had built *her* house, too. Millie, the oldest daughter and a widow, needed only to walk downstairs. Perpetually wreathed in gloom, she lived on the top floor with her dog Sandy, a mangy thing described by Joseph's father as "diarrhea on four legs," and despised by even the children. The two of them could be counted upon to descend during the height of the gaiety and dispense as much ill-will as possible.

In the kitchen, Grandma Santinori babbled in occasional English and put the icing on the cupcakes she baked especially for Dominic, as she had done futilely every holiday since the war. Then she flew off to the patio for a few quick games of *Lotto* with the children. These she enjoyed immensely because they played for a nickel a round and everyone let her cheat. In the musty living room the men crowded around a wood table and commiserated about the standard of living in New York, at least half of them promising to move to Florida within the year. A few of their wives joked about their new "smoking privileges" — until recently the old man had not permitted women to smoke in his presence, so they had had to do their puffing up in Millie's bedroom, to her infinite displeasure. Tony Bennett crackled through the smoke, and in isolated corners, the old, old men pulled silently on their crooked little cigars.

Then at the lusty cry of "Mange-a!" everyone moved under the lanterns in the backyard and the feast began. Millie's dog lunged at the first pair of red shoes he saw. At a dim corner of the big table Joseph wolfed down *canoli* with his favorite uncle — Sam — a wiry, big-nosed man who let him sip liberally from his wine glass. Joseph noticed, at an adjoining table, two old crones dressed from head to toe (not much of a distance) in black. Their faces were identical — absolutely round and white, perched on the black mound of their shoulders like cauliflower.

"Who're they?"

Sam chuckled softly. "Anunziata and Nina. Grandma's cousins."

"Pretty old, huh?"

"Centuries!"

"How come I never saw 'em before?"

"Oh, they've been here, but not much. Somebody's gotta drive 'em down from Mulberry St. One place they always show up, though, is at funerals." Sam paused to sip his wine. "It never fails, as soon as they get out of the taxi they fall all over each other and start moaning and wailing and scratching at the sky like you never seen, and that starts the whole family going. They're murder." Sam chuckled again, and went on in a raspy voice, "You'd think Jesus Christ himself fell off a cloud. Thing is, they're so old, half the time they don't know whose funeral it is. But it don't matter to them. I told your Dad we oughta rent 'em out to cemeteries."

Obviously pleased with his humor, Sam drained the wine, refilled it and offered a little more to Joseph, who was already giddy with laughter.

As the food mountains shrunk, Joseph got more and more dizzy on Sam's wine. He had just finished a plateful of lasagne, forgetting even to pick out the peas, when he discovered suddenly that the chatter and laughter had died and that heads were beginning to swivel toward the dark alley between the house and the apartment building. He climbed unsteadily onto his chair and saw standing at the fringe of the darkness two figures he had never seen before: a bald, thick-set man with a remarkably dour expression, and a younger, chic woman.

"Dominic," whispered Sam in amazement.

His presence seemed to stun everyone into silence; no one had seen him for at least ten years. Then his mother, sobbing his name, rushed to him with out-spread arms. Annunziata and Nina, as though on cue, flung up their hands and let out an excruciating wail. Millie's dog howled pathetically; Sam rolled his eyes.

But there was no chain reaction. In fact, a piercing chill in the air seemed to freeze all emotion; and as the two clutching, sobbing cousins were led off, heads began turning for guidance toward Grandfather Santinori at the head of the table. Even he looked a bit puzzled, his countenance stern but not fierce — like the moon's. Dominic stood at attention and returned the same gaze. On one of his arms was the chic woman, and on the other was his softly crying mother.

While the two men stared for what seemed an hour, Joseph noted with astonishment their almost identical profiles. Though Dominic wore thick glasses and had no moustache, on his face was chiseled his father's powerful chin, brow and grim mouth. His nose was only slightly less hooked with age than the old man's. Even more remarkably, the same pack of muscle seemed to shift beneath his clothes. The oldest of all the sons, he was also quite obviously the strongest.

"The Great One returns," Sam muttered.

Joseph wasn't sure what that meant, but he decided instantly that he didn't like Dominic at all. You had to be a pretty big rat, he concluded, to avoid your own family for a decade, especially when all it takes to make your mother happy is an occasional visit or phone call. Even a bank robber's mom must have wanted to see her son at least once in a while, to cook him a decent meal or some cupcakes.

Finally, Grandfather Santinori's expression softened imperceptibly and he extended his right hand.

"Come," he grunted.

Dominic hesitated a moment, then eased from the grasp of the two women and slowly, stiffly shook his father's hand. They did not embrace, though it appeared for an instant they might. Next to his taller son the old man looked shrunken and tired.

While the men spoke quietly, Joseph asked Sam what the big flap after the war had been all about. Preoccupied with his own thoughts, Sam mumbled something about how no castle can survive with two kings, how one must always wait for one's turn, and how bad things are if you have an ax to grind. Joseph couldn't see what it had to do with castles and kings and axes. He wondered what other kinds of mysteries were hidden in the smoke cloud over the table and in the heads of adults in general.

Dominic and his wife started working their way around the table, shaking hands, hugging, kissing — to a generally cool reception. Joseph's father, wanting no part of them, lit a cigarette and wandered off into the garden, where he stayed, a red dot pulsing slowly. Unperturbed, they moved on.

Joseph noticed that Dominic's wife was certainly not Family, not that there was anything wrong with that. His own mother, after all, was a German blond, but she had fit in and was well-liked by everyone. But he could sense this new woman would never fit in — not because of her fair skin and her small nose — but because, perhaps, of her hair, spun in a tall beehive and dyed almost as blue as her expensive-looking dress. Or perhaps because she smiled too often and too quickly. Santinoris never, ever, faked it when they smiled. So Joseph decided he couldn't stand *her* either.

Anunziata and Nina, still clutching and sniffing, were returned to their seats, and the chatter rose gradually to an almost normal level. Occasional laughter rang out in the yard, but much of it seemed forced, a strange thing indeed. Joseph imagined prickly, wraith-like things slithering in the garden and in the blackness of the alley. The wine did not keep him warm.

Sam rose shakily at his brother's approach. "Looking good, Dom," he said with no enthusiasm, his hand buried in Dominic's. "Lucille, too."

"You, too," said Dominic. "How's Evelyn and Mary?"

"Awright."

Dominic folded his arms and examined Sam for a moment, his nostrils twitching. "Still got a taste for the old *vino*, eh Sam?"

"I guess so."

"Ah, that's my Sammy!"

The too-loud, overly hearty tone of voice rankled Joseph. And what was this "Sammy" business, as if Dominic were his father? It looked like he was trying to embarrass Sam. Or something. Up close, his face unadorned with hair, Dominic reminded Joseph of a huge snapping turtle.

The turtle now looked down at him.

"And who is this young man?" it snapped.

Dizzy with wine, anger, confusion, Joseph jumped up and heard himself blurt out a stream of words: "I don't like you! I don't like you at all, or her either! You made Grandma sad. She baked cupcakes all the time and cried and cried 'cause you never came around or anything or even called, an' Grampa's a million times neater 'n you and way stronger, too! He could do the wine trick and you never could! All you are is a fat snapping turtle!"

Dominic's mouth dropped open in astonishment, and even Anunziata and Nina fell silent. Joseph immediately knew he had made a big mistake; he could feel Sam shrinking from his side. But it wasn't until he caught the hurt, angry flash of his mother's eyes that he realized that among whatever other outrages he had committed, he had mentioned the wine trick.

It was too late of course. His words seemed to rush over his grandfather like a sea-breeze, practically riffling his moustache, swelling his chest with fresh air. Everyone now looked to the head of the table, where, after a well-timed pause, the old man ground out his cigar.

"Vino," he demanded.

"Pop, no . . ." implored his daughter Tessie. "What about that sore back you were complaining about last week?"

"What back?" he said irritably, at the same time pulling away from his wife's reach.

Joseph's father was back at the table. "Don't be ridiculous, Pop, this is . . ."

"Shut!" was all he said.

Dominic, too, waves a hand in protest, but Joseph didn't think it was sincere. Not that there was any stopping things now anyway; Grandfather Santinori had the spotlight and nothing could wrench it away from him. He peeled off his jacket, vest and tie and gave them to his wife, then rolled up his sleeves. His arms were indeed large, but not as firm as they had seemed in the past, in the bedroom before dinner. The gallon jug of wine was brought up from the cellar and placed on the table with a heavy thud. As he set his shoulders and firmly gripped the jug by its neck, even the gnarled old men disengaged their cigars and leaned forward in their chairs. Grandfather Santinori was looking directly at Dominic.

"A test," he said almost tauntingly, "to proof . . . how . . . strong. Five minuto!" His left hand flipped open the gold pocket watch and placed it on the table where everyone could see it. There'd be no cheating this time.

"Please Pop . . ." said Charlie, but his protest was stifled by an icy glare.

The old man looked over the entire family, his gaze lingering here and there, especially on young Joseph, and then he fixed his eyes again on Dominic. He set his face and lifted the wine.

Joseph was sitting almost directly across the long table from his grandfather, and now that he thought back on it, he remembered the old man *had* had a tough time of it the last time he tried the trick, and that had been almost a year ago. His arm had trembled for some time before he had finally steadied it, and when he completed the trick, Charlie had had to catch him to keep him from falling — or so it seemed. On the fringes of Joseph's excitement licked a terrible sense of responsibility.

"UNO!" barked Charlie.

There was no eye-rolling or smirking this time. Joseph had never seen his parents look so pale. His father, especially, looked petrified. His grandmother wrung a napkin in her hands like a rosary. The old man was holding steady and true, his face stone.

"DUO!" said Charlie.

Joseph looked at Dominic. He, too, was nervous, but less, perhaps, than the others. Clutching Lucille, he seemed to be taking an almost radiant satisfaction in what was happening. Was he gloating, Joseph wondered, even in the face of the old man's glowing eyes? Lucille looked bored. The old man's arm held steady, but his face was reddening, as were his eyes, as though his head were actually filling with wine. The chords in his neck stood out like roots on a water oak, and his nostrils began to quiver.

"TRES!"

"C'mon Pop," whispered Sam, "Jesus God, Pop, you're gonna do it."

Someone gasped suddenly as Grandfather Santinori's arm began to quiver dangerously. A tiny snake of spittle writhed at the corner of his mouth; his eyes seemed to be turning inward. Joseph began to tremble himself. Then in one rapid, panic-stricken movement, he grabbed Sam's small wine bottle and thrust it out toward his grandfather, as though toasting him from the opposite end of the table.

"QUATTRO!" cried Charlie.

Shaking just a little, Sam stood up and lifted his wine glass, too, holding it out towards his father the way Joseph did. And then in similar fashion so did Joseph's parents and Tess and her husband, and then Millie and Charlie and everyone at the table, except Dominic and his wife. Finally, breaking from her grasp, he did too.

The old man's arm dipped low, and like a green branch relieved of its fruit, sprang back up. The trembling ceased.

By the time Charlie yelled "CINQUA!" the old man's eyes were blazing red. Incandescent, they drank everything — the tumultuous applause, the screaming, backslapping adults bouncing around like kids; and at the end of his still-outstretched arm, the steady jug of wine holding, and held by, all his children.

He winked at Joseph, and, as the wine crashed to the table, he sank back in his chair, his eyes puffy and grey as ashes.

PAT KALUZA: In grade school when they told us to use our spelling words in sentences, I wrote tiny short stories with plots weirdly contrived about the demands of the spelling words. Then my writing career declined through the years of high school, college and my job as a secretary. But a few years ago, pressed by my friend Dorothy Grupp, I took a Loft class. Everything began to change. I quit my job, and with it went my lousy self-esteem and that deadly weariness of fulltime work that has nothing to do with living a life.

As a self-employed typist, I have a new self-respect and I have time. Forget the nature of the work, forget the three-piece suits lately acquired by women; I have time. TIME. That quiet, guiltless time when one sits alone on the couch when feeling and thought wander about seemingly without aim. Thought and feeling require time to reveal themselves; they require self-esteem that one might write concretely and truthfully, that one might write at all. And if, sitting alone on the couch, feeling and thought should meet, like the collision of an egg and sperm, then perhaps the life of a piece of fiction will begin.

In support of self-employment and voluntary poverty, I offer these words of Virginia Woolf from her book, *Three Guineas:* "... you must earn enought to be independent of any other human being and to buy that modicum of health, leisure, knowledge and so on that is needed for the full development of body and mind. But no more. Not a penny more."

Pat Kaluza

IMPOTENCE

The baby lived only five months in the dark of her womb. Then, for some unknown reason, it pushed itself out to the light and died. She wrapped it in the skirt she wore that morning and left it in the kitchen's far corner on the floor. Then she cut her hair so short it looked like she had shaved her head.

When he came home that evening, she didn't answer his call. He saw the breakfast dishes still on the table and called again, something mounting in him. Then he saw her hair scattered everywhere, her thick mahogany curls on the dark wood floor, on the chairs he had painted bright green just the week before. He had to hold himself up with one hand on the table. Staring at the dishes on the checkered tablecloth, he saw long red hairs caught in egg yolk now turned to marble. He understood the baby was dead even before he found the small bloodied bundle. He seized it and hugged it to him, weeping. A long, high scream broke through from somewhere inside him. As if suddenly awakened, he quickly returned the tiny body to its corner.

Slowly and carefully he swept up the hair he had loved beyond reason, and then he went to the bedroom in search of her, numbly thinking that perhaps she too was dead. But she was sitting on the floor by the bed wrapped in blankets. She was not crying. His own shirt front was wet and cold from his tears, and she sat there like a veiled Arab woman with hard blank eyes. He could see she was shaking beneath the thick blankets, but that wasn't enough.

"Why, Alexis? Why?" he asked her softly.

She turned toward him and looking straight ahead, she slowly pulled back the blanket covering her head. He did not know this woman with her strangely shaped skull. That morning he had awakened early and watched her sleep, worshipping her and the round heap of her belly. He had gently pushed damp curls back from her nervous eyelids. This was not Alexis, and he ran from the room as if his life were in danger.

That evening he ate left-over porridge in front of a cold fire and built the casket. He went to her just once to ask for something to line the casket, but she remained hunched over and silent. Frantically searching through the cupboards of their room, he found her wedding veil. It was the only thing holy enough and he refused to ask her permission.

He spent the night at his cousin Joe's under the comforting light of Joe's moon-faced wife, and drank himself into a stupor at the kitchen table.

In the morning he returned, oddly comforted by the sickness from the alcohol. The dishes were washed and a tiny cross made of broom straws lay on top of a small pale oak box. He went to the bedroom and she was sitting up in bed; her eyes, he was relieved to see, were a puffy tender red in the white of her face. She had covered her bony head with a plain black cap.

"Do you need the doctor?" he asked, standing in the doorway.

"It happened. It just happened."

But he couldn't tell if this was really his wife's voice, though clearly he could see now that this was his wife before him. He wanted her to speak again so that he could listen more closely. Looking at her curious black cap, he understood suddenly that it was a rite of penance for her, something a nun or a condemned person might wear. It had no shape nor luster and he wondered where she had gotten it. It was like a sign for him, a mark of something, he didn't know what.

He went into the room and pulled a shirt from the cupboard.

"I have to go to work. Unless I should stay," he said with his back to her. She did not answer. Unbuttoning his shirt from the day before he saw the brown bloodstains. Something large jerked in him, and he turned toward her so that she could see the shirt. But she would give him nothing. He moved toward her to break through her staring trance, and then saw that the stubble of hair at the edge of her cap was the same color as the dried blood on his shirt. His body jerked again. He felt his teller's cage at the bank waiting for him, promising him air to breathe. He turned and hurried stumbling from the room.

Her beautiful red hair had been a gift from her Scottish father. He gave her something more: a fierce silence, a silence through which he cursed a run-away wife and a plot of land needing a son. He named her Alexis and taught her to be silent. He told her that her mother was a Gypsy: she did magic and read cards, and she had thrown something in his eyes and he married her. Wherever she was, she would be burning.

When Alexis was young, she heard him say as he lit the evening lamp, "It is to consume this darkness still with us." He would say it softly and slowly and she thought it a strange and beautiful prayer. He did not let her speak to other children; he said only the Bible was a trustworthy friend in this heathen place. She was dressed in such dark colors that children would call from the other side of the street, "Whoop, whoop, witchy," though not if her father was with her. Once he made her watch him drown a litter of barn kittens one by one in a bucket of cold water. To make her strong, he said. When she was fifteen, he sent her away to school and she never saw him again.

She told her husband these things a small bit at a time during the first year of their marriage. She would sit in the creaking rocking chair alternately sewing and staring at the fire and would sometimes suddenly blurt out, "It is a dangerous thing to be alone." Then she could speak more normally, though never at any length. He pitied her and never tried to force her from her solemn quiet. He loved her, of that much he was certain, though his own serene childhood left him feeling slender and without much substance next to the weight of hers.

When he met her she was a waitress at the diner across the street from the bank. After months of watching her hips move up and down the length of the diner's counter, he wrote her a poem, a poem no better than a schoolboy's. Waiting for her outside the diner, he thrust it abruptly at her as she walked out the door. Standing in the misty light of the diner's window, he could see her face darken over words as her finger moved across the lines. He tried to tell her that they were just for show and the poem was about love. She wouldn't believe him; he didn't know what kept her from believing him. But he loved the passion of her disbelief: it was a kind of proof that she loved him. He asked her to marry him, and she said she would, and he was never to write her such words again.

They were an unlikely match, this young man with his cheerful face and a new job at the bank and this sullen young woman with red hair the likes of which the town had never seen. During that first year of their marriage, she learned to touch his arm and then his face in the quiet evenings in front of the fire. He was happy. The town saw this and grew quiet about Alexis.

Then she found out she was pregnant and everything began to change. The doctor was with her in the kitchen when he came home that evening. A storm had threatened all day but never came. Alexis was sitting at the table crowded with bright quilting pieces and Dr. Evans was saying, ". . . young, healthy, you'll be fine." She put her face in her hands and moaned, "I can't, oh God, I can't." The doctor smiled at him over the top of her head and said, "You'll be a papa in about six months' time."

He put Alexis to bed and refused to hear her moaning, "I can't, I can't." He would not let the unnatural sounds of it kill the joy in his own breast. Everything would be different because of this child. She would lose her shyness in the work of being a mother. The baby would bring them full circle, would join the light and dark of them together. He knelt down by the bed and gave thanks to a god he had forgotten many years ago. Then he crawled under the covers more timid with her than the first time she poured him coffee at the diner. She had become sacred, a vessel of something great and holy. Later he thought that perhaps that was the very beginning of the fear.

Looking back, he could see other reasons to suspect her hand in the baby's early death. She would not help him search for a name. "Names," she scoffed. "A name is nothing." And one day he came home from the bank and told her, "I'll get a raise, when the baby comes."

"We'll see," she answered. After pestering her for her meaning, she would only say, "It came from nowhere; they weren't my words."

And still he did not believe that he was afraid of her because she might have killed it. If she wasn't ready, she wasn't. He could not ask her to bear a child if she wasn't ready. There would be others. He certainly did not hate her for it.

But one night in bed she had placed his hand on her round belly to feel the baby and ask if she could have crocuses along the front walk, white ones. He told her she would have to wait till the next spring, and he left his hand there as if he had forgotten it. She let it remain, as if she too had forgotten it. Still, it had been a terrible thing when he had to bury the child by himself. Building that miniature coffin was the hardest thing he ever did.

In the small birch grove behind the house where his father had planted a circle of white pines, he buried it. He did not know what sex it was, it was so red and bruised purple. He buried it alone and wiped the grieving from his face with dirt and sodden leaves from the winter before.

Their mourning went on and on and they passed through the summer as if drugged. Alexis wore only the darkest of her dark clothes and always the black cap. There were times he thought that if he could kill something, he would purge himself of the fear that clenched in his stomach whenever he forgot his carefulness and saw the cap. Not Alexis, not a murder like that. But to strangle something distant from himself, squeeze the crying out of a thin animal throat. He had never had such thoughts before.

When the cold of winter began, they spent every night in silence in front of the fire. They went to bed in the same silence, and sometimes it seemed to him that they were two strangers adrift on a lifeboat. It was bitter cold and their flight was hopeless.

But one night when he'd blown the light out and he could hear her begin her incessant picking at threads holding the quilt together, he reached across the bed for her.

He told her, "Stop now, be done with it."

She made no sign that she had heard. Then he said, "What's done is done, however it was done."

"However it was done?" she whispered.

"If you're hurting because you did something, then it's time to give it up. This life is meant to be lived."

She hissed, he was certain of that, low and evil, like a snake in the dark, afraid to strike.

"You!" she screamed. "You killed that baby!"

He went rigid with the hatefulness of it, the monstrous lie. She rushed from the bed crying and choking, but it was too late now for her tears. It was far too late for simple tears.

That night she left their bed for good and made a nest for herself in the corner of the kitchen by the stove. She put an abandoned door over the woodchest and covered it with a straw mat a hobo had left behind. After that she spent her evenings after their silent supper at the kitchen table playing solitaire as if hypnotized by the small machinations of the cards. He was more alone than ever, but there was nothing he could do. It was the end of their uneasy scenes of undressing for bed and his listening to her nervous picking. Her fingers plucked at the frayed quilt even when she finally slept. For this new kind of quiet he was grateful, though it brought with it a new fear that she would come into the room while he was asleep. He didn't know what she would do.

And then one night she did come. That day he had come home early from the bank because he had suddenly taken sick. He could hardly breathe and the panic choked him more. He opened the door and she was leaning over something hidden in her lap. She looked up and said, "You." Just that: "You."

He stood there holding onto the doorframe, too weak to catch the door banging in the wind. "I'm sick," he said. "Very sick." But she did not move, just stared at him with a violent look he could not decipher. Hate was too simple, though later he would come to think that hate, like love, was a whole world with no boundaries. It spilled out and mixed with everything else.

He went to the bedroom and cried as he undressed, unable to even manage the buttons on his shirt. It was more than the fever now. This was real, his need was real. These weren't just words now. Either she hadn't been able to help him or she simply would not help him. Couldn't or wouldn't, either way it didn't matter.

Late that night she came to his bed, as if attracted by the heat of his fevered body, the way some animals can smell blood by the warmth of it. She touched him with her cool fingers; in his dream he thought her a holy angel, living but made of marble. But it was her, her black cap gone and her rough skull haloed by the candlelight. An unholy angel sent to punish him.

She sat on the bed and began stroking him, lightly, slowly, on his arms and chest. He didn't know those parts of him existed until she touched them, and then they sickened him. His stomach was in revolt and he could feel his legs beginning to cramp waiting for the touch to descend. Her fingers moved down and came to a stop inside his thighs.

"I won't hurt you," she said, and lay down next to him.

He tried to stop his trembling, to think of something good, green, lush. This was Alexis coming to his bed. But he saw only himself sawing the hard oak planks, through his awful crying; he knew he brought forth that picture himself, but it couldn't be helped. He was afraid and it was all that would come.

"Please, I'm so sick," he whimpered, pitifully like a child.

She started to kiss him, pushing her tongue into his mouth. It was like a hot snake trying to get into his mouth. He jerked away and stuffed his mouth with the quilt to keep from vomiting. She left silently, as if gliding above the floor. In the eerie flickering light, he did not believe he would see the morning.

After that he came home only to sleep and cut firewood. He left money for her on the floor outside the kitchen door.

He knew he was puny and shrivelled, knew that she hated him most of all for the worm of his sex. "Cracker" she used to call it, before the baby. "Cracker" after a puppy they let her have at the school. "A fancy little soup cracker," she said once. He would laugh at her shy approach and in a quiet and strange and slow moving way, they would make love. But then, with the baby in her, it seemed like a sin to enter her body. Only the thinnest of membranes separated the grossness of his sex from the delicate life in her womb. He had heard other men speak this way about their unborn. And then the baby died.

He wanted to tell her that in the spring they would love again. They would lie belly to belly and they would make another baby. That much he could see quite clearly, though *she* refused to see it. Even though that loving to come stood between them as firm and solid as the kitchen door. In the spring they would be reborn: Alexis would fling open that door and they would be who they used to be.

He was someone different now, he knew that. Still, most of him was the same; it was only where the baby had been (yes, it had been in him too) — that part was different. It was a hole in his belly that grew and filled with a hot slippery pain, leaving him open-mouthed and panting when he thought of the baby. Not the bloody fetus he buried, but the baby from before. In the spring that hole would fill up, his sex would fill up. They could still have that baby from before.

In the spring, blessed spring, her body would let loose into womanly flesh again. She would speak to him by the fire. They would talk about planting poplars by the road. When he brought her the bulbs of carnival-colored tulips, she would move back to his bed and he would be waiting with new arms. And when the warm sweet air of spring came, her hair would grow long again, the color of mahogany, and she would trail it across his hard naked body. He would know her and never again feel her silently waiting for him, as if at the end of a long dark hallway.

Every evening after leaving the bank, he walked outside the town on the same lonely roads and watched the ground for signs of spring. A thaw in early February laid the earth bare and he saw it waiting, fecund. He looked up and saw the trees still naked, sending out their wiry fingers against an early nightfall. It was with relief that he could find no life in their hard little buds. He felt suspended high and dangerously above his own life and only spring's coming could loose him. And yet he was fearful of that spring, afraid of the first blade of grass, the first tender green blade that would slice across his heart.

So he walked and waited. The town's eyes were upon him, he knew, but they remained quiet and waiting. In late March the snow melted again, but he was suspicious and called it a false spring. There were still patches of ice down the rutted roads where he walked. He confidently maintained that it would snow again, until a man came to his teller window and said he'd just seen two robins fighting over the same worm. "Spring's here for sure," the man said.

Alexis must be told, he thought. He told them at the bank that his wife needed him, no he didn't know why. The time had come and she must be made to understand, as he understood. There would not be another chance.

Outside the bank he could hear the unmistakable chatter of newly-arrived birds, when only the day before the air had been cold and still. He ran through it, to Alexis, running like a wild man. The time had come, the man said so, and he had to run.

He threw open their front door.

"Alexis, the spring!" he called and stood waiting for the kitchen door to spring open just as he had always envisioned it. She did not answer and the door remained closed. He called again, impatient with her reluctance. Then he smelled the smoke of several small fires smouldering in their bedroom.

She did not return that night or ever again. He waited seven years and then declared her dead. He would never allow his new wife to cut her hair, though she complained in the summers and bore him all those children. At first she tried to condemn the she-devil Alexis, but he would have no word spoken against her.

ROGER BARR: I was born in Iowa in 1951 and attended a one-room country school. In 1965 I moved to a farm in southern Minnesota. I received a B.A. degree in history from Hamline University in 1973, and now live and write in St. Paul. My stories and essays have appeared in *Lake Street Review*, *Great River Review*, and other publications.

My aim as a writer is to write good stories about "ordinary" people that "ordinary" people can understand and enjoy.

"Take Good Care of Her" is one of a series of short stories about the same set of characters. Each story stands alone, yet when they are combined they tell a single, longer story. These stories are woven around the often uneasy, sometimes hilarious, but always fascinating relationship between the adult and juvenile worlds. This particular story is a funny story, but funny only to us as adults who have lived through a situation as desperate as the one the boy Jimmy encounters.

Roger Barr

"TAKE GOOD CARE OF HER"

On a Friday afternoon in early March, Jimmy leaped off the school bus into the late winter sunshine. For the first time in weeks, the icy north wind did not push him up the long driveway towards the house. Instead, a fresh southern breeze blew over the stale winter landscape, and on it he smelled the promise of spring. He pulled off his stocking cap and stuffed it into his coat pocket.

Tiny rivers cut through the dirty ice on the driveway and trickled over the shoulder into the ditch. Soon the snowy fields would melt, and the running water would wash the dirty snowbanks out of the ditches. The ice would go out of the river and he and his friend Kevin could watch the heavy ice cakes jam up against the pasture fence and flood the river bottom east of the barn. And then the yard and hills and pastures would green up, and the mud would dry, and no more heavy winter coats, boots, and mittens and caps.

He made a snowball with his bare hands, the first good one in weeks, and lobbed it into the snowy field. The thought of spring so excited him that he broke into a run and ran all the way up to the house.

Down at the barn, the cab of a strange red Chevrolet truck poked out of the haymow doors. He started down to investigate, but decided to eat a sandwich first. Besides, there might be work to do.

He kicked his overshoes off at the back step. A chance drip from the icicles above the door hit him on the neck and ran all the way down his back as he stepped through the door into the glassed-in porch. His mother had the kitchen door open to let in the heat that collected in the porch during the day. She was bent over the sink, peeling potatoes, and looked up when she heard him.

"Where's your stocking cap, young man?" she demanded.

"Ah, Mom. It's nice out."

"It's barely above freezing. You keep your cap on, you hear? I don't want you coming down with a cold. And close the door, it's getting chilly."

Jimmy hung his coat on its hook and immediately opened the refrigerator door. To his delight, there was a plate of ham on the top shelf.

"Don't touch that ham, it's for supper," his mother said.

"Ah, Mom."

"You heard me."

"I got to eat something. I'm starved."

"You can't be that hungry, you just had lunch three hours ago."

"Fish sticks," he snorted. "And mashed potatoes and butter. I hate 'm." He grabbed the carton of milk and set it on the table. From the cupboards came the jar of Skippy, a glass, knife, and two slices of bread. He built a thick peanut butter sandwich and poured a glass of milk. He took a big bite from the sandwich and washed it down with half a glass of milk. The kitchen was quiet except for the rhythmic scrape of his mother's knife.

"What's for supper besides ham?"

"Scalloped potatoes."

"My favorite."

The scraping stopped and his mother looked at him. "God must have made you with a hollow leg. Not even finished with your sandwich, and already worried about supper." The scraping resumed and abruptly stopped when Jimmy poured a second glass of milk.

"That's enough milk. You drink it all now and there won't be none left for supper. Or for breakfast tomorrow." Scrape, Scrape.

"Where's Grandpa?" Jimmy asked out of habit. Lately it was a good idea to keep tabs on Grandpa's whereabouts, and then stay out of the area.

"He's upstairs in his room, taking a nap." The knife paused for a moment. "Grandpa hasn't been feeling very good this week."

My room, Jimmy thought. Displacement from his room when Grandpa came to live with them was a wound that had festered and become infected, rather than healed by time. It wasn't fair to have to sleep on the living room sofa and have just a dresser in the hallway. Kevin had a whole room to himself, with model planes hanging by string from the ceiling and posters on the wall. And his crummy sister got to keep her room, even though she was at college most of the time.

He remembered the red truck.

"Who's down at the barn?" he asked with his mouth full.

"Don't talk with your mouth full. Some man from up by Kenyon. Your father sold him some of that old hay in the barn." A potato plopped into the kettle on the counter. "He wants you to help, so hurry along."

Automatically, Jimmy slowed down; he could make this sandwich last until bedtime if it got him out of moving hay bales.

Suddenly it dawned on him. He choked on his sandwich.

The *Playboy* magazine that he and Kevin had found in the dump last summer was in the haymow, on the top layer stuffed between two bales. They would find it. The *Playboy*, so carefully hidden, and guarded and stared at all summer, found. An egg beater started up in his stomach. Either the stranger, or worse yet, his father would move one of the bales and find it. And Christy, the centerfold, would unfold when he picked it up. Christy, his baby, his love, dressed in her white bikini of untanned skin that hid nothing, a mysterious smile on her face, in the hands of his father and the stranger. The thought horrified him. His head exploded with dizziness and a ringing rose in his ears. His father had never talked to him about that stuff. What would he say? What would happen? It would undoubtedly be terrible, a whipping for sure, maybe reform school.

He looked at his mother's back. The knife sliced a potato in half. What would she say? He considered running away. Already he could imagine a horrible scene at supper.

First his mother would leave the kitchen before the supper dishes were washed, a sure sign of trouble. Then the *Playboy* would suddenly appear on the table.

"We found this loading hay this afternoon," his father would begin. "Know anything about it?"

"No."

"How do you think it got there?"

"I don't know." A long pause as he groped for someone to blame it on. "Maybe the high school kids who stacked the hay left it."

"I don't think so. Do you?"

And Grandpa, speaking up from the doorway to the dining room. "Them two boys spent half the summer up there in the mow. Him and that boy lives on the Smith place." Grandpa still referred to Kevin that way.

"Do you think you should be looking at this sort of thing?" his father would continue. "Where did you get it?"

"They was up there in the mow every time I went out . . ." Grandpa again. "I would a said something, if I'd a known they was lookin' at dirty magazines."

"Well, son, what do you think we should do about this?"

"I know what my pa would have done if he caught me lookin' at dirty magazines. He'd a skinned me alive. . ."

He felt like throwing up. He had to go down to the barn; not going was the same as coming right out and saying it was his. His fate sealed by some idiot wanting hay.

"What's he want hay for, anyway?" he moaned.

The knife stopped in surprise. "Why to feed his cows of course! Farmers always need hay at the end of winter. There won't be any grass for six weeks."

Silently he cursed the cruel spring for what it was about to do to him. But maybe they hadn't found it yet. MAYBE THEY HADN'T FOUND IT YET!

"How long's he been here?"

Scrape. "Who?"

"The man buying hay!"

Scrape. "Oh, not very long." Scrape. Scrape. "Ten minutes maybe."

He abandoned his sandwich and grabbed his coat off its hook. The knife stopped abruptly and his mother's head bobbed up.

"Where are you going?"

"Down to help."

"Not until you change your school clothes."

He shot up the stairs two at a time to his dresser in the hall, grabbed a pair of pants and a flannel shirt, and ran into the bathroom to change, slamming the door behind him. Through the closed door he heard his mother's muffled voice. "Don't slam the door, you'll wake up Grandpa."

He did exactly that. Grandpa, stern and sour, came downstairs as Jimmy was furiously lacing his work shoes. Grandpa's felt slippers made no noise as he moved slowly across the kitchen to the table and sank into a chair.

"Hi, Dad," his mother said. "Have a good nap?"

"Did until somebody slammed a door, woke me up."

"I told him not to. Since you're up, do you want some coffee? I just made some fresh."

Jimmy saw what was coming and tried to head it off. "I'm sorry I woke you up, Grandpa."

But Grandpa had not gotten enough mileage out of his hardship. He turned directly to Jimmy, his old faded eyes pinning him to the floor.

"What's so all-fired important that you got to slam the door and wake me up, huh?"

"Dad sold some hay, I'm goin' down to help."

"Ought to make you open and close a door quiet a hundred times. What my pa would a done to me." Once he got started, Grandpa could go on until bedtime. Jimmy couldn't afford any more time — every second counted.

"I got to go," he said and slammed the kitchen door behind him. Putting his boots on, he could hear Grandpa ranting in the kitchen and knew there would be hell to pay when he came in again.

He ran through the puddles to the barn, planning what to say if it had already been found, and slipped between the truck cab and the haymow door. The high school kids were his best bet, blame it on them. I saw them looking at something, he'd tell the old man. They wouldn't show it to me . . .

"Out of the way, for Christ's sake!" Coming into the dark haymow from the dazzling snowy outside, he was momentarily blind, and almost bumped into his father before he saw him. His father swung the bale he was carrying up into the back of the truck. Heart pounding, Jimmy jumped back, half expecting his father to turn around and deal with him on the spot.

But his father simply disappeared into the darkness, and was replaced almost instantly by the stranger, who heaved another bale into the truck and disappeared into the darkness himself. Jimmy looked in the back of the truck; it was almost empty, so they had just started.

Slowly the barn began to materialize as his eyes adjusted to the dim light. At the far end of the barn the harsh yellow light bulb glowed against the rafters, and below it was a dark mass that was the hay. There was a loud thump as a bale came crashing to the floor from the top of the stack. Jimmy shivered, half with fear and half with cold; the sun's warmth had not penetrated through the barn roof and he could see his breath in the stale winter air.

His father reappeared and heaved another bale into the truck. Jimmy looked into his face for that just-wait-until-I-get-ahold-of-you look, but his father simply turned around and went after another bale. The stranger heaved another bale into the truck. Did he know? Was the look the stranger gave him when he turned around a look at someone about to go to reform school? He couldn't tell if it had been found or not, and he certainly couldn't ask.

Another bale crashed to the floor. Jimmy watched his father carry it up to the truck. "Don't just stand there," his father said. "Give a hand up top. Or better yet, jump up in the truck."

Jimmy ignored the second order and stumbled across the chaffy floor and started up the bouncy ladder that leaned against the wall of bales. Whoever was up top was the one he had to deal with. A bale sailed over his head and crashed on the floor below him.

"Hold it, comin' up!"

At the top of the ladder, he peeked over the edge at the bales under the louvered window, where he and Kevin had stuffed the *Playboy*. The bales were gone and so was the magazine. A lanky kid about his own age dragged a bale to the edge and pushed it over. Jimmy hoisted himself onto the bales and casually looked under the window. Imperceptibly, the kid looked, too, out of the corner of his eye. He had it.

"Hi." the kid said.

"Hi." Jimmy picked up a heavy bale and dragged it over to the edge, pushed it off, and heard it bang on the floor below.

He watched the kid work. When the kid picked up a bale he was rigid, bending from his chest instead of his waist. The magazine was stuck inside his coat, then, down the front of his pants. When he straightened up, Jimmy could see its faint outline under the kid's coat. You had to know it was there to see it. The kid crackled slightly when he bent over. You had to know it was there to hear it.

Giving up the magazine to his old man to save his neck was one thing. But giving it up to a kid his own age. . . . Jimmy stepped into the kid's path.

"Hey!"

The kid dropped his bale. He glanced down at the men working below. His eyes filled with silent blackmail.

"Yeah?"

They stood facing each other for a long moment.

"Where you go to school?" Jimmy backed down. He glanced down at the men.

The kid glanced at the men again, sensing his advantage. "Kenyon. We beat you in basketball. Twice."

Jimmy let the remark pass. He dragged a bale over to the edge and pushed it off, debating what to do. It was his property and already it was clear that if he was to get it back, he would have to fight for it. He glanced down at the men working below. They were too close to risk a fight. A fight with a strange kid and his dad would raise hell, find the magazine, and then he was right back where he started. . . .

The kid pushed a bale over the edge. The magazine crackled under his coat.

. . . There wasn't a thing he could do. He pushed a bale over. The kid had it and that was that. Christy, the centerfold, was gone. Anything he said would only add to the kid's glory of stealing her away. The only thing to do was ignore the situation altogether, like the magazine had never existed.

"What grade you in?" he asked pleasantly.

"Sixth."

"Me too." The conversation petered out. What could you say to someone who had just stolen your *Playboy* when you couldn't do a thing about it? Silently they dragged their bales over to the edge and pushed them off until the stranger hollered "That's enough, Stevie!"

Stevie turned around and stiffly, not bending at the waist, backed down the ladder. Jimmy suppressed the urge to push him over backwards. He memorized Stevie's face for a future time; if he and Kevin ever caught Stevie at the Kenyon swimming pool, they'd drown him. He climbed down the ladder himself.

By the truck the men stood and talked and talked. Jimmy hung around, just in case something came up. The men predicted when the cold weather would break and it would straighten up. They told each other what they were planting come spring, and what they were using for fertilizer. They complained about how prices kept climbing. They threatened to quit farming altogether.

Stevie stood anxiously on first one foot and then the other, the magazine burning a hole under his coat. No doubt he had only flipped through the pages once or twice before stuffing it under his coat. Watching him, Jimmy remembered last summer when he and Kevin had peddled home from the dump at top speed, their lungs ready to burst by the time they made the safety of the barn. He realized, suddenly, that he wasn't out of the woods yet. If Stevie wasn't careful and got caught, his old man could worm it out of him where he got it, and call *his* old man, and. . . . He let the thought drop right there. Maybe he should pull Stevie aside and tell him to take good care of the magazine, hide it where *nobody* would find it, even by accident. No, don't say anything. Stevie could have kept his crummy hands to himself and stayed out of trouble. He was on his own.

The man wrote out the check on the mud-spattered front fender of the truck. He talked about getting more hay and Jimmy made a mental note to be gone the next time he came.

The man turned suddenly to his son. "Well, Stevie! Should we go home?" Stevie jumped and jerked back as though he had been hit by a bucket of ice water. Stiffly, he got into the cab. Jimmy smiled with small satisfaction and the thought of the long, tense ride that lay ahead for Stevie — sitting next to his old man with a *Playboy* shoved down his pants.

The heavy truck splashed through the puddles and disappeared behind the house. It reappeared briefly beyond the garden and then disappeared below the brow of the hill.

"Well, there's some easy money," his father said. He folded the check in half and put it in his coat pocket. "It's a good thing he came tonight. Supposed to cloud up again and snow. Six inches by morning."

Winter again. A promising weekend ruined.

They walked up towards the house. Grandpa stood in the porch watching for them. Probably hopping mad, Jimmy thought. At least he didn't know about the *Playboy*. Nobody did. So far.

The shadows of the cedars along the west side of the driveway had already crept across the yard, almost to the corn crib. A skim of ice was forming on the puddles. Halfheartedly, Jimmy caught up some snow to make a snowball. The snow had lost that magic ingredient that made perfect snowballs.

Jimmy thought about the long summer afternoons that he and Kevin had lain in the hay mow under the louvered windows, staring at Christy. Christy, his love, his baby, always naked, like she never-ever wore clothes. Lying on her brass bed, sitting at her dressing table, rolling in the stiff, prickly hay. And the mysterious, knowing smile.

She was gone. Stolen away by a kid from Kenyon. Lately, he had grown tired of looking at the same old pictures of her, had not even looked at her through the long cold winter. But now that she was gone, already he missed her.

Way down on the road, he heard the truck's engine roar as the man worked through the gears. She was gone. "Take good care of her," he said to himself, "you thief."

IRENE TAYLOR: I grew up in Brooklyn, New York, where my mother's family had lived since the 1850's and to which my father had come as an immigrant from Ireland. In our neighborhood we were exotic because we spoke only English, but, as if in recompense, we used our one language with respect and joy. That immigrant neighborhood, as well as the beaches of the south shore of Long Island where we spent our summers, form the settings of many of my stories. Those places are etched on my mind, incised more deeply than recent places that are too familiar, too close.

After graduation from Brooklyn College, I went to graduate school at the University of Chicago, majoring in English language and literature. For nine years I taught in the Chicago junior college system. We moved to Minneapolis nineteen years ago when my husband finished his Ph.D.

I began writing two years ago after a life-time of postponement, of waiting for that time free of the demands of graduate school, teaching, and family. I joined two writing groups for the stimulus of talking to other writers about the problems of the craft and for criticism of my early efforts.

I write every morning, read whenever I can, ride my bike, garden, enjoy my friends and the richness of life my husband and five interesting children provide.

Irene Taylor

A SUMMER DAY

The sun burned down on the beach, the glistening white sand reflecting the glare and heat. Clusters of families lay languidly, oiled and shiny forms indolent on the hot afternoon. A bronzed lifeguard sat on his high perch, his nose covered by white celluloid attached to his sunglasses. Out on the water a few boats rose and fell with the gentle waves. Some were anchored for fishermen to try their luck or for children to practice diving in the deep water. Along the shore small forms, silhouettes against the intense brightness of the sun, skipped in the waves, collected shells, or dribbled wet sand on hard-packed mounds to form the delicate spires of sand castles. Swimmers, alone or in groups, cooled off in the icy water of the bay.

Jason sat apart in an unfrequented spot he had picked out for himself early in the summer. Wrapped in a striped terry cloth towel, eyes protected by dark glasses, he dried off after a swim. As he sat at the edge of a blanket he tunneled his feet, through the fine powdery sand, watching the sparkling mica bits that clung to his ankles. This was the time at the beach he enjoyed most: after a vigorous swim that seemed to empty his mind, he warmed his shivering body with a brisk rub and a gradual warming up in the hot sun. He liked to sit like this, his wet stringy hair blowing dry in the heat.

Behind him, about a hundred yards up from the water, lay a row of cottages with names like "Gull's Nest" and "Captain's Cove." It was in one of these cottages, a green one with a small front garden set off by carefully arranged lines of clam shells, that Jason was staying for the summer with his father and stepmother. He was not comfortable with them, strangers really. He arranged his days, set a pattern now respected, of spending the long afternoons alone on the beach. Here he could escape the clatter of his young half-brothers and avoid the anxious eyes of his father and the tight impatience of his step-mother, Moira. His father worried that Jason didn't seem to be doing much, didn't make friends with the local boys.

"Don't you want to go fishing with the boys next door? I'm sure they'd be glad to have you along."

Through the thin partitions of the rooms he heard Moira, tense and exasperated complain, "Don't ask me to entertain him. I've done all I could. If he wants to sit alone out there all day that's his choice."

All adults were alike, Jason thought. Here, as at home with his mother, he felt the prodding of their earnest suggestions: Do something. Find something to interest you. Make some friends.

He knew he was a burden, spoiling the family's summer pleasure. Their intentions had been kind, his father's guilt after years of neglect prompting the invitation, so unexpected to Jason and his mother, for the boy to board a plane and spend two months on Long Island. Evidently they had expected a little boy, had forgotten that he was now fifteen. Inexperienced with adolescents, they agonized over his aloneness and moodiness while he bristled at their intrusive concern.

And so the beach was his haven. Right out in the open, he nevertheless felt shielded from everyone and completely alone. The splash of the waves and the limitless wide beach and water made all sounds distant, attenuated. He sat, shut off, with the sand, the sky, and the water. His world seemed as vacant as the watery horizon. There was nothing there but him and the sand running between his toes.

When he was all warmed up and dry again, the bay lured him back for another swim. He loved to run down to the water, the hot sand scorching his feet. Racing from the waves, he felt exhilarated as the brutal cold struck his sun-baked body. He dived and tumbled in the water and laughed at the intense sensations in every part of him: his tingling skin, his smarting eyes, his gasping breathlessness. He worked each sensation to the extreme. He swam out, so far that it was almost beyond his endurance to get back in again to the safety of feet touching bottom. He dived under the waves and swam under water until his ears ached and his held breath was about to explode. And then the joy of re-emerging and the delirious feeling of filling his lungs with air. Star patterns burst before his eyes like a fireworks display, and a cacophony of piercing rings assaulted his ears. Bent over with exhaustion, having tested his body to its limits, he gasped and panted until he was ready for the next plunge. After a while, doubled over and hardly able to command his weary body, he made his way out of the water, dragging himself on hands and knees and clawing into the wet sand until he was out of reach of the waves. He lay at the water's edge until he was recovered enough to walk back to his spot on the beach and a rub down with his large towel. Then he was set for a while to gaze at infinity and warm up in the sun.

Jason heard the whistle and looked over at the high perch where the lifeguard, with sweeping motions of his arms, was beckoning some swimmers away from a danger spot, a hole marked by a buoy. All the regulars at the beach knew about the two holes, drop-offs, inexplicably carved out of the bay's bottom and long since marked by floating red and white buoys. The swimmers were diving from a boat too near the danger spot. Jason watched the romping in the boat that showed these people to be amateurs. As one swimmer tried to get back into the boat, a man in the boat playfully pushed his hands off the edge with an oar. They were all clowning and laughing foolishly at their thoughtless pranks. Strangers to this beach, they were a group of fishermen in a boat rented from a bait and tackle concession far to the east down the bay. Inexperienced as bathers and often drunk, these parties of fishermen occasionally anchored here, causing worry to the lifeguard and feelings of abused propriety to the residents.

The lifeguard blew his whistle and waved more vigorously. The swimmers went on laughing and cavorting, one man thumbing his nose in scorn and defiance at the lifeguard. People on the beach, disturbed from their naps and reading, looked in disgust at the intruders who went right on diving on top of each other and pushing each other under the water. "Crazy weirdos," Jason thought, and he turned his eyes away in contempt for their silly games.

The whistle blowing stopped. Jason looked back out on the water. The arrested silhouettes in the boat and their peering around at the water showed that something was wrong. The mute show on the water mimed the discovery that one of the group was unaccounted for. Three adults and one child, like a speeded-up movie, splashed and dived in increasing frenzy. The lifeguard sent a man to run up to the cottages to call for the water patrol, and he quickly pushed his catamaran into the water and rowed out toward the boat. Jason followed, swimming out behind the catamaran toward the troubled group.

"It's John," a man screamed across the water. "We can't find him. He didn't come up."

"Child or adult?" yelled the lifeguard.

"My son. Twenty," came the frantic answer.

The lifeguard, shown the spot where the youth had last been seen, dived deeply. Jason took a deep breath and pushed himself under water in the area around the boat to help in the search. He and the lifeguard worked their way from the boat toward the buoy, staying under water as long as they could. A water patrol boat approached with grappling hooks and divers ready to plunge into the water. Jason and the lifeguard were right at the buoy now, right over the dangerous hole. In his dives Jason could feel that the hole, about twelve feet in diameter, had almost stair-like indentations on one side and was indeed deep. Try as he did to propel himself downward, he could not reach the bottom before running out of breath and having to surface for air. Treading water while resting, he gulped air and got ready for another plunge. Each dive was deeper than the last, but still he couldn't feel the bottom of the hole. When he was above water again after half a dozen dives, he saw the lifeguard emerge with something in tow. The patrol boat approached and the men on board threw over some ropes and a life preserver. Jason saw a limp form hoisted to the deck. A diver straddled the body and worked over the inert man, rhythmically administering artificial respiration. He worked at it a long time. Jason watched attentively as he went on treading water near the side of the patrol boat. Over and over the diver pushed forward with hands pressing down on the sides of the youth's back. When the first man tired, another took up the rhythm as he moved into the first man's place. They worked for more than fifteen minutes. Then they stopped. The youth was dead.

Jason was tired. He had dived so deep that he had never gotten his wind back, and he had been treading water for a long time. The drama of the scene before him had made him oblivious to his exhaustion until, the young man dead and the activity on the boat stopped momentarily, Jason felt his heavy weariness. He wanted to stop moving his legs and arms for just a few seconds' rest, but the shortest pause made him sink under the water and he had to flail his arms and legs urgently to propel himself above the surface again.

Jason was struck with a kind of euphoria, a euphoria of utter control. The difference between living and drowning was like the flick of a switch. If he stopped paddling, he would go under, or, flick, if he started paddling, he would emerge. He tried it out once or twice for the rapture of the sensation. Never before had he had such a keen sense of power. He was right on the knife edge of omnipotence. He could swim back to shore, or he could glide down through the sensuous vastness of the deep. He gripped his way down along the stair-like projections at the side of the hole. The ringing began in his ears and the stars of darting light flashed behind his eyes. His chest was tight as he held his breath and worked his way down into the hole. When he could hold his breath no longer, he opened his mouth and gasped the water in.

On the surface the patrol boat chugged off with the dead youth to the nearest pier, where an ambulance waited. The lifeguard dried himself, panting, and resumed his place on the high chair. Families made their way silently up toward the cottages, sickened by the drowning and finished with the beach for the day. The excitement was over. The mute aftermath of sadness hung in the air. The sand, the sky, the water remained. Jason wasn't missed until dinner time that night.

EMILIO DE GRAZIA: I can remember writing stories — long ones up to twenty pages — when I was a fifth grader growing up in Dearborn, Michigan. Though the yen subsided during my high school days when nothing but basketball, and the girls for whom I performed, seemed important, it returned when I went to college, only to go under again during the six years of exile I spent at graduate school in Ohio. Then in 1973, four years out of graduate school and angry about the Vietnam war, I got up in the middle of a sleepless Minnesota night and began my first published story. Since then the urge to write has hounded me and gains strength as I write more and more.

Someone once asked me how I judged good literature. Two words came to mind: heat and light. A good story should move — in the sense that it should create emotion and in the sense that it should require us to act, even if the only act inspired is a change of heart. At the same time a good story should illuminate, help explain, the human condition, if only to bring to the surface what we take for granted or have forgotten. Perhaps no comments about literature have affected me more than James Joyce's definitions of pity and terror. "Pity," he wrote, "is the feeling which arrests the mind in the presence of whatsoever is grave and constant in human sufferings and unites it with the sufferer. Terror is the feeling which arrests the mind in the presence of whatsoever is grave and constant in human suffering and unites it with the secret cause." Even when writing a comic story I keep Joyce's definitions before me.

Emilio De Grazia

GRANDMOTHER'S SECRET PLACES

1.

It was too beautiful for a wake. All through the valley the apple blossoms had outwitted the late freezes and overnight had burst into quiet being. Everyone knew there would be no more freezes or frosts.

Because of this and because in two days I would be celebrating my twenty-first birthday, it seemed like the wrong time to be driving through the valley toward the old stone house that Grandmother Bendon now somehow would have to keep up alone. And somehow it seemed wrong that Grandpa Charlie was dead. The only thing I could imagine was that he chose this time to die because the beauty of one more apple blossoming would be too much to endure, or because he wanted to get even, somehow, with Grandmother.

Grandmother is the sort people want to get even with. My own mother couldn't endure her presence. My mother made her two or three obligatory trips down the county roads to the old stone house, and as far back as I can remember I went with her. But the visits — at Christmas and Easter and, I think, Grandmother's birthday sometime around Labor Day — lasted no more than an hour or two, and they passed in the presence of Grandpa Charlie until Grandmother got ahold of me and started telling me stories about things in her old trunk. Mother always found an excuse to leave before dark.

I always looked forward to seeing Grandpa Charlie, so it was hard to see him dead, harder than to realize anyone's dying. While I was growing up people always thought I was older than I looked; now they thought I was smarter, not only able to think but making an uncomfortable habit of it. Maybe that's why I was disturbed about driving alone to Grandpa Charlie's wake and knowing that mother, who claimed she was not feeling well, was lying. She told me she would call ahead to explain the whole matter to Grandmother, but I knew the explanation was a lie too bitter to ignore.

As my car made its last turn down into the coulee where the old house stood, I thought back to the words my mother had spoken on one of our earlier visits to the apple farm. I was only twelve at the time, but I remember the words well. I ran to her because I knew I had done something wrong, though I wasn't sure what. I only remember Grandmother yelling at me: "Don't you ever ride that sheep again!" I ran from her into my mother's arms because my father had died two years earlier and hers were the only arms I could trust. And to this day I remember my mother's words: "Don't listen to her. Don't let her make you feel guilty for her sins. You've done nothing wrong." I felt her holding me tight and I remember feeling good when she began crying with me. I saw then for the first time a sign of age in my mother's face, a deep imprint of some sorrow that curled down from her eyes over her cheekbones. I saw too that the sorrow was connected with my grandmother.

I never tried to make that sheep pretend it was a horse again, but I never really liked Grandmother from that day on. I knew something was wrong with her, even though I didn't have much to get even for.

As I turned onto the dirt drive leading to the old house, I suspected I would find out what was wrong. I watched Grandmother waving a white hanky at me from the door; from a distance she looked like anyone's good grandmother. Right then I made up my mind to find out what was wrong with her.

2.

Grandmother stood before the open door of a house that had weathered the Great Depression of the Thirties and all the lesser ones that had swept the land since the 1870's. The house had been built by Sheridan Buckley, Grandmother's grandfather, in a coulee full of trees just beneath a ridge overlooking the Root River in southern Minnesota. Buckley bought a double-section on the ridge, and though he never farmed it the neighbors considered it the richest loam overlooking the valley.

The house, partly hidden against a hillside, had stood its

ground. Buckley had built it to last. He himself had taken a dozen trips in wagons over fields to carry stones cut across the river in LaCrosse. "And then he only settled for brick for parts of the porch because he couldn't get enough good stone," Grandmother told me some time ago. "That's what he said in a diary he left. He said the stone in the valley wasn't like the stone at home. He said it would wash away to nothing after a good rain."

Not many changes, then, had come over the house. Grandmother spent two years restoring the interior woodwork that someone had painted green after Buckley died, and Uncle Charlie turned the cellar into a place for storing apples when he took up apple-growing after his years on the road as a salesman. The elms and oaks had given way on the hillsides when the apple trees came in, but everyone said it was for the better because the coulee hillsides were perfect for apples. And the habit of planting apple trees had spread to every farmer who had some hillside until the whole valley was covered with apple trees.

Though the cellar of the house seemed to lean into the side of a hill, I saw that it was Grandmother, not the house, that stood askew as she waited for me on the porch. I stepped out of my car into the perfume of apple blossoms hanging in the air, intoxicating, it seemed, the bees that fumbled indifferently from flower to flower in a busy ecstasy of fulfillment. The house seemed to hover in the haze of the white pastel of blossoming trees.

"Why, Johnny Markland, you *are* here," Grandmother said to me as I came near. "But your Uncle Bob and Betty got here about two hours ago. Even before the man from the funeral home got finished with your grandfather." She paused at the thought. "So come on in."

Grandmother wore a dark blue dress that pressed tight around her full bosom and large hips. She was big but well-proportioned, and she carried her seventy-eight years with an upright strength that allowed no sagging of her moral guard. Around her neck, suspended by a gold chain, she wore a broach studded with diamonds, and both arms were covered with bracelets of turquoise and silver that rattled like chains when she walked. Her wedding ring carried the biggest diamond I had ever seen. She looked at me out of half-closed eyes that seemed alert, though I noticed that the lipstick on her mouth was thick and smeared to one side.

She led me into the kitchen where my Uncle Bob, his wife Betty and their daughter Candy were sitting around an oak table. We said the customary things and I embraced Grandmother and offered my condolences.

"Sit," she said, and we all sat while she stood over us.

"You know," she instructed me, "your Uncle Bob drove all the way here from Wyoming in that pickup truck of theirs. And don't you think I'll forget it." Uncle Bob suppressed an obvious smile.

"The others will be here soon. I told them not to come before four, and it's almost four." She waited for a thought. "So the others will be here soon. I didn't want to take them out of their way all day, so I told them not to come before four."

"My mother —" I began.

"Sarah called before you got here. She told me why she couldn't come. She told me all about it. Your mother's committed worse sins than coming up sick for her father's funeral. I *know*," she said as though concluding the case, "so don't you worry about a thing." She offered me her hand. I took it, gave it a squeeze, and felt her press me back.

"And I don't want anyone making a mess about this whole thing. What's done is done, and that's that. That's what your Grandpa Charlie would have said. I put some coffee on for those who come, but that's all. That's all Grandpa Charlie would have wanted."

"Did you know," she looked at me after a pause that changed the subject, "that Candy here's going to college in the East?"

"That's wonderful," I said, turning to Candy, a sassy-looking blond in a purple dress who wore too much eye makeup. "What college?"

"Penn State," Uncle Bob cut in. "She's going to Penn State. We thought about Ohio State, but Penn State's got a better program in her field."

"Nursing," my aunt added with some pride.

"Oh yes, nursing. That's good," I said.

"Nursing's a good field," Grandmother said. "We've got to look to the future. Candy here's a bright girl and she'll go far."

I offered Grandmother a chair.

"No," she said. "I'd rather stand. I've been standing in this kitchen for forty years, so I don't see any reason to change my ways now. I'm not dead yet, you know."

As if the words reminded her of an unfinished task, she walked to the kitchen sink and from the window sill above it took a tobacco pouch and began rolling a cigarette. After a struggle she put it to her lips and lit it with a steady hand. At the table we exchanged glances.

"He always said I'd die of lung cancer, you know, but he was wrong. He was a wonderful man, but he was wrong." She turned away from us and looked out the window.

"You know," she said, still facing out, "this room's my favorite. And I've made something of it." She turned toward us. "I figured that if I had to live here all my life, I'd make something of it. I used to like standing here looking up the side of the coulee toward the ridge, but then Charlie put the apples in and blocked the view." She sighed deeply. "I suppose he was right. The trees are pretty in spring."

She turned toward me. "But I want to give you a tour. Your Uncle Bob and Betty haven't been here for eight years, so I gave them a tour before you came."

I *had* been through it before. More than once she had taken me into the parlor and unlocked an old trunk and oak secretary loaded with relics from the family's past while the portrait of Sheridan Buckley over the mantle stared at the wall behind us. I had spent obedient hours sitting while she showed me photographs and told stories about the stiff faces she passed through my hands. She showed me old brown photographs valuable for the stories they told about her, and once or twice revealed precious things — a small boxful of gold rings, gold coins dated from Revolutionary times, and a packet of what she called "filthy love letters," all of them signed, she claimed, "by one of our Founding Fathers."

I expected the tour to begin in the parlor where we had left off last year, and it occurred to me to coax out of her the name of the Founding Father. But all these thoughts stopped when the realization crept up on me like a bad memory: Grandpa Charlie was dead, and he was lying in the parlor. And I would have to face him.

But she did not take me there. She took me by the arm as a gentleman takes a lady down the aisle, and led me to a corner cabinet in the kitchen. "Sheridan Buckley's son built this," she said. "He was my father, and it's been in the family ever since. It's solid walnut, even the back, and it's worth its weight in gold. Why, just last week Peterson up the valley tried to sell Charlie a couple slices of walnut for twenty dollars. But here — it's what's inside that I want to show you."

She opened the cabinet doors gingerly. "These," she said. "Just look at them."

Lined up neatly on three shelves were rows of demi-tasse cups and saucers, all of them covered, in smallest detail, with hand-painted flowers. "There's over sixty of them," she said. "The first one — this one here on top — came west with the first Buckley, and we've been adding to them one at a time ever since. And they're *all* originals, all signed." She showed me one of them. Then she lowered her head to whisper. "Do you know how much they're worth?"

I didn't know if I should say thousands. She leaned toward me and whispered, "Thousands. They're worth thousands. I checked it in all the books." Then she pulled away and spoke more loudly. "And someday they'll go to someone in the family."

I saw Aunt Betty turn away from us. Candy shifted in her chair while running her hands over her hips to smooth her dress down. For an impulsive moment I hoped my hands had been hers. "But I've got a real treasure over here." Grandmother tugged at my arm and pulled me toward the kitchen cupboard. "The silver-ware. I thought about giving it to either Candy or you when you get married, but I haven't really made up my mind yet. Because you can't be sure these days. I want you both to marry right." She turned toward Candy.

"Yes, Grandmother," Candy said.

"I don't want you running off to some justice of the peace, or messing around." She struggled with a drawer in the cupboard. "You see here," she said as I finally helped her pull it out, "this here's my everyday silver. We've been using it all our lives." She paused again, leaned close to me, and winked. "But there's more. There's a secret place in the back of this drawer. Now you just pull it out for me."

The drawer seemed as heavy as a stone as I worked to pull it loose, and it was so deep it seemed to lodge in the wall behind the cupboard. Behind the forward compartment in the drawer lay a green-stained mass of forks and spoons. "See," she said, "it's all here. It's black now — just stained, that's all. But underneath it's good."

As gold. I shifted my weight from one foot to the other.

"It's solid. From France. They say it came from a palace in Paris." She paused and her eyes seemed to water. "I want you to know about these things because they're family things. Charlie's gone now, you know, and I'm getting on in years. After I go I don't want any family secrets left behind."

I pushed the drawer back in place and let her take me again by the arm. Together we took a few steps as if we were on a slow stroll in a formal garden. "The wallpaper," she continued. "I wanted to change it this past winter, but I never got around to it. The chimney runs right up through that wall. You can see a brown stain on the paper where the chimney runs through. It's from that old coal furnace. That's what Charlie said. For the longest time we couldn't afford to have it fixed, and for the longest time Charlie said he'd get around to it. But he never did, and now he's gone, you know. I suppose that someday you'll have to take a day off and drive here to look at it."

"I'll be glad to help anyway I can, Grandmother." I lied.

"I know you all care so very much." She took us all in with a sweep of her hand. I saw Uncle Bob stir uneasily, but Candy, now slouched in her chair, kept up a sullen stare out the window.

"You know," Grandmother said, "there's other things I could show you, but the real treasures are in the parlor. I never showed you half of what was in the old trunk."

I shrank from the thought that we would have to go in *there*. I dreaded listening while she retold the countless stories she had stored away with her things. But I shrank from a deeper fear: Grandpa Charlie in the parlor still waiting for me to pay my respects.

"Yes," I said. "Why don't we go in there. You don't have to, Grandmother, if you don't really want to. But I'd like to see Grandpa Charlie."

At the table Uncle Bob opened his eyes in alarm, as if to indicate that I had crossed forbidden ground. And Candy turned away from us.

"Oh," said Grandmother, "I don't mind going in there, though you're right — I don't like seeing Charlie dead like that. I'll first show you some things in my trunk, then you can go look at your grandfather."

I was confused. Uncle Bob's eyes were still wide, and Candy still turned away. I appealed to Betty for a clue, but she averted her eyes. "Isn't Grandpa Charlie in the parlor?"

"No," said my grandmother firmly.

"Did you have him taken to the funeral home?"

"No, he wanted to be here," she said.

"Well . . . then . . . ?"

"He's in the apple cellar," she said. "I fixed a nice place for him there."

3.

The people had all come and gone, and the house was quiet again. The house had been quiet even while they were present, for not many had come. A couple of long-lost relatives had come up from Iowa, an old friend of Grandmother had come from near Homer, and a half-dozen or so of the apple-growing neighbors had stopped to pay their respects, but they had come and slipped away as people do when duty rather than a mission calls. And it was a tearless affair. They all said nice things about Grandpa Charlie, and their eyes said they spoke the truth. They were not glad he was rid of her; instead what she had done had kept them from seeing to the details of ordinary duty, including tears. If Grandmother was to be so careless of forms, then they had to be guarded lest there be an utter breakdown of order.

They had confidence that she would see it through, and they knew she had her reasons. She announced the terrible fact to each of them as they appeared at the door, and she used the same words. "He's in the cellar," she said matter of factly, "I've fixed a nice place for him there." They heard the words as one reads the time of day, but feeling as if late or too early for the main event. Later, when in corners of the kitchen they awakened to the words, they gave quizzical shrugs that let the truth pass out of the house into the ordinary light of day. This was not the time for tears or talk. There would be private tears for Grandpa Charlie, and plenty of talk. I heard some of them say that Grandmother had strange ways, but that was as hard as they were on her. So no one, not even I, dared ask to see Grandpa Charlie, and Grandmother was content to let the matter lie.

Then — just as suddenly as the night had fallen — I found myself alone with Grandmother in the parlor. Uncle Bob and Betty had retired to one of the upper bedrooms, and Candy to the small bedroom just outside the one assigned to me. Sometime before midnight I decided that a glass of water might help me sleep so I stole past Candy to the kitchen. When I returned I found Grandmother in the parlor, sitting on the old sofa next to the trunk, a freshly rolled cigarette dangling from her lips. In her hand she held a brown photo of Grandpa Charlie as a young man, and I could tell she had been weeping. I sat next to her, took the photo from her, and offered her my hand. She took it, and I cupped mine over hers.

"What kind of man was he?" I asked.

"Oh, he was a wonderful man," she said. "You can see here from this picture how handsome he was." She smiled at a distant memory. "All the girls in school used to chase him."

"But you got him."

I felt her hand tighten. "Yes, I won him. And it was easy too. I was quite a looker in my day, but I won him by pretending I didn't care. I remember I said no to him four times before I let him visit the house. I figured that if I said no one more time he would lose all his anger, just give up. I didn't want that. But here — I want to show you."

She rummaged in the old trunk and came out with another photo. She showed it to me and smiled. I looked upon one of the most beautiful faces I had ever seen, a face I would have followed through a crowd for nothing but another glimpse. I wondered that a face so lovely could still smile with joy through the faded brown tint of a photograph taken more than fifty years ago.

"This is you," I said without being sure. "I can tell from the eyes." I quickly added more: "And from the lips and forehead."

"Yes," she said, still smiling, "I was nineteen then. Charlie had been courting me then a full year and a half, and we were married a year later."

"You were lovely, Grandmother."

"Yes, they all thought I was, and I suspected it too. And Charlie thought I was. Everyone thought I was, and everyone thought Charlie was the handsomest man in town."

"You were the perfect pair, then."

"Perfect." Her eyes seemed to recede, as if sinking into a past.

"My father owned half of Shenandoah. He was the banker. And Charlie's father started as a small farmer, but he worked hard and built himself a fortune. On the day we were married he owned the only mill in town and more farmland in western Iowa than anyone but the governor."

"It must have been quite an occasion."

"It was the marriage of the century in western Iowa. We had mayors from eleven towns and seven counties come to our wedding. Even my father didn't know who they all were."

"What happened?"

"What do you mean, what happened? We got married. We lived happily for a long time. Do you mean what happened to *us*?"

"Yes."

"The Depression. That's what happened."

"What do you mean?"

"We lost everything. We didn't have that much from my father because he gave it all to my older brother, but we lost everything that Charlie had — the land mainly, thousands of acres of the richest land in the Missouri Valley."

"And?"

"We had to come here. We came here after that because this is what my father gave me and we had nowhere else to go. The house had been abandoned for some years, but it was free and clear and I knew it had those acres on the ridge to go with it."

"Then what happened?"

"To *us*?"

No, *between* you. The words almost escaped me.

"Well, at first we fixed up the place. There was nothing else to do, no work. In fact we got to making this place look better than the house we had in Shenandoah. We had a little to live on, and we stretched it out. But then, of course, it just thinned out to nothing. Then Charlie wanted to start farming the acres on the ridge. That's all he ever wanted to do — just farm. But we didn't have a thing. We didn't have a tractor, not a barn — nothing. He said he still wanted to try — said he'd plow a piece by hand and horse, then take the corn in the old wagon old Buckley must have used to haul bricks. He was set to do it one day even though I thought it was stupid."

"Then what happened?"

"He got a letter from a friend in Chicago. He said I was right —
that he'd do nothing but sweat blood farming and get us
nowhere." She turned cold before going on. "He didn't even ask
me."

"Ask you what?"

"If he could go."

"Go?"

"On the road. The friend from Chicago offered him a job as a
salesman, and he took it."

"Selling what?"

"Pots and pans. I'm not ashamed to tell you it was pots and
pans. You're too young to know. The Depression did terrible
things to us. He sold pots and pans."

"Where did he do these things?"

"At first he went to Chicago for what they called his 'training.'
He was smarter than all of them, but they thought he needed
training. And then they shipped him out from there. He went from
town to town — first in Wisconsin and Iowa, then farther west.
He got as far as Las Vegas."

"How long was he gone?"

"It lasted about six years. I got him to come back for your
mother's wedding right here in this parlor, and then I got him to
stay. Oh, he came and went, you know, especially when he was in
these parts. He'd spend a week or two here, come back for the
holidays. And he made good money at it. I had everything I
wanted."

"So that's what happened between you. He left you."

"Oh, I forgave his going all right. In fact sometimes I was glad
to be rid of him. I forgave him *that*. Selling pots and pans wasn't
in our style or breeding, but I forgave him *that*. I spent those
hours here. I spent nights crying for him, and I spent nights
scared. Those hours went by. I just got lost in them and there was
no getting out. But I knew he had to go. I knew there was no other
way to get our land back."

"What land do you mean?"

"Why, the land. The land on the Missouri. We got it all back."

"You mean Grandpa Charlie's father's land?"

"Yes, that land — and more too. We added two thousand acres
to it. It's all good land too — the best."

"What's it doing now?"

"It's growing corn, I suppose. We rent it out."

"Why didn't you go back there? I thought Grandpa Charlie wanted to farm?"

"Oh, after he quit selling I didn't want to go back there. Your grandfather never would've made a farmer. All he wanted was forty acres to play around with. He was never really serious. After he quit selling he could have farmed the ridge here, but he said that was too much land for him. So he put the apple trees in, and I didn't mind though I told him there was nothing in it. And I was right, considering he didn't sell the last two years' worth of apples. But the apples kept him busy and around the house where I could keep an eye on him."

"So you never really wanted to go back home?"

"To Shenandoah?"

"Yes, there."

"You've got to learn, young man, that a home is a place you can't leave even if you want to. Too much has happened here to ever let me leave. Did you know that your mother was married in this house in 1938? It'll be twenty-two years ago next month. And you were born a year later. I'm sure about the dates because I keep such things written here." She pointed to her heart. "It was a lovely wedding, and your father, bless his silent heart, was a wonderful man. Your mother was lucky he came along. Since then I've made a home here for myself, and when it came time for me to leave I knew I couldn't go. It was that man who showed me I couldn't."

She pointed to the portrait of Sheridan Buckley hanging over the mantle. Buckley was a man of thirty in the portrait. He had black hair and a stiff proud face accented by a wry curl on his lips that was at once a smile and a smirk. Around his neck he wore a dashing red bandana, and his dark eyes looked out beyond us.

"He was a wonderful man, you know. You can see that in his face. He was the cousin of a baron in Kent, but he couldn't sit still. He travelled all over the world before he came here — even Africa — and he was a success at everything he tried. That's why he made so many enemies, and that's why they told so many stories about him."

"What kind of stories?"

"I'll tell you what. He had four wives, but my father was born to the first. They said terrible things about his wives, and they said that after he built this house he let a Dakota squaw move in with him. Some half-breed trapper spread that rumor around."

"The rumors weren't true, then?"

"Not a word of it. Oh, they all loved him — you can see how handsome he was. They say an Italian princess fell in love with him, but he turned her down. He was too much a man to settle down for long, until he came here to build this house. It was in 1876. When he built this house it was his way of settling down for good. It was his way of saying he was planting roots, that he wanted a normal life, a family, some dignity."

She paused and drew herself back. Then she leaned close to me and whispered. "I think his building this house was more than that. I think he wanted to get away from it all because he had some dark things in his past."

"You mean he wanted to hide?"

"Oh no, not *that*. They knew where to find him if they wanted him."

They?

"I know," she went on, "because I read his diary." She drew closer still. "I know I'm reading between the lines, but I think he came here and built this house because he wanted to repent."

"Repent?"

"No, not repent exactly." She backed away. "He wasn't religious until he died. I mean he wanted a new start — a home, a family, respectability. And that's why I decided to stay here. He laid the cornerstone here for a decent family. He founded a tradition. I couldn't see it all come to an end. I couldn't see boarding up this house or renting it to strangers. That's why I said no when Charlie wanted to go back to Shenandoah."

"I see. You wanted a home." I reached over and cupped my hand around hers again. "You didn't want to go back just to make more money and get more land. You wanted to make a home."

Her eyes began floating in a white sky. After a long pause she spoke again. "You are the only one, John, who has ever understood."

But there was too much I didn't understand. I had to know why this woman put her dead husband in the cellar, and I felt I had to know tonight, that to let it pass would be to risk the secret dying with her. I tried easing her back into it.

"Grandmother, I'd like to know more about Sheridan Buckley."

"Oh, he was a fascinating man." I could see she had taken my bait. "You would never believe some of the things he did. It's all in his diary."

"Could I see his diary someday?"

"Oh, *no*," she said, startled. "It's gone. It's been lost."

She was lying. "But tell me more. Tell me about Africa. You're the only one who knows these things now."

"Some day I'll have to tell you how it was. You'll have to get it down on paper."

"But Africa. Tell me about it."

"Africa. He went there on a trip at first — looking for ivory. He went all the way down the Congo River from its mouth, then went south from there overland. He was almost killed three or four times by them niggers, but he got out."

"Where did he end up?"

"In South Africa. That's where he made his fortune."

"What did he do?"

"Mining, I think. He was a supervisor in a mine down there. He worked hard, invested wisely, and he got rich."

"Then he came to America?"

"Not right away. He went into shipping then. Bought half a dozen freighters and went back and forth with them."

"Back and forth? From where?"

"Africa. To New Orleans, I think, or some city down there on the coast."

"When did he do this?"

"Oh, it must have been the thirties. Around 1820 or 1830. He said he got tired of that kind of work, so he quit. I think he wanted to settle down then, but he still was footloose and fancy free. They even said he took up with a nigger girl, but they were always lying against him, just like they were always lying about your grandfather."

"What do you mean?"

"You know what I mean."

But I wanted her to say it so I could be sure. "No, I don't know."

"They say Charlie went wild those years he was selling." She spoke the words indignantly as if untrue, then paused. "No man like Charlie could make a vow at the altar like he did and then break it. No man could do *that*. You can be sure *your* father would never do a thing like that, and your mother was lucky to get him. When your father died we all cried for a week. Even your Grandpa Charlie cried."

She shifted away from me and looked at the portrait of Buckley. "For all those years he was the only man in this house. If Charlie would have done *that* to me, I never would have forgiven him."

This time she took my hand. It felt cold and stiff. "You," she whispered, "are the only one I can trust. I know that because you've been wronged too, and I'm going to make it up to you."

She got up, opened the trunk, and came out with an old cigar box. From it she took two keys and a slip of yellowed paper. "You must promise me," she whispered. "You must promise me that what I tell you you *never* will repeat. *Never. Never.*"

I was getting close. I looked her in the eye and spoke. "Never. I promise, Grandmother."

"I promised I'd make it up to your father someday, but he died. Now you're the only one left, the only one I can trust. The others — that Candy — they're all phonies. They think they're going to get it *all*. But I've been thinking about it since you got here. You, Johnny, you're the one who deserves it all. You're the only one who understands."

"I *do* understand, Grandmother. I think you've suffered." I added an awkward afterthought. "And sacrificed."

"Yes, I know you're the one. But you must promise me. What I have here is more important than anything, especially to you. I didn't find out about it myself until long after your grandpa came back here to live with me, and I never even showed him. What I'm giving you here will hurt you, but it will also make it up to you, more than make it up. So you must promise."

"Yes."

"This is the key to the coalbin in the cellar of this house. And this smaller key will open an iron box you'll find buried under the doorstone in the northwest corner of the bin. In the iron box you'll find a secret I've carried *here* — in my heart. You have a right to that secret now. But you must promise."

"Yes?"

"You must promise not to say a word to anyone else, and never to open that box until I have passed on. Will you promise me that?''

"I promise.''

4.

I was young enough to believe that no one can be held to vows not made in perfect faith, and old enough to know that no one is perfect enough to make a perfect vow. I broke my promise because I had a perfectly good reason: I had to know.

We didn't linger long after I made my promise. To have done so would have spoiled the climax our talk had brought us to and made my promise seem less solemn. I put the keys in my left shirt pocket, as if to show her I had secured them close to my heart. Then we embraced and went our separate ways, she to the chamber above the parlor and I past Candy's to the room down the hall.

The little bed lamp gave off just enough yellow light for me to see my way. As I stood before my bed, I felt like a boy who had lost his way out of a pirate story. I thought of old trunks overflowing with doubloons and of little maps with an X marking the spot. The moment faded and left me with the realities of the last dozen hours. I lay down to sum it all up, but wilder questions flowed from wild inferences. There was wealth down there: that was certain. But why to me? Until this night there had been no sign that I was the favored one, and her decision to give me the keys seemed unrehearsed, even rash. Surely my one tender talk with her hadn't *earned* them. Unless, of course. I kept myself from the pathetic conclusion: unless, of course, there never had been another such tender talk for her. So there was certain wealth down there, but what else? I tried to recall her words: something down there will hurt you, but you'll get your money's worth. That's what it came to. But what would hurt me? Certainly she kept no black monster tied up in the bin. She was ordinary enough to keep me from feeling that I had to fear for my life. She was not insane — even the neighbors would swear to that. So if there was nothing physical, only knowledge could hurt me. There was something down there that had been kept from me, something she realized I dreaded to know.

My inferences came to a stop against this blank conclusion as I heard the grandfather's clock in the parlor strike four. I had few choices: I could wait for her to die, or I could break my vow; and I could break my vow later or now.

I stood up and tested the floor. As I stepped from board to board, they creaked like the bones of an old man in a rocking chair who in a whisper promised not to give me away. That assurance, and a light, were all I needed. I fumbled in the top drawer of an old dresser of deal and found what I wanted, a piece of yellow candle three inches long. And I had matches.

The door to my room opened at a touch and I squeezed out into the ante-chamber where Candy slept in a small rollaway bed. The light from my room fell across her face, and I could see from her slow breathing that she was asleep. I could not help pausing as I stole past her. She looked strangely younger now, almost childlike. I had an urge to slip in beside her and take her in my arms. But there were lines over her eyelids that sustained just a hint of her lineage, a hint of Grandmother herself so I slipped by her to the door. Her door was harder to try; I had to grope for the handle and it twisted with a loud snap. The sleeping girl stirred her head as I closed the door behind me, and she turned away as if ignoring a bad dream.

I sailed through the parlor without pausing even to consider the stare of Sheridan Buckley. When I reached the kitchen I stopped to consider my route. I knew that underneath the old rag rug in the kitchen there was a trap door leading to the cellar stairs. The other way in was from outside, through the door that Grandpa Charlie had cut into the basement wall when he turned the cellar into storage space for apples. Through the kitchen window I saw half a moon, and the urge to somehow be free of the house came over me. I opened the kitchen door, unlocked the screen, and found myself standing alone in the yard, the mists of dawn mingling with the fragrance of apple blossoms freeing me from the dust of the house and the smell of death. I walked around to the side of the house. Miles away a dog howled in despair.

When I came to the cellar door, I paused. I now would know if she had really "fixed a nice place" for Grandpa Charlie down there. I would know before leaving tomorrow anyway. If he was not in there, then where was he and where were we, Grandmother and all of us? Nothing would have been worse than to find nothing. I had to remind myself that it was not for him I had come this far, though it was plain that he, and the secret of his being placed down here, was tied to the other secrets.

The cellar door was freshly painted white. I found the doorknob and it turned without a sound. I stepped into the dark and was met by the rich smell of apples fermenting into cider. There was nothing of the musty odor of basement walls. I found my candle and after two matches lit it. Then I closed the door behind me.

5.

Until my eyes adjusted to the dark I saw nothing. I inched forward a few steps, my hand fumbling for something solid. Before it touched anything I began to see that I was hemmed in by crates full of apples. I held the candle up to one of the crates. The label read "BENDON'S APPLE EDEN" and the other crates piled in neat rows all carried the same label. Stacked to the top of the cellar, the crates left a narrow passageway that wound deeper into the depths of the house. My feet felt slippery beneath me and I stooped to inspect the slime. As I ran my finger through it, I knew what it was — the juice of rotting apples oozing to the floor from the stained crates piled around me.

I followed the tunnel of crates until it turned and left me standing in a blank space somewhere near the center of the cellar. I inched forward more slowly without the protection of my walls. Then, through the glow of my candle, I saw a white haze before me. The haze seemed to hover over a table covered with a sheet, and it was not until I was almost upon it that I saw what it held. There, with his hands folded over his chest, was Grandpa Charlie, laid to rest in a coffin lined with lace and silver silk and surrounded by fresh red roses. His face, caked with white powder, seemed frozen by an angry jaw stiff with determination, and the lines over his sunken eyes turned down in grief. On both sides of the coffin stood pairs of tall unlit candles.

So this was the nice little place she had fixed for him? My terror began to melt into the heat of a growing anger, and the anger gave me strength to get to the very bottom of it all. This was no time to pay respects. I saw him still among his apple trees and walking around the house with a paintbrush or a hoe. This grotesque bier was no proper altar for the dead. I turned away from him and faced the black space around me. What drew me from the spot was a pin-point of light to my right that flickered with a pathetic humanity. The furnace. I inched toward it expecting to discover a glow of coals behind its iron mask. Instead I found nothing but the small light hidden behind a thin steel grate. With my candle I closed in on the grate until I confirmed my suspicion. The light was a pilot light. This was a gas furnace.

The bin was next to the furnace. It had a simple wooden door with a latch rigged to carry a lock, and a thick padlock hung from the latch. I opened the lock and let it fall to the ground. Then I opened the door.

Spider webs, hanging like a shredded veil, draped from all corners of the bin. I put my candle to them, and they melted silently away. The room seemed barren but not empty. An iron bed covered by a thin grey mattress stood in one corner, and against the back wall, the wall near which the iron box was said to be buried, was a crude wooden toilet. Across from the bed was a small vanity dresser with three drawers, and face down on the dresser was a framed photograph. Drooping down from the one small window looking to the world outside were two dirty flowered curtains through which a small hint of dawn was beginning to glow. There were a few dishes sitting on the bed, and an old fork and spoon.

I got down on my hands and knees next to the back wall. Heavy wooden planks had been laid over the floor, but all around the toilet and against the back wall the planks had decayed, leaving the dirt floor exposed. I reached for the spoon on the bed, found the spot where I imagined the box to be, and began digging. There was, curiously, no excitement in me. It seemed absurd digging for buried treasure in my grandmother's basement, selfish even to be hoping to find some sort of wealth. Yet I scratched on, piling the sandy dirt up around my knees until I seemed half-buried in it.

By the time I had a hole almost a yard square and two feet deep, I was ready to give up. Sweat was pouring from me, even in the damp, and with each desperate scrape I gave the earth I felt a hatred so harden in my heart for Grandmother it was her very bosom I was gouging with the spoon. Dawn was showing clearly through the window, so I dug in one small spot with a final fury. Suddenly the spoon scraped across something solid. At first I thought I struck a stone, but I kept digging around its surface until I found edges. I began scratching with my nails to get my fingers under it. Finally, with three fingers I pulled out one corner and from there worked free from its grave a heavy iron casket no more than a foot long.

A sudden fear ran through me, and I jerked my head around to the door of the bin. No one was there. I felt for the smaller key in my shirt pocket. At first my fingers felt nothing but my pounding heart, but fumbling I found it in the corner of the pocket. I drew the key out, held the box close to the candle, and tried the lock. The key turned and tripped the lock, but I had to force the rusted top with the spoon handle and my bare hands.

The box opened with a crumbling sound, its hinges dissolving as I worked open the lid. What I stared at in the opened box was hidden in the dark. I drew the candle closer, and into my hands I emptied a pile of glazed stones, all of them rough and as big as bird eggs. I ran my fingers over them, and held some to the candlelight. Diamonds. These were diamonds. The box was full of them. This was my money's worth, the legacy of Sheridan Buckley's life of adventure — too wonderful to show to the dead man in the other room, too much to hide forever in the dust.

But was this it? If this was the forbidden fruit, it was not the forbidden knowledge. Carefully I emptied some stones out on the ground and probed the bottom of the box with my free hand. My fingertips found the edge of an envelope, which I lifted out and weighed in my hand. I carefully tore a corner and ran my finger-nail down the edge. I drew out a document stamped with the official seal of the state, a birth certificate bearing the name *John Bendon* in black gothic script. Inscribed below the name were the words *Born on the Twelfth Day of the Month of July in the Year of Our Lord Nineteen Hundred and Thirty-Seven. Father Unknown.*

John Bendon. Father Unknown.

It made no sense to me. I thought I heard noises on the floor above and for a moment I froze, trying not to breathe. Silence.

When I was sure no one was stirring, I gathered the stones I had left in the dirt. They made a loud clatter as I dropped them in the box. I have to get out of here, I thought, I have to get out of here.

I turned toward the door and lost my point of balance, brushing my shoulder against the dresser as I stumbled to get out. For a half-moment my candlelight flitted across the framed photograph face-down on the dresser. I picked the photograph up and set it upright on the dresser. The way it ought to be.

Then I saw her in the full bloom of her youth for the very first time, her eyes Grandmother's eyes but her face soft and smiling, perhaps for the very last time. I looked again at the bed, the dresser and the toilet. Then I knew. Grandmother had fixed a nice little place down here for her, too.

MARISHA CHAMBERLAIN: I was born in 1952, the second eldest in a large, Catholic family. My father is an English professor and a construction worker; my mother is a painter and a potter. From my birthplace in Florida, my family moved to Georgia, then on to Colorado, Texas, New Hampshire, and Tennessee. I came to Minnesota in 1969 to attend Macalester College, and have happily lived in the same small neighborhood ever since.

I began writing stories and poems as a very little girl — much as other children do, but perhaps with greater obsession. In 1971, I published my first poem and since then, have had work appear in a number of literary magazines and anthologies, including *Dacotah Territory, Crazy Horse, The Ardis Anthology of New American Poetry*, and the 1978 edition of Scott Foresman's *United States In Literature*. In 1976, I won a National Endowment in the Arts Fellowship in poetry. In 1978, I entered the Goddard MFA Writing Program, from which I graduate in 1980. My first play, *Snow In The Virgin Islands*, was accepted by the Minnesota Playwright's Lab, for whom I'm playwright in residence, 1979–80.

I've given numerous poetry readings and I co-directed Minnesota Poetry Out Loud in 1975. I directed two seasons of the St. Paul Music and Poetry Show. I'm currently writer in residence in the St. Anthony Park neighborhood through the COMPAS/Intersection program.

Marisha Chamberlain

THE ONLY CHILD

Jenese Hibner showed up the first day of our sixth grade and from that moment I couldn't take my eyes off her. It was her hair, her face, and her clothes. But it was also that her foot was strange.

Her hair was white blond, her eyes were a very light green and her chin and nose were pointed. I liked that face. She looked smart like a fox. I decided she was beautiful by my definition, no matter what anybody else thought, and regardless of the foot.

She wore new clothes but they were different from what the popular kids wore. Maybe they were home-made, but they fit like the latest fashion. She had shirts with little bands of embroidery. She had a sweater with white rhinestones around the collar. The colors she wore were not what you'd find at J. C. Penney's either. They were softer, dustier colors. When the other girls wore aqua, Jenese wore turquoise. It was like she was from another country. She had a pointed wool cap she wore in the winter, which was greyish-brown with little cream colored horses in a design around it; it had real horse hair knitted into it.

Her voice was something, too. One minute it was soft and musical, then stiff and mean like a soldier's. I loved to hear her talk, but it took me weeks to strike up a conversation with her. She looked rich and I didn't kiss up to kids who were rich and popular.

She didn't turn out to be so popular. The kids started making fun of her because of the foot. Her foot was shaped funny, lumpy and sort of rounded at the end where it should have been pointed. She had a special shoe built up around it. She could run pretty well in that shoe and she even started games at school because she could fool people into slowing down for her, and then go ahead and beat them. She looked funny when she ran, so it was confusing that she was so fast. I knew she was fast because she walked the same way home from school as I did and she was always ahead of me and stayed ahead. She was faster than she looked.

One day this girl got mad when Jenese caught her. She turned on Jenese and screamed, "There's nothing wrong with your foot, you big faker!"

Jenese raised her fist and limped after the girl, who backed toward the school door. The bell rang before Jenese could catch up and hit her. The next day Jenese didn't play with us, but instead stood off at the side with the other girls who were too stuck up or slow to play. I felt bad for her and I kept glancing over, but I didn't know what to do about it. Then something happened, because a crowd gathered around her. I guess a couple of those girls had asked to see her foot. When I got close enough to see what was going on, Jenese was tying her shoe up fast, with her head bent so low I couldn't see the expression on her face.

We were back in our classroom and opening our geography books when Jenese started to cry. She cried loud and her lip curled up and showed her teeth. Her fists were clenched on her desk, and she hunched her shoulders over and cried down onto her fists. The teacher tried to get her to talk, but she was bawling too hard. Then she decided that Jenese should go to the nurse's office and tried to get her to her feet. By then, Jenese was doubled over.

The teacher looked around the classroom. Most of the kids were pretending to read their geography books, but I couldn't take my eyes off Jenese. The teacher motioned me over to help and together we brought Jenese out of the classroom and down the hall. I was holding her arm tight. Her skin was hot and she was still crying hard. I couldn't help noticing how good she smelled.

We left her with the nurse and went back to the classroom. On the way, the teacher whispered to me that Jenese had no brothers and sisters because her parents had decided not to have any more children after Jenese. The teacher said she thought that was because of the foot, and that Jenese was a lonely little girl. She said that the father had left Jenese and her mother. The father sent money, but still the mother worked in order to provide special things for Jenese. I decided that it wasn't Jenese's fault if she was rich. She was an only child. There weren't many in the neighborhood. Right then, when the teacher was whispering to me, I felt glad to have my little brothers and sisters.

That afternoon, I didn't see Jenese when I was walking home. I guess her mother had picked her up early from the nurse's office. I walked slowly past her house, looking at everything. I didn't feel as scared as usual that she'd catch me looking. That house was the prettiest on the street, with the new lawn and the fresh white paint and trim. Above the living room window, they'd put in a little piece of stained glass with red grapes like a bunch of rubies and emerald leaves. My favorite thing, though, was the porch swing, carved in designs and painted red to match the trim. I looked around the corner of the house to see the swing on the side porch, and there was Jenese, sitting on the swing with her bad foot curled under her. She stared right back at me. I ran home.

The next afternoon Jenese accused me of following her. The trouble was, she kept slowing down, so I couldn't help catching up. Finally, she turned around and said, "Well, if you're going to follow me, you might as well walk with me."

So I did. I couldn't think of anything to say. And I couldn't help noticing the way she leaned toward me every time she stepped on her bad foot, like she was going to bump into me or fall on me.

"Do you like Elvis?" she asked.

"I'm not sure," I said.

"Presley! Don't you have a radio?"

"I'm not allowed to turn it on," I said.

She told me all about Elvis — the way he wore his pants, the way he combed his hair. She stopped on the sidewalk and showed how Elvis moved when he sang. She was wearing that rhinestone sweater and the rhinestones flashed in the sun. I thought it was wonderful, but I couldn't help laughing. She didn't seem to mind, and only wiggled her hips faster. Her voice! She could go down real low and growly, and then sob out the high parts. By the end of the week, I'd heard all of the Elvis songs Jenese knew and the plots of all the Elvis movies. We'd wait for each other at the corner of the playground and walk home together, though it took a long time because we laughed all the way.

The babysitter would be looking through the window for me by the time I got home. I was supposed to take over with the baby right after school, so the babysitter could go home. But walking home with Jenese, I kept forgetting to hurry.

During the schoolday, we didn't talk to each other. I wanted to be in the games on the playground, and Jenese was always off by herself or with the girls who didn't like to play. I was sorry that she wasn't playing. At least I had her to myself after school. Mostly I forgot about the foot and all.

One day she brought it up herself. She pointed to her foot as we were walking home, and said, "Club foot. That means I'm part of this club and you can only visit if you're with me."

"And where does this club preside?" I asked, imitating our speech teacher. I felt nervous and wanted to make her laugh.

"Nowhere in this goddam town," she replied, doing a much better imitation, with raised eyebrows and a tight smile, and only mouthing the swear word. In her own voice, she added, "Elvis ends all his nights there. Sometimes he sings a couple of songs, sometimes he just sits down with the tired look on his face, all by himself. He drinks for awhile and then he lays his head on the table."

"Does Elvis have a foot like yours?" I asked.

The dreamy expression left her face and she stared at me coldly. "No, he is honorary, which is more than you'll ever be." And she marched down the sidewalk ahead of me, dipping more than usual when she stepped on her good foot and dragging the other foot.

I hurried to catch up with her. I had to half run for a block beside her, before she stopped and turned to me.

"If you're so much my friend, how come you never had me over to your house?"

I'd never thought of that. "Well, come over right now."

"You don't do it that way. You ask your mother to call my mother and then your mother makes some cookies and we're expected."

"But my mother isn't home until late — you know, she works the split shift like your mother does. You'd have to stand around in my house while I did the breakfast dishes and took care of the baby and got the supper on." I thought for a minute. "There could be cookies. We'd have to make them ourselves. I know how if you don't. But who'll do breakfast dishes at your house if you come over to my house?"

"It won't matter. Nobody's home but me anyway. They wouldn't care if I was at your house." We walked another half block, then she continued, "My mom calls me at six or so and asks me what I'm eating. Then she tells me something about what went on at the hospital that day and I don't see her till ten o'clock, when I'm in bed already."

"Who cooks for your dad?" I asked, forgetting for a moment what the teacher had told me.

She hesitated. "He's not home right now."

That night I left a note for my mother on the table: "Mom, will you ask Jenese's mom at work if she can come over after school if that's all right with you." At breakfast the next morning, she said it was okay with her if I could still get my work done.

Two days later, Jenese came home with me. We walked past her house with its white fence, down the street to my house. I opened the gate and as we stepped into the yard, I noticed how muddy it was and smelly from the dogs, and when Rusty and Princess came over to us, they didn't look so good. I didn't want them to jump on Jenese, and I didn't want them to jump on me, either. They looked surprised when I pushed them down and yelled, but I didn't have time to explain it to them. We got onto the porch and I warned Jenese that the house was going to be messy.

It was. The babysitter left the minute I got there and Donny was sitting in the corner of the living room in a wet diaper with the toy box dumped out beside him. In the hall, the twins were running their trucks through this tinkertoy tunnel they'd built onto the pile of dirty clothes spilling down from the hamper. The diaper pail was sitting with its lid off, and I could smell it from the door. My little sister, Pammy, sat in the armchair, still in her coat and hat and with her bookbag in her lap, watching TV. I walked over to her.

"Who said you could turn that on?"

"I didn't turn it on," she said in a little voice. "It was on already."

I went over and turned off the TV. "Will you please change Donny's diaper, so me and Jenese can do the kitchen." She started to whimper, until she heard me say Jenese's name. Then she turned around and stared. She'd heard about Jenese at her school, I guess, about the foot. Jenese was standing in the kitchen doorway, looking around. When Jenese turned to us, Pammy blushed, picked up Donny without a word and took him into Mom's bedroom. On her way, I heard her tell the twins to pick up their things and go outside.

I started to pick up the toybox, but I looked over at Jenese and she was staring into the kitchen again. "Do you want something to eat?" I asked.

"No," she said. "It's just, I didn't know . . . Why doesn't your mother wash the dishes in the morning?"

"She can't. She's got to make our lunches."

"Well, why don't you buy hot lunch?"

"I don't know." We couldn't afford it, but I didn't want her to know that, or about how the school had offered us free lunch tickets but my Dad said no.

I walked into the kitchen and saw the cold pieces of egg in the frying pan and the cereal bowls mushed in with the glasses, and Donny's baby plate with carrot stuff running down the side. I took potato peelings out of the sink, turned on the water and poured the soap in. The smell of the soapsuds made me feel better. I put some milk in a clean glass and gave it to Jenese. I told her to sit down and take it easy, pointed to the chair in the living room where she could still see me and talk. She sat there and put the milk down on the window sill without drinking it.

Donny came wandering out in his new diaper. He came over to Jenese and looked at her. She beckoned to him and he came closer. He patted her knee and then sat down unsteadily on the floor. When he patted her foot, she jumped. Donny was just learning to talk. "Hurt?" he mumbled.

Jenese grabbed him and set him on her lap. His face clouded over. "Nobody hurt," she said, sternly.

I went over to them and said in a loud voice, "Donny, that's Jenese's foot that gets her into the Elvis club."

Pammy stuck her head in from the bedroom. "What Elvis club?" she asked.

Donny burst into tears and I swung him up onto my hip and took him into the kitchen. I gave him a cookie. He cried and ate at the same time and Jenese laughed for the first time since we'd come inside my house. Then she said she had to leave.

"But we didn't make any cookies, Jenese!"

She said, "Goodbye, I'll see you tomorrow," and went out the door. As soon as she got home, she called up on the phone. "Why don't you come over to my house," she said.

"I can't, I'm babysitting, can't you tell?"

"Can't they take care of themselves?"

"No, Jenese, Pammy's too little. If something happened, I'm the oldest and I'm supposed to be in charge."

"Oh," she said, and hung up.

As soon as she hung up, I tore into the dishes. I cleaned the whole kitchen and then I threw the macaroni on and got out the cookie stuff. I made three dozen peanut butter cookies and I let the kids eat them all up. I ate some of the raw dough, as well. I didn't feel much like eating at supper. I sat and watched the others, and while they were eating their desserts, I went back into the kitchen and washed the plates and pans. By the time I was done with the rest of the dishes, the kitchen was cleaner than I'd ever seen it before. After bedtime, I got up once more just to turn on the light and look around in there.

When mother came in to say goodnight, she asked if I'd had fun with Jenese. I didn't know what to say. I surprised myself, mumbling, "Old dumb, old rich Jenese."

"I thought you liked her."

"Well, I do, sort of."

"The reason I ask is that she called her mother at work tonight to ask me if you could go over to their house after school tomorrow. I'd like for you to go, if you want, but Pammy just isn't old enough to carry on without you. I'll think about it, though, if it means something to you."

Suddenly, I wanted to go so bad. I wanted to see the inside of that house, and I wanted to hear Jenese's voice.

The next afternoon, Jenese called as soon as I got to my house. "This is Elvis and could you meet me at the club?"

"Oh, Jenese, I'd love to, but I have to babysit, I really have to."

"Well, play hard to get," she said in her Elvis voice, and hung up.

In a few days, Mom decided that she could afford to have the babysitter on for a couple extra hours one afternoon, if I wanted to visit Jenese.

So the next afternoon, I followed Jenese in through her gate, across the green yard and up on the porch. I touched the porch swing with my hand as we walked in the door. Her house was as big as mine, and she had her own room all to herself with a sliding-door closet. She had a whole big dresser of her own, too. I would've liked to see inside each drawer, but she didn't want to stay in her bedroom. We went back downstairs, past her own bathroom which was all shiny and green. She turned on the radio in the kitchen and got out cokes and potato chips. She took two matching glasses down and poured the coke into them. Then she took a bottle of wine from the refrigerator, and a measuring spoon and poured out a tablespoon and dumped it in her coke. "Want some?" she asked.

"I don't think we're supposed to," I said.

"Oh, come on, a little won't do anything. Here, taste mine." I took a little sip. It tasted all right, a little bit sour. I guessed I would try some.

"But what will your mother think?"

"Oh, that's no problem," she said. She took the wine bottle over to the sink, filled the tablespoon twice with water, dumped it in, put the cork back in and shook the bottle. Then she put it back in the refrigerator.

We lay on the rug, sipping our drinks and listening to the radio. "I think we should dance," she said.

She got up and started doing her Elvis routine. I laughed. I couldn't seem to stop laughing. She wanted me to get up and dance with her. In a while I got up and did a couple of steps, but then I started laughing again. She sighed and turned the music off. "Let's go outside."

"Okay," I said. "But only for a minute. I have to get back home for supper soon."

We went out into her back yard. I'd never noticed before how large it was. It ran way back and in the farthest corner, under some trees, were a bunch of old sheds. We went through them and one had a trap door up into an attic. She put a ladder up there and we climbed up into her hideaway. She had a little table she'd made out of a board. She had some pretty rocks on it and an empty cologne bottle, plus some old lipsticks. Taped up on the wall was a letter someone had written her, sort of bleached out, plus some pictures of Elvis and country music stars tacked up around this little window that looked down on her house. I looked out and noticed how dark it was getting outside.

"I have to go now," I said, and I didn't wait for any arguments. I hurried down the ladder, out the shed door and up the street to my house.

Jenese followed after me, hollering, "Goodbye, see you tomorrow," over and over again. I could still hear her voice when I closed my own door behind me.

The next week Jenese got permission for me to spend the night with her. As soon as we got to her house, she wanted to go out to her shed. She packed up a thermos and a whole sack of potato chips, a piece of cheese and a big knife, and some doughnuts. She took the radio, put the batteries from a flashlight in it, and tried it without the cord. She fiddled with it and it came on. She got a blanket and put it over my shoulder to carry, then she picked up the box, with the radio blaring on top. We went down the hill and into the shed. She raked off a dance floor, and this time I could dance with her without laughing. Both of us wiggled and shook for awhile. Then a slow song came on and she wanted to dance cheek to cheek. It was hard to make my feet work with hers. She had her eyes closed and was leaning her cheek on mine. Every time she stepped on her good foot, I had to do a little dip with her. I had my eyes open, watching our feet without moving my cheek from hers. We danced three dances like this and then we climbed up into her attic.

She took out the doughnuts and cut the cheese with the big knife. She poured the contents of the thermos into the cup, but when I tried to take a drink, I choked. The stuff in there was strong and sour. "Jenese," I said, "This is pure wine."

"Oh, never mind," she said. "We've got to learn to drink sometime."

So I took the cup and drank a tiny sip, and passed it back to her. I'd take a sip, then she'd have a swallow and drinking the wine got easier. We ate the doughnuts and cheese and potato chips and we kept passing the wine.

Jenese said, "I think we should be blood sisters." She took the knife and cut her finger with it, and handed the knife to me. I didn't want to do it really, but my hand felt like it was floating and the knife was sharp. I just touched it, and a little drop of blood came out of the side of my finger.

"That didn't hurt at all," I said, and giggled.

She put the blood on her finger on the blood on my finger, and smeared it around. Then we drank up the last of the wine.

Jenese turned the radio on again and started to sing along. She sang soft and beautifully. I leaned against the wall beside her, unfolded the blanket and put it over our laps. I looked out the window and the sun was setting. It was starting to get dark in the shed. Through the window, the house looked like a picture in a frame. Back over at my house, the babysitter was staying the night. I didn't have to go anyplace or do anything.

Then, Jenese was shaking me. She was crying. "Look," she said, "you've got to see my foot." She'd already taken off her shoe and sock under the blanket, and she stuck her foot out at me. I was dizzy. I couldn't see so well, because it was dark in there. I reached over with my hand and felt her foot. I felt the round part and where the toes were crunched in underneath. Her foot was warm and soft, except for a callous. It was like a newborn animal, a hairless kitten, only bigger. I pulled her foot closer and petted it and gave it a little kiss.

She grabbed my hand away. "Listen," she said, "I want you to do something for me." She made a slicing motion across her ankle with the side of her hand, and she pushed the knife across the table toward me.

"Oh, no, Jenese," I said. "I can't do that. You can't do it. It would kill you."

"No," she said. "It won't hurt me. It's not good and I don't feel anything in it. I don't think it would even bleed. If I could get rid of it, they could make me a plastic one that fits a regular shoe. I know, I've seen them." And she cried again. I put my hand on the knife handle, and burst into tears myself.

"I can't see good enough."

"Look," she said, "I'll help you," and she put her hand on top of mine on the handle, and we brought it down together and drew it across her ankle.

"Ooooh," she cried, and her hand dropped from the knife. I put the knife on the table and she grabbed her ankle and sobbed. The news came on the radio and I stopped crying and took out my handkerchief and tied it around her ankle. In a little while she stopped bleeding. I put my arms around her and I guess we both went to sleep.

When I woke up, Jenese was lying in my lap and there was a flashlight shining in my eyes. Jenese's mother was standing on the ladder. I shook Jenese and we got up. The radio was buzzing and my head pounded. Jenese's mother saw the bare foot and the handkerchief, pulled off the handkerchief and saw the cut. She slapped my face. I was too tired to cry. Jenese didn't say a word. Her mother picked Jenese up in her arms and went down the ladder and out the door. I stumbled across the back yards, going home, sneaked past the babysitter asleep on the couch, and into my own bed.

At the breakfast table the next morning, I found out that Jenese's mother had called and we were forbidden to see each other or even walk home together. My parents knew about the wine and that we hadn't gone to sleep in beds. My little brothers and sisters sat quietly around the table. More than anything, my parents couldn't understand why I would want to hurt Jenese. They reminded me that they trusted me with the baby. Nothing I could say would convince them I wasn't trying to hurt her. I missed her right away. Times with her were the first times I knew for sure I was growing up. She was an only child. No one else on earth was like her, not even a blood sister. She was the first one I danced with, the first one I went away with to spend a night out of my own bed. I thought of holding her foot in my hands, how it looked, how different it was from other feet. I wish I could've been trusted with it. I did what I thought a blood sister would do, but she was an only child and I couldn't keep her.

ALVARO CARDONA-HINE: Writing is not a task given to words but to silence. It is out of silence that we fabricate life and myth. I go back a long way, to a child in the fourth grade who wrote an essay on birds and won a city-wide contest among schoolchildren. I do not recall one single thing I might have said; it has all gone back to silence. And to the rain. I do recall how I had to go see the head of the school system or someone like that, he wanted to meet me, and how I arrived at the rambling old house converted into offices with my feet drenched from the downpour. That was in San Jose, Costa Rica, back in the Thirties. The linnets must have been singing that day, they always sang when it rained. It was a sound like that of a door swinging slowly on rusty hinges. The gentleman treated me with kindness; he saw that I was frightened. He patted my head and let me go.

154

Alvaro Cardona-Hine

THE ZOO

When he was small — a boy, alone — he would go to the zoo. Whatever was to happen would happen there, that he knew. So he would go, as often as he could, in the long afternoons after school, and be lost in its maze for two and three hours at a stretch.

This zoo was unlike any other he might see later on in life. It was a dark, morose ravine by the river for which his town had found no better use. The trees didn't let the sunlight through and the air was fetid with the smell of the animals. A thousand steps led to the bottom, where the larger animals were caged, and this downward path was carved through bush and bramble. Solitude was built into that enormous prison, where only the occasional howling of an animal would break the overwhelming silence.

He loved it, he loved to go and feed jacaranda blossoms to the deer. The ground would be covered cobalt blue with them and he would simply scoop them up and let the animals lick them off his his hands through the fence. Their tongues were electric; they caressed the salt off his hands with an insistence that was sexual, echo of a possible future.

But first he would stop by the grotto where the fish were kept. This was an actual cavern dug into the side of the ravine, half way down to the bottom. He would walk in, aware that every footstep floated on its own echoes and reverberated like the reflections of the water on the ceiling. The fish would be suspended in the eternal boredom of their green water against both walls of the grotto and he would speak to them so that his voice should come back as if it were theirs:

Hello . . .

Hellooooo hellooooo . . . hellooooo . . .

Whatever was to happen would begin to happen. The fish would swim nervously, zigzagging through their spaces, and he would press his nose to the plate glass and pretend that he was one of them, a pancake of flesh with bulging eyes. Then the fear would arrive. The dim light and the echoes of his voice would bring his dread into being. He could stand his dread anywhere but in that cavern. He could not stay; he would back up, walking slowly, never turning his back on the dark end of that tunnel.

He enjoyed what dread did to his heart, making it beat faster, but he had to leave. He thought he felt the maximum fear there because the fish seemed to own all the space and what they wanted was for him to drown. They terrified him in a way that nothing else did, neither the cruel-looking eagles in their immense wire home nor the puma pacing up and down in a cage bloodied by recent meat.

To calm himself, he would walk past all the cages, past the few human beings drifting about like ghosts, tired tourists no longer looking at anything but dreaming of home, and he would reach the curving meadow where the river would be waiting. He knew the river was waiting for him because no one else ever came there. And the river would ask him about the fish up the slope, caged in their clammy grotto, at the mercy of echoes so solid that they seemed like a house of jello. Dread here was different, vast, filled with invisible, free animals whose noises were hidden by the sound of the water flowing against rock.

Here he would sit with his dread which he himself had not named and with which he could, therefore, be comfortable. It would sit by him and share time with him. It was a fugitive presence, never human, although it could have been a woman. It could have been any one of those peasant girls who came into the city to work as servants. Their laughter was as vast as dread. Their hands were always cool.

He didn't choose to name it, couldn't have. But it partook of guilt and temptation. The mystery around him was a gigantic robbery. It would puzzle him that he was there and not at the park near school, in the shade of a giant long-needle pine. That was because, whenever he found himself under that tree, he would wonder why he wasn't by the river, sensing the proximity of the blood of all those pent-up animals lugubriously waiting like himself.

Yes, he went around in his head with mysteries that were circular and which he could never resolve. They pleased him because they would make his heart beat faster and because his hands would contract and grow slightly humid, with the apprehension felt by the rest of the organism behind them.

From afar he would watch the peasant girls come walk by the road above the zoo, walk with their men friends in mid-afternoon. The men always seemed to hover over these girls. The girls were always centered; they never reached outside themselves, they seemed to be satisfied with their peripheries while the men were like arrows. He wondered if he would grow to be like an arrow, also. Would he circle something concrete then, the way he sought dread with the fish and with the river?

He would see that the men wanted to touch the girls and that this wanting had replaced dread for them. He knew why the girls were happy. He was happy when the tongues of the deer licked his hands. Strange, because he knew that he was not destined to become a woman.

That his heart should beat faster is all he sought. Not by running; not by any of the sports that the others went after all the time, in unsecret droves. Something caged, like a heart or a puma, was not free to run, it had to discover its own freedom in some other way. He would look at the captive crocodile in its shallow pool, at the far end of the zoo, and wonder where life began and ended for this creature. There was no apparent difference. Moving, feeding, everything had lost its value for the beast. He would look at the crocodile a few feet away, separated by wire and, suddenly, his heart would start beating faster. It would move up to his throat and he would have to cling to the fence. Most of the animals there at the zoo, the ones that mattered, had no mates; they were alone, ruminating, lost, dethroned. The crocodile seemed to be actually rusting. Their powerful smells told him that they would have fled instantly had they had the chance.

Still, he waited for more. More had to come, more had to happen. The crocodile told him so. Everything in the place was waiting for judgment, loaded with guilt. Like his father's guns. One did not talk about it any more than one talked about them. They were objects that guarded against danger; they were untouchable, imminent.

Imminence, had he known what it was, would have made sense to him. With everything else in the world he was waiting because waiting was an order given in a low voice by things. He went to the zoo repeatedly in order to wait where waiting was sacred and preordained. The trees waited there, and kept in their bowels the strange and savage fruit of denial. The animals waited in small circles, within themselves, like gloomy fires keeping vigil in some civil war of unknown ripening, of hopeless duration.

What was healthy about his childhood was the knowledge that something would happen. He knew that the animals were not aware of this. In countless ways he knew they knew no hope and no dread. He was attracted to them because in their presence his own sense of awful futurity became obvious and he could realize part of it before its time.

One day he went and it began to rain. He took refuge in the fish grotto. He moved silently, so as not to create any more echoes than he had to. Had he frightened the fish these would in turn have frightened him. While the rain poured outside, he went from tank to tank, scrutinizing the old familiar faces. Suddenly he heard a footstep, then another. He turned and, from the dimness where he stood, he saw a man enter the grotto. He had the immediate sense of being trapped, of being at a loss. He tiptoed further into the interior of the grotto, made darker by the darkness of the day.

The man had not noticed him and that was to the good. Maybe if he stood very still he would not be seen and the man would go away. He didn't want to be seen; something told him he should remain invisible and silent. He watched.

He saw that the man was not interested in his surroundings. Had he come just to get away from the rain? He did not once look at the fish, nor did he attempt to explore the grotto. He was dealing with himself, talking to himself in a low voice. He was younger than his father, this man, and well dressed; clearly not a bum or a beggar planning to stay there for the night.

How strange: now the man had a rope, and he was throwing it up, to the ceiling. There was an iron grill there which the rope finally looped. With the two ends of the rope in his hands the man fashioned a noose. He worked a long time at this, tugging and perfecting his work. It was all he could do to reach it with his outstretched arms, but this seemed what he wanted. When he was satisfied, he did something so spectacular that the boy let out a scream: it was to jump against the wall, holding the rope with one hand. Bouncing off, at a certain altitude, the man was able to slip the noose around his neck. It caught as he came down and the bones in his neck cracked under the weight of his body. He stopped moving instantly, but his body continued to swing back and forth at the end of the rope.

The echo of the man's neck as it snapped lasted almost as long as the body took to stop swinging. That was awesome. And as long as the body was in motion, the boy could not move. He couldn't think. Dread had come to touch him with what had had to happen. It was too marvelous and too frightening, and this paralysed him completely. But eventually the body ceased to swing; it stood perfectly silhouetted against the bright mouth of the grotto, a thing as limp as the large clump of bananas perennially hanging from a rafter in the back porch of his house.

Even after it had stopped moving the boy did nothing. Not for a long time. He watched it, filled with increasing regret that what had had to happen had been this. For it was not marvelous, not any more. It was confusing. He felt obligated to run and report the incident to someone. But obscurely and devotedly he had wanted an end to guilt, and he knew that telling about this would fill him with more guilt than ever, as if he had somehow been the cause of it. He felt angry that this man had come and stolen the magic of the zoo from him.

His anger was such that he finally decided not to report anything. He would just go home, as if nothing had happened. This might save him the zoo. Even though he instinctively knew that what he had waited for had happened, he hoped against hope that it might not be so and that subsequent visits might restore him to a sense of dread once again. He needed dread, he needed another future. This man had robbed him of one and he would have to fight to regain something equally valid.

All right. He would go. But he remembered his scream and this bothered him. Had the man heard him? He had lost all sense of privacy by that. A great unhappiness invaded his being. It made moving difficult and he had to fight and impose his will in order to stir.

He did it. He moved towards the figure dangling in mid-air. It was unhappiness and not fear that he felt, like a weight in his belly, making his movements clumsy and feverish. Why couldn't he move faster? He had never realized that one had to be happy in order to move.

His unhappiness was so profound that it made it almost impossible to get past the man. He went slowly, methodically, placing one foot and then another ahead of him, his eyes focused on the man's contorted face. Then, all at once, the face drew him, it called to him, and the boy moved with ease towards it.

When he was close, the face became his own all at once and he lost all sense of time. He was staring at his own face, at his face as it would be later on in life. This and nothing else was what had to happen. He moaned with self pity then, and abandoned the grotto.

Down below, under the pouring rain, the crocodile opened his heavy lids, blinked once, went back to waiting.

EMILIE BUCHWALD: The facts are these: I was born in Vienna, Austria; grew up in and around New York City; married someone whose warmth, wit, and love are central to my life; received degrees from Barnard College and Columbia; and have spent the past twenty years in Minnesota, teaching, acquiring a Ph.D., writing, and being a part of the lives of our four children.

In college I took a course in fiction writing. I thought of myself as a poet and when I wrote prose I felt like a novice knitting a sweater without a pattern or a clue to the shape of the finished garment. My teacher, John Cheever, gave me this: "Tell the story. Make it as unified, as rounded, as verbally complete as you would a poem. Not a word more or less than is needed." That is such good advice and so hard to do that I offer it freely.

As a reader and a writer, I am interested in: words and the mystery of human behaviour. I love verbal play, the power of the word to suggest, to connect, to bring into being what we feel and imagine. I struggle to make the best walls and windows of words that I can.

I admit to being a voyeur of the imagination. I like to look into lighted windows at twilight, wondering about the lives being lived within, their uniqueness, that which makes each of us self-contradictory and ultimately mysterious. I try to describe that which I believe has emotional truth.

Emilie Buchwald

STATIONS

Helen's jokes about pioneering didn't survive the first day of the drag and lurch of the U-HAUL IT behind the Plymouth, of changing Davy's diapers on the front seat, of greasy paper sacks, soda bottles and used diapers bulging the litter bag.

The KC 135 jet tankers were starting the pre-dawn engine-revving that made the walls of the Wherry housing units vibrate when they locked their unit and slid the key under the Columbina's door. Karl returned the guard's salute for the last time as they drove through the Richter Air Force Base gates; the stars were still out. By the time the northerly suburbs of San Antonio lay behind them, the sky was brassy blue, a fierce glistening arc of light from horizon to horizon. They stopped for dinner at S*C*H*U*L*T*Z***C*A*F*E, letters in blue neon, stars in red, grateful for the languid breeze from the wooden ceiling fan, though it only ruffled their hair.

"Right out of *Casablanca*," said Karl of the fan and the twilight room full of silent men intent on their beer.

"Hardly," said Helen.

They chewed wearily at their steak sandwich specials.

Driving across Oklahoma the next day they zigzagged from one detour to the next under the weight of the hot December sun. Helen forgot the candy bars she had set on the dashboard that morning. The car smelled of melted chocolate and peanut butter all day. The stubborn heat and the leanness of scenery, the windmills and the green oil pumps beaking up and down making money for invisible shareholders in the wilderness, reduced them to a sweaty crankiness.

They tried eating lunch at the top of one of the desolate hillocks rising like breakers from the blowing flats, but the wind toppled the thermos every time they stood it up and stripped them of every lightweight object they didn't hold or sit on. Their faces stung from a fine red dirt that fell out of their clothes that night and stained the shower water as they scrubbed themselves.

They were forced to sit in the deadly baking car after all. Mercifully, the heat lulled Davy into a state of continuous drowse.

The third day they drove wearing their coats, the heater turned to high heat/high fan. Gas station attendants in summer-weight coveralls had disappeared with the other southern fauna. For the first time in two years Helen believed in the reality of winter.

Karl drove slowly, leaning forward, squinting into the blowing snow-twilight of the afternoon. Helen retrieved once again the string of plastic chips Davy delighted in shaking jerkily up and down and dropping from his car seat into her lap.

The bundled corn husks were powdered with new snow. Good dirt, she thought, rich and black, stronger than Texas soil, as if it could take the worst of sun and frost, shelter the fittest bugs, sprout the tallest weeds and still manufacture endless plenty. The snow fall began soon after they passed the sign, NEBRASKA WELCOMES YOU. It was just a wafting of isolated heavy flakes at first.

"We need to find a place," she said quietly. "Let's stop soon."

"Don't nag, damn it," he said, but without heat, and she was not angry because she had said it just to say it; she knew they were involved in something words could not remedy. They were both anxious to find a motel for the night. They were both almost convinced that the road ahead would not provide one. For an hour they had seen nothing but fields without farm houses and the side roads that cut off into who knew where. The one gas station they saw was boarded up. So was a wooden vegetable stand whose crayoned sign promised MELONS AND BERRIES CHEAP.

Helen leaned forward too, trying to see past the windshield wipers, as far as the blowing snow allowed her to see. There were drifts directly in their lane which required careful maneuvering; the U-HAUL IT shimmied ominously behind them as Karl turned the wheel slightly, moving out of his lane and back again. They had seen no other car for a long time. They seemed to be, she thought, the only people stupid enough to be out driving in this storm. She searched ahead for a house or a store or a gas station, something to offer them refuge from this road which seemed to be only their road.

They came around a turn and saw the blinking stars of gasoline pumps. Karl applied a slight additional pressure to the accelerator. The car leaped forward and spun. The tires thumped over something. Helen clutched for Davy. She fell against the car seat with a force that numbed her elbow. Then they were stopped, wedged into a snowbank, at a tilt. Davy kicked his legs and laughed, waiting for another, similar pleasant diversion.

They both tried their doors. Helen could open hers only enough to squeeze out, shin-deep into the snow. She had the urge to move, to do something. There on the highway, like a giant's misplaced toy box, the trailer sat, undamaged. She ran toward it, wondering if they could move it without help.

"Don't leave the baby alone!" Karl yelled, running to catch up with her.

"Don't tell me what to do!" she yelled back. "Why don't you stay with him!" She glared at him, her socks sodden inside her icy canvas sneakers. I'll get frostbite, she thought. He glared back. He put his arms on her shoulders and leaned his forehead against hers. They stood thus, eyeball to eyeball and she could feel him laughing. She put her numb hands into his jacket pockets and laughed. It felt good. She leaned back and looked at him. There was a drying splotch of purple-red over his left eye. She felt her own forehead; it was sticky.

"You're hurt!" he said, examining her face.

"No, you are," she said. "That's your blood," He put his hand up to his forehead.

"I guess so," he said.

"We were lucky," she said. She remembered that her elbow hurt. She was very cold now.

"O.K.," he said, "let's try it. Get behind it on that side." But even together, with shove after thrusting shove, they were unable to roll the trailer closer to the car.

It was hard to estimate the distance to the gas station. "Maybe it's only a quarter of a mile," Karl said quietly. He dug his muffler and lined gloves out of the heavy clothes duffle. "I'll be back soon" he said, but as he slammed the car door she wondered how far he would have to walk through the blizzard. There was no denying the fact that this was a blizzard. Storm was not big enough a word for what was raging around them. In the torrent of wind and snow and dark she lost sight of him almost at once.

One bottle of formula remained in the insulated bag. She decided not to use it until she had to, but when Davy cried, though it was only an experimental cry, the tentative first stirring of hunger, she lifted him from his car seat and fed him. This was so irrational an act that she realized her brain wasn't in charge at all. She had imagined herself calm, but it was a calm her brain imposed by suppressing the facts. The rest of her needed help. She was feeding Davy to comfort herself, for the physical reassurance of holding his firm heaviness and watching him watch her with that look of perfect confidence in his existence. One of his hands was on her hand holding the bottle. The other he moved delicately back and forth brushing the wool of her coat with his fingers, putting himself pleasurably to sleep.

Snow covered the windows white except for the one side window in the back shielded from the wind's full force. The windshield wipers were frozen to the glass. Her jokes about pioneering came back to her with a thought that years of American History in the classroom had not prepared her for: "I could never have survived," she murmured to Davy, "never." Without the shelter of the dead machine she would die, as other women walking the frozen fields carrying their babies had died.

She was not too cold, except for her feet. She thought about starting the car. Would carbon monoxide kill them before Karl came back? It also occurred to her that the car might not start at all. That was too frightening a possibility for her to risk trying it. When would her family start worrying about them? How many days before they started asking questions and making phone calls? Too many. And besides, they were busy with Christmas, calling each other up and planning the dinners and finding the tree lights. They were running errands downtown where they stood on long lines for everything and the parking lots were full until closing time and the tree lots were picked over for the least scrawny Black Hills spruce. Here there were no trees, nothing important enough to hinder the wind.

In the white blank of the windshield she saw a glow, an increasing brightness. She kept herself from hoping much. In a few more minutes there was a scraping at the frozen door handle. Karl forced the door open. His face was bright red, his eyebrows frosted white. She noticed a tow truck pulled alongside.

"You all right?" he asked, taking in the baby asleep in her lap. He reached behind her, pulled out slacks, extra socks from the heavy duffle.

She nodded. "You're the one who had to walk."

The driver of the tow truck dropped down beside the car, squatted, examined the way in which the wheels were wedged into the snowbank. When he turned his face she saw that he was a boy, probably no older than twelve.

"Can you take the trailer, too?" Karl called to him as he attached the chain hitch to the frame.

"Later," he shouted back. "I'll need Pa, anyways."

He motioned to them. "Come ahead!" and Karl helped her out and up into the truck cab. The wind wants to kill us, she thought. The boy at the wheel was short. How much can he see? she wondered. She peered out; the road's divisions were lost in the seethe of snow. The boy's hands on the wheel were red through the grime, the knuckles scraped and crusted. In the blowing veil of snow, the modern contours of the gas station were concealed. It reminded her of an old-fasioned cottage surrounded by a ragged hedge of snow. The boy jumped out and ran around to open their door. He glanced at the baby she held close against her coat.

"Is that a boy or what?" he asked.

She leaned close so that she could speak without shouting. His eyes were curious but not friendly. "His name is David," she said.

They hurried inside. Any fanciful ideas about cottages were immediately dispelled. The gas station was furnished in petroleum-modern: green tile walls, dark speckled linoleum, two vinyl chrome-arm lounges facing one another, separated by a green metal table. On one wall were shelves of Gold Star Auto products. On the opposite wall, a print of a smiling service attendant tipping his hat hung over the vending machines of cigarettes and candy. The boy pushed aside a curtain in the back wall, motioning them to follow. The next room must have been, Helen thought, the station's first quarters. A system of tall radiators was set against the far wall. Tires and spare parts were heaped in a corner. Rags and jacks of varying sizes, burlap sacks of potatoes and onions, leaned against an old gas range. A man was seated at the chipped formica table reading a newspaper.

"Well, Mel?" he said, acknowledging them with a nod.

"Had to leave the trailer, Pa."

"Let's get her," he said, rising, marking his place by folding back a page.

"I'll go back with you," Karl said.

"Don't need you, lieutenant. Thanks just the same." He pulled down the fur earflaps of his hat. "You're not dressed for this," he said, jerking his head at the door. He pulled a down jacket from a peg.

"Coffee's there on the stove. Help yourself." They tramped away in their heavy boots.

Helen still held the baby. He was awake, blinking at the fluorescent light's humming lustre. Where could they sleep? "There must be a house, bedrooms, where they live," she said.

"I think they live right here." There was another curtain in the rear wall, only partly closed. Karl swept it back for her.

She could see what there was: unpainted dresser, unmade cots, large-screen tv set facing the beds.

"How can people live like this!" she said. "No one has to."

"We could sleep on those couches out there. Cover them with blankets and it won't be bad. Don't frown. Would you rather be out there in the car?"

"The boy's filthy. He's certainly not old enough to drive. His father should have more sense."

"Be glad the boy can drive," he said, his voice harsh. "What in hell is wrong with you?"

She wanted to cry. Why? Why care where they slept? They were alive. Tomorrow would have been too late, except for the announcement on television news. She imagined a camera panning in on the car and on Karl's frozen corpse. Impossible to think of him dead, he was so thoroughly, competently alive. Given time and a few tools he could fix anything. She took his existence for granted and hers, too. She would die, of course, everyone died, but later. And Davy's life was of such an order of seriousness to her that it was incredible to imagine anything interfering with it.

"I don't know," she said. She was also shrinking away within herself from this pitiful room and lives that did not know how to go beyond the barest kind of existence.

"It's not like you," he said, meaning that she was sensible and understood how to deal with most situations.

"I'm tired I guess." She was tired from holding herself rigid against this place and against the knowledge of what had almost happened to them.

"Let me take him for awhile." He gathered Davy from her stiff arms. "reach into my pocket for the extra socks. Wash up, get warm." The baby transferred his gaze to Karl's face, scanning, absorbing the familiar contours.

"What about you?" she asked.

"In a while. I'm fine for now. Leave the diaper bag. I'll change him." He put Davy down on the formica table and undressed him in the leisurely but careful way in which he did everything.

Her legs were stiff too, the muscles tense. In the waiting room she stared out, watching for the lights of the truck. The snow whirled down in funnels of white.

The key to the Ladies' Room hung next to the door. Like the rest of the gas station it was tiled in green. It was clean. There were paper towels, there was pink soap in the dispenser. He does his best, she thought. A bluebottle fly on the mirror ledge flew past her, sluggishly circling the stalls, while she ran water in the sink. In the mirror she observed herself. She ought to look different, she thought, but she just looked tired and the light reflecting off the tiles gave her face a sickly greenish tinge. The fly careened to the floor, buzzed, lay still. The wrong season to wake up, she thought, and the wrong place. She stripped the socks off her feet and wrung them out. It was a painful pleasure to lift each foot up and run warm water over it. Her feet tingled in the clean dry socks. She held hot water to her cheeks, her eyes. She slapped her cheeks and dried herself harshly with the rough brown paper towels. It helped. She felt a little silly, but she was awake again.

Karl had the baby against his shoulder, jiggling him gently. He hadn't put Davy back into the quilted snowsuit and that made her feel that they were settling in for the night.

The tow truck pulled up, their trailer behind it. At least they would have the comfort of their own things, blankets, extra sweaters, shields against the strangeness of the place, an extension of home.

She took Davy, holding the neck that occasionally still bobbled.

"We'll set his car bed between those lounges. I just have to move that little table out of the way." Karl hurried out to help with the unloading. He carried in one duffle and the bag with the cans of formula and the supply of diapers. The boy brought in the car bed and set it up for her, checking to make sure the catches were locked. By the time she finished making up the lounges into their blanket beds, Davy was asleep on his stomach, his hands balled into fists up by his head. A faint sweat on his forehead proclaimed the effort of sleeping so profoundly.

The boy, Mel, stopped to look down at him. "Sleeps a lot, don't he?" he said. "He's lucky."

"You don't want to eat them" their host said when he saw their bag of sandwiches spread out on his table, the drooping lettuce and dried luncheon meat between the stiff triangles of bread. He swept them into the steel garbage bin and gave them plates and cutlery. From the refrigerator he brought arm-loads of food, ketchup, pickles, and beer, until the table was crowded with jars and containers.

He sat back in his chair, his paper in his lap, and watched them eat.

In the back room Mel lay on his cot in front of the television set, divorced from the proceedings.

"I thought I wasn't hungry," Karl said, making himself a second generous ham sandwich.

"That's right, there's plenty. You eat." Their host watched them with satisfaction. "You headed for the squadron at Reinholt?"

"We're going home. Back to Minnesota. I'm finished."

"Is that so. Well, there's another good day's drive once the roads are open. The plows'll be out when it lets up. This ain't too bad."

Karl glanced at Helen. She smiled. "It seems pretty bad to us," she said.

"The wind's the worst part. When it blows like this, it's mean."

They were full. Their host had brewed another pot of coffee, "egg coffee," he told them proudly. "It's smoother."

"Want a mug, Mel?" he called.

The boy came out and took the coffee, laced it with cream.

"Pa, that program you like's coming on."

"I'll be there. I've got to look around and lock up yet."

"Just telling you."

"I don't forget."

The boy pulled the curtain closed behind him. There was a loud roar of laughter and applause, music, and an announcer's voice, carefully pitched for gaiety.

"Turn that down, Mel. I'll be there." he reached for his hat.

"He gets lonesome," he said, an explanation.

"This is a pretty quiet place for a child," Helen said.

"The school bus takes him when he wants to go. Some days he don't want to go. Not that he's dumb. Says he misses me."

He was watching them to see if they would allow him to say more. People to talk to were a luxury. Having them here to himself pleased him. Helen saw it in his face.

"I had a girl too. Our house was back of the station there. Burned right to the foundation. The furnace went, just like that. My missus was burned too bad."

Helen wished he hadn't decided to tell them. His story demanded they give him something in return, sympathy, some kind of response. She was so tired. It was hard to deal with his disaster.

"That's horrible," she said. "I'm so sorry."

Karl nodded. What could anyone say?

"I better lock up now," he said. He seemed to understand that they were at a loss.

When the station door slammed shut, Mel stuck his head out from behind the curtain as if he had been waiting there.

"Did he tell you she's dead?" he asked.

"What?"

"I heard it, part of what he told you. Burned, right?"

"I'm sorry," she said, alarmed at the anger on his face.

"Me too. I hate it when he tells that lie."

Karl said coldly, "What are you saying?"

"He lies. About her. My ma. She wasn't in any fire. She just took off with my sister. She left a letter, but I never got to read it. He tore it up."

For just a second Helen wondered if the boy was making up his story. For just a second. His look was scornful but very steady.

"There was no fire?" Karl asked.

"Sure. There was a fire all right. The night she left, Pa burned down the house back there that she was so fussy about. He wasn't drunk, not at all. That part's real."

"Why are you telling us this?" Helen asked.

"I hate it when he lies. He tells that lie to everybody who'll listen. Why not tell the truth? We don't need her. We make out all right. When he lies like that, I know he's still missing her. I don't miss her."

The station door opened and closed and they heard the lock being turned. Mel retreated. His father came back rubbing his hands, his face still smiling a company smile. Snow glistened on his jacket. They watched him, feeling suddenly shy.

He poured himself more coffee. "I keep thinkin'," he said. "Maybe we should move." He glanced at them, seeking a comment. "See, look at this here." From his back pocket he pulled a Gold Star dealer's wallet-sized atlas. They saw the name, Oscar Peterson, written on the flyleaf. He opened to the centerfold map of the United States. He had made circles around a few cities in red pencil.

"These are the places. My sister's husband retired down here in St. Pete." There was a heavy red band around St. Petersburg. "She brags a lot about her weather. The trouble is, I'm used to this place. My pa farmed outside of Holden."

"Do you grow any crops?" Helen asked.

He laughed. "Crops! Not to speak of. Just tomatoes and onions and a few rows of sweet corn. Just enough for us."

"Pa," shouted the boy. "You are so missing the whole show!"

"O.K., Mel. Be right there." He turned to them. "You all right? Got enough blankets?"

"I just need a large pot to sterilize some bottles and water," said Helen.

"Sure thing." He rummaged in the cabinet under the sink and brought out a black and white speckled roasting pan like the one her mother had used years ago.

"Perfect," she said.

"Pa!"

"Coming, Mel." He put his palms on the table, leaning close to them. "A man would be real dumb to sell his place, not knowing if he could make it somewheres else." It was a question.

He was so close to her that Helen could see the large blackheads on his broad nose, the individual stiff gray hairs sprouting from the corners of his ears.

Karl said, "A man can make a go of whatever he wants enough."

"That's so," he said doubtfully. "That's so. Some men can."

He pulled the curtain back. Mel was on his stomach, head propped up on his hands, intent on the screen.

"Say goodnight, Mel."

"Goodnight," said Mel, not turning his head.

"Well, goodnight again, lieutenant and missus. We better have a real good look at your right front tire in the morning."

Helen worked quickly, sterilizing water and bottles. She measured out formula, thinking that Oscar Peterson was not a lucky man, thinking about the woman who had lived in the burned-out house. Karl cleared the table and washed up. They moved quietly, busy with their thoughts. They didn't undress. They put on heavy sweaters and hugged wordlessly before crawling into their separate heaps of blankets.

Helen lay in her cocoon thinking about the apartment Karl's brother had rented for them. Their furniture would arrive. They would start their new jobs. Rising on one elbow she felt Davy's cheek, then his neck. She pulled back the top blanket and settled herself again.

It no longer seemed strange that she was lying looking out a full-length plate glass window. Snow had risen against the door. From the back room there was still muted music and excited voices, Mel and his father warmed by magic in their outpost. The snow spitting against the glass made almost the same sound as a good fire in a fireplace. The gold stars in the globes over the gas pumps were lighted but no longer blinking. Helen fell asleep but dreamed she was watching them.

KENNETH GOODMAN: was born in Cleveland, Ohio, May 21, 1954. He made the decision to become a writer at the age of 7, after completing his first short story in a first grade classroom. Since then he has passed through various stages of creative development, and is currently working on a novel entitled, *The Best of For Today.* He wonders why he is writing this statement in third person.

Kenneth Goodman

DATING THE GIRLS IN THE OFFICE

I am the fastest typist I know — 85 to 100 words a minute and rarely an error. It's really a sight to see. I can do it in rhythm, if need be. I have had emotional affairs with typewriters. This baby I'm working on now, well, we have an understanding. I type in secret messages with the power off, before the working day begins. This morning, for instance, I let it know, "I understand, my love. I know you'd rather be used for poetry and literature instead of this rat race crap, but abide kid! Maintain! We'll get through it somehow!" While other typewriters in the office have gone on the blink at least once since I've been here, mine has remained healthy. Somebody cares.

My skill landed me a job in this office involved with a federally funded project calling for massive amounts of typing. The first thing I noticed when I began was that I was the only man around. I worked intensely at first to make a good impression, but kept gazing out of the corners of my eyes. Women! Women! Everywhere! And no men. Anywhere.

At first I couldn't believe it. I roamed the hallways, exploring other offices involved with mine, assuming I'd run into another male somewhere. I didn't. There was no doubt about it. It was me and forty females, forty hours every week. I did discover later that there was one other man, The Boss.

The reactions of my friends and family to the situation were what I expected. The word "harem" was used profusely. My brother in Wisconsin told me over the phone, "Boy, you've got it made!" An old high school buddy sent a pornographic anecdote clipped from a men's magazine describing a sexual encounter right in the office. Apparently I was in for a treat.

Now I am a shy person, as a rule. Oh, let's face it. I'm terrified of women — passive putty in their hands. Past relationships have found me the manipulated plaything of hedonistic females — so much that I finally declared an end to it as hazardous to my health. This brought about long periods of loneliness. Soon I began to enjoy this state, contrary to the Playboy philosophy. The morning I first set foot in this bevy of femininity I had been so long without erotic contact (embarrassed to say *how* long) that I felt like a diabetic in a candy factory. But this was my secret.

I deliberated that in terms of sex, I would definitely not initiate, but certainly not refuse. I became a silent beggar: my eyes beseeched. I was sure my first opportunity had arrived when Rhonda Krantz invited me to a New Year's Eve party.

"A-ha!" I thought. Here was an extremely cute young woman verily asking me to make love with her. I recalled some wild New Year's parties of my past and accepted at once. The rest of that week my heart fluttered whenever Rhonda walked into the office. I had eyes for no one else. The week flew by.

"Pick me up at 8?" asked Rhonda, Friday afternoon.
"You bet!" I answered.

I danced around like a fool getting ready for the party, choosing the most flattering clothes, the most macho aftershave. Of course, I wondered, "Will I be able to 'do it,' after so long without?" I decided to wear loose boxer shorts instead of the restricting jockey type, to allow better circulation.

Rhonda seemed very cheerful as she directed me to the evening's destination. "What kind of a girl wears the shoulder strap and the seat belt on a date?" I wondered.

I found out. The New Year's party I fantasized about for a week turned out to be a Christian Fellowship meeting. The main activity of the New Year's night? Biblical charades. No kidding. Everyone left before 12:00.

My balloon of desire for Rhonda Krantz popped into a thousand pieces, though after I dropped her off I must admit feeling relieved. After all, if we had attempted to make love and I had failed, how could I ever have gone to work again?"

As I became more familiar with the office, other personalities made their impressions on me. I was often amused observing the automatic reflexes of my own mind, for I was absolutely unable to control silent replies to statements and questions put to me. These were sentences I would never say, yet my mind thought them. Once, as I was filing papers in a cabinet, a female comrade asked, "Can I just stick this in there?" filing a paper of her own. I was aghast as I heard my mind think, loudly, "Can I just stick *this* in there? Heh-heh." Can you imagine what it's like to have a female supervisor look you in the face and declare, "Boy, you sure pulled a boner!"

But once I got over the initial fantasy period I began to discover that blanket sexual expectations applied to all the girls in the office blinded me to their individual personalities. Once I lifted off my blind, I could see each one of them differently, uniquely. I began to make friends.

In a moment of rare self confidence, I forced myself to say, "Want to go to lunch with me?" to Alisa Scott, who sits at a desk adjacent to mine.

"Sure!" she said and smiled.

Her mere consent erupted waves of contentment from my waist into my rib cage. At two of twelve I symbolically turned off my typewriter and looked over at Alisa. She winked at me. Together we took our coats off the hooks and made for the exit.

"Ah! One hour of freedom!" she said with a wild look in her eyes, her long black hair waving in the wind.

"What shall we do?" I asked.

Visions of Alisa and myself sitting in a fast food place eating burgers didn't quite appeal.

"I don't eat red meat," she said.

"How come?"

"Because!" she said, shocked at the mere question, "Who wants a brain full of lard?"

"Huh?"

"It's like a lamp," said Alisa. "How can you see the light if your lampshade is smeared up with grease?"

"You've got a point there."

"I know what we shall do!"

"Whatever you say, baby!" my mind thought.

"Let's go to the bakery and smell!"

"That sounds nourishing."

Alisa led me to a small bakery in an old brick building.

"By now they've just baked the breads!" she said, wiggling her eyebrows. "Now, I want you to concentrate only on smell. Let it be like a glowing jewel in the middle of your face."

Not only had they just baked the breads, but the cookies as well. For the next thirty minutes all I could say was, "Mmm!"

When we first walked in, nobody was behind the glass counter, but soon a man resembling Santa Claus dressed in a white thermal undershirt, white apron and white pants with a thin black belt exploded through two swinging doors carrying a tray of just-baked rye breads.

"Hey there!" he said robustly.

"Mmm!" I replied.

"He stoned?" the baker asked Alisa.

"Just on the aroma!" she said.

I began thinking, "Ah, Alisa! Woman of the old towns! Wearer of cotton and wool! Reader of literature! Eater of foods of beauty!"

On the way to the bakery she had confided to me that where she *really* wanted to live was in a small town in Vermont. I saw her sitting on a front porch in an antique rocking chair. A warm rain of big, bulbous drops would fall, suggesting a naked rain dance in the back yard with the lilacs and honeysuckle on a bed of caressing mint leaves.

"Well, are you ready for an afternoon of routine behavior?" she said, snapping me back to reality.

Oh, but it wasn't so bad at the office, not with the wonderful, rich nourishment I had for lunch generating me. At quitting time I walked out near Alisa, fresh with the relief of a working day thrown off like a scratchy sweater. But she seemed distant now. When we neared the street she suddenly smiled broadly. I perked up and opened my mouth to speak when an English sports car in mint condition roared up and stopped. The right door fell open.

"Hi, honey!" said Alisa, getting in.

I stood with dropped jaw as the MG sped away.

"Hi!" I heard behind me. I didn't turn around. Who would say hi to me? "Those MG's, heck!" I thought. "Always breaking down . . . always have to be tuned. . ."

Peck peck! Something was tapping me on the shoulder. I turned, recognizing the face.

"Oh! You're uh, uh, you're . . ."

"Janice!" she said.

"Oh, yeah! Well! Hm!"

She smiled, nodding her head. I nodded mine back. We stood there nodding heads like a couple of birds.

Janice was one of the more mature women in the office. She

spoke rarely, but when she did it was always something pleasant. She had simple, straight brown hair and a nice face on which one could detect traces of worry around the eyes and mouth. We started walking together instinctively.

"I don't mean to pry," she began, "but I couldn't help but notice a copy of *Sonnets to Orpheus* on your desk."

"Oh yeah. Rilke."

She warmed immediately.

"Oh! Any friend of Rilke's a friend of mine!"

"Yeah? I uh, hadn't even started it yet . . ."

"You know how he wrote that book?"

"No. How?"

Her face grew somber.

"He climbed up an old deserted tower in Germany and sat at an ancient desk . . . There he stayed for a week, eating nothing, writing the *Sonnets to Orpheus*!"

"Wow! How'd you know that?" I said, feeling an urge to read the book.

"I know!" she said. "You know what else I know?"

By now we had walked past the bus stop.

"No. What else do you know?"

"I know how every poet died. Sylvia Plath stuck her head in an oven. Shelley went out to sea in a storm. He never came back. Randall Jarrell ran in front of a speeding car, and John Berryman . . ."

Suddenly she stopped walking. I went back to her.

"John Berryman?"

She gestured with her eyes over the side of the bridge we were standing on.

Below was the frozen Mississippi.

"You mean . . ."

"You are now standing on Berryman's Bridge," she announced.

"All right. Enough of this suicide stuff. Want to go get a cup of tea?" I suggested. "Or do you have to get home to your old man?"

"I'm divorced," said Janice."

The mist of Ceylon tea rose to Janice's chin, crawled up her face and was seemingly absorbed into her hair. Her eyes were very pale.

"When my husband left me I lost the kids, I lost the house . . ."

"Where did you live?"

"Edina."

"An now?"

"An apartment in South Minneapolis."

"Quite a change."

"At first I was shattered . . . still am . . . but, I went to a poetry reading one night . . . there were friendly people there . . ."

"Hm!" I said. That had not been my experience.

"The poetry helped me," she said. "It kept me sane."

"HM!" I said. That had *definitely* not been my experience.

"You and I like poetry for different reasons," I said. "For you it takes you closer to life. For me it . . . well, I don't know."

"Tell me!" she said, placing her hand on mine.

"A-hey you two!" Suddenly our table had a third party.

"Diane!" I said. (She sat at the desk behind mine.)

"Well, it's nice to see the *front* of you for a change!" she said. Diane was drinking whiskey.

I could tell Janice was taken aback at being "caught" with me after working hours. I was powerless to stop her as she politely excused herself and left, leaving me alone with Diane.

"What's that tea stuff?" she said. "How about some skee?" ("Skee" as in *Whiskey*.)

"Sure, baby!" I said. But she had already ordered me a shot. A waitress set it down in front of me. The more of that hot amber liquid I sipped the better Diane looked. I began to loosen up. She talked about people in the office.

"Can you believe that Sally?" she said. "What a dragon! What a witch!"

"Well, you know, she can't help it," I said, trying to be compassionate. "Some people are just like that."

"Well why do they have to make the rest of us suffer just because they've got bees up their butts?"

"Misery loves company?" I tried.

"You know, I think Wanda's a lesbian," said Diane, finishing her skee.

"What gives you that impression?"

On and on we gossiped. Diane confided that Jody Trigg, a quiet, shy secretary "had a crush on me." Because of that statement my behavior toward Jody would no doubt be forever stilted.

"Next skee on me!" I rhymed, ordering two more.

By the middle of my third shot I was aching with desire for Diane. She had rested her bare foot on my shoe. I could feel her toes drumming.

As it turned out, Diane threw up on the bslkr

Boy am I typing fast now. Perhaps you noticed the typo. I was sitting here in the office typing, which is not unusual, except for the fact that it is Saturday night. I let myself in with my key. I own a broken down manual at home which would just not do for this, you see . . . and who should pop in, but Jody Trigg? Thus the typo was produced.

"What are you doing here?" she asked, a look of bewilderment on her face.

"Oh, just some personal typing."

"I forgot my gloves here last night," said Jody.

"Oh."

She stood there, grinning, leaning on the door.

"Almost finished?" she asked.

"Yeah! Just a few more lines . . ."

"Oh." She kept standing there, smiling.

"You doing anything now?" my mouth said.

"No."

"Oh. Well uh, why don't you go get your gloves, and . . ."

"And . . ."

"And!"

"Okay!" she said and disappeared.

Her office is way down the hall. I figure I've got just a few seconds left. Jody is the shy type. So am I, I suppose. Trouble is, how do two shy people find each other when they're both too busy being shy?

Bye-

Hi. Jody and I walked aimlessly up and down the icy streets, frenzied party goers flowing by us like wind, their voices whirling and running together. Torrents of people ran down sidewalks. Jody and I entered the flows like cars on a freeway, adjusting our accelerations accordingly.

"Can you tell by looking at me I'm depressed?" asked Jody.

"Well like I always say, depression can be either quicksand or a trampoline."

"It's quicksand," said Jody, "and only my fingers are showing."

"Strangers in the night, exchanging glances . . ." sang a potbellied man leaving a bar.

"Do you ever feel you're going insane?" asked Jody.

"All the time. Let me ask you something. Do you feel like you're losing it? I mean like you're losing control?"

Jody nodded in agreement.

"I know what you're going through," I said.

"Do you ever get suicidal?" asked Jody.

"Oh yeah. I even tried it once."

"Really?"

"Yes."

"How?"

"Barbituates and whiskey."

"What stopped you?"

"Well it's really kind of funny. It was mosquitoes. I was in the woods at the time, and when I started popping pills, I was suddenly attacked by a cloud of mosquitoes. They chased me out of the woods."

"I wonder who notified them?"

"I don't know, but I'll tell you this. When I was walking to the woods, taking those final steps, I uh, well I hate to use the word 'soul,' but, I swear I heard my soul crying."

"Really?"

I suggested to Jody that we go over to her place. Jody lived in an apartment in an old house. A spooky house. The stairway especially was spooky, intricately carved wood, winding and creaking with a musty odor. Try as I might, I couldn't get her off the subject of depression. She poured me a glass of warm port wine and placed a record on her stereo. The singer's voice was low and mournful. It made me feel uneasy. I noticed that her bathroom didn't have a door, but a shower curtain draped across the entrance.

"Do you think suicide is wrong?" asked Jody.

"No, I don't think it's wrong *per se* . . ."

"Did you really try to kill yourself?"

"Yes, Jody, you are obsessed with this depression thing! You're letting it fester. You know I look back on the time I tried to die, and I can't for the life of me remember *why*. It all seems so absurd, now. If you just ride this thing out, you'll laugh at it later, though it seems impossible now."

"I know I know I know consciously, but deep down I can't shake it . . ."

"What?"

"Two months ago I had an abortion, and it felt like my whole self came out with that fetus."

"Well, you know, I caused an abortion once."

"I keep getting haunted visions of that kid calling out to me from the void . . ."

"Jody, do you mind my asking, what religion are you?"

"Catholic."

"So you think you've committed an unpardonable murder?"

"The guilt is so deeply planted . . . there's other things too . . . my father . . . a horrible alcoholic . . . he said . . . and did . . . things that scared me very much. You don't know how horrible, how very horrible alcoholism is till you witness it first hand."

I felt an urge to change the subject.

"Yeah, well, it's getting late. I'd better be going."

"You can't stay?"

"Well, I *could* stay . . ." an involuntary smile spread across my face.

"No . . . no . . . don't. I don't think I could stand another sexual relationship."

I was going to say, "Oh, we don't have to have sex. I could stay to just be with you . . . so you wouldn't be alone to torture your mind . . ."

But I didn't.

Jody wasn't at work the following Monday, Tuesday or Wednesday. She hadn't called in sick. I recalled our conversation and became worried. Her landlord refused to open her apartment door, though the bedroom light was on three days and nights. Finally we called the police.

I came into work early Thursday morning and saw my supervisor crying. I knew immediately why. Everyone was called to a conference room where it was announced formally. Rhonda Krantz burst out crying. I went for a walk by the river.

I kept seeing Jody's face, her turned-up nose, her smile, the way she swished her hips when she walked down the hall. Jody lived alone. Her apartment had no phone. Would she have tried to call someone if it had? Or was there a moment of terror, when she realized she had played the game too far and there was no way to call out . . . oh quiet!

An hour later I walked back to the office. Diane was typing furiously. Rhonda stared at me, pouting. Alisa handed me a brown envelope. Her eyes were red. Written on the envelope was "If you wish to contribute for flowers or a memorial for Jody's funeral." I searched my pockets.

"How can we work today?" I said to the girls in the office.

Janice walked over and put her hand on my shoulder. She spoke very softly — "There is a poem about a family farm. One of the children is killed in a tractor accident. But the chores go on. The father gathers hay, the mother collects eggs. It doesn't mean they didn't suffer . . ."

An anxiety drew me to Jody's desk. Perhaps it was her presence which remained. Unanswered notes lay there like abandoned kids — "Jody, _____called," "Jody, _____ stopped by . . ." I resisted an urge to crumble them up. One side of her coffee cup displayed a gold-colored chrysalis. On the other side was a swallowtail butterfly. A plastic bottle of hand cream had been barely used. "Kneading Lotion" was printed in red letters on the label. Jody's typewriter seemed alone and muffled, sheathed by a black plastic cover. I grabbed the machine quickly and brought it to my desk. In urgency I lifted off the cover and saw a thousand messages in the keys. I typed a silent message with the power button off: "Now I will care for you."

My fingertips are warm upon the keys.

JOHN SOLENSTEN: teaches literature and writing courses at Concordia College in St. Paul. Before returning to college teaching at Concordia in 1977 he was a public information writer for IDS in Minneapolis and his stories generally have Minneapolis settings. He has published poems in a number of Midwestern publications, including the 1979 Midwest Poets edition of the Carlton MISCELLANY. His first play, WATONWAN, was produced by Centre Stage in Minneapolis in January of 1978. He has recently completed THE TOWER AND THE SHADOW, a collection of short stories with the IDS Tower as both central setting and primary character.

"Very often I get short story ideas from a kind of roller-skate reading of newspapers — a habit I developed at IDS. 'Minnehaha' is really a fictionalized news event, but the news — that human selfness is both horrifying and admirable — is old news, of course."

John Solensten

MINNEHAHA

Kneeling there over the kitten, he felt the thick plaster alcoving of his basement apartment pressing down over the edges of his shoulders — pressing him down so he couldn't breathe — and he felt a quick chill of terror tremor up through the back of his neck and out into his ears. But in the new rays of the morning sun slanting through the half windows above him, the kitten teased and cuffed and clawed the tufts of the green shag rug, mewing and rolling on its back with the tireless joy of a kitten. Sliding his elbows out on the rug, he lowered his face to the kitten's little world of play. "You are something," he whispered to the furred motion near his face. "You are sweet and dumb like a fuzzy worm in the grass."

The kitten mewed and then, caught by one of the threads in the shag, engaged itself in a desperate battle to escape, flip-flopping on its back to gnaw at the thread trap and spinning its body over to box in blurring jabs with the air. Then, escaping suddenly, it ran around in a ragged circle, its tail up stiff like an antenna, before it padded with leonine smoothness toward his face resting on its right temple in the carpet.

"Did you know your tail has three times as many muscles in it as my finger!" he exclaimed softly, stroking its white ear with the little finger of his left arm and blowing on its whiskers. It blinked. "Kitty can't go to my house because I'm not getting any. And you can't play with my kids because she won't let them come to this dirty place. And you can't go over there because it's *a*septic. No kitty fur allowed."

He was lifting the kitten up, reaching over it with his fingers, the thumb pressing on the fragile bones in its back. "And one more thing," he said, "— you are not supposed to be here. Pets are creatures non grata here. You'll have to learn to be very quiet like I am. Silence is staying alive."

It was not a friendly knocking at the door: it was precise and measured like a gavel falling in a court chamber. "Crap, crap, crap!" he snarled, pitching the kitten gently under the unmade day bed and lugging the tank top over his deep belly as he smoothed the fringes of his hair around the baldness. Standing before the door he saw himself in the full length mirror. He was paunchy and white, his mouth too small and tight, his legs thin and tapered like blue-white furniture legs. The steady modulations of knocking continued. He twisted the door knob and swung the mirror image of himself away.

They were so tall, so brown and green and tall standing there — Ruth, his wife until two days ago and her mother. Both wore green suits and flesh-colored blouses. Both held their heavy brown purses under the left arm, tucked up high under the armpits.

"Are you being cute, David?" Ruth asked, opening her purse and digging deeply through tubes and pens. The lipstick on her mouth was bright red and wide and the teeth were very white inside as he looked at her.

"What?"

"Are you playing tic-tac-toe with your ex?" her mother asked. "Ruth and I have been standing here an hour."

"Have you got someone in there?" Ruth asked. He couldn't bear to look at all of her anymore. It was too much. By looking at her mother, whom he hated totally, or by looking only at Ruth's eyes or her mouth or her hands he could stand it. Otherwise it was more than he could take and thinking about losing her made him feel like he was blowing up inside. While he was thinking about it they were past him and into the room.

"Whew!" They said it almost simultaneously. Ruth's right arm, waving, was tapered beautifully, the downy hair Titianesque in the light. The bone opening for his genitals began to hurt, but he could not feel that his genitals were there at all.

"Well?" he asked, feeling sick.

"Father is bringing your things up, but he doesn't want to see you." There was a noise of a cardboard box being dumped on the carpet outside and then hangers clacked as the clothes slid down and the footsteps went away. Then the silence was like a heavy black wing slowly moving between them. Her mother went out and he could hear her straightening the hangers.

"Don't you dare, mother!" she called over her shoulder, pursing the right side of her mouth to help the sound go around the corner. The straightening noise stopped and he could hear her mother throw the clothes down and walk down the hallway.

"Not much!" he said it to her right eye which sometimes, he recalled, twitched when she was tired.

"You didn't have or make much, Davey."

"I guess not," he replied. She was so tall to him that sometimes he wished his shoulders were wider and not so tapered so that when she pressed her voice down on him he could shrug his shoulders and resist. He always felt that everything could fit over him easily — a rope, a cage, a box — a winter cave for rosebushes, if he was a rosebush.

Out of the silence she said, "I have to go back to work."

"You could have brought it tonight. It will be kind of bad tonight."

"The University," she replied. "I've got class tonight. I'll be done in August. I get done with things I have to."

"Sure, you get done with things and over things."

"Don't start that with me, Davey. This is what you wanted you know." She was jubilant, really very jubilant. When she wanted to emphasize something she blinked both eyes at him. When she did, he felt her driving her nose into him, penetrating him. He could only stand one thing at a time, especially the nose.

"That's not true."

"True? True? You lied about having a job for three whole months. I could not forgive you for that and for letting me fix sandwiches and tell people about your job while you were in the public library goofing off. And I cleaned up your shit, Davey, while you were exploding on the can in the morning because you were stewing about a job interview. You hung us all up — two children and my parents and me. I hope someone will want me after you. It's a bad start but now I'm getting another chance."

Looking at her hair — reddish gold in the morning sun — he wanted to wind it around her throat so she would stop, but it was beautiful and his forearms felt thin and delicate. He fluttered his arms like a bird, but he didn't say anything.

"Dear God, stop that, will you?" She was crying and submerged in her kleenex so he couldn't see her face but only her hair. As he raised his hand to touch it, she suddenly turned her face on him, contorted and flushed with anger. The voice became teeth and the teeth pain.

"It is sickening to see you here, Davey, and to have anyone ever connect us and to smell this place and to have to allow those beautiful children to see you on Sunday. Oh, but I'm going to see it done right. They won't come here. You meet them at the theatre. You don't call. You have no interest in my car or anything else my father gave us. That is why you got off easy."

"Easy?" he interjected. In the brief silence that followed his question the kitten mewed a long whiney mew.

"That's it!" she cried. "That's it, isn't it — a kitty-cat. Does it believe in you? Can you handle all that responsibility? Can you provide for the pussy-cat in the manner to which it is accustomed? Will you clean up its little crap? Most of all, will you clean up its crap?"

"Davey lost to Goliath," he mumbled.

Then she was gone, closing the door and slamming his image in the mirror back in front of him — the plaid walking shorts, the belly, the sloping shoulders, the face narrow, the chin small.

"Appalachia!" he cried to the mirror. "I came from a long line of sparrow faces in Appalachia to dwell among these big-faced Nordics." He opened the door and stepped out into the hall. The old sport coats and cords were there, twisted from the hangers, and the boxful of things. The box cover was inter-folded neatly and tightly, but he pulled up the center to look in. There were red, white and blue envelopes addressed to her from APO 25 in Japan and among them the black oblong gold trimmed box with the Bronze Star in it. He closed the cover and slid the cardboard box into the apartment.

Then, coming outside again and bending down to get the clothes, he had the terror. She was there beyond the front door talking to the manager. He could not bear to look at any part of her again and she was too far away to look at one part of her, so he turned away. He threw the clothes on the rug inside the apartment and took the kitten with him out the back entrance, folding it into the opening of his shirt as he whistled blindly down the alley.

Standing there on the stone bridge at the top of the falls he felt taller and fuller. The green, frothing current below the bridge tugged at the safety wire strung upstream from the bridge and surged in deep, hydromuscular eddies. He could feel a humming, galvanic buzz through his blue canvas shoes.

The kitten nestled in his arms as he leaped over the torrents of water churning on the downstream side of the bridge to the head of the falls. Sometimes the kitten scratched his arms as he held it and when he looked down he was surprised to see red scratch marks crossing the blue veins. On a little island near the bridge there was a small, bronze statue of Hiawatha and Minnehaha. Hiawatha was carrying her, one hand high on her waist, the other over her left thigh, pulling her up to his chest. Her moccasins dangled and her arm was over his shoulder. They were both smiling. Together they looked strong — invincible on the statue rock.

"Do you know what Minnehaha means?" a voice at his ear asked. It was the voice of a retired schoolteacher. He knew it.

"Not really," he replied.

"Laughing Water. Laughing Water" the voice said very authoritatively. "It's all in Longfellow."

"That man is holding a kitty!" shouted a little girl. "But not in Shortfellow," he mumbled. The chocolate stains from the Cheerio she was licking spread down her pink sundress as he turned to look at her. As she pointed at him the thin chocolate shell of the Cheerio split and fell on the grass. She screamed at him.

He touched the kitten soothingly, folding it over one arm and petting its mewing head. He wanted to swim, to wash, to wade — to do something. He liked water. It had an isolation of its own: it could be a very private element. Upstream he could see children sitting in the shallows laughing and poking their toes up to examine them in the sun. They were together except for a black boy who hooked his chin over a flexing tree limb and rode there in the water staring at him.

Then she was there in the brown dress, thrashing about, then standing wide-legged among the children, moving like a crazed and wounded animal. She swung her thin shoulders in a writhing dance motion crying, "Ohah, ohah, ohaaaaa" in an old women's voice. Then she sat down in the water and as she kicked her feet with frenetic childlike petulance she began to float down from the children frozen in silence and immobility above her.

She floated toward him and he couldn't move. As her hand hung on the safety wire he reached toward her but it was too far.

"You! You!" she screamed. "Nobody and nothing!" she screamed. He looked only at the eye, angry and frightened and gray-green, dilating so widely he recoiled from its vortex as if he might drown there.

Then, crying little bleeps to himself as he felt the kitten cry in pain with his steps, he ran to the side of the falls, stumbling over the brush and scratching his face. As he dropped to the little limestone shelf next to the falls she came over in a stiff, brown boney cartwheel — the purse spinning off, the shoes dropping, the dress folding into her crotch, then flapping to cover her face, the hair witch-strung and gray, the mouth bloody, the teeth biting at the water too.

The thump of the heel of hand at his back. The dark little man was shouting, shouting, "You swim? You swim?"

Yes, yes, he swam. Why?

"Get her in the pool. See!" He was being jostled to the edge. Below him there was a brown rag floating in the water.

"My kitten! My kitten!" He was reaching out with eeking little cries inside his throat as he did it. No one was taking it. No one took it.

"Take her! Take her!" Now he heard himself screaming. Then, "Please, please, please." He held the kitten out into the space, but no one took it.

"She's gone! Dear God, she's gone!" someone shouted. He could see the brown rag drifting toward the river and he felt the people turn away from him and follow the drift of it down the swift current through the ravine to the Mississippi.

For a long, long time he stood there. Then he found that he was sitting on a wooden bench in the pavillion. Under the pavillion he felt the heavy presence of plaster and timbers above him. The kitten was very still.

He knew, when he heard voices again, that they were bringing her back. It was a wet lump in a picnic blanket. They brought her so close to him he thought one hand would claw him with its bloody fingernails. He bent down, waiting for stones or words on his head, but no one stopped. The crowd receded in his ears as if they were under water or passing to another place. There was a great flutter of blankets and a closing of picnic baskets and choruses of complaining children.

Once, close by, two people paused. "It's horrible, isn't it?"

one said. "It is, it is, but it's got to be cooler tomorrow," the other one said, adding quietly, "Shitty picnic! Really, now, two weeks of baking heat."

Then a voice, even closer by and a whirring of television cameras. "We're the Action TV crew," the blonde young man said.

"Go to hell!" he cried. He was shaking, but his voice was level and steady. "All of you can go to hell — with all of us! You and us can go!"

"Come on, now," the boy voice coaxed. "You're the one."

He walked away. He could hear someone talking into a microphone like he was reading something.

"You'll see yourself on TV tonight at 6:00," the boy voice said. "Channel 7 at 6:00!"

Then another older, deeper voice touched him, bringing him up short. He saw the Minneapolis Police Department badge — almost walked into it — as the officer held it out toward him.

"Me, you have to talk to," the officer said. "Are you the person they say could have attempted a rescue here?"

"No one," he said resignedly, "would hold my kitten. It would have been lost."

"A kitten?"

"I begged and begged." He hated his begging then.

"That won't do it, of course."

He looked up at the right lens of the policeman's glasses. The red beacon of the ambulance pulsed on it. His own heart beat thickly in his throat.

"Your name and address?" The policeman was writing in a small notebook. His fingers were thick and strong.

"David Just, 1612 Mason, Apartment 3-B, the low rent district."

"Not funny here."

"Not for anyone."

"You refused to attempt a rescue?"

"Not really."

"You can swim?"

"Yes, but not really just the same. I didn't really refuse."

"O.K. I'll have to talk to you later. Stay around, please. There will be newspaper people in a minute."

He could feel the policeman's eyes looking at him but he kept his eyes on the lens. He heard a siren and the ambulance beacon stopped pulsing in the lens and the door closed with a heavy thump like something was being put away.

"Some kitty — some goddamed cat," the policeman said, closing his notebook with a quick flap!

"I asked and asked. Why me?"

"Sure. There'll be no charges so you can sleep all right."

He began to walk away from the policeman, holding the kitten's skull gently in his fingers. The head was warm and the teeth turned to bite at his fingers. On the crest of a little hill he turned to look back at the falls. The policeman was watching him, but new visitors were parking and the motion of people began to flow quickly again. The kitten scratched and mewed. Comforting it, looking into its clear green eyes, he felt very calm and strong. Then he began the walk back with short, hard steps like someone beginning a climb.

PEGGY HARDING LOVE: born in Chicago, August 20, 1920, moved with her family to Minneapolis in 1923. She graduated from the University of Minnesota High School in 1936, and received a B.A. degree from Swarthmore College in 1940. During 1940 to 1942 she studied with Joseph Warren Beach and Robert Penn Warren at the University of Minnesota. From 1942 to 1947 she and her husband, John Love, worked on pacifist cooperative farms in New Jesey and Pennsylvania. They returned to Minneapolis in 1948 and ten years later moved to northern Minnesota. She died in 1976.

Most of her stories were published in mass circulation and literary periodicals. "The Jersey Heifer" was included in the O'Henry Prize Stories for 1951. She also did editorial work and collaborated with other authors principally on children's books about animals. She loved to take contemplative walks in the woods observing all its creatures, especially birds.

Peggy Harding Love

THE JERSEY HEIFER

In October the cows went apple-crazy. The sweet, sun-warmed apple smell drifted down from the orchard, tempting them unbearably; and by afternoon one or the other — the heifer usually, she was the mischief-maker — would have nudged down a rail from the old wooden fence around the pasture. Once, only once, young Phoebe Matthews looked out the kitchen window and caught them in the act, but the picture stayed forever in her mind, an image of transcendent innocence and freedom. Leaping negligently, her hoofs tucked up delicately, the Jersey heifer went over the lower rails like a deer, and close behind, clumsy but with drooling haste, Daisy, the three-year-old Guernsey, stepped clumsily out, one stiff leg at a time, banging her plump udder with shocking heedlessness against the bar.

They trotted eagerly along the quiet dirt lane, turning their wary heads from side to side; and later, near milking time, Phoebe and Joe, her husband, had come upon them drunk with bliss in the long grass of the orchard. Each time they were discovered there, the cows stood perfectly still, their red and tawny coats bright against the blue sky, their soft wide eyes looking out innocently among the apple branches. Long threads of saliva trailed from their velvety muzzles and glistened in the late sunlight, and under their hoofs the crushed and rotting apples gave off a heady fragrance.

Always at the sight of them there Phoebe's heart leaped in delight. She hated to drive them out; but Joe, slapping lightly at their smooth, hard flanks, would chivvy them back to the pasture with a slow-moving, gentle stubbornness that matched their own. "Apples cut down Daisy's milk," he told Phoebe firmly. "I've got to wire that fence," but he lingered beside her, smiling to see the tipsy heifer prance off down the pasture.

"Let them go," Phoebe pleaded, begging as earnestly as for herself, "let them have a little freedom. I'll bring them back when they get out." "Well," Joe said, musing, "well," and he looked off over the fields that were so newly theirs. "The apples will be picked pretty soon now anyway," he said, and running his thumb lightly down Phoebe's arm, he headed back to where he had left the horses hitched to the spring-tooth harrow.

By the end of October they had picked all the apples on the trees and stored them in barrels in the cellar. They were Baldwins, small, tart and juicy, the best-flavored apples anywhere, Joe insisted; and though the trees were old and shamefully neglected, though curculio and scab had made their inroads and no one bought Baldwins any more, still Joe and Phoebe knelt carefully in the long grass, collecting even the windfalls and hauling them up the wagon ramp into the upper story of the old bank barn for cider-making.

They were pressing cider the afternoon the county agent stopped by for his first visit, and the first thing he told them was that the orchard should be cut down. Those old trees would never show a profit, he said, no matter how they were pruned and sprayed. Joe walked around the farm with him with a pocket edition of Thoreau sticking out of his hip pocket — he liked to read it while he was resting the horses or waiting for the cider to drain. Pax, their springer spaniel, raced ahead while Phoebe, trailing behind, listened uneasily to the agent's suggestions. The orchard should go, the horses should be replaced by a tractor and modern equipment, new fences should be built, the chickens not allowed to run; and when Phoebe said in alarm, "But we like horses!" the agent smiled like a wise, indulgent uncle.

"You know, I'm always glad to see city folks coming back to the farm," he said. "A fine young couple like you, not afraid of hard work, and I can see you've done a lot here already, why, there's no reason at all why you shouldn't have a good, solid return on your investment. But you've got to remember, first and last, farming is a business."

"We figured farming was a way of life," Joe said. For a long moment they all were silent, and Phoebe, kneeling suddenly, gave Pax a fierce, quiet hug. After a minute Joe said: "I guess you better not put us down as farmers. We're grateful for your advice and we sure need a lot of it, but maybe we're aiming at two different things. We don't want a business, or an investment either. We just want to live right and do right by our land and animals." Joe's smile was apologetic and a little troubled, but his voice was earnest. "Put us down as shiftless no-accounts or crazy damn fools," he said, "but I guess we'd rather live peaceful than make money."

"No, son, I'll put you down as two romantic dreamers and come around again next spring." The agent got in his car and was starting out the dirt lane when he leaned out the window again, grinning like a paternal old tomcat and pointing to where the pasture fence rail was down again. "Your cows are out," he called. "Who's boss around here, you or bossy?" and, laughing slyly, he jounced away in his dusty sedan.

For a little while Phoebe and Joe stood where he left them, quiet and abstracted in the pale, slanting sunlight. Phoebe's hands were cold and sticky from the apple juice, and she held them up in the sun to warm them. At last she said, "I'd better get the cows." The orchard was stripped now, completely appleless, so she wouldn't find them there; but the scent of apples still hung everywhere in the air, filling the cows with yearning, and searching restlessly for fulfillment they still broke out of the pasture. Joe looked at Phoebe as if he hadn't heard her. "What if he's right?" he said broodingly. "Maybe it's all an impossible dream." But when Phoebe protested, "No, he's wrong! We've never been so happy," Joe smiled and touched her reassuringly, because of course it was true.

In a minute Joe went back to the barn to finish pressing the last batch of cider, and Phoebe started down the lane. "Co' ba, co' ba," she sang out dreamily, taking comfort from the sound of her voice in the quiet air. It was a call for cows she had read in a book, but of course they never came. Back in the barn she heard Joe snort with laughter, and off behind the orchard great rustlings and upheavals in the underbrush signaled that Pax was on his way. "No, not you, foolish," she cried before he even got there, but he bounded out through the sumac beside the road, grinning and panting, with dirt from his diggings all over his face and tongue and his long, silky ears matted with burrs. She was going to let him greet her before she sent him back, but after a token snuffle at her legs he ignored her utterly. He zigzagged wildly across the lane, nose in the dust, and in a minute he was off again, hot after a recent rabbit.

Phoebe walked on past the fenced-in vegetable garden, nipped now by frost but still green with broccoli and parsley, still orderly and serene; past the cropped-down empty pasture that sloped gently to the stream. The woods beyond flamed with color in the horizontal sunlight, and in the pasture the fierce old pin oak stood all alone in crimson splendor among the hummocks and the browning grass. Up the lane two sets of hoofprints lay guilelessly in the dust — one set large and clumsy, moving ponderously after the smaller, dancing crescents that led the way and among them, steaming faintly in the cooling air, three insolent small cowflops on the rutted road. "They can't have been out long," Phoebe said out loud to herself. "That minx, that little devil," and, smiling ruefully, looking all around, she walked on after them.

Ever since they moved to the farm eight months ago she had started talking to herself. She wasn't lonely — even when Joe was working off in the fields she had the animals for company; but she talked to them the way she talked to herself, loving, reassuring and scolding in calm, sensible words that vanquished any wayward feelings of uncertainty, any possible tremor of fear. Yet she wondered sometimes — she wondered now, with an unreasoning, anxious moment of panic as she walked down the lane — why she should ever be uncertain and afraid. After the lost, dismal years when she had followed Joe from one Army camp to another, the farm seemed like a paradise. Joe had been hopelessly miserable in the Army, putting in his whole three years as cook's helper in vast base kitchens in the South. With dogged non-cooperation he stayed a p.f.c. throughout the war, unable to adjust to necessary evils and ridden by a constant sense of guilt, of being party to an infinite wrong.

Phoebe suffered with him in nearby furnished rooms, clerking in five-and-tens or typing in sweltering, alien offices. On weekends they rushed together in joy and despair, and lying in some mildewed, roach-infested haven they talked with helpless longing of the North, of the small New England college where they had met, of the good life they must find away from all this. It seemed to them that love and innocence had been destroyed everywhere, and that all the values of the world they knew had become false and unreal. Without their knowing quite how it happened, the good life of their desperate Sunday longings gradually came to mean a small farm of their own, in a climate with decent, changing seasons, where they could raise their own food, earn just what they needed and no more and live in honesty and freedom. Only there, starting a new life from scratch, did goodness and integrity seem possible. It didn't matter that they were both city-bred: the last few months before Joe got his discharge they pored in fierce absorption over the Strout farm real estate catalogues, and Phoebe took out every book in the public library on vegetable crops, dairy management and poultry-raising for profit.

They bought the farm on a GI loan — ninety rolling north New Jersey acres, a quarter-mile back from the highway and no improvements. There were plenty of reasons why it was cheap — the sagging clapboard house, the long dirt lane that drifted shut in winter and ran with mud in spring, the hand pump at the sink and the dirt floor in the stable; but Joe and Phoebe looked at the mulberry tree and the maples, the lush curves of the hayfields, the broad shallow stream in the pasture, the thirty acres of well-grown woods so silent you could hear the mushrooms growing. They bought it in November and moved in in February. They had a mortgage Joe felt they could handle and enough money saved up to buy some stock and tide them over the first year.

For Joe the core of the farm was the fields and topsoil and green crops making their intricate, purposeful growth — he had been going to teach botany once; but from the beginning it was the animals Phoebe loved most of all. She saw the whole farm as a combination Eden and Noah's Ark, where she and Joe and Pax and the cows and horses could live together as joint tenants on equal terms in innocence and mutual respect. In her heart she could not believe that God had made her truly different from the animals she loved, born in sin with a heritage of guilt; and she would gladly have traded all her human knowledge and foresight for Pax's trustfulness or the Jersey heifer's wild, free spirit. "There's a serpent in your garden," Joe had teased her one day in May, holding up a wriggling five-foot black snake he had found behind the barn, but Phoebe's faith had not been shaken. She knew black snakes were harmless and ate lots of rats and mice. "Or chickens or eggs," Joe added dubiously; but he had built a fine tight henhouse, and he let the snake writhe peacefully away.

Up by the jog in the road Phoebe found the cows. They were off on the edge of the woods, nosing around in the faded goldenrod and wild asters under two ancient, half-dead crab apple trees. There was nothing there but a few dried-up, worm-hollowed crab apples, and the cows seemed apathetic, sunk in depression. "Don't look at me like that," Phoebe said, "it isn't my fault." The Jersey stared at her with great accusing eyes, her long fringed eyelashes sticking out beneath the gentle curve of her pale, sharp horns. She held her head low, petulantly, the warm black markings on the dainty face shading away to the velvety umbers of her chest and back, her broad saucy nose thrust out and her nostrils working slowly. When Phoebe touched her muzzle, she tossed her head and leaped sharply back.

"All right, if that's the way you feel," Phoebe said. "Come on, Daisy, we'll let her sulk." Phoebe put her arm across Daisy's broad russet-patched rump, and obediently Daisy lumbered back to the dusty road. She plodded slowly back toward the farm, now and then stopping in her tracks and turning her shy, hornless forehead to look around at Phoebe. When Phoebe clapped her on the hip she went on amiably, switching her tail rhythmically behind her in the late chill air.

Before they had gone far, Phoebe heard the Jersey scrambling back onto the road and the quick, light thud of her hoofs coming after them. Phoebe smiled to herself and kept on, purposely not looking back; but in a moment she became aware of a strange, unnerving silence. The quiet struck her suddenly as deeply suspicious, even terrifying, and for a long, disoriented instant she felt herself walking down an endless alien road surrounded by unimaginable hidden dangers. She stopped, whirled quickly and found the heifer so close behind her that her horns could not have been an inch away from the seat of her jeans. "What are you doing?" Phoebe cried sharply. "Go on, you get in front of me." But the Jersey stood her ground stubbornly, head lowered and eyes rolling with audacity. After a moment Phoebe went on, walking stiff and wary, driving Daisy before her and turning her head every minute to look distrustfully behind. "Cut it out now," she ordered fiercely, stopping, turning and going on uneasily; but all the way back to the barn the Jersey followed a hairbreadth behind, the bracketed horns lowered and dark eyes rolling boldly while her hoofs stepped delicately in perfect silence in the soft dust of the road.

"She threatened me, she threatened me all the way," Phoebe told Joe when she got back. She was laughing, but hurt and outraged just the same, and the strange nightmare feeling had not quite worn off. She had fastened Daisy in her stanchion in the stable below, on the ground floor of the barn, brought her hay and grain, jockeyed the heifer out through the stable door into the pasture and replaced — how many times now? — the fallen fence rail. The sun was nearly gone and she was shivering in a sweater when she went up the steep crude stairs from the stable to the upper story, through the narrow trap door where they threw down the hay. Joe had finished the last batch of cider and was lining up the clear amber jugs beside the door, ready for loading on the Model A tomorrow to take to town. Discarded apples and the pressed-out apple cakes lay in a heap below the haymow, and in the cavernous gloom the autumn smell of apples, sweet and sour, mingled with the summer smell, dusty and sweet, of tender-cut green timothy and clover.

"That heifer thinks she's pretty cute," Joe said, pulling on his leather jacket, getting ready to go. "I think I'll keep Daisy in tonight after milking. Maybe the Jersey won't wander without her." Leaving the wide wagon doors open to the last rays of the sun, they went out of the barn together and up the path to the house. It was time to get the milk pail from the kitchen, time to start the fire for supper. "What are we having?" Joe asked, putting his long arm across Phoebe's shoulders. "What do you think, silly?" Phoebe said wearily, dreamily. "Apple fritters, apple butter, apple pie."

It was late that night, so late it was early morning, that Phoebe woke up suddenly with her heart pounding heavily. She sat up in bed listening tensely and in a moment she heard it, a terrible bawling cry from somewhere outside. "Joe, Joe," she cried, shaking him frantically, "somebody's crying terribly. He struggled up and in the dark bedroom they listened for the sound. At once it came again, a strangling, agonized bawl rising hideous with pain and terror through the cold black night.

"It's the heifer," Joe said, leaping out of bed and searching in the dark for his clothes. "That's not Daisy's voice, it's the heifer, somewhere near the barn." He was pulling on his pants and shoes blindly, fumbling in haste. "Oh, hurry," Phoebe cried, "please hurry," and she scrambled wildly on the cold bare floor trying to find the place where she had dropped her clothes.

"Light the lamp first, Phoebe," Joe said. "No, baby, please, light the lamp first so I can get down there fast. Then you can dress." His voice calmed her a little and in a moment she had found the matches and lit the kerosene lamp that stood on the old pine dresser. Joe's back and arms made great black shadows on the ceiling, flailing into his heavy sweater, and then he picked up the lamp and clattered out, down the narrow boxed-in stairs. Dressing as fast as she could, shivering with cold and fear, she heard Joe downstairs unhooking the big flashlight that hung in the kitchen. His footsteps strode across the kitchen, Pax's claws clicking behind, and both of them rushed out into the night. In a minute she was dressed herself and running for the barn, a lantern in her hand, through the clear, chill blackness.

The bellowing grew closer, more localized, and she headed up the wagon ramp and through the wide door of the barn's upper story. On the other side of the floor Joe's flashlight lay on the rough boards, throwing an arc of light across the shadowy loft. The apple heap was trampled, disarrayed, and the scattered fruit rolled, thumping hollowly, under her stumbling feet. Pax stood stiffly, cautious and curious, and beyond him Joe knelt beside the open trap door, the trap door for forking hay down to the stable. Phoebe saw the opening filled with a grotesque, meaningless shape, and then she saw it was the heifer, hanging head down in the narrow stairwell. All she could see was the slender rump and lower back wedged tight in the aperture, the hind legs caught on the floor boards, kicking feebly, and the long fringed tail thrashing blindly back and forth across the pitiful, terror-soiled buttocks. From below, the gasping cries came up in rhythmic agony, hushed a little but not stopped by Joe's quiet voice talking and talking to her as he crouched at the opening, trying to see how she was caught.

"The apples," Phoebe moaned, flinging herself down beside him, "she smelled the apples and came to find them." But Joe had jumped up, taking the flashlight, and was running out and around to the stable door below. Phoebe ran after, her heart hammering, the lantern swinging insanely from her hand, and Pax eager at her heels. The low, oak-beamed ceiling and thick stone walls of the stable made a warm, cozy cave, and in it the heifer hung crazily upside down, her head and one foreleg wedged at an impossible angle between two treads of the heavy, ladder-like stairs. The wedged foreleg was broken, bone thrusting through the skin, and in her struggles she was slowly strangling herself. In the lantern light her eyes rolled whitely, blindly, and the helpless, rasping cries grew steadily fainter. Beyond the plank partition the horses stomped restlessly in their stalls, and through it all Daisy stood facing the stairwell, shaking her head in her stanchion and shifting ceaselessly in troubled bewilderment on her clean straw bedding. She lowed nervously, swinging her hindquarters from one side to the other while Joe and Phoebe worked desperately with the tortured heifer.

"If we could saw the stair!" Phoebe cried in anguish. "Wouldn't that free her?"

"It's no use," Joe said. "The weight of her fall would snap her neck. Phoebe, you'd better get the gun."

"No, Joe, oh, no! Can't we lift her, can't we try again?" she begged frantically.

Joe's face was drawn and despairing. "It's no use. She's close to six hundred pounds and there's no way to lever her up." The heifer bawled again, a hopeless choking cry, and in the lantern light her free leg kicked futilely in the air. "She's suffering, Phoebe. Get the gun."

Phoebe had turned, blindly, and was rushing out the door when Joe called, "Phoebe, bring a knife too, the sharp knife in the kitchen." For a moment she didn't understand, and then she turned back whimpering in horror. "No, no, we can't. I won't!" Across the shadowy stable Joe's voice rose in furious torment. "Get the knife! You know we can't waste food." He stared at her relentlessly. "We wanted a farm, didn't we? To make our own life, our own food? We've eaten meat all our lives, now we've got to earn it."

Wordlessly Phoebe went out, Joe's voice, soft and exhausted now, calling after her, "Hurry, baby, I don't want to leave her." Running mechanically back to the house, Phoebe kept thinking dully, the gun and the knife, the gun and the knife. The .22 rifle for shooting rats, used only twice even for that, and the long clean knife, the knife for slicing cabbage from the garden, for cutting the fresh-baked bread she was so proud of. With the flashlight she found the gun and the box of cartridges on the parlor mantel, the knife in the kitchen drawer, and not thinking at all, moving in a desperate, mindless agony she ran with them back to the stable. Joe still stood beside the heifer, his arm under the tawny, gasping chest in unavailing support, still comforting the Jersey in a hoarse, gentle voice, while Pax lay quiet in the straw, alert and watching, and Daisy lowed uneasily.

Phoebe laid the knife, the gun and cartridges beside Joe and turned away. She went to Daisy quickly and unfastened her stanchion, turning her toward the door out to the barnyard. With clumsy hands she got the door open and Daisy out, the stiff cow legs hesitating as always before the step over the doorsill. She walked beside her down the slope of the pasture, and they were well away from the stable when Phoebe heard the shot. She stopped then, letting Daisy swing slowly on by herself into the darkness, and for a long moment she stood quiet, shaking in the cold.

She was still standing there when Joe shouted from the stable, "Phoebe, call Pax." Numbly she walked back to the door, and in a fleeting glimpse she saw the heifer hanging limp in the lamplight, a dark stain on the stairs beneath her head, and Joe shoving Pax roughly away from a bucket that stood on the floor. Pax came reluctantly when she called, and holding him wearily, detachedly, without love, she took him with her back to the house.

When Joe came in they sat in the cold kitchen for several minutes before they went to bed. At last Joe said, "I'll try and get Mr. Myers first thing in the morning to help me butcher." He looked at Phoebe sadly in exhaustion. "You know we had to, don't you?" She looked at him hopelessly, nodding slowly. "It was all my fault," she said, "all of it. I wouldn't let you wire the fence. I killed her, I killed our sweet Jersey heifer," and when Joe put his arms around her she finally began to cry. "No, baby, don't say that," Joe said painfully. "It was a crazy accident and no one's fault." But Phoebe shook her head. "I killed her. I laughed when she pushed down the fence rail, I didn't care. I liked her to be saucy. And only when she threatened me," Phoebe sobbed, "only her horns, only her horns made me afraid."

After her tears Phoebe slept, but she woke early, long before milking time. She lay quietly in bed, her body aching, her mind calm but filled with a clear despair. Beside her Joe slept deeply, and for a moment she felt a bitter, shocked wave of resentment that he still slept, escaping so easily; but turning her head stiffly on the pillow, she saw the anxious lines tensing the sleeping eyelids, the jaw clenched tight and grinding faintly in a dream of agonized effort. Looking at his sleeping face, she was washed with shame and wracking love — beside his goodness, his unforced selflessness, she was a monster of childish frailty. Oh, it's easy, it's easy, her mind whispered, to scream and run and cover your eyes, but how much harder to pull the trigger in love, to bleed the dead for the sake of the living. Always, always Joe had had the hard part and she the easy mournings, the easy joys. For a moment in the cold gray light she thought hopefully: It will be different when we have children. Then the hard part will be mine, our life will be fairer; but when she tried to vision it she saw with aching conviction that even then it wouldn't change. After the painful hour of birth all would be as before, and she saw herself a wayward, feckless mother, overemotional, given to reasonless euphorias and panics, unable to provide that calm and certainty that children need.

Just before sunrise Phoebe got up and went down to start the kitchen stove. Pax slept curled tightly in his wicker chair, but when he woke he unwound happily, yawning and stretching down onto the floor, and came up wagging his wavy-haired rear. At first she looked at him with horror, unable to touch him, remembering in a flash his avid interest in the bucket in the stable. He came to her like a friendly, handsome stranger, and even when she knelt, suddenly humble, and stroked his soft liver-and-white coat and burr-brocaded ears, she went on thinking: But how can I ever really know him, know the real meaning of his life?

She went on out for firewood and kindling, and coming back from the woodpile with her arms full she stopped above the pasture, shivering in the still, gray light. Below the pin oak Daisy lay placidly on the drying grass, her head held high in quiet dignity as she chewed faithfully on her cud. The fence rail was still down where the heifer had got out last night, but Daisy ignored it, content by herself in the deserted pasture. Like Pax, she met the morning serene, untouched by tragedy, and for a long time Phoebe stood watching her from another world. Of course they can't care, she thought, watching all alone; it's part of their innocence. She thought of all the innocent ones — the horses and chickens, the black snakes and the rats — and she knew at last that she was hopelessly excluded, forever responsible. The serpent had been there in the garden all the time, a thousand apples joyfully offered and taken. She heard again the county agent's wise, indulgent voice, and already she saw the barbed wire strung along the wooden fence posts, Daisy's next calf born and sent away, flock after flock of chickens in their biennial cycle of birth, production and early, practical death. She turned away, lonely and chilled, but with her armful of firewood she went on resolutely through her own human cycle, up the steps and into the kitchen to kindle once more the comforting fire for breakfast.

JOHN MITCHELL: When President Kennedy was killed, I had been in Sielo, a Kissi village in Liberia, for six months as a Peace Corps teacher. It was just dark when a knock interrupted my lesson planning, and I walked to the door with my kerosene lamp.

A student named Gabriel said, "I am sorry to announce that President Kennedy has been shot." Incredulous, I drove a motorbike into the village to borrow a portable radio from Blackie Howard, the tribal treasurer. I listened to the Voice of America all night, drank a bottle of cognac, wrote letters and cursed.

About a year and a half later the experience happened on which "The Volunteer" is based, and that night I began to write in earnest.

As a writer I am fascinated and bewildered by all the possibilities for saying the same thing twice. For me writing is concentric, a laborious, unlikely effort to reach the point of no return. I rewrote "The Volunteer" about a hundred times over the years because I was afraid I would make an unforgivable mistake.

I was born in Alabama during the Second World War and still regard myself as being "from Alabama" rather than "at" the other places I have lived. I write poems, and am making personal films. Since 1968 I have been teaching at Augsburg College in Minneapolis.

John Mitchell

THE VOLUNTEER

In the silence I opened my eyes to the mosquito net that hung over me like a folded web, as if I had been sleeping in a tent made by a spider. And then, as my sight wandered across the mud walls, I saw two large curious eyes staring at me through the low screened window of my bedroom. I was startled, just as I had been the first morning in my new home when I discovered myself strangely observed.

"What do you want, Sumba?"

Her small hand fell from the open shutter and she replied, "I got sore, teacha," as if that explained everything.

"You know I don't dress sores on Saturday! Why didn't you come yesterday after school?"

How well I knew the silence that followed, a silence that made all questions rhetorical. Yesterday meant nothing to her, nor tomorrow; she knew I would have to do it today because she was there today.

"You go around back and sit down. I'll be out in a minute."

I lifted the net and crawled out of bed. After putting on my pants and sandals, I entered the dark narrow hallway to open the backdoor, and stepped out into the heat. It was almost noon.

"Teacha, you too lazy today! I come here early in the morning, but I can't find you. You sleep too much!"

"Yes, but I stay up late at night and you go to bed early."

"You know *plen-ty* book!" She shook her head like one of the old women, as if she meant to confuse the meaning of what she had said.

"There's plenty book to know, I guess. Sit here on the steps and I'll get the medicine."

After making some antiseptic solution, I tore off a piece of cotton with a pair of long tweezers and dipped it into the cloudy liquid, and began washing the country-sore on the inside of Sumba's foot. Her thin legs were mottled with gray scar tissue from previous sores.

In two years I had dressed thousands of these tropical ulcers, some of the larger ones almost daily for as long as six months. They never seemed to go away. The first year and a half I had liked doing it, because I could see what I had done. But in the last six months dressing sores had become the bane of my existence. Now I could hardly bear the sour swamp smell that came off the sores like an odor from a sick flower.

And I had no patience for the dozen interruptions each day, since the students invariably failed to come during the hours I had scheduled for medical treatment. I was ready to leave, never to return to the misery that warped my fascination for West Africa.

I dug into the whitened flesh and Sumba jerked abruptly. "Ah yah! You can hurt too much, teacha!"

She whistled and rocked as I watched new blood ooze from the rawness inside. I began again, working more gently and giving my full attention to the sore so that she could wipe away her tears.

"Why you can't let me wash my own sore?"

"You know why, Sumba. Look at you now! You wouldn't get it clean once you felt the pain, and the medicine can't do any good unless the sore is clean. Someone who can't feel the pain must do the job, not so?"

Whatever she thought, she mumbled it in the Kissi dialect, and added, "Your eyes are dry too much! You can't feel sorry?"

"Yes, I can feel sorry, but I've still got to clean the sore." Then I took my revenge. "Besides, I stay up too late at night and sleep too much and the darkness dries my eyes so that I can see better the next day. And that's why I clean sores pretty good. Okay?"

She was sufficiently perplexed, at least until her next visit, when she would come with a clever way to trick an explanation out of me. In the meantime she had forgotten the pain, and I felt better.

I dried the edges of the sore and applied some penicillin ointment, then taped on a dressing, but knew that it would soon fall off or be removed once it became dirty and embarrassed her.

"All right, Sumba; I'm finished."

"*Ba'-li-ka'*, teacha," she said, to give me a chance to use the little dialect I knew.

"*ba'-li-ka' chu-nun'-ti*," I replied, and she smiled. "Remember, no sores on Sunday!"

I smiled, and once alone, regarded the sun, furiously reaffirming itself. What a place, I thought; two seasons, dry and wet, sun and rain, with hardly anything between.

I walked to the rain barrel, set up on four posts to catch water from the drain that ran under the eaves of the zinc roof. After sounding the metal to see how much water was left, I turned the faucet and let the sun-warmed water trickle through my fingers. It felt good and would be just right for a shave. But soon I would need to go to the swamp to refill the barrel.

I boiled some water while I dressed, drank a cup of coffee, and left without eating breakfast. I wasn't hungry yet and wanted to get some fresh grapefruit in the Foya market.

I drove fast down the laterite road since there were no people walking along its sides to complain about the dust and the danger of a sudden slide in the gravel, just a few cattle egrets that flushed near the weeds, flapping their white wings into the harmattan sky. But I slowed down as I neared the immigration check-point. The cracked bamboo pole, weighted on one end with a large granite stone, was sticking up in the air like a think alert insect, but there were no soldiers attending the gate, so I went through without the usual palaver and delay.

Not far beyond the gate a small settlement of Lebanese general stores lined the dusty road that passed by the market, which spread out randomly behind the stores on one side of the road. As I parked the jeep, I was curious at the lack of greetings; no small-boys came rushing to salute me, grinning, "Peace Corpse! Peace Corpse!" It had been more than a year since Kennedy had been killed, but the small-boys hardly knew the difference. Already in the city some of them were calling us the Piss Corps.

I went into Rashid's store to buy some matches, cigarettes, and a mantle for my kerosene lamp. The store was not crowded, which seemed to account for the frown on Rashid's face as he leaned over his cash register. Only small-small dollar business today, I thought. Rashid shaved, because he had no beard, but I never knew when, because he always looked as if he had shaved the day before.

As he handed me my change, he grinned and said, "Two men fell in a well."

"When?"

"This morning, in the market."

"Are they still there?"

"Well, I can't say."

I wondered how two men could have fallen into the same well and began to worry that one had fallen on top of the other. As I walked outside and lit a cigarette, I imagined two drunk men in a well, indignant with the sober world peering down from above and offering ludicrous advice. When I turned the corner of Rashid's store and entered the thruway between two unfinished Lebanese stores, I saw the market spectacle swirling under the dry-season sun, and stopped, then moved cautiously to one side.

A drunk soldier, smelling of cane-juice and soiled American khaki, was driving an old man backwards toward me. The old man retreated stubbornly and grumbled repeatedly, "You abuse me, man! Let us settle this the way of olden times!"

But the soldier came on, shouting and thrusting his rifle before him; and each time he shouted he snapped his head upward, causing his oversized helmet to fall down over his eyes, making it necessary for him to snap his head up again to see. The two of them passed and would continue to go on that way until the soldier tired and left the old man with a curse, or struck him with his rifle.

Before me the people murmured in a large circle. I moved closer to one of the buildings which formed part of the circle. As I peered around the back corner, I heard a man in front of me remark, "Some kind of gas in that hole!"

"I believe so," his companion replied. "Myself, I can't go near it!"

The well, about four feet in diameter, was not far from the rear of the mud brick building whose future occupants it would serve. Beyond the well a man groveled in the dust as he begged two soldiers who were threatening him with the butts of their rifles. The man on the ground was bare chested but wore loosely fitting pantaloons. I guessed the soldiers were ordering the man to go down into the well, and I presumed he was a Mandingo because of the garments he wore and because Mandingos dig wells — they have strong medicine to protect themselves from the genie who lives in the ground. The man cried and begged, but refused to move.

Thinking the two men in the well were somehow all right, I wondered how long they had been there waiting for rescue, and two hours came to mind from some comment vaguely overheard in passing. It was entirely possible, and the likelihood made me angry, given the absurd panorama before me.

Impulsively, the handful of local soldiers on the inside rushed the contracting circle, stampeding the people through the marketplace, with scores falling over each other and scattering the stalls and produce. A marvelous insanity prevailed. An orange rolling across the ground tripped the feet of a terrified man, who fell throwing his arms protectively over his head and face. A huge woman, not as quick as the others, threw herself convulsively to the ground and began bawling as she squirmed. Although unnerved myself, I was curious at her behavior, because no matter which way she turned, she managed to keep one eye on the nearest soldier.

As I moved carefully along the outside of the reforming circle for a better perspective, I noticed that Father Parkinson had joined the bystanders at the well and appeared to be seeking information or giving advice. He looked clean in his white robe, and the ebony cross that hung from his neck stood out boldly on his chest.

Nervously, I pushed through the circle of confusion and walked as confidently as I could past the tense soldiers toward the well. Father Parkinson was listening to a Lebanese man explain how he had gone down into the hole but had surfaced immediately because of bad air.

"What happened?" I asked.

"I don't know," the Father answered; "I just got here myself. They say a man and a woman fell in. . . ."

"No, a small-girl fell in and her father went down to help," someone corrected him.

"Excuse me." The Father leaned forward to speak to a short man who had just arrived and was earnestly tying a thick heavy rope around his thighs.

At first I thought he was Lebanese too, but when I saw his wife standing nearby, a small pale-skinned woman hugging a straw hat, I recognized him to be the American missionary from Koindu in Sierra Leone.

I remembered the time he had arrived late as guest speaker for a Sunday service at the nearby Swedish Pentecostal Mission; breathless, he had explained his delay to the congregation because that morning the Koindu butcher had hacked to death one of his wives in a fit of drunken anger. The missionary had delivered his message and then prayed for humanity in these troubled times. After Church, while he sat drinking tea among white friends, he had shaken his head and with grievously downcast eyes had uttered, "A terrible thing, a terrible thing." And then he had arisen briskly and said, "Well, I must be on my way."

"I don't want that rope!" For the second time the missionary told his nervous assistants he didn't want a smaller rope tied to him; he would take it down in his hand.

He called for prayer as I stepped forward to suggest that perhaps he could use the smaller rope to signal when he wanted to come up. As I spoke, I leaned over and peered down into the well and saw two dark forms, motionless, about twenty feet below.

"O, it isn't so deep," I excused my intrusion, and felt foolish about having given advice.

"Let us pray." He addressed the crowd again, lowering his head. When there was sufficient quiet, he spread his hand to incorporate the people and shut his eyes, praying aloud for all to hear.

"All right!" he said after the *amen*, echoed by a few in the crowd.

I watched as he was lowered on the rope and felt uneasy as he neared the bottom. When the rope stopped with his feet dangling above one of the heads, I felt a horror beginning to rise within me, but could not look away.

"Lower!" he shouted breathlessly.

He dropped a few feet and jerked to a stop almost face-to-face with a sitting body, his feet still dangling and turning awkwardly. Frantically he began to tie the small rope around the larger body and I thought, God, he's tying it around his neck, but realized that it probably didn't make any difference.

"Up! . . . Up! . . . Up! Up! Up!" came an unholy crescendo, as if he had suddenly been abandoned by everything sane and true, as if something invisible and dark had grabbed his feet.

The men near me began to pull the ropes like men under judgment, as if pulling the very earth over their heads, and the missionary shot up the hole, and I alone saw the body follow him up as if hanging from him.

The missionary scrambled spastically out of the hole and waved his arms like an alarmed fool, his wildly rolling eyes disjointed in chameleonic madness. His momentum carried him far beyond the well's edge until he stumbled and fell as someone grabbed at him. Around us the marketplace moved as a blur, as if hundreds were dizzy at once and about to faint. Father Parkinson rushed to his side and tried to offer assistance, while others fan-fanned at him, but no one knew what to do except lay their hands upon him.

I had not moved from the well's edge. My cheeks felt cold, as if my face were beginning to freeze, and the strength went out of my body as my eyes glazed over with tears. I just stood there and looked at the body near my feet. The man's eyes were rolled back, drawing the whiteness after them. His ribs broken in their stillness, and his mouth gaped open, all jaw. The world under me felt heavy, clumsy in its balance, and everything seemed to slide a little.

The missionary had calmed himself, and his wife, who had rushed to him after her initial shock and begun fanning with her hat, was asking for a soft drink. "He wants Fanta! He wants something to drink," she implored, but no one moved except to look at someone else, until someone willing to spend the money could be found.

"I almost died!" the missionary assured us. "Another five minutes and I would have been dead . . . I couldn't breathe."

Father Parkinson appeared with a bottle of Schweppes, and the missionary hesitated as he held it up to read the label. He drank a few swallows, wiped his mouth with his wrist as he read the label again, and then tried to brush the dust from his stained clothing. He spoke briefly to a bystander as he looked back at the well, shook his head finally, and left for his appointment at the mission.

A smaller body still lay at the bottom of the well. And the people, having witnessed the missionary's exit — they had swayed like a cluster of bamboo in the wind and a universal moan, interspersed with cracking sounds, had risen — were murmuring suspiciously, as if everything they believed had been confirmed, and no one was safe.

"There a spirit in that hole!"

"For true! Something very bad there!"

"What we need is a hook." Father Parkinson had spoken to me, and I turned to him. "Do you have any kind of hook in your paraphernalia?"

"No, I don't think so." I lied, imagining a broken child on a hook, and focused my attention on the soldiers, who had charged the people again, grabbing three men as they fled to force them to carry the body away from the well's edge. The men twisted and cried in the grip of the soldiers, looking at the body and for a way of escape, but there was no way.

"That man die for goodness sake." I turned to the voice, and when the speaker was sure he had an audience, he continued, "The man take off his robe and say, 'Here, take my bundle and hold it; I will go down to help.'"

"The girl's father?"

"No, he not the girl's father, he from Guinea. He was coming here to sell his coffee. Now he can't go back no more again."

"Ah yah! Plenty palaver be coming to his family when Government find out he cross the border and bring his coffee here for dollar. Guinea people like money-palaver too much!"

The body had been shrouded with palm branches, already attracting flies, and soldiers began to cover the well with planks, one by one, as they were able to find them. Women were wailing, tearing their hair upward in Medusan tangles of despair, beating their bared breasts, and leaning their bodies and pleading with their hands, first towards the corpse and then toward the well.

I stood for a moment, wiping the sweat from my eyes and trying to think. I knew that I would have to go for the hook. I drove back to Sielo, found the hook, and returned quickly, now curiously afraid that I would be too late.

But little had changed. Some of the grieving women had withdrawn to a dark room in one of the unfinished buildings to wail in unison, as if to reinforce their grief until it burst from them and left them in peace. The area around the well was calm, almost deserted, as two soldiers completed the business of covering it. No one else stood near the well and many people had left the market to walk home.

Vainly looking for a familiar person who had helped retrieve the first body, I called one of the soldiers at the well and showed him the hook, a gleaming piece of aluminum about four inches long, with a short chain leader attached to it. Finally understanding my intentions, he reported to the Immigration Officer and pointed back at the hook, which I then held up. There was some hesitation, and I found myself hoping they had given up.

When the two soldiers began dragging the lumber away from the hole, I walked to the well. As I fumbled with the small rope, which had been abandoned like a tainted thing after the Guinea man's body had been removed from it, and tried to tie it to the chain leader, the crowd in the market became quiet with renewed interest, and Father Parkinson reappeared. I was grateful for his company, but embarrassed by his presence.

"Where did you get the hook?"

"At the house. I had forgotten about it."

"I got this clawhammer; I thought we might be able to use it to hook onto her clothes. I went to Rashid's store to look for a hook and he said, 'Leave her there, it's a good place for her.' Can you imagine that! How did you happen to have the hook?"

"I got it to fish for crocodiles."

I walked to the well's edge and, meticulous about my balance, lowered the hook toward the girl's body. I noticed a piece of crumpled zinc partially under her and then understood that the zinc had been placed over the hole expediently by the well-digger and the girl had stepped onto it unknowingly. There was no water in the bottom of the well.

Too quickly the hook caught something. My God! I tried to shake it loose.

"Father, I think it's in her face. I can't get it loose."

"Well," he shrugged, "it doesn't matter if she's dead."

It must matter, I think it must matter.

"All right."

Testing the rope, I began to pull with one arm and, finding instant movement, thought strangely what a light easy thing death was. Instead of pulling hand-over-hand, I turned and walked away from the well, pulling over my shoulder. I didn't want to look — I imaged the hook in a bulging eye — but knew that I would look, but slowly.

Behind me I could hear and feel the body nearing the surface as it rubbed and banged in its crazy turning against the dry walls. I felt its stiff, angular exit, and then Father Parkinson cried, almost happily in his reassurance, "It's in her hair!"

Below the braids, her eyes were closed, and I felt grateful for that.

The crowd was delighted and several men rushed up to me and slapped me on the back and shook my hand.

"Thank you, teacha! That good trick!"

"Thank you, yah! You do good work!"

I didn't know what to do or say, and stood there in silence, with the bodies and the wailing women, dust-covered and grief-stricken, until finally I drifted away, wondering at the man from Guinea.

PATRICIA HAMPL: My first book, *Woman before an Aquarium*, published in 1978, is a collection of poems. And for four years I co-edited a poetry magazine with James Moore. I've taken up fiction writing "rather late in life," as we used to say in my family of people who married after 30. My only other published short story, "Look at a Teacup," was reprinted in *The Best American Short Stories 1977*, edited by Martha Foley.

I love short stories, and on certain days of the week think Chekhov had the answers to all life's problems, but I find the story form the toughest of all genres, requiring the most flawless narrative grasp. Or maybe I just have trouble maneuvering people in and out of rooms in such a short space.

I was born in St. Paul in 1946 and still live there. I've taught at the University of Minnesota, worked at the St. Paul *Pioneer Press* and for Minnesota Public Radio as well as in various free-lance writing and editing jobs. I've also made my living by giving readings through the country and by conducting workshops. I'm currently a recipient of a Bush Foundation Fellowship and, during this grant year, will travel for the fourth time to Czechoslovakia and will spend a lot of time at the North Shore — the subject of a new book I have in mind.

Patricia Hampl

MARTH

We were talking about where Marth was buried. Somewhere outside Los Angeles, my mother said. That was the town she loved.

She had married young, a Canadian millionaire — at least that's what she thought he was at the time. He was older than Marth, a flashy kind of guy, my father said.

The handsomest man, Mother said, passing us the coffee. He'd been married previously to a French bicycle heiress.

"French Canadian or French French?" I asked.

"Oh, French French," Mother said.

"Definitely, he was a drinker," Dad said. "Not an alcoholic — he'd drink right in front of you at 10 a.m. He and Marth travelled all over together — Europe, Canada, you name it. Then he died and the money ran out. I mean, he died and the money ran out at the same time *exactly*," Dad said. "It was like timing."

Marth discovered all she had left was some little piece of land in Milwaukee that nobody wanted, and black Linda; that was their Cadillac. "They always named their cars," Mother said dreamily. And then, Marth had the jewelry. She was just heartbroken, according to Mother. Also destitute.

Black Linda was repossessed; that's when Marth came to stay with us in Minneapolis. "For the weekend," according to my father. "Get that — for the weekend."

"The invitation," my mother said, turning to me, "had been open-ended."

"What invitation?" Dad muttered.

Marth did stay with us three years, so he has his point. But I can't help it, I'm on the other side. Marth was Mother's friend from way back; they grew up together. "We made mud pies together," Mother would say to me when I came into the kitchen and found them fixing dinner together. I always imagined them, two plumpish matrons, seriously saucing up lumps of dirt on catalpa leaves. I couldn't *see* them as children, not even when Mother showed me, delightedly, the pictures: Marth blonde and plump, staring chicly into the camera at an angle, Mother with her dark cap haircut looking solicitously at the smaller blonde next to her. In one picture Mother had her arm joyously around Marth's waist. Marth had her hand on her hip, as natural as a starlet.

I liked to think they were friends, had always been friends, had once been these small, unlikely figures. As I looked at the pictures I sensed, obscurely, that I too would grow. So Marth became my first friend, setting me forever and for the first time, off to the side of my father. She was my first *person*, not just my first friend. The first person from outside that you let in — that's important.

That first day she came to us I followed her upstairs. I watched her unpack her yellow leatherette suitcase. I sat on the edge of the bed and traced with my finger the designs in the pale chenille bedspread. "Just the one suitcase," my mother said with a lyric fall to her voice, turning to my father. "That's all she had in this world." She gets back at him, one way or another.

Marth was putting away her underwear that day. "Thank God, I still have my jewelry," she said as she put some peach-colored silk panties in the newspaper-lined drawers of the bureau that we were going to share. My mother and I wore white cotton underwear that got stretched out in the wash and flapped against our thighs. Maybe Mother still wears that kind. But Marth always said, "Silk for silk" when she drew on those pale coral things edged in what I still believe was real lace.

She wanted to show me her jewelry. "Here," she said. "I keep it all in my *booz-um*." She had a curious, insinuating way of saying the word; her doughy voice made that future ripple with naturalness. I admired her more than I could say.

She fished into her blouse and brought out a triangular sapphire pin. Then she handed me an opal ring that looked like a bead of skim milk. "You can try them on, honey," she said. And I did feel we were somehow equals.

Marth didn't have dreams of striking it rich again. She was something of a realist, and she was fat by then. There was an urgency in her bright dyed hair that, much as I personally admired it, I sensed did not promote love. But she had trooped around Europe on somebody else's money and had lived it up at private resorts. She'd even been to a spa. That kind of fun marks a person.

Maybe that's why she came up with all her nutty ways of earning a living. She couldn't just go out and get a job. She was always looking for the small lit candle at the center of things. Which is just crazy if you're trying to find a job. It really got on my father's nerves.

Marth had read in some magazine, Mother said, about how you could address envelopes in your home in your spare time and make a living. "Now, that certainly showed initiative," she said pointedly to my father.

For three months our dining room table was covered with stacks of white envelopes. They reminded me of miniature grain elevators, like the ones Marth and I could see from our bedroom window. I used to think those elevators were depressing. On summer nights Marth and I sometimes woke up from the sour, mousey smell of them. Mother didn't like me to be critical of things. "Just think of the elevators as great big cookie jars," she would say, when I complained of the smell. "Just don't dwell on things. If you start dwelling, where will it end? You do dwell on things, darling."

I asked her if thinking would stunt my growth. "Don't get sophisticated with *me*," she said. But on Marth we agreed. Each of us saw her in our own way, but we agreed. Mother said Marth had a certain something; she could just tell Marth was going to get somewhere. "You don't hear Marth complaining," she would say.

Marth took her envelopes seriously. She had special work dresses and she wore only her single strand of pearls on the job. She set herself morning and afternoon quotas, she took a precise lunch break. "Just a peanut butter sandwich, Allie," she would call to my mother in the kitchen. But Mother gave her a peeled tomato, cut like a tulip, filled with chicken salad. She was anxious to do everything possible for Marth's future.

After a while it became clear that Marth was not happy. She had discipline, she met her deadlines, she even got grouchy — everything to make it seem like a real job. But it didn't work.

"Sweetie," she said to me one afternoon when I came into the dining room to visit her, bringing a plate of cookies and two glasses of milk (even regular offices have coffee breaks, she had said on a previous occasion), "I've got better talents than this. I'm just not fulfilling myself. This is for somebody else." It wasn't a moment of despair, but she was low.

I couldn't have agreed more: she had to make a move. It had made me sad to see her at her envelopes. Between ourselves we had started calling them Pillsbury's Best. Marth stood up to my mother on the issue of the grain elevators, in fact. "They're not something you think should be in a *neighborhood*," she said. "That's a rancid smell coming from there," she said pointing out the window. "You can't tell me that's good, Allie, that rancid smell."

The envelopes went. Not long after, the table was covered with the makings for paper flowers. "You have to admit," my mother said to my father as she poured him some more coffee, "those flowers looked very real."

The flowers, far more than the envelopes, were the sort of thing you could see Marth doing. That was the year we bought a television set. Marth sat with her flower-makings right in front of the set, watching the Americans and the Koreans sit down at a big polished table and sign their names, hour after hour, diplomat by diplomat, to the truce. This was not at all boring to her. "Just think," she said to me as I sat with her at the table, "we can see history happening right before our eyes in our own homes. Remember this moment."

Unfortunately, the paper flower trade was pretty well mopped up by the time Marth set up shop at our dining room table. Even she was worried. "This is no cottage industry," she said, half in pride, half in sorrow; "the real center for this business," she said gloomily to my mother, "is Los Angeles."

She had big plans, though. "These flowers are a real future," she told us.

"Remember that?" Dad said. "She had the gall to sit right in that chair" (indicating mine, as if the impudence sat there still), "and tell me right to my face that the best part about her angle of the business was — there wasn't any *overhead*."

Mother let it go.

Marth's favorite flower was the red rose. She twirled gorgeous, funereal bouquets of them into existence on long, *gros-grain* stems. "Stems are hard," she said. She always felt they were no match for her blossoms. Her roses were wonderful, plumped like little horsehair sofas on top of the stiff, very green stems.

"I bet I could market these for weddings — bridal bouquets," she told us one day. "I mean, when this new velvet paper has revolutionized the flower world. Lots of people would give anything for a lasting bouquet like this from their weddings. How about you, honey," she said, looking over her blossom to me, "Would you like a fancy bouquet like this when you walk down the aisle?"

I didn't say no, although my father was frowning.

I don't remember what happened to the roses in the end. "It all sort of fizzled," Mother said. "Then she took some course and got a job as a housemother at that college in Wisconsin." But although the girls there loved her, as we had at home, Marth wrote back that she was crazy to get to L.A. These bread towns and beer towns, she wrote us, everything smells of one thing. She needed a town, she said, where you could live. Mother and I knew what she meant. "I wrote her," Mother said. "I told her, Make your move, Marth. I said, Don't get stuck."

She finally made it to Los Angeles. She got a job in an exclusive pet store. She waited on a movie star or two, people whose faces you'd recognize, Mother said. "You've never even heard the names of some of those birds she sold out there," Mother said. But gradually, we lost touch with her.

Then Marth developed some kidney ailment they can cure you of like nothing now, according to Mother. She was dead within two months.

Everybody in the hospital loved her. Mother says they'd come in and give her back-rubs at the drop of a hat. "You know how everybody loved Marth," Mother said. "All the stories she could tell." But I don't remember Marth ever telling any stories. It was Mother and I who did that.

"You know," Mother said, "I think Marth missed her calling." She was talking again to Dad; she had forgiven him. She was inviting him back, back into the human circle where history gets written and rewritten, endlessly, endlessly. "I really do think Marth should have been an actress, a dramatic actress."

"Are you kidding?" Dad said, pushing his cup back, rising to go to the football game on the T.V.

"Lloyd," Mother said severely, banishing him even as he freed himself, "Marth really had ability."

MICHAEL HARVEY: At ten I quit cigarettes and hopping freights for short rides family moved to a small town twenty miles away wind on the lake didn't care much for school stayed up late reading under the blankets with a flashlight became obsessed with basketball began to enjoy solitude, walking in the dark and the lake at night, listening to rock n' roll on the radio at twelve I wanted to be a writer kept it to myself.

Ran away at sixteen, hurt by a girl made it to the east coast a week without sleep and I landed in jail outside Chicago. Brought home ran away west forever, returned to play football, tennis graduated, traveled, went to work, didn't like it started college to escape the war, stopped a year later, went to Europe. Saw Hendrix in London, never recovered, got a guitar back to school traveled dark nights alone, a guitar next to silent highways, hoping for beautiful strangers.

Was lucky with friends. Against all hopes I hurt them and they hurt me tried to understand gave up on writing, forever; stopped playing the guitar unemployed teacher lives alone. Quit found a girl, she took me to Chicago to see dylan wrote a book worked at Stillwater Prison moved to San Francisco saw movies, played basketball, wrote a book, made long phone calls drove to Virginia came back hid out broke down I thought I was Albert Einstein till I find out I am Marilyn Monroe.

Improvise day by day no good at plans anymore but I know what I want. Selfish too careful cruel poor hopeful determined alone proud do the best I can been lucky but worked hard too.

Michael Harvey

PURITY OF HEART IS TO WILL ONE THING

On the first day of school Richard Wilkes stood among a group of boys in the back of the room by the windows. They all wore light blue shirts and dark blue corduroy pants. By the blackboard Sister Rachel sat at her desk waiting for the bell to ring, the students to take their seats. At the door appeared Sister Bernadine, the principal, with a girl, a new student. Sister Rachel rustled to the door, smiling, eyes eager.

The volume of conversation increased through the room though everyone was careful not to attract the attention of the murmuring nuns. The gathering by the door was noticed in the corner by the windows.

"That's the new girl. Her dad's a major in the Air Force."

"Is he a pilot?"

"I don't know. Maybe."

"She's sorta good lookin, doncha think?"

"She's okay. Skinny."

"What's her name?" Richard asked.

"Laura Wakefield."

"You should see her sister in eighth. She's beautiful."

"You in love, Ratsy? You wanna get married?"

"Shut up, snothead."

"Where's she live?"

"I don't care if she's skinny."

"Tamarack Street."

"That's not far from my house."

"Hey, what's for lunch today?"

"Slop. Like always."

The bell rang. Sister Rachel turned sharply. Students scurried to their desks. Sister Bernadine watched from the doorway with steely eyes. Order established, the nuns conferred a moment, then parted. Laura was directed to an empty desk near the door.

Sister Rachel welcomed them all to the seventh grade. She introduced the new girl, then called names to help with the distribution of the books.

From his desk by the windows Richard studied the girl. She was his height, slender, lithe. Her hair was deep brown and long to her shoulders. She wore glasses with silver and brown frames. Her eyes glistened attentively. Her face was oval with high cheekbones and her features were balanced, elegant. Her expression combined serious and studious. With a quick inquiring glance she startled him away.

Richard went home after school instead of playing football. His mother stood at the ironing board in her blue apron working over one of her husband's white shirts. He got a glass of milk and a piece of German chocolate cake.

"Get a napkin for that. I just cleaned the kitchen."

"Okay."

Janice Wilkes was a short, plain, cheerful woman, not quite forty. Her hair was light brown, softly curled, all in place. She took pride in keeping the house neat and comfortable. Richard thought she didn't have anything better to do.

"Aren't you going to change your clothes?"

"Yes. Hungry now."

"How was school?"

"Okay."

"Do you like Sister Rachel?"

"Sister Marie is nicer. I wish I had her again."

"Too nice maybe. I hope you're going to work hard this year."

"Yeah." He washed out his mouth with half a glass of milk. "There's a new girl."

"Really. What's her name?"

"Laura. She lives over on Tamarack."

"Up on the hill? The last house?"

Richard shrugged.

"I'll bet that's it. That was the Stewart's house. Your father was hoping to sell for them, but Paul Stewart went to Mr. Dobson instead. Where are you going?"

In his room he put on his old jeans and a dark green sweatshirt. He removed his school shoes for tennis. His mother was putting the shirt on a hanger when he went through the kitchen, out the screen door and down the steps two at a time. He didn't hear the door slam or his mother call: "Where are you going?"

Tamarack was a narrow street that ran for only a quarter of a mile behind the houses that fronted that part of the lake. 'Wakefield' was freshly painted in white on a black mailbox by the driveway of the last house. A lot thick with trees and high grass ended the road. The house was white with a red roof and sat up on a hill. Keeping to the trees, Richard circled the place. A drab green military car was parked near the back door. There were screened porches in the front and back. In the front on the second story were dormer windows. He saw no people, wasn't sure if he did whether he would stand or run. There wasn't much to see and nothing more to do; his curiosity was satisfied. Standing where the road met the trees he felt calm, at ease. It looked okay. With the sun still warm in the sky, the blue jays toying with one another, he set off down the road, the trees arched above him. Squirrels ran as he came upon them and he felt good.

The school year proceeded. Day by day he watched her. He had to make sure she was right. He didn't want a dummy like Sandra Latemba. She was very smart he discovered. It worried him for a while, until he saw her playing basketball during recess. He was much better. And he wasn't dumb; it was just that school and homework were so boring. He knew he could get straight A's if he wanted. Sister Marie had told him so last year. Before she gave him his report card with a C in math and a D in attitude.

But if grades were given for getting girls, he wanted an A. Subtle, he decided, slow and careful, that was the way to do it. Let her discover him he thought. She could notice how fast he ran, or how smart, or how many friends he had. But before long he was disturbed that she hadn't noticed already. She was new though and he understood that it might take a while. But he needn't be impatient forever. Because he had a plan.

On a Monday morning in November he arrived at school a half hour early. The few who had come earlier were surprised to see him, he who most often arrived within a few minutes, one way or the other, of the last bell. Hanging up his coat he decided that he would wait until more people showed up. He'd be too conspicuous now. He sat at his desk and took out a library book. Sister Rachel at her desk nodded pleasantly, trying to encourage this extraordinary behavior.

Minutes passed slowly; gradually the room filled. The faces he feared to see remained absent. Stay away a few minutes more, he said again to those he hoped were still eating their breakfasts, Laura first among them.

It was getting late. He had to move. He got to his feet and moved in the direction of her empty desk. The room was more than half full and rattled with morning conversation. He tried his hardest to be invisible. Walking up the row to her desk he noticed, with gratitude to what he already recognized as a capricious God, that all but one of the adjacent desks were also empty. Slipping his hand into his pocket, he glanced at the door one last furtive time. He drew the folded square of paper from his pocket. No one was watching. He edged it into the desk and continued up the aisle, relieved, ecstatic. Proud and shocked by his audacious genius, he returned to his desk. To wait; to watch; to be flung sickeningly by a slow wave of anticipation and apprehension. He wished she would come now. The waiting was the worst of it all. He prayed for it to end; the bell startled him, his opening eyes darted to the desk still empty. She was never sick; where was she? Sister Rachel nodded to the front row, the sign for the class to stand. A clatter of feet and desks was followed by the hum of practiced voices speaking practiced words. Prayers done, math class began.

The morning ached past. He kept hoping she would arrive. Disappointment became frustration, then anger, pain. He wished he had waited. All it meant was one more day of waiting, he told himself. But it was not that simple he knew. It had gone wrong, a bad start, and he feared the wrongs that might come before to- morrow. During lunch he resolved to get the note back, to try again another time. Walking back to the classroom he felt the comfort and relief of his decision.

Entering the room he saw Jennifer Wakefield, Laura's eighth grade sister, sitting in the desk copying down the assignments that Sister Rachel standing nearby was reading to her. Instinctively Jennifer's head came up, Sister Rachel turned. He closed his mouth and swallowed.

"What are you doing here, Richard?"

"Nothing."

"Nothing? Richard, what are you doing here?"

"I forgot something."

"Well get it then. And do try to stand up straight. You'd be such a good-looking boy if only you'd make the effort."

"Yes 'ster."

He rummaged in his desk, keeping a fearful eye on the two across the room. They did not appear to have gotten to the books yet. He cursed them both, then himself, then Laura, and Laura again. Sister Rachel might have heard him muttering, she threw him a cool suspicious stare. He grabbed a book and walked out of the room praying passionately that they would not find the note. The nun watched him go, perplexed again by the boy's unusual behavior.

On a playground filled with scrambling children he stood alone. It was going wrong. He didn't want it to be like this. He didn't know what to do. Or what he could have done. Confusion. He didn't understand. And he feared whatever might happen next.

The bell rang and he returned with the others to the classroom. Looking for even the least warning he glanced at Sister Rachel as he came through the door. She was writing on the blackboard, seemed not to notice him. He sat at his desk. He couldn't be sure; he, and others he had seen, sat smugly safe, confident of having gotten away, then black words and a knifing stare cut away the sheen of pride revealing guilt and fear. He waited. But the sword did not fall. The afternoon was nearly over before he began to feel it might not. Not that he was safe, but he might yet have a chance. At the end of the day, during the confusion of banging desks, jackets and sweaters, he got to her desk, opened it. A panicky shuffle produced no slip of square folded paper. Uncertain, relieved, worn, he looked to the nun bent over her desk writing. He could only think that Jennifer had come through for him. A true miracle; he could laugh to himself, still anxious but with a prayer of hope.

Numb, free at last, he walked step by step out to the playground. He spent an hour running frenzied with his friends, energized by the excitement of his escape and the possibility of success.

His cousin Fred found him leaning against the standards of the basketball court gasping happily for breath. Soft, slow, portly Fred was solemn, worried, slightly more than usual. Fred was a year older but cautious and diligent, susceptible to the tyranny of the nuns. Richard often mocked him for weakness.

"Sister Bernadine asked this afternoon if you and I are

cousins.''

"Yeah? So what?"

"Well," Fred began, "it was just after she took a note from Jenny Wakefield. And she, Jenny I mean, said there was something about you in it."

"Oh?" Another deep swallow.

"Yeah. But she wouldn't tell me what it was. Do you know?"

"No. What'd the note say?"

"I don't know, I told you. She wouldn't tell."

"What'd 'ster do with the note?"

"She kep' it."

"Huh. Now we'll never know, will we, Fred?"

Fred looked at him with frustration, suspicion. He had been put on too many times. "Nope, I guess not." With a finger he pushed his glasses back up on the bridge of his nose. He wandered off scratching his shoulder.

Richard collected himself, waves to his racing hooting friends, and trudged to the side of the building where his books lay in the grass. Gray flat clouds covered the sky. He kicked through the fallen leaves that covered the sidewalk. Birds lined the telephone wires. By the time he got home darkness had fallen.

He went to school the next day expecting anything. But nothing happened. It was ten days before he was persuaded that danger had passed. Even so he watched and hoped warily for a sign from Laura. Her eyes touched his now and then, but mostly he saw her listening attentively, her studying dutifully, her staring out the window.

Weeks passed and winter came on. At night sometimes he would walk to her house and stand outside in the dark. Not with purpose or intention, he was simply drawn to the copse of bushes and trees where he could watch in the windy dark unseen. He had discovered that Laura shared a room with Jenny on the second floor in the front, the lake side. He knew they were often on the other side of the drawn yellow shade — talking, studying, sleeping. The certainty of their presence together nearby, so commonplace and unextraordinary, excited, confused him. And drew him back.

On a day with the crisp snap of sheet ice, with puffy clouds skidding across the sky, Richard and Matthew Evans kicked their way along the railroad tracks by the edge of town. A dim white sun sharpened the morning. Richard walked with his red coat open, his black rubber boots flopped and the buckles jingled. School was out, Christmas a few days off. Matthew, taller, huskier, lumbered over the ties telling Richard with vivid speculation what his high school sister and her boyfriend had been doing in the living room the night before. Astonishment alternated with anxiety. He had begun to see that the future was going to demand of him more than he was willing to give. Richard, patiently sympathetic, took a positive and adventurous view. No escape, he said. Besides, it was something you got used to, you had to do it a few times, like riding a bike or swimming. Still, he felt his own apprehension keenly. Though he tried he could not imagine how it would be. The comfort of shared feeling deepened as they walked thoughtfully, far from houses now, approaching Richter's pond. When they broke past the trees they saw Linda Radburn and Laura skating in fits and starts on the clear dark ice bordered by reeds and dark cattails. They strode toward the girls across the dry snowy field.

The girls kept skating. Twenty yards from the ice Matthew broke into a trot. Richard kept walking. Matthew reached the one open space of shoreline where the girls' boots and shoes lay. He picked up a shoe and moved to the center of the pond.

"Matthew, leave us alone," Linda whined, as she skated toward him hesitantly.

He dangled the shoe in the distance between them. "Is this yours?"

"Yes. It's mine. Give it to me."

"Okay." He held it out. As she reached he pulled it away. Her momentum kept her coming. He put the shoe behind his back and she stumbled against him keeping her balance only by hanging on.

Righting herself, she said, "Matthew, give me my shoe."

He smirked, stepped back, she followed. He stepped back again, she kept with him. He broke into a run sliding and stumbling, chased by the red-jacketed girl around the circle of the pond. And around.

Richard came onto the ice and walked directly to Laura. She was watching the other two. It was the first time he had seen her up close in clothes other than the navy blue jumper and white blouse that was the girls' uniform at school. She wore jeans, a sky blue winter jacket with a white fur collar, a white stocking cap, and a long white scarf.

"Hi," he said, trying for her attention. She seemed not to hear. "Hello?"

She turned.

"He'll give it back. He's just foolin around."

"I know. But he doesn't have to."

Richard glanced at the two stumbling against one another. "Yeah."

"What are you doing out here?"

"I don't know. Just walkin. I couldn't take sittin in the house again all day.

"Did you finish your report already? And the other homework?"

"Ahh, no. I didn't start yet."

"What are you doing it on?"

"Ummm. I'm not sure. I gotta couple a ideas. I haven't decided yet. I wanna pick the best one." He shifted his feet. He'd forgotten that report. He didn't believe in homework over Christmas. "How 'bout you?"

Matthew was yelling now, skipping unsteadily away from Linda a step behind. He slipped, flew bodily into the air, landed full on his hip, rolled, lay groaning.

With a squeal Linda slid past him. He lay rubbing his hip, she came back, reached down for her shoe on the ice. They both grabbed for it. Each pulling, Matthew won, dragging her down on top of him. He began to wrestle with her, laughing, then tickling. She laughed too and began to hit him in the head with the shoe he had let go of to tickle her.

Richard and Laura watched nearby. The other two got on their feet arguing. Linda called him an ass, Matthew gave her a shove. Her feet got lost and she fell on the seat of her pants.

"Why don't you go away," Laura said sharply. "You bully." She skated to the shore, sat down with a thump, and began to untie her skates.

The other three watched her, not having expected this.

"C'mon, Linda. Let's go home."

Linda, shoe in hand, perplexed, looked from Laura up to Matthew.

"C'mon," Laura said. "Why can't you just leave us alone?"

Linda got to her feet.

"Jeez, what a bitch," Matthew said. Then to Richard: "C'mon, let's go."

The two boys walked back toward the railroad tracks and attacked with determination the biggest tree. They stopped halfway up. They saw Linda point at them and then watched the girls cross the barren white field to the brown dirt road that led back to town. When the girls were out of sight they climbed limb after limb down the tree. They walked back to the pond. Fifteen yards from the bare shore Richard saw Laura's black mittens on the ground near the reeds. They consulted, decided it would be best to bring them to her. Make her feel good about yelling at them. They trailed a mile behind the girls all the way to Laura's house.

Linda answered the door. She smiled wryly. "What do you want?"

"These're Laura's gloves," Richard said. "We found em by the pond an thought we ought to bring em back."

"Oh. Thanks. Here, I'll give em to her."

"No, no. I'll give em to her myself."

"Hmmm." She wasn't unwilling but she hesitated.

"Linda, who is it?"

"Two boys, Mrs. Wakefield. From school."

"Is there a problem?"

"NNNOOO."

"Bring them in then. If they want to come."

Matthew and Richard came in smiling and were introduced to Mrs. Wakefield, a tall slender red-headed woman in brown ski pants and a wine-colored sweater. Pleasantries were exchanged and she directed them to Laura who was in the living room watching television. She was curled on the couch and looked up calmly as they entered. Still in jeans, she wore a light green sweater that emphasized the flatness of her chest. On her feet were gray and red skating socks. White bows decorated her hair.

"I found your gloves by the pond and um thought you might want em."

"Thank you. Where were they?"

"Right on the shore there."

Matthew watched her accept the gloves, his eyes narrow.

"Thank you. These are my good mittens. Would you like to stay and have some hot chocolate?"

"Yeah, sure."

"Sure."

"You can watch tv while we make the chocolate."

"Okay." She got up and they took the couch for themselves. The girls went to the kitchen.

"She didn't look sorry to me," Matthew said. "You'd think she'd apologize after she treated us so rotten."

"I s'pose."

"What's this?" Matthew turned to the tv. The soap opera didn't interest him; he switched channels until he discovered cartoons on eleven. Richard heard rattling metal in the kitchen; voices, laughing.

Linda returned to take their coats and clear off the coffee table. She asked Matthew what he hoped to get for Christmas. Richard took the opportunity to slide out to the kitchen. Laura stood at the stove, stirring. She looked up, kept stirring.

"Hi."

"Hi."

"Did you really finish all the homework already?"

"No, I did the reading assignment and the report. I have the religion questions left. There wasn't anything else, was there?"

"God, I forgot about religion. Shit, I mean uh sorry. No, that's it, I think. How come you study so hard? You sure must like school."

"It's okay. It's easy."

"Sure, but it's so boring. I hate it."

"I don't mind it. I get bored sometimes but we've got to go."

"I guess. I wish we dint." She kept stirring. He could hear Matthew and Linda talking in the living room. He hoped she would stay there. "Where'd your mother go?"

"She's upstairs."

"Oh. What's she doin'?"

"I don't know."

"Mmmm." He didn't know what to say. He felt stupid.

"Do you think Matthew likes Linda?" Laura asked flatly, looking down into the swirling milk.

"Jeez, I don't know." The question stunned him, it was so personal. "Maybe. I never thought about it."

"Does he ever say anything about her?"

"No, ah, I don't remember. He doesn't talk about girls much." She looked dissatisfied with his answer. She turned to the cupboard behind her, rose up on her toes, reached for the dark brown tin of chocolate. "I'll ask him."

Her head whipped around. "No. Don't do that."

"Okay. But I thought you wanted to know."

"Don't tell Linda I asked you either."

"Oh, she must like him, huh?"

"Sorta. Nothing special. Don't you tell her. Or him either."

"I won't."

"Promise," she insisted.

He agreed gladly, pleased to share a secret with her, feeling it bound them together. He liked her more than ever and he was encouraged that she was being nice to him. Maybe she liked him too. But he couldn't quite bring himself to ask.

"Would you get four cups down from that cupboard?"

"Sure."

"When's your birthday?" she asked softly.

"July third."

"No it's not. You're just teasing me."

"I'm not. Really." He set the cups on the stove.

"Your birthday is the third of July?"

"Yes."

"When's mine then? Did somebody tell you?"

"No. When is it?"

"You don't know?" He shook his head. "The third of July."

"Really? We're twins."

"No, but it's funny we have the same birthday."

"Why did you want to know?"

"So I could know what sign you are."

"Like astrology?"

"Yes."

"But that's wrong. The nuns say."

"I don't believe in it. I just like to know. It's okay if you don't believe in it."

"Oh." It seemed a fine distinction to him. But she knew more about it than he did. "What does it mean? That we have the same birthday."

"I don't know about that. But being born in July we have the same sign. Cancer."

"Cancer? Like a sickness?"

"No. It's just a sign. I don't want to talk about it anymore.

Here, take this to Matthew. Tell Linda to come here."

"Okay."

He did not get another opportunity to speak to her alone. The four of them drank hot chocolate and ate cookies. Then Richard and Matthew were escorted to the door. But Richard was ecstatic; finally he had made an impression. And she had been kind, confiding. He thought that she might like him, or at least come to like him eventually. Through Christmas and into the new year he thought of her and persuaded himself that it was different between them. Nights especially he looked forward to school and seeing her there every day.

But when school resumed she was as distant and formal as before. It was as though they had never spoken. She did not ignore him; she was friendly, polite, but she gave no sign of her feeling for him. He tried to be familiar, to find her alone, but she eluded him. He felt she was trying to avoid him. He didn't understand.

One day in the spring he surprised her on the playground apart from the others during a game of kickball.

"Why do you always run away from me?"

"What do you mean?"

"You know."

"I don't."

He looked straight into her brown eyes. The day was gray, windy. Her red scarf fluttered beside her arm.

"Is there something wrong with me?"

"No. Nothing."

"Why won't you talk to me?"

"I . . . I do."

"No you don't."

The bell rang. Others around them ran for the door. She kept looking at him, scared. Her lips moved, her mouth opened, she turned away, left him standing. He watched her run to the green doors and go in. He walked away from the playground, away from the school. He walked home, told his mother he didn't feel well, went to bed.

If she did not care for him he would not give her his time, his thoughts. It was hopeless. He did not stop going to the house evenings, though he went less often. Through the spring he buried his hurt in baseball, too much school; days and nights he ran through the town, free and wild.

The summer was different than it had ever been. He swam and played ball with the school team; he rode his bike around the lake and stayed out late at night. But he kept to himself, preferred to be alone. Instinct kept him apart from the others, made him feel alone and on his own. At night he walked away from lights and streets. He loved the darkness and the wind. His father yelled and his mother worried but he paid no attention. His parents could think he was strange; it didn't matter, he was. It hurt but he accepted it, took it as a curse with honor — he couldn't help the way he felt. He was different, let it be, he would fight the world in his own way. He kept them all at a distance as the only way he could decide for himself how he wanted to be. He began to see his life ahead of him but with no clear way to go. He felt adrift and empty, he felt the fear of power and sadness. He wanted to be where he was going without having to find the way and know the place. He knew that escape was not available; now he could see, he was trapped, neither questions nor emptiness went away. The power of choice was weak compensation. He was lost and he knew it.

He slept until noon and stayed awake nights, wished she or someone were with him but knew it was hopeless to wish, hopeless to forget. Lying on cool grass, the waves washing the shore, he looked up to the dark starry sky. Raised on his elbows, his knees up, he wasted the hours, unequal to his confusion, hoped the air might clear, but was convinced that despite quiet nights with a full moon and a kind girl close by neither he nor anyone had a chance. She was up there now and he here, wanting her wanting him, so he might feel less abandoned. She'd never understand the words he'd use to say this, he'd never get it out really; but the effort might be enough to get her to share the feeling — but she'd run when it got too strong. Run like she had last winter, unable to answer, run to be away from him. The light behind the shade went dark. If it weren't for Jenny he'd climb the drainpipe to the roof and go to her window. She'd scream, he'd run, they'd chase and shoot him. He wouldn't let that happen; he'd keep it to himself and never be a fool. Lost beyond hope but never a fool, never a coward; he was going to be a man somehow.

He waited a half hour more, thinking her asleep. The moon shifted, stars fell, a wind rose off the lake. He stood, stretched himself. Stiffly he set out along the shoreline across the yards, a silhouette alone moving on the edge of land that dropped down beneath the water. All summer long.

The weeks passed him by and he hardly noticed. School came again, worse than before. On the first Friday of September he fought Dominic Mojeski on the playground. Dominic was called the toughest kid for his age in town. At the end Richard's lip was swollen, bleeding; he had a dark bruise on his forehead. Dominic's nose bled to his chin and the side of his face was scraped and torn because Richard had pushed his head along the asphalt. All the boys and a few girls had surrounded them. The judgement was a draw.

In school he worked enough to get by and endured the prodding of his parents. Sister Bernadine harassed him for his refusal to wear the black oxford shoes that were approved for the boys' uniform. He chose his black cowboy boots with the red and white design on the sides that he had begged for and been stunned to receive on his birthday. Some days the tall nun ignored him, some days she grimly stood him up as a bad example till he hated her, but never did he respond with more than "yes" or "no" to her abuse. He would not ever bend to her, show fear or remorse, only stubborn quiet rebellion.

He began to run with Dominic and Larry, his tenth grade brother, though even they saw him as somehow outside, too reckless, dangerous. His parents said they didn't understand the change in him, a turn for the worse. He knew it was beyond explanation, he didn't even try, just took the pain as his fate. But when it stabbed him he fought it with all the wildness and fury within him, then found pride in the fear he helped others to discover. When punishment came he took it.

Still he kept an eye on Laura and she kept an eye toward him. His reputation dismayed and impressed her. Each was attuned to the other, but neither found a way to move across the hurt between them.

On a Saturday in the middle of the fall Richard walked the windy shore. Thick gray clouds whipped across the cool blue sky. The waves on the lake were dark except for whitecaps. Huge shadows slid over the surface reflecting the clouds above. Richard stopped and turned into the steady wind. A single sailboat was the only craft on the water. It was coming toward a dock down along the shore. The lone sailor waved at him. He couldn't tell who it was. He moved along toward the dock. When he got down to the water he saw that it was Nurk Morrison. Nurk had sailed in the races every weekend that summer and even won a couple. But he was so round and pudgy that people teased him now for always carrying a life preserver. Nurk called and asked Richard to come out on the dock to catch the rope and pull the boat in. Richard didn't mind helping; he'd never seen a sailboat up close before. When the rolling boat steadied a bit Nurk jumped free of the flapping sails, took the rope and tied it to a post.

"Hey, Nurk. Whatta ya doin?"

"All right. Windy, isn't it?"

"Yeah. Whatta you doin here?"

"Wendy Rachlis and some friend of hers want to go sailing. They're waitin up at the house." Nurk flung his arm out toward a house.

"Who's Wendy Rachlis?"

"She goes to public school."

"Oh, one of those."

"Yeah." Both laughed in conspiracy, and with a twinge of uncertainty. "What're you doin, Rich?"

"Nothin. Just walkin."

"You wanna come?"

"Sure. Thanks. I never been in a sailboat before. It looks neat."

"It is. But hey, you can swim can't you?"

"Shit. You want me to push you in. I'll give you a half hour an still beat you across the lake."

"Okay, okay."

"An I don't need no inner tube either."

"Just makin sure, Rich." The corner of Nurk's mouth twitched. "Well, we better go get em."

"Aw, I don't wanna go up to the house an meet Mom an Dad. You get em. I'll wait here."

"Okay, I guess. Leave the dirty work to me. I'll be back in a minute."

Nurk was almost to the shore before Richard called out, "I'll do my own dirty work. You just hurry up."

Five minutes passed. Richard walked up to the crest of the slope and watched the whitecaps on the windblown water. Nurk called from a distance. Richard turned to see him coming through the grass with Wendy and Laura. When they met at the stairs she smirked, avoided his eyes as though she were embarrassed at being surprised by him. Both girls were barefoot with their jeans rolled almost to the knee, the tails of white shirts flapped at their waists. Under Nurk's sensitive direction they set off from the dock with hull splashing, pulleys, whining sails slapping. As the wind caught the sails they glided with a solitary squeal between two anchored boats that dipped and rocked. They sped toward open water.

The lines tight to his satisfaction, Nurk kept to the stern, his arm around the rudder. The girls took the low side of the angled deck. Richard on the high side was excited and wary, pleased and shaken by opportunity. The girls sat close together, laughing, looking to the waves ahead. Wendy was blond with pink cheeks, too cute Richard thought; he wondered why she wanted Nurk. Laura's hair was pulled back in a ponytail, her skin pale with the chill but still glazed by summer tan. A hesitant half-glance, she smiled as he brushed the hair out of his eyes, then she looked ahead again. He tried to speak but only raw sound came out, no words. Wendy turned and they tittered together.

In the middle of the lake the wind was at its strongest and the waves were high. The water slapped at the bow as it cut across. Nurk did his best to hold the boat to a brisk steady pace, skimming bumpily, splashily along.

"In a minute now we'll come about. You two watch out for the mast. You'll have to duck when it shifts," he explained.

He moved the rudder, the sails lost wind, fluttered, flopped. He grabbed the boom to move it to the other side. A line slid past Laura's face, caught somehow on the frame of her glasses and almost slowly pulled them away. Richard saw them catch her blouse just above the breast, then slide down onto the deck, bounce, careen toward the space beyond wood above water. He lunged, brushed against Nurk, caught his jacket on the rudder. Instantly the boat turned, the sail snapped and filled with wind. Nurk yelled, a scream. Richard felt himself thrown between the girls and into the frigid water. He surfaced, the sail collapsed like a wet sheet around his head. Nurk was cursing. Richard submerged and swam out from under the sail. The boat was on its side. Nurk swam about grabbing at the life jackets none of them had thought to put on and tossed them at the girls who were crying out as they gripped the mast. Richard sensed again the glasses drifting across the top of his hand and his spastic empty grasp. He looked at disaster all around and felt himself the sole cause. He wished he could sink painlessly to the bottom of the lake. He shivered, shook his head to clear his eyes. Nurk yelled at him to help. They began the business of righting the boat.

It was ten minutes before they got it up, half sunk, the waves rippling over the deck. The girls weren't much help. Wendy snapped at Nurk. Laura kept silent, her eyes wet and cold; she did what she was instructed to do. Finally an outboard arrived. A man watching from a window had seen them go over. He got the girls into his boat and gave them a blanket. Nurk was quiet suddenly and the man took charge of towing the sailboat to shore. It took slow chilly minutes.

They docked in front of a house that was only a couple hundred yards from Wendy's. Shivering, the girls struggled from the rolling outboard onto the wooden dock. They thanked the man and then, still dripping water from their hair and clothes, hurried to the shore and across the wide green lawns, past the somber white houses. Richard watched them go until Nurk yelled at him to help bail water. Neither of them was happy and neither enjoyed salvaging the boat. It took an hour of work before Richard felt free to escape. He drifted home dismal and depressed. A curse had settled on him, a curse he did not deserve, could not understand, might never escape. He wished she would go away and knew as he said it that he was lying to himself. It was all beyond his power to control and it hurt. Against his will, suffering, he kept his distance from her through the year.

On a day in early spring Sister Bernadine called him up to her desk. He was tired, numb, irritable. He had not slept the night before, had lain in bed considering his life and circumstances. She offered him a weary stare, then spoke quietly with venom. He stared back. Her voice rose to a thin yell heard freely in the room. A shivering silence wavered behind him. She pointed to his boots. He looked down, tuned out the words; his hate, concentrated on the colors and the pattern on the boots.

"Look at me when I speak to you, Richard Wilkes. I said look at me."

He was aware of noise but not words. He looked up calmly,

stared out the window and saw branches weaving in the wind. Hands on his shoulders shook him angrily. She slapped him with force. He wrenched out of her grasp, slapped back as hard as he could hitting her high on the side of the face. He turned to the class: disbelief, shock. He was calm inside and showed no emotion. He stepped away from the desk. Recovering, she reached, he lurched from her hands on his arm, ran to the door, down the length of the hall, his feet clopping, down the stairs pushing out the heavy metal doors. He realized the sleeve of his shirt was torn and didn't know when it had happened. He ran from the school, toward the woods, into the trees, through lingering dirty snow, sucking mud, ran till he fell and could not rise, only lie on the ground panting, heaving like a deer exhausted by chase. The dirt was cold, damp; it felt so good to surrender to pain. He started to cry and could not hold back.

After a while he wiped his nose with the remnants of his sleeve. He sat up, leaned back against a tree. The sun broke through clouds and warmed the space around him. He didn't know what would happen to him now.

That evening after the phone call, his parents conferred at the kitchen table with worried voices. Richard kept to his room. He knew what was coming long before the three wooden taps on the door. Jim Wilkes came into the room; his tie was loose and the top button of his shirt open. He was a tall man, slender, with bushy red hair and fair freckled skin. He was a man with his anger under control.

"We're going to have a talk, Rich." He came over and sat on the bed. Richard felt the pressure as he sat down. "What happened today, son?"

"Didn't they tell you?"

"Yes, but why did it happen?"

"She hit me first."

"But she's a nun."

Richard scowled, turned away. He didn't have a chance.

"What's the matter, Rich? Are you so unhappy? These last few months I don't know you anymore."

Richard shook his head weakly.

"These fights, and your grades are terrible. Your mother and I can't let this go on. You've been brought up better than this."

He looked at his father with hurt in his eyes, fought back the softening impulse of tears.

"Rich, if there's anything I can do I will do it. Just tell me."

There was nothing he could say.

"All right then. It's up to you to straighten out, and quick. Understand?"

"Yes, sir."

"There'll be no more going out after dinner until your homework is done. And you'll be in every night by ten o'clock. I want you to come directly home after school. I don't want to hear about you getting into any more fights."

"I don't care."

His father gave him a sharp look, his lips pursed. "The three of us have a conference Wednesday at seven-thirty with Father Warnes. You can't go back to school until after that so you're to help your mother during the next two days. Tomorrow you'll scrub the kitchen floor. And you can get the yard raked, too." Jim Wilkes stood up, ambled stiffly to the door, turned back. "There's going to be some changes in you, son. And I mean soon." He closed the door behind himself.

The conference was at the rectory, in Father Warnes' office. The priest, heavy set, red-faced, balding, sat behind his desk and clasped his hands over his stomach. With his parents there, Richard listened to the discouraged priest. He had become a problem, a lost soul. He must see the pain he was bringing to himself and those who cared about him. Repentance. Confession. Mercy. Self-discipline. The words floated past him and joined the million others that had blown by without impact. At the end he said he was sorry, it wouldn't happen again, no more fights. Yes, he wanted to come back. It was nowhere near as bad as he'd expected. The priest and his father shook hands, shared a moment of anxiety. Richard walked ahead with his mother to the car. No conversation disrupted the ride home. He went to his room.

When he got back to school Sister Bernadine left him alone. He was asked no questions, he offered no answers. The hours passed tediously. For a week he wore the black shoes, then returned to his cowboy boots.

After school he rolled up his sleeves and wandered warm afternoons through the town. He stole cigarettes from the supermarket. He bought a knife, six inches long, white mother of pearl sides. He kept it in his pocket, turning it over and over in his hand, not hungering to use it so much as keeping it ready for the time that someday would come. He did not expect it soon, preferred to keep it far off in his thoughts, but he would not be surprised again.

In the last weeks of the school year he put effort into schoolwork. He felt the necessity of proving to them and to himself that he could do as well as he liked; that if they had made it worthwhile he would have tried. It wasn't easy as he was far behind with too little time to retrieve all the ground lost. But the change was obvious and suspicion became uncertainty in Sister Bernadine's eyes. She did not attempt to shorten the distance between them. She could only fail; he would have relished that final insult. His daily grades improved considerably. On the last day of May his report card showed some improvement. His parents were pleased.

Graduation was held in the church with Benediction afterwards. Thirty-four students filled the first three pews; parents and relatives sat behind them. The gathering was small beneath the hollow resonance of the vaulted ceiling. Richard wore the sport coat that had been bought for him. His tie was tight around his neck.

Laura sat in the first row. Her dress was white. She listened to Father Warnes in his gold vestments. The address wore on; coughing, muffled. Richard heard nothing; he reflected on the red rose in Laura's dark hair. He felt hatred but did not curse her; she was a weakness that stung, that he would never overcome. He knew it and would not lie.

When the ceremony was over, a casual reception was held on the lawn in front of the school. The evening sun settled over the trees. There was no wind. Clusters of parents stood chatting among themselves or with the nuns. Pink punch was served from a bowl that sat on a long lunchroom table covered with plastic. The graduates floated free of their parents and moved around with their friends. Sister Bernadine spoke amiably with Mr. and Mrs. Mojeski.

Richard stood alone. Across the way his parents talked with Father Warnes. Jim Wilkes had worn his best gray suit. His arm was around Janice Wilkes and he nodded at the priest's words. Laura came from the table with a glass of punch, walked directly to him.

"Hi," she said calmly. "Want some punch?"

"Sure."

"You don't look very happy."

He shrugged. Her dress was lacy with a full skirt that fell just over her knees, as it was supposed to. The red flower was like a hammer on his eyes.

"You're going to public school next year, aren't you?"

"Yeah."

"I hope it's better." She looked down at the grass between his shoes. "It was hard for you, wasn't it?"

He shrugged, looked away. "No."

She shifted, uncertain of herself. Her eyelashes fell, rose. "Richard, you're so different. I like you but you scare me."

He sort of laughed, with a mixture of irony and disbelief. "What?"

"I'm going away. We're moving to Virginia. . . . My father, you know."

He couldn't think of one thing to say, just kept looking hard at her. He might have kissed her if he had known that was what he wanted. "Take care of yourself."

She reached out and took his hand, shook it formally, embarrassed but resolute. She left him, crossing the grass she turned to wave. "Good luck."

"That was a pretty girl. Who was she?" His mother startled him.

"Hmm?"

"Who was that girl?"

"I don't know. Just a girl."

"Oh. I see." She appraised him, cautious and curious.

Jim Wilkes joined them. "This is almost over, Janice. Let's get on home."

"Are you ready to go, Richard?"

"Yeah. I'm gonna walk. I'll see you at home. Here take this." He pulled his arms out of the jacket and handed it to his mother. Disappontment wet her eyes. He unbuttoned his sleeves and rolled them up to his elbows. He pulled his tie loose and removed it. "It's all over now. I'll be home soon."

They watched him cross the lawn to the sidewalk in front of the church. His head was up, his hands were buried in his pockets. He'd always remember. He wondered if in ten years she would remember him. He expected so.

DAVID KYSILKO: I was born in Duluth in 1950, grew up in Hibbing and Minneapolis, went to Oberlin College, served a stint as co-director of a free school in Wisconsin, then retired again to the Twin Cities to earn dollars in ways that left plenty of time to write and travel. I am presently working full-time on an MFA degree in fiction.

I write because I feel compelled to capture life in some way, and words are my best tools. I understood this one day when I was touring the island of Crete, and spent an afternoon at the museum in Iraklion looking through Minoan artifacts. There were statuettes of snake goddesses, birds and other animals, drawings of octopodes and bulls, axes and saws. Everything had a touching simplicity, and I felt very close to the Minoans, though I wasn't sure why. Then I came across a well-preserved vase decorated with a large drawing of a double axe that was surrounded by tall blades of grass. It was so finely and sensitively done that I felt I could see across 3000 years into the Minoan mind, feel his desire to communicate what was important in his life, his compulsion to say, "This is it." I felt his need to get it outside so it could be looked at concretely. He, too, knew that life slips away quickly. Perhaps I was only projecting my own feelings, but at least I'd grasped what those feelings were. I'd known before then that I wanted to write, but from then on I knew why.

245

David Kysilko

BURT'S BAIT

It was just past midnight, and Burt's OK gas station sat in an island of light in the forest. The highway, U.S. 61, that borders the North Shore of Lake Superior, was empty except for one pair of headlights blinking through the trees to the north. Hands in pockets against the early autumn chill, Burt leaned against one of his tin soldier pumps and watched the car hit the straight-away in front of the station. It slowed, and he stood up and started to tinker with a loose bolt on one of the handles, so he looked like a man with barely enough time to pump some gas for a hundred dollars. Then he saw it was neither customer nor friend, but his mother in the familiar old Chrysler, and he cursed out loud.

It wasn't unusual for his mother to show; he was used to putting up with her once or twice a week, usually after she'd had a few at the Sundowner. Normally she was driven to the station by Leonard, a man Burt had dubbed "the chauffeur" because he had spent ten years in that Chrysler carting his mother up and down the North Shore. But that night there was no sign of Leonard. His mother was at the wheel, and she drove the car over part of the curb, seemed to hang in the air a moment, then crunched into the gravel and stopped within inches of the pumps.

Burt jumped out of the way. "You drunk," he shouted. He was in a sour mood: he had just spent five futile hours waiting for a car to stop; and he did not want to see his mother because lately she reminded him of something distasteful, though what it was he couldn't say. Besides, Jeremy was back. Burt looked into the car from the passenger side. His mother was short and fat and he wondered how her stubby legs managed to reach the pedal.

"Where's Jeremy?" she called out the window. The top of her head was level with the backrest, and she looked like an astronaut strapped in for takeoff. She raced the engine a few times, and the exhaust blew a little swirl of dust and smoke across the drive.

"He ain't come by yet. Where's your chauffeur?"

"Too damn drunk to drive," she said. The "d's" sounded more like "t's." "Maybe I just wait a while. You give a lady a drink?"

"Go home," he said. He didn't even want to look at her. He turned to one of his pumps and read, on the tiny meter at the top, the total gallons pumped through. He tried to remember what he'd started the day with, then he tried to think how he was going to get rid of her before Jeremy came. When she was drunk, she often got the idea Jeremy was her lover, and then she was so ridiculous he couldn't do anything about it.

He heard her make a move to get out of the car, so he quit staring at the pump and hustled over to stand in front of the door. It hit a few times against his thigh; then, with rare docility, and looking very tired, his mother sat back again and stared through the spokes of the steering wheel. "How's business?" she asked without interest.

Burt flicked a thumbs-down.

"Well, better that than wearing out the furniture in front of the tv, like you used to."

"Sure, now I sit next to the door here and wait for cars."

"Thanks to my money."

"Thanks to my old man's life insurance." Burt stopped before the well-worn conversation could get any further. The problem was that the money for the gas station really had been an unexpected bit of generosity on his mother's part, which she never let him forget. "You wouldn't know what to do with it," was his usual answer. He knew this was true: all the money in the world would not change his mother's lifestyle, except for adding a bit of silver plating that would soon tarnish and look like hell just like everything else. Going to hell, he thought, was maybe what she reminded him of. They lived in a square, five-room house that was in constant danger of being overrun by the forest and by the discarded junk that never made it to the dump. An old pick-up in the back yard looked like a sinking freighter as the grass grew up over the windshield. Burt could barely remember the days when it ran.

Off to the north more headlights flickered through the forest, and the car sounded like someone going along ripping boards off the fence posts, so Burt figured it must be Jeremy's souped-up Malibu. He wished he had gotten rid of his mother. The maroon

Malibu pulled into the driveway and parked off to the side. Burt noticed that Jeremy had put on a new set of wide tracks. Jeremy, who worked at the taconite plant, made three times what he could with no family to support, no bills to pay. He was just in from Canada, where he could hire a plane and a guide without thinking about it. All because his old man knew one of the foremen at the plant and could get him in. Burt didn't bear Jeremy any grudges, exactly, but he wished his own father had made a little more of himself before he died.

"Jeremy!" his mother called, suddenly coming to life.

"You rich sonuvabitch," Burt said, breaking in. He saw the girlish expression on her round face, and he knew they were in for it. Jeremy got out, waved, and stopped to light a cigarette, cupping his hand against the faint breeze. He was still wearing his work overalls, a plaid hunting jacket and hat, and he sported a new mustache that was barely visible under the station's floodlights. He got his cigarette going and walked up to the Chrysler.

"Hey Burt," he said, looking significantly into the car, "I thought I'd help you clear away some of your business."

"Shit," Burt laughed nervously. "Business is going as good as your whiskers."

"What you want to hang around here for?" his mother asked Jeremy. "Come with me." She patted the seat next to her.

"Ohh." Jeremy raised his eyebrows. "You mean . . . ," and with his thumb and index finger he formed a ring that he penetrated with the middle finger of his other hand and accompanied with slurping sounds. Then he leaned his head through the window, smacking his lips, and made as if to kiss the old woman, but with his left hand he reached across her and put the car in drive. The transmission caught and the car began to crawl away. Jeremy laughed, sputtering like a faucet. "Darling, don't leave without me," he shouted.

"Shut up," Burt said. His mother found the gas pedal instead of the brake, and the car lurched forward. Twenty yards later it stopped, grinding the gravel underneath.

"Sweetheart!" Jeremy called, and he fell on his stomach and began humping the ground.

"You bastards!" she yelled. Her voice came muffled from inside the car, which lurched forward again.

"Go home!" Burt said. This time the car spun out of the drive and onto the highway. Jeremy rolled on his back and howled. Burt sniffed. "Why are you such an asshole," he said.

"It's a good time, man," Jeremy said. He got up. "Anyway, with you pussyfooting around she would have been here all night."

Burt sulked, but he could not deny this. Jeremy beat the dust out of his hunting cap and readjusted it on his head. "Forget it," he said. "Come see what I brought you." Burt thought that forgetting was easier said than done; and even though he wanted to forget her, he found himself mentally defending his mother against Jeremy's pranks, though he couldn't get much beyond how you shouldn't kick someone when she was down, and how the old lady had a spark of life in her yet. He followed Jeremy to his car and watched him take an ice chest out of the trunk. It was filled with northern pike cut into steaks like salmon. In spite of himself Burt whistled appreciatively.

"Nothing in there that was under twelve pounds," Jeremy said. "And they got this old arthritic guy that did all the cleaning. He comes up to you wearing these bib overalls and chewing something, and he says, 'That'll cost you twenty-five cents a fish, depending though on how many you got.' But you know, I could never figure if you had a lotta fish if that cost you more, or less, or what. And the guide, he did most of the cooking and building fires and all. Hell, I thought he was going to dig a hole for me to shit in." They went into the station and Burt sat in his swivel chair next to the door. Jeremy lit another cigarette and perched himself on the counter next to a pile of oil filters, and went on about the fish he'd thrown back, the plane ride over the endless puddles of lakes, and what a tough sonuvabitch the guide was. He stared up toward the ceiling, as if waiting for the guide's face to appear in the rising cigarette smoke. "What he was," he began slowly, "was like a cross between a bear and one of them French Cannucks, and I think he's got some squaw pussy somewhere, so you can imagine. He had these big old hands, too, brown and tough, that you could hang your extra hooks on. At night, I swear, I saw him rub them with saddle soap."

He laughed at his own story, but Burt stared glumly out at the empty highway. He had been looking forward to this talk, but now Jeremy's chatter oppressed him: first, because of the way they had kicked his mother around; and second, because it made his own life look dull unto death. As he watched, a car flashed by, like a northern that missed his lure, and he counted it in his peculiar way. That is, he didn't keep an exact tally (though he did think of trucks with four axles as counting two), but he observed them, noted them, marked the passage of each vehicle in his head, so that by closing he had a definite feel for the number that had gone by, and who was driving them: fishermen, hunters, canoeists, tourists. Soon, with the fall rush, there would be a change, and the old people would start arriving in their big Buicks and Caddys, driving up and down the shore looking at leaves like they were made of gold. "Gosh, isn't it pretty," they said. "Well, it's different, anyway," he said in return, but to himself.

What he could do about his mother he didn't know. For years her worst had merely created annoyance, on the order of mosquito bites, rashes, hangovers and diarrhea. But lately she made him feel like a cesspool, collecting scum and going nowhere. He wished she would marry Leonard, so she would be off his hands, but the chances were slim. Leonard had retired ten years ago from nothing in particular, claiming a bad back, and now lived on veteran's disability. Aside from being affable and harmless he had nothing going for him. No one rejected him, but no one really wanted him, either. His mother wanted Jeremy, or thought she did. He tried finding it humorous, but couldn't.

"Some poor sucker broke his wrist down at the plant tonight," Jeremy said.

"Yeah?" Burt usually found this sort of information interesting, and was himself something of an encyclopedia on people who drove off the North Shore highway, especially if they landed in the lake. But he felt that Jeremy had noticed his moroseness and was attempting to cheer him up, so he tried to look bored.

"This dumb shit dropped a crate on him. You should have heard him screech, we thought somebody'd dropped a cat into a machine again. Some asshole did that once, you know. Anyway, we race over and he's standing there like a faggot, all pale with his wrist limp." Jeremy demonstrated, and Burt couldn't help a quick grin. Then he smothered it and wondered why nothing interesting happened to him.

While he was brooding about this, a pair of headlights beamed into the office. "Here comes your pot of gold," Jeremy said. The car, a beat-up Ford with a canoe on top, drove past the pumps and parked next to Jeremy's Chevy.

"Shit," Burt said, though he knew it could have been worse: it could have been his mother again.

"From the Cities, I bet," Jeremy said. They saw two people in the car: a man driving, and a young woman sleeping next to him.

"Betcha they ain't married, either," Burt offered. He had to admit that men from the Cities had a way with women that remained a mystery to him. He wondered how they could get these young ones with breasts busting out of their shirts like in *Playboy* to go camping and canoeing with them, share sleeping bags, walk about with hands glued to each other's ass, and then be so damn casual about it? Like it happened every day. Maybe it did. He spent plenty of time at the station thinking about it, especially in summer. He was often tempted to ask them how they did it, just like they asked him where was the best place to eat or camp or catch walleyes, but he hadn't gotten around to it yet.

The man got out of the car and walked toward the office. He had muddy boots and pants, a week's worth of beard, and he walked with a muscular stiffness. But Burt figured him as not over twenty-five, and despite the grime he had an underlying cleanliness (got from spending too much time indoors) that marked him as a city dweller. The man stuck his head in the door and grinned a fresh, trusting grin. "Howdy," he said with shy confidence. He seemed aware that he was young, healthy, and had a promising future, but at the same time thought this counted for very little in his present circumstances.

"Looks like you been in the woods," Burt said.

The canoeist nodded, then blushed. "Hey, I'm sorry I can't be some business for you," he said, "but I sure could use a cup of coffee if you've got one. Every place around here seems shut down." Then he added apologetically, "I've got to get my girlfriend back before morning."

"Always keep a pot going," Burt said, and he pointed to a little automatic perculator and a stack of styrofoam cups.

"You from the Cities, hey?" Jeremy asked aggressively as the canoeist poured his coffee, and he nodded and blushed again.

Most of the people Burt knew didn't like slickers because they tried to run everything in the state. His mother was good for nearly an hour a day on this topic, starting with how they controlled all the money and jobs, and usually ending with how they'd killed his father, because it was a man from the Twin Cities that had shot his father in a hunting accident (though he hadn't died until two years later, and then of a heart attack). "They shun't let 'em nort' of Duluth'," was her final word. Burt, though he generally agreed, was tired of hearing about it, even if it was worth a good snort when someone at the Sundowner told of an upstate legislator who'd proposed turning the Cities into a wilderness area, banning cars and snowmobiles and industry. His own policy was to treat them all right when they stopped at his station, so maybe they'd remember and stop again; and this canoeist looked like he could be trusted. Burt thought he might ask him about women, if he got the chance.

The canoeist was quiet, but alert and self-conscious. He sipped his coffee silently, as if slurping was obnoxious and out of place in a gas station. "How's business?" he asked. "You get a good piece of the tourist trade, I imagine."

Jeremy snickered at this, making grinding and whining noises that sounded like a car trying to start in forty below weather. Burt suddenly noticed how his sense of humor thrived on everyone else's bad luck. "Slow," he told the canoeist, and he gave Jeremy a dirty look. "But I ain't hardly started yet. And next year I'm going to open a bait shop in the back room there. I got a line on some tanks already. Suckers, shiners, chubs, nite crawlers, you name it, Burt's Bait'll have it."

"You catch a lotta fish up there?" Jeremy asked, cocking an eye up at the canoeist.

"Enough," he said. "Plenty to eat, anyway."

"You ought to take a gun with you," Jeremy continued, as if everyone in the world knew that, and it was like putting pants on in the morning. "All the grouse you can stomach in those woods. I get a little tired of fish, myself."

The canoeist looked at him skeptically. "I don't know . . ."

"Nobody'd catch you," Jeremy insisted. "I bag'em whenever I can." He gave Burt a wink. Giving slickers a hard time was standard recreation, and he assumed Burt's business wouldn't be called a bait shop for nothing. Burt's bad mood continued, however, and he resented Jeremy busting in and taking over the action.

"You couldn't bag more than popcorn," he said.

Jeremy looked surprised. "Hell . . ." he said.

There was a silence until the canoeist picked up the thread. "Well, maybe I could've used a gun this time," he said seriously. "A goddam bear came running out of the woods just last night, I don't know why. He charged the fire, circled it a few times and ran off. I was hauling my ass into the canoe and my girlfriend was off at the latrine. She never saw him."

"Sure, bears are no problem," Burt said quickly. "I got one last Friday with my .22 pistol."

Jeremy looked up in disbelief. "A .22? You could hardly kill my grandmother with a .22."

"I got him all right."

"Where, at the Duluth zoo?"

Burt swiveled around to Jeremy. "Out at the garbage dump. Me and Fergy were out shooting rats and drinking beer. You just wait 'til their eyes catch the moonlight," he explained to the canoeist, "Then you've got 'em. Well, we'd barely started when this big brown mother comes lumbering in, looking for dinner. And all we had, see, was our .22's. So I told Fergy to go start my pick-up and be ready to beat the hell outa there. Then I made sure my clip was full, and aimed, and put one in her. And hardly anything happened. The bear looked up kinda startled, like she was asking, 'What the hell's going on?' So I kept firing, and that bear, she must've thought there was bees or something stinging her, she got up on her hind legs and started swatting around and roaring. I put the whole clip in her and she began spinning around like a dog chasing its tail, so I began to edge back to the pick-up; I mean, you couldn't tell what she'd do next. And what she did was, she just fell over. So I reloaded and went to take a look. She was gone all right, but I put a couple more right through the eye socket just to make sure."

Burt stopped; he felt light headed and out of breath. That the real story would eventually get back to Jeremy, that it was Fergy doing the shooting while he kept his hand on the pick-up's gear shift, didn't matter. "Just wanted to shake the slicker up," he could say. For once he'd gotten the jump on Jeremy, and he looked up at the canoeist to see if he was impressed. He knew that with some tourists one hardly had to walk into the woods to take a piss and they were ready to sign you up as a guide. But the canoeist was only staring at the floor.

"Well, did you skin her?" Jeremy asked.

"Naw. We just let her sit." Burt was sweating. He wiped his forehead with the side of his hand, and wiped his hand on his pants.

Jeremy leaned back, shaking his head and thinking. "How about that," he said.

"Christ, you guys are real killers," the canoeist said suddenly. "Real heroes." His voice was even, but he was still staring at the floor, his hands devouring the styrofoam cup. Burt was confused. Jeremy looked indifferent, perhaps ready to crack a joke, but Burt wanted to know what the canoeist was thinking.

"What do you mean?" he said. "You think it's crazy we didn't skin the damn thing?" he asked, though he knew that wasn't it. He believed the canoeist had something to say, and he waited for him to speak, his senses keyed-up, suddenly aware of the gas and oil stench that always clings to a filling station, and clung to his hands as well, so he had stopped thinking of it as distinct from himself.

But the canoeist said nothing. He flushed and stood solemnly in a posture suitable for a funeral, his hands folded in front of his crotch, the mangled cup (instead of a hat) dangling from two fingers. His back twitched slightly. Finally he threw the cup in the trash can. "Forget it," he said. "Thanks for the coffee." And he walked out.

Was that all? Burt thought. He was suddenly angry and felt betrayed, and he got up and stood in the doorway, watching the man walk to his car. "A pussy," he mumbled, just loud enough so Jeremy could hear. The canoeist banged his door shut and turned his engine over, and it churned and whined but refused to start. "Sucker probably flooded it," Burt said, still talking to himself. "I'll give him something to get him going." He went to his desk and took out the .22 pistol he kept there in case of robbery.

"You crazy or something?" Jeremy asked as he watched this, and he slid off the counter but did not move toward Burt. Burt stood in the doorway again and watched as the canoeist's old car finally fired, rolling a cloud of exhaust across the driveway. When it began to move he lifted the gun and took aim at one of the rear tires.

"Give him something to talk about," he finally answered Jeremy. "Give us all something to talk about."

"What the hell is wrong with you," Jeremy said, though he remained still. "You want the sheriff in here? Gunfight at the OK gas station? How'd that be for business?"

Burt wavered and lowered the pistol. He saw it was no use; he wasn't crazy, yet. The car backed onto the highway, and he followed the taillights as they disappeared to the south. He remembered that he was going to ask the canoeist about women, and he began to despair. Though he remained angry, the feeling grew in him that he was worse off than the slicker. He had just proved it to himself, by not shooting at the car.

As Burt gazed idly past the pumps he saw another car driving toward the station. It was Leonard's Chrysler, back for round two. This time, though, Leonard himself was at the wheel, and his mother sat as far to the other side as her fat body would allow.

"Christ, don't she get enough?" Jeremy said, but with a trace of glee.

His mother was the last person Burt wanted to see. The same memory of something distasteful came back to him, so acrid and real that he felt he could lick it off his lips and spit it out. This time he knew immediately it was the same feeling the canoeist had given him: it was simply the death of his own life before he had even begun. He had been dying for years, and he blamed his mother. He felt he was destined to take Leonard's place, driving her around as she grew older, fatter, more immobile, but never died.

Burt raised the pistol that still hung in his hand and pointed it toward the Chrysler as it drove past the pumps. He fired three times over the car, and the cracks echoed six times against the Sawtooth Mountains that formed the edge of the lake. Leonard, who had looked ready to pass out on top of the steering wheel, jerked up, and his red face lost its color.

"Go home and fuck!" Burt shouted, and he pulled the trigger once more. Leonard did not look toward the station again. He gunned the car so it spun around on the gravel, and kept it floored. Like a playing card flipped over, Burt's mother appeared on the opposite side, waving her fist out the window and alternately cursing Burt and telling Leonard to stop. For once Leonard didn't listen, and the car sped off to the north.

Jeremy was laughing so hard he had to wipe away some tears. "Now that's more like it," he shouted to Burt. "That's taking the bull by the horns. You see old Leonard's dome, pale as the goddam moon?"

Burt stood humbly hanging his head, not sure he had done anything. At the sound of the shots time had split open, and in that space he did not think anything could exist. Then he felt the pistol, and it was hot, and he knew he must have fired it. He turned and glared at Jeremy.

"Don't blame me it went off," Jeremy said. "Now why don't you forget about 'em. Forget about this fuckin' station, too: ain't nobody else gonna stop by here except maybe a moose wants a drink of water outa your biffy."

The hardness left Burt's face, and he put the gun back in the drawer. "I suppose . . . ," he said.

Jeremy looked steadily into Burt's eyes, then suddenly turned jocular and punched him in the shoulder. "Hey, we've put in our days," he said. "I've got a pint in my glove compartment, and a couple magazines. Shut off the lights out there and get some 7-Up from your machine and we'll put it down."

"Well, I suppose," Burt drawled, and he walked to the fuse box. He felt that the whole night he had tried to be someone else, and he was suddenly tired of it. "I suppose that's all this night is good for, anyway." He flicked a switch and the island of light disappeared.

"You bet," Jeremy said. "You bet."

LAWRENCE SUTIN: Fiction is human truth conveyed by means of a complex ventriloquist's act. When I read what I like the illusion is that I am being spoken to by an author. In fact the author is long gone and the book is the dummy on my lap. The dummy shows me our script and I read it aloud in my head until I begin to believe it. That's the dummy's cue and it starts to talk back. In good stories the dummy *always* has the best lines.

When I write I learn how very subtle that dummy is. It can induce the saddest and silliest thoughts without sense or warning and may even try to rework the plot on its own. While I am making the finishing touches, painting its wide innocent eyes, the dummy blinks impatiently and practices inducing sad and silly thoughts in me. It would prefer to be out of my hands by now. It no longer feels sufficiently appreciated. It imagines a stranger suspended in disbelief in a small room with a single lamp. The stranger is reading carefully page by page and neither his nor the dummy's lips move even once.

I would like to express my heartfelt gratitude and awe to four writers whose books made me realize why I had always wanted to write: Henry Miller, John Cowper Powys, Isaac Bashevis Singer, Blaise Cendrars. I would also like to thank my friend and teacher Judith Guest for her kindness and shared knowledge of the storyteller's craft.

Lawrence Sutin

WHAT IS A THING?

"Each flight of imagination is rewarded by a moment of delight.
It is not surprising that such a method of existence should grow
upon one."

— Stendhal, *On Love*

That night Henry took a bus to the bus station. He and Susan
shared the car as well as the apartment, but all that was due for
change. The last hellish week had left Henry on the brink of
exhaustion. Susan had fallen in love or, in her own terminology,
had developed a strong interest she could no longer ignore, in the
bartender at The Situation; there she worked as a waitress, wearing a long dress and letting her dark hair fall to her elbows. She
had beautiful eyes, large, luminous almonds of brown and white.
Through her he had discovered his utter weakness for delicate
perfume dabbed behind the ears. What was best was to kiss one's
way slowly up the tender vine of the neck, past the loose lock of
hair which encircled the cheek, and finally into the delicate, tender swirls of the uplifted ear, tongue teasing and tasting, while the
scent of sultry, radiant night blossoms filled his senses. Sex
might be better with someone else someday, but not soon.

Now he was late. Susan, in a fit of flaring anger which emerged
as he once again urged her to reconsider, refused to drive him to
the station and insisted that she have the car for work. Henry,
head held low as a mongrel's, capitulated. It was over. But he
could not forget how he had loved living with her these past few
months. Her calm tides smoothed the rough span of his days. He
enjoyed laughing with her, or watching her while she danced to
phonograph music. On her off-nights they went to movies, then to
their bar, then came home teasingly happy, removing each other's
coats as the door closed behind them. It was over. His stomach
turned and pressed against his abdomen, wanting out. And I'm
late too, he realized again. Heading cross country to a funeral,
and I'm late. He ran out of the bus into the bus station but the big
bus, the Streamliner bound for Chicago, had departed five min-

utes before. The next was due in three hours, at ten-thirty. He had a night to spend in a bus station.

Gratefully he felt anger emerge to stifle his anguish. If she hadn't been such a bitch I wouldn't be waiting here right now. It isn't unimportant to get to your uncle's funeral in decent shape at a decent hour. It wouldn't have been any great sacrifice for her. At most she would have been fifteen minutes late to work. But now that she had the bartender in tow that surely would not matter. He could cover for her. Henry knew the bartender. He was handsome, but conventionally so: easy smile, white teeth, dark, thick hair. Was there no subtlety to her tastes? But then, Susan herself was hardly an abstruse aesthetic puzzle. Her beauty drew waves of attention, always. And now I'm here for three hours and she's with him, and the next week in my life will include the funeral of a remote uncle, a family gathering after the funeral during which I will have to explain my lack of life plans to pesty relatives, two days back in the parental nest with still more questions and revelations of inescapable identity and difference, and then back here for the final separation with the woman of my dreams, all this to be sandwiched between mirror-image trips in a God-awful air-conditioned tin tube with people smoking cigars and popping aspirins and barfing, and little kids crying, and weird old ladies starting conversations, and everyone sweaty and smelly and miserable all through the night, unwrapping peanut butter sandwiches to console themselves. His anger was gone again and he was standing in the main waiting room of the station; overhead through the public address speakers came a blurred chant of cities, all of which seemed to end in soft vowels.

Large fluorescent fixtures, like illuminated waffles, filled the room with tense, humming light. There were row upon row of plastic seats, all attached to cross-beamed metal frames. Several servicemen in uniform occupied one of the rows, reading papers and magazines, eating candy bars and chips, or simply slumping, their caps pulled down over their eyes. A mother balanced a little girl on her knees while she bottle fed an infant strapped to her chest. There was a young couple, the man's left arm around the woman's shoulders while she leaned into him smiling, that reminded him of the happiness he had lost. An older pair, presumably married, sat side by side, she squinting at a teen-age girl sitting cross-legged in a short skirt, thinking perhaps what she had been and how she had looked at that time, at the doorway of life, while he, and this, Henry suspected, no one his own age did any longer, and why was that?, peeled an apple. Those who were alone sat with their belongings piled on one and sometimes both of the chairs alongside them. Henry understood. It was not callousness, he knew, just that the risks were too high. He laughed at his own thought. What risks? What is wrong with us all in here, anyway? Who wrote this script? Wouldn't we all like to travel together in a nice, friendly, cuddly bunch, singing songs and passing opened bottles of red wine over our shoulders? Why are we made so that getting along amounts to a miracle? "Oh someone," he said to himself, pacing now his second circle around the rows, "someone come and hold this poor boy's hand. He may not be able to make it."

Enough. Sit down. He chose an end seat, slid his satchel beneath the chair, and tried to breathe slowly and so calm himself. It was difficult. Things wanted to jump. He could not explain it better than that. Nothing fit. The phone booths wanted to spring into the air. The columns supporting the roof would crack. Long lines of people waiting for tickets readied themselves for an assault. The thin glass walls protecting the vendors could not hold. Everyone had places to go, urgent aspirations, but the schedules were mere columns of random digits. Look at us all sitting here! Do we look as though we can wait much longer? God knows there's not enough gossip in the papers to see us through. Stupid sheep grazing on the nub-ends of other people's once green desires. They cut down trees for that? The damn ashtrays are filled to their brims with sucked-out, filthy filters. It's all designed to turn us into nervous wrecks who can't inhale without coughing.

He took a book from his satchel, a familiar friend, one he had chosen carefully to nurse him through his travel. After five minutes of attempting to read it he knew he had made a disastrous choice. It was a paperback, elegantly designed, an import, a tasteful, chubby little anthology he had once found in a pile of discards in a second-hand bookshop, entitled *A Book of English Verse*. Within it, over a span exceeding five hundred pages, was the spiral portrait gallery of the English poets.

Henry had always treasured poetry, and by reading aloud from this volume had passed many a tremulous evening. But this particular crisis was beyond the power of even the amassed poetic tradition to assuage. The distance between his plight and the polished verse on the pages could not be broached. These poets had no inkling of the passion and despair of modern uprooted times, in which spirit meant spunk, soul was barroom music, the pangs of love mere cries of criblike dependence and the call to fidelity only the confession of a warped libido. Henry looked about him. Fat Ben Jonson would have gagged on the hot dogs those children ate with their father's approval, and humped, dwarfish, Pope would hawk pencils there in the corner in these our times. He shut the book. What I need, he thought, is not to come to grips with myself, but to escape, pure and simple. He replaced the book in the satchel, walked over to a coin locker in the wall, placed a quarter in the slot and withdrew the key, put the satchel inside and slammed the door. The clock hanging from the ceiling like an upsidedown lollipop said 7:48. Over two and one-half hours to kill. He left the station, walking rapidly through the double set of glass doors into rain.

The grey, lidded sky had just now burst asunder into a downpour. There was no place to step that did not shine. Pooling rain gleamed in cracks and dents of the sidewalk as the street lights caught upon it. Henry's feet splashed while his face bobbed suddenly three feet before him in a shimmering puddle. He stopped and puckered his lips, extended his elbows and quacked. Rain drops on the reflection ruined the effect, but he saw there that Susan was peering over his shoulder with her large eyes open wide. He turned to her, shuddering from cold, and said aloud, "I am doing all this for you." She disappeared. In the rain you come, Susan. Even in the rain. It will do you no good. I know you are not loving me any more, and I will not love you either. Go away. He wiped his eyes with his knuckles. She did not care.

It was hard and cold now, with a wind. He needed a scarf, a hat, shelter. When he looked up, the rain, showing clearly in the light, fell sharply, curved slightly by the rushing wind. He opened his mouth and shivered as one chill drop struck directly upon a filling. Another, larger shudder overtook him, and at last he knew firmly what was happening. He was nearly soaked through, standing on the curb, not moving, waving his arms. This part of town he barely knew, but he was certain that there would be a small cafe nearby with coffee. A warm place to sit. Anyplace but the station, that buzzing alarm clock of humanity. He ran, bounding across an intersection against the light, toward a blinking neon display sign hanging above a doorway, the only such sign in his line of vision. The doorway was open, surprising enough during a rain. He moved inside and began, in the new warmth, to shake convulsively. Was there a towel, a hot drink? Around him he saw only amusement machines.

"Hey chief, could you close the door please? It just blew open and we're losing heat."

Henry shut the door quickly, not bothering to first trace the voice to a visible body. Escaping the rain and cold was sufficient. He scanned the room. Pinball machines: Space Shot, Big Chief, Galaxy War, Hot Rodder, Ace of Spades, Mask of Evil, Dealer's Choice, Lucky Loony, You're the One, Blast Off. Electronic rifle shoots, submarine chasers, auto races, tank battles, fighter dogfights. A handgrip strength test. A four for a quarter photo booth. Vending machines with charms and medallions. A man in a metal cage smoking a cigarette watching him. Water dripping at his, Henry's, feet. More machines stretching out on behind the man, but Henry was looking downward now, observing with numbed awe his own rainfall onto dirty linoleum. He shook his head and spattered the floor for yards around him. The one about the guy who didn't have enough sense to come in out of the rain ran through him. "Excuse me," he said, forcing himself into high volume, "do you know what time it is?"

"Clock's on the wall. Eight-twenty-five. The floor's getting wet, chief. You want a towel?" He held up a grey cloth. Henry moved toward him, calculating his time in the downpour. What had he done for one-half hour? It was lost to him; he remembered only that after he had spoken to Susan he had been quiet and it had been quiet, very pretty really, tiny full moons shining all about him and marble-firm aura coating his body until it was broken by what? What woke him? Susan again? She didn't care; that was resolved. Keep it so. Let up now and I'll be whining in my sleeve all the way to Chicago. As it is I'm guaranteed jammed sinuses and possible high fever. Buy aspirin before I leave. Drink it down with what? I need a canteen too. I'm in the wrong place. The man handed him out the towel through the bars. Henry brought it immediately onto his hair and pressed down hard, closing his eyes.

"I could give you some coffee if that would help."

"Thanks, I'd like that a lot." He opened his eyes, catching at the same time the stale, piercing ammonia odor of the towel. Something in his face wrinkled.

"Yeah, I use it to wipe the machines, Sorry, it's all I've got."

"That's o.k. I'm sure I must look pretty crazy to you anyway."

"No, man. You look really natural to me." The man's face did not smile. Behind the grill in the poor light it looked like a green grape, than changed slowly into something more drawn, like a pear. His eyes rested comfortably on Henry's chin, a practiced glance for the changeling public. Should I give him my name? Is he trying to be friendly or waiting for me to spend money? He brought the towel over the back of his neck; the sudden sweep released crystalline drops clinging to his hair ends and sent them scuttling down his back. He patted at them several times through his shirt. No good. The man had turned aside from him, reaching for a coffee pot standing on a hot plate. He appeared again. Very narrow eyes, Henry noted. Like seeds, little dark ones. What color were those irises, brown or black?

"You'll have to use my cup."

"Oh that's o.k., I can do without."

The man's mouth puckered. No wrinkles at the edges. Early thirties. Have I made him angry? "Suit yourself," he said.

"No. That's not what I meant. I just thought maybe you wouldn't want me using your cup. I don't want to put you out."

"I offered," he answered, shrugging. "It's beans to me if you use my cup unless you're sick or something."

"I'm not sick yet," Henry said. "But I guess I will be."

He poured Henry coffee; then sent an arm below the counter, all the while holding his face impassive. The arm returned with peach brandy.

"Great."

"Nothing better," the man agreed. "A snort slows everything down, including germs."

"You're being very nice to me," Henry told him as the spiked cup reached his hand. "Thank you. My name's Henry."

"Sam, Henry."

"Thank you again."

"It's o.k." Sam leaned back, arms on his belly, which was not very large, Henry thought, just protruding, and eyes on Henry's chin again, service rendered, passivity restored. At least I'm not dripping any more. He drank the coffee, sharp peachiness coating his tongue. I'm not cold here either. He found the clock himself this time. About two hours. Progress. Plus hospitality. I should play something to be nice. Does he own this place? It was a long, narrow rectangle lined by machines, the cage itself the width of a machine and inserted among them. No one else here but me. I should eat. But, drinking the coffee, Henry knew that he should play, for the sake of Sam's kindness and the benefit of his income, Henry's eyes now focused upon large red words painted upon the yellow walls: SAM'S SUPER EMPORIUM — FUN AND GAMES THAT AMAZE. What better time? He flexed his fingers. For Sam's sake and my own. A small excitement spoke to him.

"I'm on my way to my uncle's funeral," Henry began. Sam looked up from his *Popular Mechanics* and nodded; the vocal tone had precluded condolences. a disturbance in the air, yes, but hardly mournful. Henry paused to brush the guilt of indifference from his thoughts. "And so I'm waiting for a bus. Maybe I could play some of these. They look fun."

"Amazing too," Sam added flatly. It was late. Henry gauged the depth of the sympathy and concern before him and rather suddenly struck rock. Better play a lot.

"So could you change these two ones for me?" The bills were wet and felt like raw potato slices. They were pulled from between his fingers. Change fell into a kidney-shaped bowl.

"Thanks."

Sam lifted the magazine. Henry felt his skin prickle beneath his damp clothing; the withdrawal, sudden as had been the kindness, left him anxious and doubly alone. The glowing machines vibrated. Why do I want to cling to him? Am I queer tonight? Just lonely. I don't want to shoot Indians or Japs. Try pinball. He pushed a quarter into one called Wheel of Fortune. Automatic ball appearance on this one; he himself preferred a hand plunger to set the ball before the opening shot, but that was that. He sent it medium force up the alley into the arena. As he had hoped, it plopped, after some bouncing that was somehow oddly skewed, due perhaps to the placement of the magnets, into the bonus set-up alley. Two more such hits in the adjacent alleys would light the free game target. Random free fall. He poised his fingers on the flipper buttons, used the right flipper to send the ball up against an unexpectedly strong side cushion which sprang it against a one-hundred point nodule and then into the left gutter. 8,000. Free game if he hit 65,000. Accelerate. Second ball did badly: no alley, scattered scoring against minor targets. 17,000. Pathetic. Henry rallied with number 3, a strong finish, a sucker ball to get you to play again. My heart's not in it; my reflexes are shot. And only one three-ball play for a quarter. I can remember getting three five-ball plays for the same price. I'm getting old. Someone somewhere said once: when I was a young man, time ran. It's like that. Not tonight, though. Plenty of time tonight. Because I don't want it. He moved to Elephant Hunt and again scored poorly. Use up my change and get out of here, he vowed. But he could hardly resist Love's Disguises, with its heart-patterned lights of red, blue and yellow. Henry shot fiercely, barraging the prime targets with flipper-delayed bullet shots. A free game on a machine match with the final two digits of his score produced a heart-thump sound and a relighting of the scoreboard. Overanxious, he frittered the free game away.

As he passed by Sam's cage, bound for the rear of the room to see what $1.25 would be good for, he ventured to maintain contact. "Got a free game," he said, not prideful, really, just puppylike, lonely.

"Which machine?" Sam asked, the magazine on his lap. He had not been watching. Why did I want him to? What's wrong with me?

"Love's Disguises."

"Tough machine. Nice going." Sam lit another cigarette.

Henry walked on, vowing to rein himself in from further attention begging. It was now clear to him why Sam had taken on such importance. Someone had to hear his story. He was poisoned by the loss of Susan; he needed to bleed to clean himself. Sam might understand. Who knew? Henry was ready to try, ready to spill his soul completely. I'm just drawn to her, he wanted to say. Sam would nod knowingly. It's like that with women, they would agree, certain ones claim you and you can't say why. With Susan, of course, there were obvious reasons, but they were neither necessary nor sufficient. Beautiful, buoyant, laughing, yes, but it was more than these qualities could ever convey. A gestalt, maybe, a whole greater than any summation of the parts. A gestalt so good it makes you hot just watching, huh? Sam would jibe.

Yea, Henry might admit, but it was never all roses even so. She had some quirks that were driving me crazy, the flirting, the sloppiness, the bubble shell of selfishness that made her smile when she should have cared. Like now. He could see her approaching a table, tired, maybe, but a knowledge there somewhere of her effect, her movements, males squirming; drunken droolers, she once called them, but she still smiled, a Circe, after all. What could she do if she made her living from tips? Fine. Let her. Slap on the shoulder from Sam and then an old adage, tried and true. Plenty of fish in the sea. Forget her. They're all the same. Then, a bit rueful, Sam takes out a billfold with plasticene photo holders, flips to the last, points, there is a woman, her, he says, she got me, you know? More nods. Yeah.

Henry then noticed a narrow passage branching off rightways at the rear of the shop. At its end was a large sliding door to accommodate incoming machines. Against the wall, hidden from view from the rest of the arcade, was something that looked like an oversized pink refrigerator. Food? Henry's hunger jumped through the burning hoop of his conscience. Could he possibly take a look, grab a quick bite? No, he corrected himself, moving closer. You'd have to pay, but you shouldn't even look. But now that he stood before it he shook his head. It wasn't a refrigerator at all. In scarlet letters, painted in italic script across the pink, ran the question: What's Your Pleasure? A full three-quarters of the front of the thing was a door. Yes, but there were two nozzles, an inlaid speaker unit, four square buttons and, at ground level, a protruding metal plate with indentations shaped for human feet. Henry craned his head around the corner to check out Sam. Reading and smoking still. Henry stepped up onto the plate and read the directions which were set forth in reduced italic:

PUT QUARTER IN SLOT.
PUNCH APPROPRIATE GENDER
AND PREFERENCE BUTTONS.
REMAIN ON PEDESTAL
THROUGHOUT.

A foot massage, Henry wondered? But he doubted it. The two pair of buttons were labelled M/F, He/Ho. God. Should I fake it? Why do it at all then? He pushed a quarter into the slot, punched M, He, and waited. A humming began and grew in the pink monolith; after a slight shudder, the plate took up the vibration and sent it through Henry's body. This is too goddamn loud! he thought, ready to bolt. A soft, sneezing sound occurred, then another. Henry's nose tickled. A third sneeze. Perfume! Henry was inundated! A mist of fragrance clouded over him, excessive, sultry, gaudy, he realized, but delicious. Susan. Henry yielded to the urge to inhale. His body swayed upon the plate. A voice spoke to him, a low, hazy, quickening voice, speaking through a pink boa, Henry guessed. "Hello," she said. "I'm pleased to meet you. It's so nice to find someone who isn't ashamed to want to feel and to play." A pause. The vibration intensified, causing Henry's legs to numb most pleasingly. His hands had been held against his waist; he let them fall. "Of course there's only so much you and I can do out here in the open like this, and my time is nearly up. But if you've got a dollar and the inclination, there's a place inside where we can get to know each other. Please don't be shy. Nothing that we want so naturally should make us shy." An added hiss of perfume formed the conclusion. Henry felt it on his cheeks. His lower torso now experienced the glow of his legs. He leaned forward against the machine, slightly weak, slightly dazed. The humming stopped. A red light set in the doorway flickered on. Henry moved away, rubbing his thighs, and peeked again at Sam. No change.

There is really no reason not to, he told himself. I'm alone. I've got time to spare. Who can it hurt? Who would care? Who would believe it? It's like a movie, that's all. Movies make you get it on, why not this? He gently fed a one to the slot. Like a tongue it disappeared. A click; the door opened slightly. Henry made a final check over his shoulder and went in, closing the door behind him.

There was one seat, wide and cushioned, cream-colored, comfortable. Recessed lights allowed for dim but steady vision with the door closed. Before him was a panel of crimson velvet fitted out with a variety of knobs, holes, bumps and grills. A nervous giggle overcame him. "Hi again," she said. "I'm so glad you decided to stay a while. I'm very sure we can enjoy ourselves if we can just relax and let things flow. This is just a place for us to dream. Don't we dream every day, really? I do."

A supple leg extended from the velvet, sheathed in a black net stocking. The lights dimmed into darkness. Breaths of perfume came soundlessly now. "Feel," she said. Bright pinpoint blue stars appeared in the velvet; curtains withdrew from the sides of the booth revealing mirrors which caught the stars and draped them effortlessly into widening patterns of a night sky. Henry tapped the outstretched limb with a finger, expecting firm mannequin plastic. But there was a give, a resilience, even a tension. He touched again, this time with his open palm. The smooth mesh of the stocking invited more. His hand followed the upward sweep of the calf and reached the thigh. "Feel." His second hand followed the first. "It feels so good," she said. "There is no reason not to let yourself enjoy what feels so soft and smooth and good." That's true, he thought. That really is true.

"Yes," Henry said at last. He listened.

"Yes."

A slight stirring. His chair came alive as the plate outside had. He leaned gently backwards. Through his legs and up his spine came the tingling. The rippling tension within his body gathered and subsided. A sweet peace made him sigh. He stroked the leg slowly, his hands flowing along its sides. Vague drum beats reached his ears. They coalesced into a writhing rhythm, the accompaniment, with tambourines now, to a sinuous dance at the banquet of a Pasha. The leg moved closer, touching against his chest, moving downward.

"Please stand." The voice was yearning, not demanding. He stood.

"Come closer to me. This way." The leg retreated. Henry followed. A Volcanic shape in the panel glowed starkly, rose red. "There. To your right." He glanced downward. A drawer emerged; inside was a condom. "Please. It's best that way." Henry tested the door. It was shut tightly. He undid his belt, removed his pants and underwear, pressed forward and in.

"Gently at first. I like that best. You'll soon learn what you can do." Henry felt a caressing power.

"Oh yes, you're fine. Strong and fine. Can you feel me? Let me have you soon, very soon."

Falling back into the seat, Henry shut his eyes, letting darkness engulf him. Faint breathing sounds. He strained. His own. He would not let himself think, though his mind seethed. Rubbing his knuckles against his eyelids he transformed his vision into a kaleidoscope. The two eyes became one; before him was a horizon of dancing, luminous spheres. "Thank you very much," he heard her say. Then a sliding noise. He opened his eyes. A second drawer had appeared. "That card will let you know where you can find me again." A click. Bright lights beamed from the ceiling of the booth. Fighting an urge to lie back and sleep despite them, Henry dressed. Before opening the door he examined the card. Three locations, all named Sam's. All machines designed and constructed by one Samuel Mazucca. Then he knows! Henry started. But of course he knows! He must know where I have been all this time. Henry pocketed the card and clambered into his pants.

On the way out he waved quickly at Sam, affecting cool. Sam winked. The clock said ten. Once on the sidewalk Henry broke into a run, then stopped. Why? he asked himself. Well why not? Why the hell not? What the hell anyway? Damn, it felt good. Admit it. Yes I do. Good somehow, I don't know how, I don't care how. He whooped, a loud lungburst that was swallowed by the shifting mist hanging like a Chinese lantern after the rain. A cat ran past his feet, its eyes blazing. He lost it as it ran into an alley, but shortly thereafter there was a yowl, a find, obviously, a triumph. Thank you, Sam. Goodbye, Susan. Time to mourn my Uncle. I never knew him. He hated my father and my father won't say why. A sad muddle. But he's dead. Mourn the dead. Because it was, it is, after all, wonderful. The world turns. Things happen; they do happen. And there is enough for everyone.

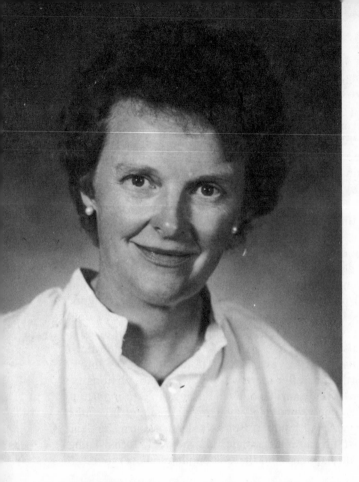

CAROL BLY: She is one of the four theme planners of the National Farmers Union's "American Farm Project" and the proprietor of Custom Crosswords, Odin House, Madison, Minn.

Her published work includes translations of poems and a novel from German, French, Norwegian and Danish; original short stories in *American Review #19* and *The New Yorker*; and a forthcoming book of essays with Harper & Row. Most of the essays originally appeared in Minnesota Public Radio's *Preview* and *Minnesota Monthly*.

She is the mother of four children: Mary, Biddy, Noah, and Micah Bly.

Carol Bly

BROTHERS

The St. Matthew's Vestry had little in common; like most vestries, it was made up of rich men and poor men who were fortunately neither brave nor crazy, so they were able to carry on a nervous, lively conversation together. If the Senior Warden, a worn-out young man named Mosely, had been brave or crazy, he would have shouted at Forsyth: "It is infuriating! infuriating that you work only three days a week, and sail your big shot boat the rest of the time! While I hold one full-time job and one part-time job and my wife has to help down to the Gopher Pantry — and we don't make a third of what you make! And that carpeting you sell — it's no good! You even sold the church bad carpeting!" Forsyth would have shrugged (if he, in turn, had been brave or crazy) and remarked, "Well what do I care? You're just not somebody who'll ever make any money! You just aren't — well — you just aren't the kind of man that makes money — don't bleat!" But niether man said anything like that.

The six vestrymen were sitting in a little circle of folding chairs in the choir room, waiting to do the last planning of tomorrow's bazaar. It was Friday morning. They talked about fatal accidents together; they worked up to some gaity about it, while their priest strode around the choir room behind them, finding the paper cups where someone had left them under a pile of surplices to be ironed. Father Bill gathered up easel and newsprint; he unplugged the coffeemaker and brought it over to the men.

They all liked Father Bill Hewlitt, who was forty-one. All their other rectors had been very young men who composed letters late at night to the Bishop, explaining that they surely enjoyed their rural parish work at St. Matthew's, Amos (Minnesota), but they were available for a metro parish if one should come free. What they liked especially about Father Bill was that he seemed content to stay there in Amos. He belonged to them. So they felt he took their church seriously.

Higgins was telling about a UCC minister from St. Anton Lake, the next town, who had been called to the accident two weeks ago on Minnesota 371 and Minnesota 200 and hadn't known the man was dead. The conversation moved unerringly from mere death to especially grisly death.

The little circle of men drew in; their voices sagged joyfully lower. In 1975 Elmira Inman's half-brother fixed up a chainsaw to the fly wheel of his old John Deere and opened himself up all the way lengthwise before they found him. Then there was that bailing accident on the Pierce farm back before the law you had to use string instead of wire. Before they found him, this man was half-bailed up as good as his own flaxstraw. And speaking of *finding* people dead, Beske told how it was ten days before they found old Wolfmeyer, not the one in the hospital now, but his cousin. He'd been shooting in Amos Slough over near the Refuge and they found him lying in the water. Those undertakers really knew their job all right, Beske remarked. Amazing what they can do. Then each man had a story about embalming or making up a face on top of stocking plaster and how good they could make you look. Each man waited sombrely for the man ahead of him to finish before he would start his own anecdote.

Bill Hewlitt let it go until they got to the 1972 outboard motor accident involving two young girls. Then he stalked over and said firmly, "The Lord be with you," "And also with you," the men had to return. They prayed and had to work fast to wind up all the last-minute arrangements of the bazaar.

Bill served them as usual, standing at the newsprint, writing up their comments, but he wasn't paying any attention. He was thinking of his older brother Francis, who was coming late that afternoon. They weren't close. They had scarcely seen each other since they grew up; only once, six years ago, and the reunion had not been successful. But now Francis had called from Washington, he had chosen to come, he wanted to be met in Duluth in the old way, and Bill found himself delighted.

He half-heard the Vestrymen. They were now estimating to one another which stall would make the most money at the bazaar. It was always the mouse roulette wheel that made all the money. Men gathered around it, watching the mouse moving, confused, with that surprising liquidness of mice; and rolls of money passed hands on the side, in addition to the pot St. Matthew's made on it.

Bill half-heard the Vestrymen talking about it, but he was remembering dozens of the evenings of his adolescence in Duluth. He and his brother would steer their father's great Packard through the heavy fog off Lake Superior. They drove their father and his old friends home from their club. One by one the old men were let off at their houses, Francis sitting behind the wheel with the engine running, Bill jumping out and opening the car door. Sometimes a maid opened the lighted, oak door. She would stand to one side to let the old man go in, and then smile and greet Bill before he jumped back into the car. "Goodnight, Landers!" "Goodnight, Harris!" the old men still in the car would shout hoarsely, as they let off each man. Bill would jump back in, his face cleaned by the night fog; behind both boys, the men gradually sobered, coughing, belching quietly, bursting into little laughs over remarks remembered from the poker table.

In 1970, when their father was long dead, the house long ago sold, and all their father's gifts to them invested elsewhere, or in Bill's case, spent on seminary, Francis and Bill had one reunion. It was hastily got up. Francis had called Amos from Duluth and suggested Bill drive the two-hour trip in.

"O but come out to us!" Bill had exclaimed. "You'll get to meet Molly! And come see the baby — and I'll show you my parish and all!"

"God, I'm sorry, Bill," Francis had said. "I just got in last night and I've been tied up all morning with conferences here — and I've got to get the morning flight back to Washington. Could you possibly get free and drive in? I'm at Lander's house — you remember Dad's old friend Landers? At least we can have a drink and go out for dinner somewhere."

Bill had obediently done the drive, at eighty miles an hour, arriving a half-hour before the time. Dazed by memories, he had driven up the perfect, curving asphalt driveway, between the perfectly groomed trees, each standing in its own circle of spaded earth. Then the house appeared, shockingly large, shockingly beautifully built of brick. "I'll tell them you're here, Father Hewlitt," the maid said.

He said, "Don't announce me. I'll just walk in. I'm early, but they expect me."

He went down a cool hallway. Men's voices rose from beyond double-doors ahead and to the right. "O yes — I remember — the

Landers's living room was here — and to the right," Bill told himself.

The men's voices were triumphant, he thought, and excited. "I don't see any reason why that won't shape up at this end without any griefs," a strong voice said. That must be young Landers, Gorham or Gorston, whatever his name was. "I'll figure out a spread of regular American holdings for you, Fran," the voice went on. "We'll phase out the Anaconda or Kennecott or whatever touchy stuff you come in with — no matter how the politics go, and I'll check out my suggestions with you at that time. Now — on any extra cash input —"

"Sounds good, Gordy," another voice said, and Bill, pausing in the dark hallway felt his hair rise a little. My brother! he cried; he had thought he was looking forward to seeing Francis; now he knew he was looking forward to it more than he had begun to guess. In a single split second, as a single impression, he thought: it is ridiculous for two men to be brothers all these years — it is ridiculous for any men to be brothers for even five minutes — without being close! If it didn't come naturally, how did we fail to do it at least just as an act of will! What idiots! What a waste!

"Sounds good, Gordy," his older brother's voice was saying, adding with a laugh, "Christ! Chile could get to be a madhouse down there if it goes the way they think it will. And once more, Gordy, let me just say this might not amount to anything for you — or for me — but it could — it just could — go over the top of the page!"

A quiet rejoinder: "I'm indebted to you, Fran. Don't think I won't do my level best for you at this end."

Bill deliberately rattled the double-doors as he opened them. After the hallway so full of shadow, he was rather dazed by the white, opaque light in his face.

Beyond the room's immense window, Lake Superior lay covered with solid white fog. This fog filled the room with impersonal white light, neither cheering like sunlight nor doleful. Two men rose energetically from a long davenport in front of the window. Because they were in silhouette to Bill, he couldn't tell which one was his brother. Both came right towards him, stepping over the long coffee-table, both with right hands stretched to him.

"Bill Hewlitt, damn it! Marvelous!" cried Gordon Landers.

"Hello, Bill," said Francis. "It's been a million years."

They all stood shaking hands, touching one another's shoulders. "You remember baby Gordy Landers, that squirt kid we beat at Monopoly all the time?" Francis said, laughing.

"And look at Bill!" Gordy Landers said. "Clerical collar and all," said in a tone called respectful, which was in fact absolutely not respectful. Then, glancing down at the low table, which was neatly laid out with piles of papers, a china figure having been shoved down to one end, Gordon bent and began collating the papers into groups, and slipping them all into a chrome and leather case. He then poured a drink for Bill. Both men asked Bill if he wanted to be filled in on some one-liners from Washington. "It is my hope," Gordon said, handing Bill a highball glass, "That your brother doesn't darken our consulates and embassies in South and Central America with these stories. I'm encouraging him to get them all out of his system here!"

They all laughed and sat down.

This falling aircraft, Francis told them, had only three parachutes on board, but there were four passengers — three famous men and a Boy Scout. As President Nixon jumped out he grabbed a chute and shouted that he in particular should be a survivor for the sake of preserving the moral values of freedom and democracy in the Western World; then the second man, Kissinger, explained that he must survive as he represented the brains of the free world, and he jumped, leaving the Archbishop of Canterbury and the boy. The Boy Scout said reassuringly, "O go ahead, sir, take chute. That last one grabbed my rucksack!"

Bill listened with a smile on his face, taking good strong sips of his scotch, thinking, how triumphant Francis' voice sounded! and, how cheerful these two guys sounded as I came in — how cheerful they still are!

But their cheer had to do with whatever their business was with each other. He felt good humor spilling over from both of them to him, but it was good humor left over from something that was nothing to do with him. They were both excited, they were in excellent humor with each other, and now they didn't want to be serious at all. They had obviously *been* serious; now the seriousness was used up and so their attitude was genial and playful.

Bill kept listening to his brother, thinking about him, gradually giving up any idea of a serious conversation. He kept on his face the amused, inquiring expression with which people listen to jokes, and he accepted some more drinks. After a while the scotch was comforting inside him and his face held its animated expression easily. The other men eventually asked him some questions about his life. Bill heard his own voice telling them about St. Matthew's Episcopal Church, about his wife Molly, about their year-old son and the baby expected midwinter. Then Bill longed to leave the huge sitting room lighted by the lake fog. He longed to drive home fast and angrily, yet somehow his voice kept talking on, another ten, twelve minutes: he was even chattering. At one point, unable to stop himself, he had even pulled out a picture of Molly and little George. Part of him said, "Get up and go, you great ass!" But another part of him kept him stuck, chattering away at his well-travelled brother and that Landers kid who had grown up into some kind of shrewd broker and exporter.

Hours later, driving gingerly through the cold night mist, Bill had cried aloud in his car, remembering his garrulity.

Now, six years later, he was sure this visit would be entirely different.

After the Vestry meeting, Bill had two appointments. Since the first was not until two o'clock he went across the St. Matthew's lawn, had a look out over the sky-colored, slightly misty lake, and entered his study, a small building attached to the rectory garage. He pulled over the pile of letters to be answered.

The telephone rang. In the receiver, Bill heard gigantic background noise of steam and metal, then a very loud voice shouted directly into his ear: "This is Elmira, Father Bill. We're getting a lot of feedback down here in the kitchen. Some of them are saying we ought to make the hamburgers bigger, the way they used to of, but I said we ought to keep them in line with what they're serving in uptown Amos. There's no point in making a lot of enemies for nothing, Father. People don't need no big hamburgers if what they're used to is what they're serving in the Gopher Kitchen and they *been* serving and with this here inflating if we're going to make a cotton-picking nickel off this bazaar —"

"Elmira," Bill said, imagining walking leisurely through the bazaar tomorrow with his brother, imagining Francis with the cordiality he had even as a teenager, squandering a mint at all the good stands: "Elmira, let's go ahead and make the hamburgers huge — wouldn't that be all right? Elmira, let's let the word get out that the St. Matthew's Episcopal Church bazaar has the most generous, most terrific hamburgers of any church in a twenty-mile radius!''

"What about the money?'' she said. Then there was a pause during which Bill heard something like steam escaping from a sinking liner. It was followed by a sharp hoarse cry from Elmira, who had turned away from the receiver: ''Louise, for cat's sake don't grab that thing in yer bare hands,'' and then more sizzling as if now an entire boiler had poured out onto hot metal. Someone, no doubt Louise, Bill smiled to himself, trying to think, Louise who? uttered from somewhere near the receiver a very clear rude remark.

Bill said, ''We aren't just giving away hamburgers! Great big good ones, Elmira! 50¢ each, not 10¢ — we'll make money!''

''Okay, Father, you're responsible. It's over my dead body!''

He said with a laugh. ''O go on, Elmira, make them whatever size you think best.''

Now his desk buzzer went off. The parish secretary Coralie said, ''I've got Lorrain Mosely on the outside line, Bill.''

''O all right,'' Bill said gaily, thinking: only two more hours until I can get some tea with Molly and then go to the airport and pick up Francis.

''Father Bill,'' came Mrs. Mosely's sombre voice. She said very significantly, ''I would like to *share* about Jesus at the bazaar tomorrow.''

''No sharing at the bazaar,'' Bill said.

''I can't believe what I'm hearing, Father! I can't believe you're really saying to me that we wouldn't have sharing at a big gathering of Christians like that! In my Prayer Group they're already talking about our church! You know what they'll say, Father? They'll say, 'Yeah? Where else but at an Episcopal Church would you get together four or five hundred Christians without one mention of Jesus Christ during the whole thing?' is what they'll say.''

Bill said, ''We always have a blessing at every bazaar. So there will be mention of Jesus Christ. No sharing, Lorrain.''

He was annoyed when his two o'clock appointment was still not there at ten after two. The young man who had called saying he wished to make a *confession* had said he would come by boat; so now Bill went outside, and waited, scowling, at the top of the rise over Lake Amos.

Bill knew him by name. He was Duane Wolfmeyer, the grandson of Neil Wolfmeyer, a very old parishioner now dying in Amos Hospital. The Wolfmeyers were a type of Episcopalian that exasperated most rectors; they only showed up in church for some baptisms, most marriages, and for their own funerals — for hitching and ditching, as people described it at Diocesan coffee breaks. But Bill felt comfortable with such people. His own parents had seldom gone to church. They were intellectuals, and if they sang every Christmas Eve mass they were also given to describing Jesus as a megalomaniac on Low Sundays. Bill did not embarrass his brother by inviting him to his ordination.

Now the young Wolfmeyer grandson followed Bill into his study, and wandered without shyness over to the bookcases. "What a terrific place you've got!" he said. "Terrific funky study, sir! I love it! Beautiful!! beautiful!" The young man went easily around the room in his tennis shoes, touching bindings with tanned knuckles. "Christ, you've got everybody! Merton! Evelyn Underhill! Underhill's fantastic! Christ you've even got volume eighteen of the collected Jung and I didn't even know it was out yet! And the *Bogi Hokjhar Shetar!* Terrific, Father Hewlitt!"

Bill had sat down at his desk. "Sit down, Duane," he said, after a moment. "Sorry," he added, aware that he didn't like the man at all and would have to consider that fact all the while they were talking. "This is one of those days when we have to run on schedule." Practically all the while he spoke, he kept looking out the window, nervous with pleasure, anticipating the drive into the city. The wonderful basswood forest, with its straight, black trunks and the clumsy leaves, so surprisingly clumsy and moving, was already going yellow although it was only the middle of August. The mist that had lain over the lake all morning now began to fill the woods. Its gentle windings were full of ease.

Duane Wolfmeyer had begun a long narrative of his life as a surveillance man for the C.I.A. He explained he had joined students' groups in Colorado, and also helped organize 4 × 6 cards on selected people around Boulder in particular. He had found the money useful, he explained, because he was doing some writing, and really more important, he said slowly, regarding the priest significantly, he was doing "a great deal of spiritual work." It was just so damned practical, he said to Bill, and frankly, he hadn't seen where anybody had been harmed by it. "What makes me mad at myself, though," Duane continued in a frank tone, smiling, "is that no one tried to deceive me about it. I knew perfectly well this guy came from an intelligence group and I knew what he wanted me to do — well, for starters anyway — to inform on those students' groups, and then he said they would see what else turned up. Sometimes weeks and weeks went by and there wasn't anything to do, but I still got paid. Obviously I knew I wasn't getting all that money for nothing. . . . still, I did it because it was so darn practical. It meant I didn't have to write home to my dad for money — and in a way, of course, it was really sort of a good thing. It gave me time to take in some Meditation, and I did a lot of really good reading, too. Father, would you mind if I smoked?"

"Yes, I'd mind," Bill said, looking out the window.

People kept going by, now, with paper flowers and twisted crêpe about their heads and necks. Some of them carried 2 × 4's for bazaar stalls, and large boxes which Bill knew were filled with fairly wretched Anglican trinkets. There were tiny nylon flags printed with the Cross of St. George, which ravelled at a child's first handling of them; buttons to wear; magic tricks with a mother and father rabbit made of felt. Duane Wolfmeyer's voice rose and fell. He explained his experience as an informer over again, and then over again, warming to it, using different reminiscences to illustrate.

The whole question of C.I.A. informers was not new to Bill. The year before he had discussed it around the dining room table at Lane House, the Minnesota Diocesan headquarters, with five or six priests. Bill had thought through the problem of C.I.A. people, and faced with this problem he would tell the informer to work off the bad job done, something like atonement.

There is no profession, Bill recalled leisurely from Conrad, deciding he would repeat it to Duane, that fails a man more completely than that of a secret agent of police. But when the priest looked over at the courteous, relaxed, conversant young man in front of him he realized: far from being *failed*, this fellow was not even repentant. In fact, as he wound up, Duane was now suggesting that he was money ahead and to all intents and purposes, no harm done.

"How many people have you told this to?" Bill now asked.

"Let's see," Duane said. "It's been a while now, you know.

Let's see. I did tell my apartment-mate at the time; but he said it was a damned sight better than sweating a teaching assistanceship. Then, I told this Quaker workcamp leader that I'd worked with — that's a man you'd like, Father Hewlitt. Then I did tell Rinpoché — that's my meditation teacher. And I told a guy I knew that's a Congregational minister."

"Anyone else?" Bill said.

"I'm trying to think," Duane said in a frank, cooperative voice. "O yes! I participated in a Massich Group seminar and during Sharing I think I may have mentioned something . . ." He added, "People have been helpful."

"But you still want my opinion?" Bill said, smiling slightly.

"Yes, sir — it's why I came, I guess."

Bill looked out the window. "The important thing is that the conversations now come to an end. You've had enough talk. What I think, what your roommate thinks, what the Friends Service Committee man thinks, and so on — all that is past now. Now you need to *do* something."

"I would like to hear any suggestions you have," Duane said. "My grandfather thinks very highly of you, sir."

"First," Bill said, now turning from the window, "I suggest you obey simply all the advice you've ever received on the subject. If the Buddhist gave you some exercise or discipline to do, do it. Do whatever the Quaker told you to do. Whatever the Congregational minister told you to do, do that. Then I want you to do what I'm about to tell you to do, too. The point is, Duane, to do something, do something. The talking is over — forever. You absolutely must not tell any more people about it. Not one. If you meet a girl, don't tell her."

"Wow," said Duane. "For sure?"

"For absolute sure," Bill replied. "You've talked enough. From now on you carry it alone. Now — do you want to hear the rest?" He smiled. "Or is that enough?"

"No, hell, please," Duane said. "Please go on."

"You were well paid," Bill said. "Add up as well as you can the actual number of hours you worked as an informer and write it down. Then work it off, hour for hour, at volunteer work, scratching off each hour in some simple, completely visible way — such as on paper or wood. This will show you that *that* mark on the left, say, was an hour of bad work, this mark through it, on the right, is an hour of *good* work. This will give you some secret structure of your own. It'll also help you," Bill added wryly, "not to take another job of the same kind — which they would probably offer you on a higher level this time."

"You don't mind laying it on a person, Father Hewlitt!"

"Well," the priest said mildly, "did you tell them you would never work for them again?"

"Well, no," Duane said.

"That's all I meant," Bill said glossily, having trouble with anger for the first time during the counselling.

After another moment he threw Duane Wolfmeyer out because he was expecting a ten-year-old acolyte named LeRoy Beske who had called for an appointment.

When LeRoy showed up at the screen door, Bill got up and opened it for him, and shook his hand. He pointed out to him a gigantic chair placed for guests. "I'm glad the mist is coming up again, LeRoy," Father Bill said. "I've always liked fog. I was brought up in it. In fact, in the harbour of my city, Duluth, there used to be this big foghorn that bellowed like a sick cow all night and half the morning all summer — to keep oreboats from smashing into the bridge, I suppose. Come on in."

"But that fog better not ruin the bazaar tomorrow, though," LeRoy said. "My mother baked all them pies; she's going to go straight up if that bazaar gets called off."

"And your dad's got the David-and-Goliath slingshot booth this year?" Bill said.

"Yeah," LeRoy said.

LeRoy didn't seem to be getting around to what he wanted to say so Bill offered, "Well, last year's slingshot booth was crooked. You couldn't knock those things down with a road-paver."

"It's cleaned up this year, sir," LeRoy said. "And I wanted to tell you something, sir. We want to clean up the mouse roulette wheel game."

"Fill me in on the whole thing," the priest said.

"It's the mice for the men's mouse wheel," LeRoy said. "They have this wood roulette wheel, you know the one, Father; they made it about a yard across and painted into all these pie-wedge piece shapes, red, orange, like that. Then all around the outside edge it's got these holes cut out, same size as a beer can. They have the cans stuck onto the wheel, under the holes, so when they spin the wheel, they drop the mouse on it, and when he gets sick or something, he dodges into one of them holes and then whatever man got bets on that color of a hole, he gets half the pot and St. Matthew's gets the other half, is how it works. Anyhow, the problem is this is a very popular thing at the bazaar, Father, like you get ten, twelve men standing around paying into the roulette wheel all the time and we sometimes have to kind of force people to hang around the slingshot booth and the other games. You know, Father, I seen you herding bunches of ladies over to the booths a lot of times.''

Bill winced.

"Here, Father, we got this here for you;''LeRoy stood up and wrestled a piece of paper out of his jeans pocket.

PROTEST AGAINST MOUSE ROLET WHEEL

Bill read at top, and under it:

> We the undersined protest the mouse rolet wheel because it is mean to the mice. Also it isn't just one mouse, they use a lot of them. We think it should be stopped. Sined:

> Janet Higgins, E.S.N. Forsyth, Brett Forsyth, Verone Mosely, and LeRoy Beske.

With the lightning speed of an experienced rector, Bill noted that all the names belonged to children of his strongest churchmen — Vestry members, Sunday School teachers, tithing donors, the Senior Warden. Terrific, he said to himself with a sigh.

When he was alone again Bill looked at his appointments list and wrote "See about mice" opposite LeRoy's name. He could still hear Duane Wolfmeyer's 350 Chrysler I-O motor howling uplake. He crossed off Wolfmeyer and picked up the phone.

When the nurse on duty at the hospital answered, he said, "This is Father Hewlitt, Debby. How is Mr. Wolfmeyer doing?''

"Holding his own, Father. We'll keep you in touch.''

This whole pleasant world of forest and lake where Bill was rector of St. Matthew's Episcopal Church was tottering now, nearly wrecked. Whenever Bill looked out over the peaceful water he was aware, for example, that Lake Amos, which looked so immutable, showed in fact on engineers' maps in St. Paul as part of the gated chain of lakes which could be tapped, opened, whenever Minneapolis and St. Paul needed water. Bill was aware, too, that four sharp young Episcopalians who had summer places on Lake Amos, and who showed up every Sunday for church and could always be counted on for the alto, tenor, and bass of Vulpius, Williams, and Bach, were all of them counsel for mining interests in Duluth and Scranton. These companies laid out schedules for years and years ahead, showing when they would begin to take the ore under Lake Amos. Their public relations departments projected a timeline for publicity to inure the public to the stripping when it came. The photograph was to suggest bliss; it would show young and middle-aged people, sailing well hiked out on Lasers, men and women in golden lifebelts, plenty of sky, plenty of very clear water — the overall tone much like that of the flowery-meadow photographs utilities firms used when they were telling Americans how the west would look again — after all the coal has been taken.

Bill knew that family corporation offices in Duluth kept huge stiff maps with pale blue lines on them, like the veinwork of tiny animals. The legends of these maps written beautifully, in a surprisingly feminine hand, like the legends on treasure maps in children's books. These huge maps were opened out onto standing-height lecterns to fee owners like old Neil Wolfmeyer, Bill's parishioner who now lay dying in the hospital. Elderly women laid their sky-color gloves to one side of the map and asked their executors to show them the reserve mine known as Wiggin-Amos No. 5. These people had very likely not heard of the town of Amos, Minnesota, itself, and certainly not of St. Matthew's Episcopal Church, with its cheap, carpeted rectory and its rector's study tacked to the garage and the bright grass running down to the lake, and its altar still smelling of incense on Monday mornings. Yet all this lay over their holdings.

Each morning in August, the lake gave comfort like granite, under its mist. One felt the easy presence of old, uneducated men fishing, scarcely moving their wrists over the worn boats' edges. There was ease in how the line lay over their bent index finger, pinned by the thumbnail, and ease in how the line dropped with no movement into the water.

Bill's parish was half such people — a local populace that could still make a living in wooded country. They serviced snowmobiles, ordering parts from Brainerd; they ran roadside plumbing repair services; they tongue-and-grooved logs for cabins. The other half were the rich, who bought up the failed dairy farms.

Finally Bill got into the car for the two hours' drive to Duluth Airport. He travelled in a lovely mist. It was impossible to feel that this wild country of Minnesota was endangered. Among the basswood trees must be dusk enough and room enough for millions of mice and impractical ferns to find some sort of a living. What is interesting, Bill thought, is how we all secretly want these to outlive our species, mankind, because they are nicer. He drove in an alien, fresh way, enjoying car and mist.

At the airport he stood around for a while near four or five other people.

"Nah, you can tell he's a Catholic," a woman's voice said expertly, somewhere behind Bill.

"Nah, he isn't though," another woman's voice said, with exactly the same intonation of expertise. "He's an Episcopalian, I know, because he's from my hometown."

Now a crowd was growing around Bill; the air filled with the incoming jet's shriek. Everybody seemed pleased with the noise. People lifted up on the balls of their feet, and leaned over other people's shoulders. The air carried a waft of fuel oil, and close at hand, chewing gum.

The passengers began coming into the waiting room. The very first man made Bill lurch forward a little, it seemed so like a thinner older type of Francis; then Bill saw it wasn't he and began studying the others as they came off. That's right, he considered, Fran would take his time. He would not muscle into the aisle. It would be like him to help ten women get their coats down from among the pillows overhead. So Bill was waiting composedly when a hand touched his shoulder. He turned to see a shocking, emaciated face. It belonged to the first man he had seen come up the ramp, his brother Francis.

They shook hands in the old way, then drew back, their hands not fallen to their sides. They had never embraced and they didn't now. Bill saw instantly that Francis was dying, and the brother saw that Bill saw it and nodded. "Give me the baggage tags," Bill said, in a shepherding gesture he would not have made otherwise.

They stood waiting for the baggage, as rigidly and normally as they could. Their eyes were silver-coated with tears. Everything they saw was zigzag and crystal with tears, but Bill darted forward at the right moment, grabbed the bags, took Francis to the car, and they drove away.

II

When men and women think of becoming Episcopal priests they tend to imagine themselves in heavy, quiet rectories, with small panes at the windows — but in real life, a Minnesota rector is often proudly offered a modern, gimcrack ranchhouse. The sashes swell quickly after every rain.

Bill and Molly's rectory was carpeted with speckled aqua nylon from room to room. The speckled aqua was endless. It led out to the guest room on the first floor; it led up the staircase to the second; it led to the kitchen, where it joined a speckled aqua linoleum meant to suggest piazza tiling. At all the windows hung drapery in a complicated pattern called "Florentine," which the St. Agnes' Guild had voted for 12 to 3. A giant wooden salad fork and spoon were pinned at a certain angle to the wall. Things broke rather easily. Then the Vestry came and peered, especially Hayden Forsyth, whose firm had laid the carpet. Sometimes three or four women arrived in a flurry to "see about those drapes." They gently lifted and set things down." I remember the year we all made these!" someone would exclaim, holding up a rose-colored artfoam doily, scalloped at the edges, on which one was to set a figurine or a bowl of plastic fruit. All about the room were gifts to priest and family from one parishioner or another.

Molly and Bill made a joke of all this for Francis. It was Saturday morning, the day of the bazaar. They were sitting in the living room rather surprisingly early. Molly had expected the sick man to be tired from travel, and to sleep late, while she and Bill caught a moment of peace before the day was on them. But, in fact, like many people in crisis, Francis was highly charged. He had waked many times in the night and finally allowed himself to rise at six-thirty, wishing not to disturb anyone. When he came into the living room, all dressed, and found Bill and Molly already there, with a coffee urn between them, an expression of euphoria lighted his face. They both saw instantly that he had had a bad night and was delighted it was over. Bill held him out a thin, flowered cup, from a set the little boys were not allowed to handle, and thought: this is my blood relative — how nice he is here. Everyone smiled at every single remark made. Molly understood it was a crisis — everyone understood.

The telephone and the doorbell rang at the same moment. Molly went to the door, Bill to the phone. Molly returned with a beaming, respectful young man. "This is Duane Wolfmeyer, Francis. My husband's brother, Duane — Francis Hewlitt. He just flew in from Washington last night."

"Good to meet you, sir," Duane said, reaching across the coffee table to shake hands. Francis half-rose and then sank down again.

"Are you one of my brother's parishioners?" Francis said, smiling.

"Not exactly. I came over early to see if I could help with any last minute things about the bazaar. I'm just visiting my grandparents' home here, and Father Hewlitt has been wonderful to my grandfather, who's sick."

Francis said, "I never darkened the door of a church when I was a young fellow. I don't think I'd have known what a bazaar was, much less offer to help at one." He crossed his legs. "Can't say I missed it."

The younger man caught the tone of superior, more manly activity than his own. He didn't sit down at all.

Bill appeared quickly from the kitchen doorway. He had a white stole slung over one shoulder and he carried his communion box in one hand. With the other he fumbled at the stole, putting the lavender side nearly under, the white up. "How are you today, Duane?"

The gathered, competitive expression Duane had worn with Francis Hewlitt disappeared; now he looked vulnerable, in the way of people who have been counselled. "Can I drive you?" he begged.

"Nope, but thanks," Bill said, leaving. "Why don't you stay? You can get filled in on United States South American policy from my brother here."

Molly followed Bill to the car.

"I'm taking communion to old Wolfmeyer," he said, putting the box into the front seat, and sliding in after it. They talked for a moment, the idling car sounding very modern, very mechanical, the man in the lace-edged stole looking very old-fashioned.

When Bill returned an hour later everyone was at work on the bazaar. Francis had helped the people raise a makeshift flagpole at the beach, with the Episcopal flag — cross of St. George in red, the white background, the baby-blue field with nine small crosses — and now it was fluttering over the dock. Francis held cordon for little girls who were threading it through the wobbly stancheons to make the David-and-Goliath slingshot shy. A Lutheran electrician had kindly offered to arrange the outdoor wiring. Bill noticed that the summer people, who were lawyers, stockbrokers, and retired people and the all-year-round people were working together with jerky gaiety. They seemed to like handling the rougher, poorer poles, blocks, bolts; when something broke from old age, such as ropes of tents, they noisily got up ingenious ways of making do. This aspect of the bazaar always made Bill grumpy. He found their comraderíe phony. After every bazaar the people said, "How wonderful the way it brought us all into closer fellowship!" But Bill knew that the three men and one woman lawyer, who were asking LeRoy Beske (as they all worked setting up a water tank for the Senior Warden to be dumped into) how you could tell a Polish bachelor's bathtub from a French bachelor's bathtub, would return on Monday to plan tax benefits for mining interests. These mining operators would strip off not just LeRoy Beske's dad's trailerhouse lot, with its bit of jackpine scrub; they would also strip off the cemetery where LeRoy Beske's grandparents' bodies lay shrinking.

At lunchtime the Hewlitts had only tea, because they must eat bazaar food literally all afternoon. Francis was in the guest room with his door closed. The little boys looked at Bill, from where they sat on either side of Molly, afraid he would interrupt the story she was reading aloud.

"Keep reading," Bill said, smiling. He lay back in his chair and listened to how Trouble dogged one brother until that brother finally tricked Trouble into a hole with a heavy stone near by, then rolled the stone over so Trouble couldn't get out. But the other brother nagged the first brother to tell him where the treasure lay; finally, the younger explained that one must roll aside such and such a stone. The older brother raced to the place, heaved away the stone, Trouble leapt out and rode on *his* back for the rest of his days. Since that was the venal, wicked, elder, cruel, mean, coarse, uncaring and unscrupulous brother, the little boys were immensely pleased, and they bent over Howard Pyle's illustrations carefully. They loved all the tricking and lying, they loved the plain greed, and then they loved justice winning in the end.

Outside, the loudspeaker which was to play waltzes all afternoon had been hooked to its tree. Someone asked it over and over, "Testing?" Inside, the house was introverted and calm; even the bad furniture looked heavy, and calm, and decent.

Bill and Molly talked lazily, putting off gathering their cheer and general affection to go outside. The children had toppled over on Molly's knees, beautifully asleep like baby birds. The doorbell rang. Duane Wolfmeyer came into the room. Everyone whispered so the little boys could sleep another few moments. At last Bill stalked out to find a clean collar, and returned, still fastening it.

"If there's anything I can do at all?" the younger man said, following the priest with his eyes.

"Duane told Francis that the C.I.A. was a very bad organization," Molly said, smiling. "You should have heard him!"

"I thought I told you to keep quiet about the C.I.A.," Bill said. "In fact, that was the first thing I told you to do, was *shut up* about the C.I.A."

"Sorry, Father Hewlitt, but frankly, your brother kind of drew me. He kind of surprised it out of me. He was so interesting, talking about places he's been and things he's done — and the people he knows, my God. And then I was so surprised when he said he'd been associated with C.I.A. projects from time to time — I'm afraid he surprised it out of me, sir."

Molly and Bill both looked up. "O I doubt he had much to do with an organization like that," Molly said at last, in the tone she used to break up quarrels in the St. Agnes' Guild. "I don't think I heard him say anything like that — of course I wasn't there all the time you two were talking."

Duane said agreeably, "Oh he didn't do a lot. Mostly he just arranged premises for them in different places at different times. It sounds a lot more interesting than most jobs I've heard of. He said he just did useful things, like, if they needed a small import firm in Santiago, say, for engineering equipment, he'd see that one got set up. That sort of thing."

Feeling confident, and seeing that he had their interest, Duane remarked, in a manly way putting down any emotional aspects,

"No, I doubt he did any very exciting cloak and dagger stuff. He said himself — as if it were just a joke — that he was hardly much of an asset to them. Mostly he told me the places he's been with the State Department — Athens, Cambodia, Mexico City, Santiago. I hope I wasn't rude, Father Hewlitt, but I did share your thought about moral responsibility. Sorry, sir."

Now the hall door opened. "Well!" Francis Hewlitt cried, raising his hand in pretend Buckingham Palace salute. "I'm ready to do the bazaar, by God! I've promised George and Timmy I'll buy them three shots at every single game in the place, and two hamburgers apiece if you're selling 'em anywhere!"

He had rested. He must have rinsed his ill face with hot and cold water: he looked shining and friendly, and he had combed his always handsome hair into a neat wave. Francis wore a white linen coat and an ivory polo shirt. He gave off a kind of blazing good will that nearly hid the dreadful look of illness.

They woke the children. Everyone went outside. A little numbly, they began to go about the bazaar. The Strauss played from the loudspeakers. Women already sitting at TV tables overlooking Lake Amos caught Bill by the elbow and one cried, "Oh, Reverend Hewlitt? Oh, Reverend! This is something you Episcopalians do so well!" Near the garage someone in a Midwest, nasal accent began to do a good job of squawking Punch's voice as he threatened the baby. The Senior Warden, a rich carpet salesman from Minnetonka, perched fully dressed on the edge of a drum full of water. He was ready to be promptly dropped in if you threw a ball so it tripped the mechanism.

Down on the beach there were a few people taking the sailboat rides but mostly, their owners conversed quietly at buoy. They were middle-aged men and women whose fingers kept touching along the stays and shrouds even when they were just waiting for riders. Most of the young people leaned, smiling and commenting, over Duane Wolfmeyer's big Crestliner.

Duane now wore a button that read KISS ME I WENT TO THE ST. MATTHEW'S BAZAAR. He ambled down to the dock and took all the kids out in groups of four. All the rest of the afternoon the big boat's roar went around the lake. The waltzes kept tinkling out of the birch leaves.

Bill was drawn into groups here and there; he could be seen everywhere rocking on his heels, his head bent to listen, his face getting sunburnt afresh over the black shirtfront. "You don't know me, Father Hewlitt," a woman cried, placing boneless fingers on his arm. "But I have always admired you and your nice wife and when I saw you at the airport yesterday in Duluth I said to my cousin who was with me, 'Why, that's our Episcopal priest from Amos, of all people; I'd know him anywhere!' I was meeting my sister." Bill shook hands with everybody, he laughed at all the jokes.

III

Sooner or later they were going to have to have a serious conversation. The dread of it began at supper and clung to them all, except the children. When Molly had read to the boys and put them to bed, she returned to the living room where they all sat a moment, watching the evening mist rising from the lake. For them all, they felt, it was the blessed evening after enforced cheer. Whatever communal dancing meant to Breughel, church carnivals don't mean that now.

Francis set his own stage. He had offered to lay the fire himself, and now he lighted it, and then moved deftly around the room. He brought in from his suitcase expensive liqueur which Bill and Molly would never keep. He had gone and poked about in the kitchen until he found some glasses stuck behind a pile of 9×13 cake pans with women's names printed on adhesive-tape on them. He brought out a brass tray painted with orange wavy lines, on which stood six thinnish glasses, also painted with orange wavy lines — a gift from someone in the parish.

"Well," Francis said, looking briefly into both their faces, and then addressing the fire in a light, ordinary tone: "Actually this isn't just regular United States leave for me. In fact — in fact, as I think you have guessed, I retired. About two weeks ago. I've been more or less taking care of details. The Bethesda apartment. That sort of thing." there was a pause. Then Francis said, "I have a serious health problem." Another pause. "The fact is, I've got a prognosis of either six weeks or longer that'll be what the doctor calls 'good' weeks, and it might last longer but she didn't think so. So here is my plan, and I want your opinion of it. See what you think! And if you know a better alternative, for God's sake, tell me." He kept talking, in a practical, expressionless tone, making it unnecessary for them to interject pity. "I thought I'd spend the six weeks here — oh, not at your house!" he said with a grin. "In a rented cabin — all arranged with some people I met at your bazaar this afternoon! Rather neatly, if I say so myself!"

"But Francis," Molly said, "we'll take care of you."

"That's another thing," he replied. "I don't know how much trouble I'll be — maybe not much — certainly there shouldn't be any problem for a bit; and then, when there is, I'll head for the hospital."

"We'll fill all the gaps, Fran," Bill said. "And Fran, you haven't said what you've got, but I take it it's been properly looked at? And if there's a course of treatment you're doing it . . . ?"

"I've been the route," Francis said wryly.

"Well then," Molly said, "I can see why for the while you'd rather be alone in peace and quiet. But if you get sick and don't want to be all the way across in Amos or wherever you've gotten the cabin, come to us. It won't always be quiet, but sometimes it will be quiet — and we're here."

Francis smiled at her, then turned to Bill and said, "I rather like the idea of my own family seeing me through like this. We haven't done that much, have we?" He looked pointedly at Bill's collar, and the cross hanging on his chest. "You might even do your thing with me."

No matter how detachedly Francis had told them his news, no matter that they had been accustomed to the idea of his sickness for a day and a night, they were still all stiff and motionless, like people making a point of sitting bolt upright, although in fact they were lounging backward in sofa and chairs. The sense of Francis' death floated into everyone.

"Well," Francis said, "that isn't all I came to tell you about. That was the bad news, as the kids say! Here's the good news! You think of me," he said in a clowning rhetoric, "as just a stodgy member of the United States' State Department, bent over my desk during the siesta hours, filling in the mindless evenings under the Southern Cross in white tie, telling Polish jokes to the wives of dictators so they will understand our democratic culture—"

Molly and Bill smiled dutifully.

"But actually," Francis went on, "I have built up a little

portfolio of sorts — nothing momentous, mind you — but it's all looking in fair shape now anyway, and since I don't seem to have a spouse to leave it to — I would like to leave it to you and your nice George and Timothy.'' He kept talking so they would not have to express any gratitude immediately. "It's a mix," he was saying. "Some mining stuff — some of the obvious things — we can go into all that tomorrow. And in Duluth, on Monday, I have an appointment with a guy named Gordon Landers: Bill, do you remember Gordy Landers? He will fix it all up for you, in trusts or whatever you think best — Some of it was guesses I don't mind saying have worked out pretty well! Nothing to challenge the Arabs with, but enough for four years apiece at Harvard or wherever for both kids, unless the country goes absolutely crazy — crazier than we are already," he added genially, loping on casually in his monologue in the able way of people accustomed to taking meetings through their agenda.

But even Francis, who had spent half a lifetime conversing with uncongenial people in crisis situations, could not be expected to garble on and on. "Well, hell," he said, eventually, "you guys could say *some*thing, anyway." Then he added neatly, "Oh, and the portfolio was worth one and one-half million this morning."

Francis leaned back looking ill and also pleased with himself, his pale hands upright, prayer-fashion, on the manila envelope. Bill knew he was thinking: it isn't every day an Anglican priest with a two-bit parish in the middle of the Minnesota northwoods gets a cool million and a half in stocks dumped into his skinny lap. Bill waited until he controlled the stiffness in his throat and then said, "Listen, Francis, you told Duane Wolfmeyer something about the C.I.A. this morning . . . I gathered you had done some work with them? I'd like to hear about that."

"Oh, for the love of Christ," Francis said in a bored way.

"Molly and I were very surprised," Bill said. "We didn't know you were doing anything like that.

"Ah, that drip Duane," Francis said. "You have a marvelous patience about you, Bill. You must have dozens of people like that Duane hanging around. But you keep up a straight face with him! And you, too, Molly! I'm all respect! I have to confess we talked for about twenty minutes and then I more or less told him to go to hell — or at least not to wax so damned moral before breakfast. I'll tell you one thing we really do learn as we get older:

we learn not to be in such brilliant form before breakfast! It's an imposition on the other human beings in the room!''

"He said you told him you had done work for the C.I.A.," Molly said.

Francis gave her the smile that confident men save for unpleasant women. "And so I have," he replied mildly. "Most infrequently, I may add, and admittedly, nothing very interesting. I was hardly what they call an asset. It's just that my face logically belonged in certain places at certain times, so I could manage trivial arrangements without fuss. I'm no expert, you know. I suppose they make use of a few thousand people like me from time to time. I am sure the Soviet Union does the same sort of thing," Francis added sensibly.

"One and a half million dollars," Molly said. "You must be on the receiving end of something very big!"

"Let me relieve your mind, Molly," Francis interrupted, keeping a firm, still affectionate tone. "There is no way — please know this! — there's no way the most corrupt broker with the most inside information in the world could parlay a $10,000 inheritance — the same as your Bill here got — into one and a half million on the fluctuations of Kennecott, ITT, or Anaconda or anyone else's stock — at least not while I was in the area."

"Then how'd you make it," Bill said.

Francis said coolly, "I arranged for importation of heavy machinery into Chile. They needed it. Does that sound terribly wicked?"

Francis now tapped the manila envelope on his knees. "I think there are a couple of things," he said, "that you two had better think about before you ask such holy questions about where I got what, who've I been consorting with — all questions that are very easy to ask. There are other questions, it seems to me, that you haven't asked, such as: what makes you think Timmy and George will want to go to Bemidji Junior College or Brainerd Vo-Tech and marry someone who will nail up plastic salad spoons and forks on the walls, and khaki reproductions of the Praying Hands? You two make a joke of it, but you *chose* this life! And, you chose this life *after* you tucked away Harvard and lots else of the world! I'll hand it to you," he said, a smile returning to his face, "there's some sort of moral force in your life — but you might well find that Tim and George will have their own ideas. And I don't want to imply that you just live a simple, easy existence out here, Bill, with nothing worse to fret about than a morning's quarrel with your Vestry, but frankly — and Molly, you ought to think about this, too — there are a lot of tough people around in some unpleasant places, some in danger all the time, and these very tough people are looking out for *your* well-being. If some of these people — and now we are getting close to your question — discover that certain concerns abroad, due to pressures like shortages deliberately created by a foreign power, are willing to pay fairly handsomely for harmless importation of simple capital equipment they need, well, frankly, I feel, myself, I haven't too much complaint to make! I do not regard it as scandalous to ensure machinery for industry — for perfectly harmless civilian repairs and replacements — to businessmen trying to run operations under such trying circumstances! I don't expect you two to understand what a nightmare it is to do business in sensitive countries — with or without inside political information! Your young friend Duane, now, was kind enough to quote me that line from Conrad you gave him about "secret agents of police" having unrewarding lives — rather an emotional term, I'd say — but let me just point out that I found many of these people to be gentlemen among gentlemen."

They were all quiet a moment. Then Francis thumped his manila envelope again. "What's in here," he said in a tone public speakers use, an obvious relief, when they can return to the subject after some idiotic question from the audience, "is a simple listing of the properties I am turning over to you and your sons. They are a perfectly predictable, ordinary spread of American interests. Gordy Landers made some of the suggestions, and I think they're very good. Burlington Industries, Con Edison, Telephone, MacCabe and Janus, Ashland Oil, Wheeling Steel, First Bank Corporation, some Great Northern Iron Properties — that last ought to appeal, Bill — the holdings mostly right around here, I think." Francis added, "Now — do these sound like the work of the devil to you? They don't to me." He leaned back again, his cheeks and bloodless forehead gleaming.

It was most difficult to break into this manly, sensible-sounding monologue and say you didn't want your brother's money for you or your kids. All the time Bill talked his own voice sounded shaky and false to him, like the voice of Marchbanks. It sounded like a mixture of callow righteousness with callow unfamiliarity with "the world men have to live in, after all." He heard his own voice like a fool's voice, sailing on, in high, nervous timbre.

Then, marvellously quickly, he heard his wife's voice come on. In a daze, in a daze something like his feelings as a new bridegroom, he heard her voice begin without any pause after his own stopped: he heard Molly tell Francis that she felt exactly as Bill did. And all the time, on the surface of it, her voice, as his had, sounded portentous and stupid.

Then Francis was saying, "But you can't have talked this over! I only just told you about it!"

"All the rest is the same," Molly said. "You know that. We will take care of you. We are still standing by. That hasn't changed."

Francis said, "Well — that's good of you, Molly! Standing by! How easy the Prayer Book used to make it sound! The fact is, you don't know what dying is until it's your own dying." He gave a brisk laugh. "You had better take it from me, what a very special quality one's own dying has! I seem to have a very special feeling toward mine anyway!"

He got up now. "Nobody can say you two are chicken! It's not every day someone turns down a million and a half from his own brother or brother-in-law! And to his face, too! And without sleeping on it!" He went to the hall door and turned. "Now, some soft-headed types would have thanked a person and taken the gift in the spirit in which it was given, and knowing that the brother was on the way . . . down, as the kids say. These softheads might have felt they could afford to spare his feelings a little. They might have felt the guy'd been trying to serve the United States somehow, and now that he was dying he didn't have to have a bunch of someone else's assassinations and coups d'etat or whatever you two have on your mind laid at his feet! They could have given the money away to some goddamned left-wing charity later! But not you two! Not you two!"

From the pulpit next morning Bill wound up his sermon. He was saying "What we have to consider on absolutely every occasion is, who's *invisible* in the scene?" As he spoke, he saw Duane Wolfmeyer creep into the back pew, pale with the gleam of a well-washed hangover. He decided to throw in an example just for Duane. Then he decided that was too vindictive. Then he changed his mind and did it anyway. "Even if we get paid just to change the towels every morning for an organization that is cruel it still means" (Now he saw Duane listening with his left-over prep-school manners) "we aren't keeping our invisible brother properly." Then Bill asked for their prayers "for Neil Wolfmeyer of this parish, and for the Whole State of Christ's Church."

In the choir room, priest and server helped each other lift off chasuble and surplice. Behind them, the people had just finished No. 346 and were waiting on their knees, for LeRoy Beske to reappear in his red cassock and snuff the candles.

LeRoy said, "I changed serving with Brett Forsyth especially to serve with you this morning, Father."

His eyes were bright — not in admiration for the sermon, Bill decided.

"We made you this, Father. You got rid of the mouse roulette wheel, so we made this here." The boy handed over a piece of unusually clear birchbark. On it, a mouse was well drawn, in brown ink. The mouse looked up from its bark, its whiskers merged with the lines of the birch; its forefeet were slightly raised, dangling close together, its insubstantial jaw hung open, concentrating, the way mice do hang their jaws open. Bill thought it was the face of an animal that never, so long or so hard as it studies its enemy, will ever be able to grasp how dangerous that enemy really is.

That morning Francis had borrowed the car and driven to Duluth to see his old friend Landers. All afternoon a few people hung about the lawns of St. Matthew's. They were dragging away the last of the bazaar gear. To everyone he came across, Bill showed the birchbark with the mouse on it.

Then, around dinnertime, he fell into a terrible mood. He told himself again how grateful he was that Molly and he had agreed on the only major material decision of their life together, but it didn't do any good. He was in a terrible mood. This was not a gentle mood of grief for his brother. It was a pure, bad mood.

He hunched past his study bookshelf and silently flung at Merton and Jeremy Taylor and John Donne, "Ah, easy enough to talk!" He went back outside and was rude to a perfectly nice Lutheran electrician who had put in hours sorting out the bazaar wiring and still wasn't through. He strode angrily across the beautiful lawn and didn't give a glance even to the lake. He thought: I'll never be seconded by anyone's state department to anyone's secret power group. No one who has any real say in who shall die and who shall live and what shall happen to any sizable portion of the earth's crust is ever going to turn to me in some sweaty meeting and say, "Damn it, Father — fill us in on the moral side of this thing, will you — are we okay?"

The priest flung himself into his house and dropped down beside the little boys in the living room. He read aloud to them a lot for the next two days. The boys clung to him on the Sears Roebuck couch. He kept reading everything over again instead of saying okay but this is the last time. He got up a falsetto for the witches' voices. He made the animals, when they spoke, howl and snarl and bellow twice as loudly as he ordinarily took pains to do. And as for the dragon, when it dragged itself up to the boulders where the princess was tied down, he gave out such resonant, such coarse and greedy hissing, the boys crowded against their father's middle-aged hips, and they pressed their ears against his shoulders.